"I'm beginning ⬛⬛⬛⬛⬛⬛⬛
mistake. It's im
anyone when no

I want to know you. Max was suddenly aware that her breast was pressed against his side. He breathed in the scent of her hair, and something about the combination of coconut shampoo, perfume, and warm skin set his body on fire.

Emma's eyes glittered in the lamplight as she turned toward him. "Thanks for letting me cry on your shoulder." She stood on tiptoe and leaned toward him. She was going to kiss his cheek. Without pausing to think, he turned his face and caught her full on the mouth.

Her lips softened, then opened, then moved under his. She was kissing him back. Desire, hot and dark, kicked him in the gut. He deepened the kiss, losing himself in it, in her. She moved against him, her mouth wet and responsive. She stepped back, drawing her purse in front of her. Her pupils were huge, her breathing fast.

"Look—this is a bad idea. This is the last thing I need right now. And you have an election . . . I've— I've got to go." She opened the door of her Saturn and climbed inside.

This time Max didn't stop her. Because, damn it, the person he should have stopped was himself.

BETWEEN THE SHEETS

ROBIN WELLS

FOREVER

NEW YORK   BOSTON

Copyright © 2008 by Robin Wells
All rights reserved. Except as permitted under the U.S. Copyright Act of 1976, no part of this publication may be reproduced, distributed, or transmitted in any form or by any means, or stored in a database or retrieval system, without the prior written permission of the publisher.

Forever is an imprint of Grand Central Publishing. The Forever name and logo is a trademark of Hachette Book Group USA, Inc.

Cover design by Diane Luger
Cover photograph by Herman Estevez
Book design by Giorgetta Bell McRee

Forever
Hachette Book Group USA
237 Park Avenue
New York, NY 10017
Visit our Web site at www.HachetteBookGroupUSA.com

Printed in the United States of America

First Printing: February 2008

10 9 8 7 6 5 4 3 2 1

*To my husband and personal happy ending, Ken;
my two terrific daughters, Taylor and Arden; and my
wonderful parents, Charlie Lou and Roscoe Rouse.*

---

*With special thanks to Erica Spindler and Nancy Wagner
(aka Hailey North) for the parsley mojo.*

BETWEEN THE SHEETS

CHAPTER ONE

B.C. (Before Catastrophe)

December 5

The call girl's naked thigh made a sucking sound on the limousine's black leather upholstery as she scooted her miniskirted bottom closer to President-Elect Ferguson. "You're a lot handsomer in person than you are on TV," she purred.

Oh, give me a break, thought Special Agent Allen Gromstedt as he peered in the limo's rear-view mirror and saw the brunette press a silicone-stuffed breast against the gray-haired man's arm. With his huge honker and flabby jowls, Ferguson was about as handsome as a scabbed knee.

Gromstedt turned his attention back to the traffic on St. Charles Avenue and tried to ignore the couple in the rear of the limo, but their presence was inescapable. The hothouse scent of the woman's perfume wended its way through the lowered partition to the front seat. It was expensive perfume, not the drugstore stuff like Gromstedt's wife wore. Hell, it ought to be expensive, he thought as he steered around a double-parked utility truck. For three hundred dollars an hour, she ought to smell like gold bullion.

"You're taller than I thought you were." The woman's hand squeezed the old man's bicep through the jacket of his dark navy wool suit. "Ooh—and bigger, too. I just lo-o-o-ve big men. I bet you're big all over."

Oh, brother. Gromstedt braked for a red light at the Napoleon Street intersection and stared straight through the windshield, deliberately avoiding eye contact with John Stokes, the dark-haired agent seated beside him. The Secret Service had trained them to act as if they didn't see or hear any of their VIPs' conversations, but this was so cheesy that Gromstedt was afraid he couldn't look at Stokes without accidentally smirking or rolling his eyes.

It wasn't like he hadn't been warned. Stokes had worked the Ferguson detail during the campaign, and he'd given Gromstedt all the scoop on the plane flight from D.C. to New Orleans that morning.

"The old man keeps the partition rolled down because he likes to show off his lady-killer prowess," he'd told him. "He thinks he's impressing us or something."

To Gromstedt's way of thinking, it didn't count as prowess if the woman was bought and paid for, and all of Ferguson's were.

"He says it's not adultery if he hires them," Stokes had explained. "He says if he pays for it, it's just a business transaction."

Gromstedt could imagine how well that logic would go over with Mrs. Ferguson. But then, if he were married to the hatchet-faced old broad, he might look for ways around the fine print, too. The image of his own wife flitted through his mind. He'd hit the jackpot when he'd married Sara, that was for sure. Twenty-two years of marriage, and he'd never once been tempted to stray.

"What Ferguson does is his own business, I guess," Gromstedt had replied.

"It's kinda our business, too."

Something in Stokes's voice had made Gromstedt cut him a sharp look. "What do you mean?"

"It's our job to get him the girl."

"*What?*"

"Well, he can't just go out and hire one himself," Stokes had said.

The light changed. Gromstedt lifted his foot from the brake and eased it onto the gas. This whole call girl thing made him uneasy, but it wasn't the old man's ethics that bothered him. It wasn't even his own.

It was the idea of getting caught. He had twenty years invested with the Secret Service, not to mention a wife, two kids in college, and a mortgage. He couldn't afford to get busted for hiring a hooker.

Stokes was the one who'd handled the actual hiring transaction, but Gromstedt was driving the limo, so he was in just as deep. They'd picked her up at the Hyton Hotel on Canal Street an hour earlier as Ferguson addressed a national conference of teachers, then made her hide under a tarp in the far back of the limo as Ferguson climbed in.

"Does agency brass know about this?" Gromstedt had asked Stokes.

"Oh, yeah."

"And they're okay with it?"

"Let's put it this way—our job is protecting Ferguson's physical safety, right?"

"Right."

"Well, he's a hell of a lot safer with a call girl who gets into the car thinking I'm her john for the evening than he'd be with a gal who knows she's about to do the next president. Left to his own devices, he could end up with a kamikaze terrorist with anthrax in her twat."

Stokes had a point. "So . . . the agency will back us up if this ever gets out?"

"Hell, no. They'll hang us out to dry."

"But . . ."

Stokes had shrugged. "It's part of the job. You want the plum assignments, you gotta expect a few pits."

Gromstedt glanced in the rear-view mirror again. The woman was whispering something in Ferguson's ear.

The old man laughed and stroked her thigh under her short black skirt. "How about cameras, sugar?" he murmured. "You like doing it on video?"

"Ooh," she breathed. "Just the thought makes me hot."

Just the thought makes me gag. Stokes had warned him about this, too. Apparently the old man loved to make tapes of himself in the sack.

"Is he crazy?" Gromstedt had asked. "Man, if one of those tapes got in the wrong hands—"

"I know, I know. But that's how it is with these power dudes—the higher they climb, the more invincible they think they are."

It was true. Gromstedt had driven enough heads of state, visiting dignitaries, and vice presidents over the years to know they could behave with surprising carelessness.

"Have you watched them?" Gromstedt had asked. "The tapes, I mean."

"Nah. But Murphy did. Said he nearly puked. Apparently the old man keeps the camera primarily trained on himself."

Oh, boy. It was going to be a long four years, what with hookers and videos and the old man popping Viagra like peanuts.

"I don't think I got your name," Ferguson said to the call girl.

"Amber," the woman replied.

"Pretty name for a pretty lady."

And about as likely to be real as her oversized boobs, Gromstedt thought, glancing in the rear-view mirror again. As far as call girls went, though, she wasn't half bad. She fit the prototype Stokes had said Ferguson preferred—slender build, big rack, shoulder-length straight brown hair.

The old brownstone mansion that housed the public library loomed on the left. Recognizing the landmark, Gromstedt shifted to the left lane. A block later, he caught sight of an enormous white-columned mansion. This was it—the Mullendorf estate. Gromstedt had stopped by earlier to familiarize himself with the route and to scope out any potential hazards.

He braked for a left turn and punched a button on his headset phone. "Eagle One on the approach."

"Got you spotted," came the reply. "We'll open the gate after the streetcar passes."

A pea-green and brick-red streetcar rattled down the center median, the windows brightly lit, the bow of a Christmas wreath flapping in the damp New Orleans air. He was glad to see the streetcar up and running; from what he'd heard, it had been out of commission for a year and a half after Hurricane Katrina. As soon as the streetcar cleared the intersection, Gromstedt steered onto an oak-lined side street. Right on cue, the electronic iron gate beside the mansion swung open.

"Ooh, this place is beautiful!" the call girl squealed as

Gromstedt guided the limo past the agents at the entrance and up the narrow brick-paved drive. "Is it yours?"

"No, sugar," Ferguson said. "It belongs to a friend of mine."

"Do you think he might want a girl? Because if he does, I have a friend who's not busy tonight, and—"

Ferguson chortled. "I'm sure he'd appreciate the thought, but my pal's out of town."

"And he's letting you stay at his place? Must be a good friend."

"He is."

No kidding. Mullendorf had raised more than four million dollars for Ferguson's campaign. But then, the tycoon probably stood to make a hundred times that in defense contracts or some such. None of these rich guys ever gave away anything that didn't somehow end up back in their pockets in spades.

Gromstedt carefully steered the limo around a silver Saturn LS parked on the side of the narrow drive and spotted Agent Bill Clarkson just inside the open warehouse-sized garage. After Clarkson flashed the prearranged "all clear" signal, Gromstedt slowly drove inside and killed the engine.

The call girl reached for the car door's handle as the hangar-sized garage door began to rumble down.

"Slow down there, sugar," Ferguson told her. "We've got to wait till the garage door's down. Never know when a photographer is lurking in the bushes." He patted her thigh and leered. "Besides, a pretty little lady like you should never have to open a car door herself."

The woman giggled. "Ooh, you're such a *gentleman*. You really know how to treat a lady."

Ferguson chuckled. "I sure do, sugar. I sure as hell do."

Oh, Christ—I hope you wait until you get to the room before you try to prove it. Keeping his expression wooden, Gromstedt climbed out, waited until the garage door thudded closed, then opened the limo's back door. The woman's legs, long and slender, stretched out through the opening. The rest of her followed, her black skirt hitched high enough to reveal scant red panties. Ferguson struggled out behind her, breathing hard.

"This way, sir." Agent Clarkson opened the door to the residence. "The stairs are to your right."

Ferguson wrapped an arm around the woman and looked at Stokes. "Can you get us to my room without any of the help seeing us? Mullendorf's wife and my wife are close friends, and if word got back—"

"We've already taken care of it, sir, but I'll double-check." Stokes lifted his walkie-talkie. "Miller, are the domestics out of the way?"

"Affirmative," replied a gravelly voice through the receiver. "We sent everyone home but the butler, and she's with me in the front room. The back stairs are clear."

"Thanks." Ferguson put his arm around the call girl's waist and winked. "See you fellas in the morning."

Stokes closed the door to the house behind the president-elect, then turned back to Clarkson. "Did he say the butler's a she?"

"Yeah," Clarkson said. "A good-looking one, too—and just Ferguson's type. Straight dark hair, big tits, slender build."

"Maybe he could have saved some money," Gromstedt joked.

"Nah. This girl's not that sort. Besides, he likes to pay, remember?"

"Yeah." Stokes exchanged an amused glance with Gromstedt. "It's not something we're likely to forget."

Fifteen minutes later

Thump-squeak. Thump-squeak. Thump-squeak. Thump-squeak.

The odd overhead noise made Emma Jamison pause in the middle of her refrigerator inventory and frown up at the crown-molded kitchen ceiling of the Mullendorf mansion. *Please please* please *don't be a problem with the plumbing or the central air,* she silently implored. She was responsible for ensuring that President-Elect Ferguson had an enjoyable stay, and there was nothing enjoyable about plumbing problems—especially not at eleven at night.

The noise subsided as abruptly as it had begun. Emma held her breath and listened for a moment, then blew out a relieved sigh. It was probably just air in the pipes or some other benign cause. The big old house had survived two centuries and Hurricane Katrina, so hopefully it would make it through one more night.

"Got any coffee?"

She turned from the open Sub-Zero to see a middle-aged Secret Service agent saunter through the arched hallway of the enormous black-and-white kitchen. He wasn't a member of the advance team who'd been poring over the mansion for the past two days, so he had to be one of the six who'd arrived fifteen minutes earlier with President-Elect Ferguson. Emma usually had a good eye for faces, but these agents were so numerous and nondescript it was hard to keep them straight. The most notable thing about them—aside from their dark suits and ties—was their total lack of notability.

Except for this one. He was older than the others; his rust-colored hair was flecked with gray, and he had a slight paunch.

"Help yourself," Emma said, tilting her head toward an industrial-sized stainless-steel coffeemaker on the black granite countertop. "I just made five gallons."

"Five gallons, huh?" The man's face buckled into a smile as he crossed the room. "If I ration myself, that might just see me through the night."

What do you know, Emma thought. *An agent with a sense of humor.* She'd begun to think the government performed some kind of personality-extraction procedure on them all before they let them out in the field.

"I'm Allen Gromstedt," he said, reaching for one of the twelve white mugs lined up in two precise rows by the coffeemaker.

"Nice to meet you. I'm Emma Jamison."

She turned her attention back to the interior of the paneled refrigerator and finished comparing the chef's list of breakfast ingredients against the contents. *Two gallons of two-percent milk—check. One pound unsalted butter—check. Sharp white cheddar—check.* It was all there. She'd done the shopping herself, but she wanted to double-check, just to make sure.

It was the sort of behavior her psychiatrist ex-fiancé used to call neurotic, stemming from a lack of self-esteem. The thought of Derrick made her shoulders tense. Well, who wouldn't have self-esteem issues, after being engaged to a jealous two-timing liar who psychoanalyzed her every move?

Besides, Derrick had been wrong. Sure, she had a few

issues, but she wasn't neurotic; she was meticulous and detail-oriented, which were good traits for a butler to have. And she wasn't all that lacking in self-esteem, either—at least, she hadn't been before Derrick. What she lacked was good judgment in men.

Well, never again, she thought, shutting the refrigerator door with a definitive thud. Never again would she be blinded by charm and good looks. The next time she fell for a man, it would be someone trusting and trustworthy who loved her just the way she was.

She turned to find Agent Gromstedt looking around the immense restaurant-grade kitchen. "This place isn't too shabby," he remarked.

For an enormous mansion furnished with priceless antiques and every convenience known to man, it wasn't too bad. She was tempted to say it aloud, but butlers never gossiped about their clients or commented on their belongings.

The agent put the coffee cup under the spout and lifted the spigot on the coffeemaker. "Do you live here?"

"No. I'm just working here temporarily."

He furrowed his brow. "I thought you were the butler."

"I am. I'm with a temporary butler service." She happened to own the service, but there was no need to get into that.

"No kidding." Agent Gromstedt shoveled three teaspoons of sugar in his cup. "How does that work?"

"Like any other temporary-employment service. Clients call when they need extra help."

His spoon clicked against the side of his cup as he stirred. "This might sound kind of ignorant, but what the heck do butlers do?"

"Manage households, basically. We handle things like

hiring chefs and caterers, running errands, supervising the housekeeping staff, keeping the kitchen stocked. Whatever needs doing."

"So what's your assignment here?"

"Well, the Mullendorfs are out of town, so they hired me to open their home and make sure Mr. Ferguson has everything he needs."

His eyebrows rose. "Wow. Big responsibility, hosting the next president of the United States."

Yes, it was, and Emma was thrilled that she'd been entrusted with it. She'd worked for a lot of important people in her career, but the newly elected leader of the free world had to be the V-est of all VIPs.

"How'd you get a gig like this?" the agent asked, taking a tentative slurp of his coffee.

Emma opened a cabinet and pulled out a paper towel. "The Mullendorfs are regular clients," she explained, wiping some water off the countertop. "I manage their New Orleans home whenever they're gone, and I handle special projects when their live-in butler needs a hand." Which was pretty often. The Mullendorfs had repeatedly tried to hire Emma to replace him, but Emma liked the freedom of self-employment.

Besides, she made a good living—good enough that she'd recently bought a new car and a little gingerbread-trimmed cottage on the edge of the Garden District. Her career was in terrific shape.

It was her personal life that sucked.

"I always thought butlers were stuffy old men in tails," the agent said.

Emma tossed the paper towel in the trash can under the sink. "That's the movie image. We come in all kinds of packages."

The agent leaned a hip against the counter and eyed her over the rim of his coffee cup. "Well, your package is a big improvement over the stereotype."

He wasn't coming on to her, exactly, but there was an element of masculine appreciation in his gaze that made Emma's hand flutter to the top button of her dress. Derrick used to say she was uncomfortable with her sexuality. Well, she wasn't; she was just uncomfortable with the way men looked at her chest. Ever since puberty, it had drawn an unwelcome amount of attention. It wasn't Dolly Parton–esque, but it was generous, and even though she wore clothes that downplayed it, like the tailored black coatdress she was wearing now, her bustline never escaped male notice.

The top metal button wobbled loosely under her finger. Uh-oh—it was dangling by just a few threads. She hoped it held until she made it home.

"So where are the Mullendorfs?" the agent asked.

"At their home in the south of France."

"Must be nice," he said.

Emma nodded, but she was only being polite. The truth was, Emma didn't envy her clients. From what she'd seen, some of the most miserable people in the world slept on thousand-dollar sheets. Her daydreams didn't revolve around opulent mansions or expensive cars; they centered on minivans with baby seats and a man who loved her as much as she loved him. Her parents had had a close and loving marriage, and she'd always dreamed of having a relationship like theirs.

Her grandmother kept telling her that divine providence was at work, that there was someone for everyone, and that when the time was right, Mr. Right would appear. Well, her Mr. Right needed a providential kick in the butt, Emma thought ruefully; her thirty-second birthday was rapidly approaching, and she couldn't keep hitting the snooze button on her biological clock forever. It didn't help matters that her last single girlfriend had gotten married and moved away last month.

Thump-squeak thump-squeak thump-squeak. The racket overhead started up again, louder and faster than before. Emma glanced up. "I wonder what's causing that noise."

The agent stared into his coffee cup. "What noise?"

Emma pulled her brows together. The agents all had wires coming out of one ear, but Emma thought it was a communication device, not a sign that they were hearing impaired. "You don't hear that loud thumping sound?"

Thump-squeak thump-squeak thump-squeak.

"Oh, that." The agent took a leisurely sip of coffee and shrugged. "Probably just the hot-water heater cranking up."

"It's never made a noise like that before." She'd personally run the showers, turned on all the faucets, and flushed all the toilets to make sure they were in good working order before the president-elect arrived, and she hadn't heard anything that sounded remotely like this. "I'd better go upstairs and check." She turned and started for the hall that led to the back stairs.

The agent stepped into her path, body-blocking her so rapidly that she ran into his chest. Emma gasped and jerked back.

"Sorry, but you can't go up there," he said firmly, his arms spread across the doorway.

"But that noise—"

"It's nothing to worry about."

How could he possibly know that? Emma stared at him. "If the hot-water tank leaks or explodes—"

"It won't." His voice was hard and certain, his expression steely. "It's fine."

Thump-squeak thump-squeak thump-squeak.

"It's *not* fine," Emma insisted. "That's not the way the water heater normally sounds."

"Well, then, it's probably not the water heater." The agent dropped his arms and nonchalantly strolled back to the counter. "It's probably just the house settling or something. Old places always make weird noises."

"Not this weird." Even weirder was the agent's complete lack of concern about it. "Look—if I can't go upstairs and check it out, would you please go up and take a look?"

"Don't worry." The agent took a calm sip of coffee. "It'll stop in a moment."

Emma planted her hands on her hips, frustration simmering in her chest. The thump-squeaks were coming faster and harder now, and her alarm was growing by the second. "How can you know it'll stop if you don't even know what's causing it?"

"I just do."

Thump-squeak. Thump-squeak. Thump-squeak. THUMP-SQUEAK . . . louder and faster, until the pots and pans hanging on the iron rack over the stove began to vibrate.

What was wrong with this man? "I don't understand how you can just stand there and do nothing," Emma said, fixing him with a hot glare. "You ought to be more worried than I am, because it sounds like it's coming directly from Mr. Ferguson's bedroom."

The moment she said it aloud, it hit. *Bedroom. A bed.* That's what was causing the noise. A bouncing bed, banging against the wall.

Which meant the wall wasn't the only thing getting banged.

Mortification scalded Emma's face. Judging from the way agent's eyes glimmered as he raised his coffee cup, he could tell she'd figured it out.

Oh, *jeez*.

She was standing there listening to the president-elect do the nasty with someone, and it wasn't his wife. The future first lady was in Sacramento, California, attending a highly publicized symposium on health care.

Turning abruptly, Emma opened the refrigerator again and pretended a deep interest in its interior, her mind swirling. So the rumors about Robert Ferguson were true: he was cut from the same hound-dog hide as Clinton. Instead of young interns, though, Ferguson was said to prefer high-class call girls—a description that Emma had always thought was an oxymoron.

The Secret Service must have smuggled a girl into the house along with Ferguson—which explained why an agent had kept her in the front parlor while the president-elect sneaked up the back stairs. It also explained why they'd requested that no domestics stay overnight.

Great. The Secret Service was aiding and abetting the president-elect's illicit sex romps. Nothing like your tax dollars at work.

THUMP-SQUEAK   THUMP-SQUEAK   THUMP-SQUEAK THUMP-SQUEAK.

Now that she knew what was causing the noise, it was painfully uncomfortable to stand there and listen to it. She closed the refrigerator door and stiffly turned around.

"Will Mr. Ferguson be needing anything else tonight?"

THUMP-SQUEAK   THUMP-SQUEAK   THUMP-SQUEAK.

The agent cleared his throat. "I believe he's got everything he needs."

Right. Emma felt her face flame. She was no prude, but this was downright embarrassing. "Well, then, I'm going to head on out."

"Don't blame you. Got a husband waiting at home for you?"

She shook her head. "I'm not married."

"Bet you've got a hot date lined up, then."

Oh, that was a good one. It had been so long since she'd gone on any date, let alone a hot one, that she couldn't even recognize a thump-squeak.

"Just a lonely Yorkie." She headed for the coat closet on the other side of the room. "I'll be back around five-fifteen to let the breakfast chef in. If anyone gets hungry, there are all kinds of things in the fridge—pizza, cold chicken, pasta salad, and muffulattas."

The agent's eyebrows flew up. "Muffa what?"

THUMP-SQUEAK   THUMP-SQUEAK   THUMP-SQUEAK. Why, oh why couldn't the chef have prepared chicken salad? *Muffulatta* sounded like the first cousin of Pussy Galore. "It's a local sandwich made with olive relish."

The thump-squeaks abruptly ceased. Emma wouldn't have thought it possible, but silence was even more embarrassing than the bed-banging.

The agent shifted his stance and cleared his throat. "There is one thing Mr. Ferguson's likely to be wanting."

Let me guess. A cigarette?

"Ice cream," he said. "He sometimes gets a late-night sweet tooth."

The president-elect's aide had told Emma as much when she'd called Ferguson's transition headquarters. She nodded. "There's a half-gallon each of Cherry Garcia and Chunky Monkey in the freezer."

The agent raised an appreciative eyebrow. "Wow. You really did your homework."

"That's my job." And she took pride in doing it well—in anticipating her clients' needs and wants, and exceeding their expectations. Emma opened the coat closet by the kitchen door and reached up to pull her purse off the shelf. As she stretched forward, the loose button popped off her dress and clattered to the white terrazzo tile.

Emma clutched at her gaping dress, glad her back was to the agent. The button rolled noisily across the floor.

"I've got it." Agent Gromstedt scooped up the metal button, then crossed the room and handed it to her.

Emma's fingers closed tightly around it. "Thanks. I'd better go pin myself back together."

She scurried to the powder room in the hall. Closing the door behind her, she undid the rest of the buttons, stepped out of the dress, and surveyed the damage. The button was the kind that attached from the back, so the easiest course of action was to pin it back in place. She opened her purse, pulled out a safety pin, and was working the sharp tip through the metal loop when a loud rap sounded on the door.

"We've got an emergency," the agent barked. "You've got to leave."

Alarm shot through her. "But . . . but—"

"We've got to clear the premises." His tone was grim and urgent. "Now."

The button and the safety pin both pinged on the floor. Emma scrambled back into her dress, but before she could fasten any of the remaining buttons, the bathroom door burst open.

"Hey!"

"Sorry, but I've been ordered to get you out of here." The agent snatched her purse off the counter, grabbed her arm, and pulled her out of the bathroom.

"Wh-what's wrong?"

"No time to explain. You just need to go."

What was happening? Possibilities swirled through her mind, each more terrifying than the next. A bomb threat? A terrorist attack? Emma's heart pounded hard enough to bruise her ribs. She stumbled as the agent half-dragged her to the kitchen door.

"Where are your keys?" he demanded.

"W-what?"

"Your car keys. Where are they?"

"In . . . in my purse. Side—side pocket."

He extracted them and handed them to her. She struggled to keep her dress together with her one hand, but it was virtually impossible—especially when he thrust her purse at her, opened the door, and practically shoved her out into the cool, damp night.

Awkwardly clutching her gaping dress, her purse, and her keys, she staggered toward the steps off the back landing, only to be blinded by a sudden flash of light. She paused on the narrow stoop, trying to catch her bearings, when the light flashed again. A camera. The thought registered vaguely through her daze of panic; someone was taking pictures through the bars of the iron fence.

"Hey, lady! Who are you?" called a man's voice from the vicinity of the camera flash.

Sirens screeched through the air, close and coming closer. Another Secret Service agent appeared out of nowhere and took her by the arm. "Hurry up!" he ordered, pulling her toward her Saturn, which was parked in the delivery entrance drive. "We need the driveway cleared."

Fumbling with her key chain, she unlocked her car and climbed in. It took a moment, but she finally found the ignition key and started the engine.

The electronic gate swung open. An agent stood by it, motioning for her to leave. Emma's legs shook so badly she could barely press her foot to the accelerator, but she somehow managed to drive out the gate and onto the side street just as an ambulance and half a dozen police cars screamed around the corner.

What the heck was going on? A dozen doomsday scenarios played out in her mind—bioterrorism, an airborne attack, a dirty bomb. The house was her responsibility, and for all she knew, it was about to blow up.

It occurred to her that she should call the Mullendorfs, but she didn't have a clue what to tell them. How could she explain what was happening, when she had no idea herself?

Her fingers shaking, she turned on the radio and pushed the button for WWL, New Orleans' all-news station. "The school board passed a new resolution . . ." a reporter droned. She impatiently hit "scan" and cycled through Carrie Underwood, Christina Aguilera, Norah Jones, and a commercial for a jeweler.

Nothing. It was still too soon.

Well, any event involving the president-elect was sure to be rapidly reported. She'd go home, turn on her TV, and find out what the heck was going on. Once she had the facts, she'd figure out her next move.

CHAPTER TWO

*E*mma's heart was still pumping like a fire hose nineteen minutes later when she clambered up the porch steps of her white shotgun-style home and unlocked the door with shaking hands. Her five-pound Yorkshire terrier ran to greet her as she stepped inside.

"Hi there, Snookems," Emma said, scooping up the little dog with one hand and grabbing the television remote with the other. Snookems gave her a wet kiss on the side of the face as she plopped onto her beige camel-backed sofa, leaned against a scarlet and beige-striped pillow, and clicked on the TV.

The anchor on CNN was talking about a celebrity trial, so Emma switched to MSNBC, then Fox News, then the local stations. Nothing but regular programming.

"Maybe the whole thing was a false alarm," Emma said to her little dog. "You know what they say—no news is good news."

Snookems jumped off her lap and yapped.

Emma smiled. "No dinner is never good news, though, is it, girl? I'll get right on it."

The Yorkie barked again, then padded into the sunny yellow kitchen, her long gray hair dusting the floor. Emma followed the little dog, her ear tuned to the TV. She'd just finished filling the dog's red ceramic bowl when the imposing strains of "breaking news" music interrupted the CNN newscast. Emma dashed back to the TV.

"This just in," the anchor said. "Sources in New Orleans report that President-Elect Robert Ferguson has been taken to a hospital after suffering what apparently is some type of coronary incident."

"Oh, no," Emma murmured. Her own heart did a funny skip.

"There's no official word on his condition, but early reports are that it's very serious. Chris Smithers is in New Orleans with a live update. What can you tell us, Chris?"

The image shifted to a reporter standing in a doorway under a glowing red sign that read "Emergency." "I'm here at Ochsner Hospital, where President-Elect Ferguson was brought in an ambulance about fifteen minutes ago. He was staying at the private home of Marvin Mullendorf, the head of Mullendorf Oil, when he suffered what appears to be a heart attack. We're awaiting word from the president-elect's spokesman."

"Chris, do you know if his heart actually stopped?" the anchor asked.

"We don't have any details about that yet."

"Can you tell us what he was doing when it happened?" the anchor asked.

"Again, it's too early to have any kind of official word. One source indicates that he'd already retired for the evening. Another report says an unidentified woman was seen rushing from the home just before the ambulance arrived."

That must have been his thump-squeak partner. Had he collapsed while doing the deed? When the thump-squeaking had stopped, had his heart stopped, too? "Oh, wow," Emma murmured, sinking onto her couch.

"Any chance of foul play?" the anchor asked.

"No indications of that, but I'm sure all possibilities will be explored."

"Mr. Ferguson's wife is in Sacramento for a meeting about health care," the anchor said. "Has she been notified?"

"We've had no word on that. We can assume that's taking place, however. It's standard protocol to notify the family before any statements are issued to the press."

For the next twenty minutes, Emma sat glued to the tube, flicking the remote, channel surfing for updated information. It finally arrived, in the form of the somber-faced reporter standing outside Ochsner Hospital. "Doctors have just confirmed that President-Elect Robert Ferguson died at approximately eleven-thirty this evening of what appears to be massive coronary arrest."

Died? He was *dead?* Emma's hand flew over her mouth.

"Mrs. Ferguson is on her way to New Orleans," the reporter continued. "She will fly with the president-elect's body to Washington, D.C., where an extensive autopsy will be conducted."

Emma's mind churned. She needed to call the Mullendorfs and let them know what was going on, but first she'd better get back to the residence so the place wasn't unattended.

Hurrying to her bedroom, she peeled off her damaged

dress and scrambled into a navy pantsuit, then dashed back to her car.

When she pulled up to the Mullendorf mansion twenty minutes later, it was lit up like an airport. A Secret Service agent stood at the closed gate, so she parked on the street and walked up the drive. He checked her credentials, then let her in.

She entered the home through the same door she'd fled less than an hour earlier. The downstairs was deserted, but she heard movement upstairs. Curious, Emma headed through the kitchen to the garage foyer and climbed the back stairs, then paused under one of the six lantern chandeliers that lined the high hallway ceiling. Low male voices rumbled from the guest suite that Ferguson had occupied—the Gold Room, the Mullendorfs called it, because the heavy tasseled drapes, the bed canopy, and the bedspread were all made from a buttery silk velvet, and the mahogany floor was covered with an enormous gold-toned Aubusson rug. The antique Persian carpet runner in the hallway softened her footsteps as she walked past the gallery of gilt-framed ancestral portraits lining the vellum-colored walls.

The guest-room door was open, but a strip of yellow crime scene tape stretched across the doorway. Emma peered into the lushly appointed room and drew in a shocked breath.

The canopied plantation bed was stripped to the mattress, and two Secret Service agents in plastic gloves were cutting off the pillowtop. The plush gold velvet bedspread was crammed in an enormous plastic bag, along with the Egyptian cotton sheets and the mattress protector.

"Wh-what's going on?" she asked.

The agents looked up, their expressions alarmed.

"Hey—you're not supposed to be up here," the shorter, younger man barked.

"It's okay. She's the butler," said the agent with a dark receding hairline.

"What are you doing?" Emma asked.

The older agent turned to Emma with a conciliatory smile. "We're collecting evidence."

Evidence? Why would they need evidence if President-Elect Ferguson died of a heart attack? "For what?"

"In case there's an inquiry later."

"You mean . . . about the woman who was here?"

The shorter agent abruptly straightened, exchanged a glance with the other man, then looked her hard in the eye. "What woman?"

"I—I heard there was a woman seen leaving the property."

"Did you see a woman?" he demanded.

"Well, no. But I heard . . . noises."

"What kind of noises?"

"A-a banging sound." The moment she said it, she realized how it sounded. Her face heated. "I mean, a thumping. Like . . . like . . ." She drew a deep breath. "Like a bed rocking."

The two agents looked at each other. A moment of silence beat between them. "Oh, that must have been Mr. Ferguson doing calisthenics," the older man said.

The other agent nodded. "Right. Calisthenics."

"I see," Emma said. And she did. She saw that the agents were closing ranks to protect Ferguson's reputation.

And she understood completely. Butlers adhered to a strict code of confidentiality about their employers, and the Secret Service no doubt did the same. She couldn't fault them, because they were simply doing their job. They'd been hired to protect Ferguson, and they were continuing to do so, even after his death. They probably figured there was no point in upsetting Mr. Ferguson's family or tarnishing his name, now that he was gone.

A video camera on a tripod by the bed caught Emma's eye. Her pulse skyrocketed; she had a phobia about video cameras. She knew it was irrational, but just the sight of one sent made her stomach tight and quivery. As long as the lens was pointed away from her, she could function, but a camera turned in her direction could bring on a full-fledged panic attack.

This camera, thank God, was aimed at the bed. "Were you taping something?" she asked.

The agents looked at each other again. The older man cleared his throat. "Yeah. We were taping our search of the premises."

"Yeah." The younger man nodded. "Agency protocol."

Emma's brow knit. "The Mullendorfs don't like pictures taken inside their home."

"It's a required procedure," the shorter agent said. "To prove we processed the scene correctly."

"Yeah," said the other agent. "But it's just for intra-agency use. It'll never see the light of day."

If it was an agency requirement, there was no point in arguing about it. The Mullendorfs had told Emma to accommodate the Secret Service in every way possible. All the same, she hated seeing their guest room destroyed. "That bedding was custom-made. Is it really necessary to take it?"

"I'm afraid so."

"Why?"

The agents exchanged a glance. "You know how

rumors and theories get started when a head of state dies," the taller agent said. "We have to be thorough in case any questions arise later."

"I just don't understand why—"

His smile faded. "It's protocol." His eyes flashed with impatience. "Now, if you'll excuse us, we need to finish up here."

His tone and body language clearly indicated that she was dismissed. Well, fine; there were plenty of things Emma needed to finish up, herself. She had to call the Mullendorfs, cancel the breakfast chef and kitchen maid service, rearrange the housekeeping schedule . . . a list started forming in her mind. "I'll be downstairs if you need anything," she said, turning toward the door.

By the time the agents cleared out and Emma closed up the house, the sky was streaked with the first rays of daylight. She'd been up all night, Emma realized. A wave of exhaustion swept through her as the electronic gate hummed closed behind her at the end of the driveway. Yawning widely, she climbed into her Saturn, started the engine, and pulled away from the curb. She couldn't wait to get home, take a hot shower, and crawl into bed. She absently scanned the radio dial for further news about Ferguson as she drove down the deserted streets toward her small home.

"This just in," said a deep-voiced radio newscaster as Emma neared her home. "An unidentified hospital source said President-Elect Ferguson had a large dose of Viagra in his system when he expired."

Well, well, well. That little piece of news probably meant the Secret Service wasn't going to be able to cover up Ferguson's illicit activities, after all. Emma turned up the volume.

"We also have an unconfirmed report that a half-dressed woman was seen leaving the Mullendorf compound shortly before President-Elect Ferguson was transported to the hospital."

Emma shook her head. The woman with Ferguson hadn't even had the sense to put on her clothes before she left.

"The woman, who was wearing an unfastened black dress . . ."

Black dress? The breath froze in Emma's lungs. No. Surely not. Every woman had at least one black dress.

". . . allegedly climbed into a silver-colored car parked inside the compound and sped away," the newscaster said.

The hood of her silver Saturn gleamed mockingly through Emma's windshield. Panic flushed through her veins like water down a sewer line as the dots connected into a mortifying picture. They thought *she* was the woman with Ferguson?

Emma was still trying to wrap her mind around the concept when she turned the corner onto her street and saw three TV satellite trucks parked in front of her house. Seven or eight people stood on her lawn, holding cameras and microphones and notebooks.

Fear, sick and clammy, crawled through her gut. *This wasn't happening. This couldn't be happening.*

Her fingers shaking, she pulled her car into her narrow drive and drew a deep breath. This was all a mistake—a simple misunderstanding. She'd explain what happened and straighten everything out.

A photographer raced toward her, snapping pictures before her vehicle even stopped rolling. A burly man with a video camera on his shoulder turned a light on her as she hesitantly opened the car door and climbed out.

She stared at the TV camera, fear stampeding through her veins. "Miss Jamison?" called a blond man in a gray suit whom Emma recognized as a local TV reporter.

Sweat beaded her upper lip as she gazed at the video camera. *Relax*, she ordered herself. *Think. Talk.* She couldn't afford to have an anxiety attack now. "Y-yes?"

The reporter thrust a microphone in her face. "I understand you were at the Mullendorf residence when President-Elect Ferguson died."

She clutched her jacket together and swallowed back a wave of queasiness. *Talk. You've got to explain,* she ordered herself. She shifted to the side so she wasn't looking into the camera. "Y-yes," she managed.

The cameraman moved so that he was once again directly in her line of vision.

"What were you doing there?" the reporter asked.

"I-I'm the butler." Her mouth was so dry that her lips seemed to stick to her teeth.

"Do you care to comment on why you fled the house, undressed, moments after Mr. Ferguson's heart attack?"

Oh, God—the camera was focused right on her. Emma's pulse roared in her ears as she fought the rising tide of fear. "I-I wasn't undressed! My—my dress had popped a button, that's all, and I was fixing it . . . and then the Secret Service said there was an emergency and I had to leave and move my car, and . . ."

The heavyset cameraman stepped closer and squatted down, thrusting the large video camera about a foot from her nose. The wave of fright became a tsunami. She was drowning in it, choking on it. She raised her hand defensively and stepped back.

The cameraman took a step forward. Another TV cameraman moved in beside him, along with another microphone-wielding reporter.

Breathe, she thought. *Just breathe and talk.* She gasped for air, but her throat felt paralyzed. She gasped again.

"President Ferguson had a large dose of Viagra in his system," the second reporter said. "Would you care to comment on that?"

Air. She had to get some air.

She sucked in a thimble-full of oxygen. "N-no. I-I mean, I-I don't know . . ." *Think. You have to think.* "I-I don't know anything. I nev-never even met him."

The camera lens glared at her, a cold, mocking, one-eyed beast. The pack of reporters closed in like starving wolves.

"How long have you known Mr. Ferguson?" one asked.

"What were his last words?" called another.

"Why was he taking Viagra?" yet another demanded.

Oh, dear God—she was about to pass out. A primitive reflex propelled her wobbly legs into motion. Starving for air, she turned and tore up the steps to her stoop as the reporters bombarded her with more questions. She tried to fit the key in the door, but her fingers shook so badly that she kept missing the lock. She was on the verge of collapse when finally, finally, the key clicked into the keyhole.

She opened the door and dashed inside, then leaned against it and slid to the floor, gasping for breath. Snookems ran to greet her, barking frantically. The little dog climbed in her lap and stood on her hind legs, trying to lick her cheek. Emma sucked in long gulps of air, waiting for her heart rate to slow and the paralyzing panic to subside. It would, just as soon as the reporters left.

But they didn't leave. The doorbell rang, then rang again. The ringing drove Snookems into a yapping, squirming frenzy. Emma held him in her quivering arms, until the combined racket of the doorbell and the yipping dog had Emma's nerves as frayed as the bottoms of her favorite jeans.

She rose to her feet and leaned against the door, her eyes closed, and tried to gather her courage. She'd worked for celebrities before; she knew that if she asked the paparazzi to leave private property, they had to comply. She just had to work up the nerve to do it.

She'd pretend she was doing it for a client, she decided. Still holding the snarling dog, she drew in a lungful of air and cracked the door open. A video camera stared her down.

She drew back, closed her eyes, and fought against a rising tide of fresh panic. "P-please stop ringing my doorbell," she said, putting as much authority into her voice as a woman cowering behind a door could muster. "And get off my property. If you don't, I'll call the police and file charges for trespassing and harassment."

"Is it true you were with Mr. Ferguson when he died?" a reporter shouted through the crack. Emma slammed the door, threw the deadbolt, then leaned against it, breathing hard. Snookems was still growling, but the doorbell, at least, was quiet.

Her phone rang. Great—now they were calling. She crossed the room, ready to yank the cord from the wall, then paused when she saw the caller ID. It was her grandmother, who lived in a retirement center in the tiny Louisiana town of Chartreuse.

Emma squeezed her eyes shut. Oh, jeez—Grams was a TV junkie, and she always watched the early morning news shows. Drawing a deep breath, Emma lifted the receiver.

"Emma, dear—are you all right?" her grandmother's worried voice warbled through the phone.

"Yes, Grams. I'm fine."

"I just saw you on TV, and you didn't look fine. In fact, you looked plumb awful. Did that man molest you?"

"What?"

"That Ferguson man. Did he do something to you?"

"No, Grams."

"You sure? You wouldn't defend that fat turd just because he's dead, would you?"

When Grams started using the T-word, it was a sure sign she was upset. "No, Grams. I never even met him."

"Well, they're saying that man was full of weenie starch, and they keep showing this photo of you leaving the Mullendorf spread with your dress falling off. It doesn't put you in a good light."

A new wave of anxiety shot through her. "There's a photo of me leaving the Mullendorf home?"

"Yes, indeed, dear. You're on every station."

Setting Snookems on the floor, Emma picked up the TV remote. It shook like a divining rod as she struggled to click it on. "I-it's all a misunderstanding, Grams. I lost a button on my dress. I was trying to fix it when the Secret Service said there was an emergency, and . . ."

The TV flickered on. Oh, dear God—a photo of her filled the screen, and it was worse than she'd imagined. Her face was scrunched in a terrified grimace, and her dress was open all the way down the front, exposing her black bra and white thighs. It would have exposed even more, but her purse was mercifully clutched over her groin.

Emma felt as if the floor had risen up and tilted sideways. She flopped down on the sofa, the phone in one hand, the remote in the other.

"No," she gasped. The photo stayed on the screen for what seemed like forever. It was horrid. It was mortifying. It was humiliating.

And it was on TV for all the world to see.

The anchor's words began to sink into her consciousness. ". . . has been identified as Emma Jamison. Speculation is circulating about her relationship with Ferguson amid unconfirmed reports that Ferguson died with Viagra in his system."

It was a nightmare. It was a catastrophe. It was the worst thing she could ever imagine, taken to the tenth power.

"Emma?" Grams's voice quavered through the receiver. "Are you there, honey?"

"Y-yes. I-I just turned on the TV." She felt nauseated. Her hand shaking, she clicked the remote. Her picture was on the next channel, too. And the next. She clicked it again.

". . . identified as Emma Jamison," Matt Lauer was saying.

Matt Lauer was talking about her? Emma sat there, feeling cold and numb, as if she'd been packed in ice.

"Emma?"

"This is awful, Grams." Her voice shook. "What am I going to do?"

"Tell those goobers they've got their facts wrong."

"I tried. They won't listen."

"Well, try again," Grams said. "Once you explain what really happened, I'm sure everything will be all right."

But Emma had the horrible feeling that nothing would ever be all right again.

CHAPTER THREE

A.D. (After Disaster)

Seven months later

Emma Jamison, the woman who shagged President-Elect Ferguson to death, has reportedly closed her failing butler business in New Orleans and moved to the tiny town of Chartreuse, Louisiana. Apparently she's taken a job as the director of housekeeping at a retirement home.

A retirement home, ladies and gentlemen! All we can say is they better lock up the Viagra and make sure they have fresh batteries in the defibrillators.

—Jay Leno, The Tonight Show

"Hey—you're her!" The convenience-store clerk's mouth sagged open to reveal a clump of gray chewing gum resting on yellow molars. He leaned across the stained Formica countertop and stared. "You're her, aren't ya? You're Emma Jamison!"

Emma cringed. She really ought to be used to it by now. After seven months of being ogled everywhere she went, she ought to just take it in stride and not let it bother her. But she couldn't. Every time it happened, she felt pinned down and exposed, like a bug in an exhibit case.

She didn't have a life anymore. Her business had folded, she'd been forced to sell her home, and she'd spent all her savings on futile attempts to salvage her image. She couldn't go to the grocery store, couldn't walk her dog, couldn't buy stamps at the post office without somebody accosting her. Apparently she couldn't even stop at a run-down convenience store in rural Louisiana to buy a box of tampons without being recognized by a slack-jawed store clerk.

Emma drew a steadying breath. The unair-conditioned store smelled like stale coffee and the overcooked boudin sausage rotating on the counter rotisserie.

The clerk scratched his greasy hair and gazed at her in fascination. "Y'know, you look just like that photo."

She didn't need to ask which one. That awful photo of her running out of the Mullendorf mansion in her unbuttoned dress had flashed on TV screens around the world and blazed on the cover of every newspaper, every magazine, every tabloid on the planet. It was etched in the nation's collective memory, like the astronaut planting the American flag on the moon.

That photo, along with confirmation that Ferguson had died with Viagra in his system and traces of condom spermicide on his executive branch, had made the whole world jump to the same conclusion: the butler did it.

And ever since, Emma had been the main course in a media feeding frenzy. Reporters and photographers followed her car, camped on her front lawn, trailed after her into ladies' rooms, peered into the windows of her house, and even tried to take pictures through the tiny doggie door in her kitchen. They banged on her door, yelled at her as she crossed the street, and called at all hours, begging for interviews.

She'd tried to set the record straight. Her fear of video cameras prevented her from attempting TV interviews, but she'd talked to several print reporters. She might as well have saved her breath. No one believed her—not about losing the button on her dress, not about never meeting Ferguson, not about being in the kitchen while the old man shook the chandeliers upstairs.

"The Secret Service can verify it," she'd insisted. "An agent named Graw-something was with me in the kitchen."

But the Secret Service remained silent, citing a code of confidentiality. Out of respect for the deceased and his family, the official statement read, they would release no information about Mr. Ferguson's private life.

Emma's private life, however, was up for grabs. She'd had no idea there were so many forums for humiliation: late-night talk shows, news programs, political commentaries, radio programs, editorial cartoons. She was the laughingstock of the country—the subject of comedians' routines, the focus of *Saturday Night Live* skits, the butt of a million jokes. She was satirized as an adulterer, a man-killer, and—worst of all—a liar.

She hated the liar label the most. "I never even met him" had become a national joke, ranking up there with Clinton's "I didn't inhale." Since no one believed anything she said, it was impossible for Emma to defend herself.

She'd hoped that the frenzy would die down after Ferguson was buried, but it just took on new life. A controversy raged over who should be installed as president. Since the Electoral College had already convened, the Constitution said that Ferguson's running mate was supposed to take office, but a groundswell movement to hold a special election grew. And every time Ferguson was mentioned, Emma was mentioned, too.

She'd emptied her bank account trying to clear her name. She took—and passed—a lie detector test, but the press dismissed the results, citing the unreliability of lie detectors. She hired a private investigator to find out the truth, but the Secret Service thwarted him at every turn. She took out a second mortgage to pay a public-relations expert to "rehabilitate" her image, but it was like trying to drain the ocean with a bucket; every time she spoke to a reporter, her words were twisted and mangled and used as fodder for new comedy material.

Just when she thought it couldn't get any worse, conspiracy theories started to swirl. Ferguson hadn't really suffered a heart attack—Emma had been paid to kill him. She'd injected an air bubble into his aorta, poisoned him or suffocated him. The Secret Service, his political rivals, and the mob were all in on it. Ferguson's blood samples had been switched to hide the murder.

The rumors became so rampant that officials called for an investigation. Emma prayed for an official inquiry so the Secret Service would have to reveal the details about that evening. But just when an investigation began to look likely, a video turned up on the Internet—a video that showed, without a doubt, that Ferguson had indeed died in the act. Explicit enough to make the Paris Hilton tape look like an episode of *Teletubbies,* the video showed the back of a naked brunette with shoulder-length hair like

Emma's, riding the president-elect like Seabiscuit in the final stretch.

The woman's face was never shown—just Ferguson's. Thanks to the sexual position and the camera angle, the world at large now knew that a man having a heart attack looked very much like a man having an orgasm. The only difference, apparently, was what percentage of his body went flaccid immediately afterward.

The video put all the conspiracy theories to rest. Unfortunately, it also sealed Emma's fate, because everyone believed that *she* was the woman in the video.

Never mind that the woman with Ferguson had darker hair, wider hips, and a dragonfly tattoo on her left buttock. Emma produced a letter from her doctor stating that she had no tattoos anywhere on her body, but the pundits only scoffed. Temporary tattoos could look just like the real thing. An industrious reporter even dug up an old photo of Emma wearing press-on tattoos as part of a Mardi Gras costume years ago, proving she was no stranger to temporary body art.

It was hopeless. If a picture was worth a thousand words, a video was worth a million, and people believed what they thought they'd seen. To Emma's utter chagrin and complete mortification, the whole country—no, the whole freaking *planet*—believed they'd seen Emma bang the president-elect to death.

Including this cretin of a clerk. His open-mouthed gawk shifted into a leer. "You look reee-al good on that video."

"That wasn't me."

"Yeah, right." He gave a rude snort, then shouted over his shoulder. "Hey, Coquille—you'll never believe who's here!"

"Who?" called a woman's voice from the storeroom behind the counter.

"Emma Jamison."

"Get out!"

"If I'm lyin', I'm dyin'. Come see!"

Emma glared at him. "Would you just ring up my purchase, please?"

"What? Oh, yeah." He picked up the box of tampons she'd placed on the counter, then stood there, holding them, as a heavyset woman with stringy black hair lumbered out of the storeroom.

The woman's eyes grew large. "Hey—you're really you!"

Thanks for the clarification. Emma considered walking out, but she needed to make the purchase and didn't want to go through the same humiliation somewhere else. Mustering her best imitation of a patient smile, she pulled a credit card out of her wallet. "If you don't mind, I'm in something of a hurry."

The woman just stood there and stared. "Ya know what I don' get, *chère*? Why ya keep denyin' it."

Emma went into blank-faced butler mode. "I'm not denying anything. I'm just trying to make a purchase."

"I'm talkin' 'bout Ferguson. Why you keep sayin' you didn' do him?"

"Because I didn't."

Coquille and the clerk looked at each other and sniggered.

Exasperation bubbled in Emma like hot lava. She'd moved to her grandmother's hometown in southern Louisiana two months ago, thinking that if she could just lie low and stay out of the spotlight, eventually people would lose interest in her. Eventually, she'd thought, the furor would die down and she could rebuild her life.

But how could the furor die down when morons like this kept stoking it?

She was sick to death of it—sick of being judged, sick of being ridiculed, sick of being called a liar. She was sick of putting up with smug superiority from strangers who didn't know a thing about her but thought they'd seen her in the most compromising of positions. Most of all, she was sick of the futility of it all. Nothing she could do or say would change anyone's opinion.

The woman eyed her challengingly. "Ya might as well admit it, hon, 'cause the whole world's done seen it."

Maybe it was the condescension in the woman's eyes or raging PMS, but suddenly Emma had had enough. She plopped her hands on the stained Formica countertop and leaned forward. "Okay—you've finally broken me. It's true. It's all true. And if you want a real scoop, how about this." She lowered her voice conspiratorially. "The president-elect gave me crabs."

"Oh, wow." The man's jaw went slack again. "Really?"

"Really. Crabs and clap and genital warts and Bangkok crotch rot."

"Wow," the man muttered.

She should have known they'd believe that. They wouldn't believe she was innocent, but they'd readily believe the worst. She pulled her hands off the counter and blew out an annoyed breath. "Would you please just ring up my stuff?"

"Yeah, yeah, yeah—in a moment. Coqui—grab my phone and take my picture with her, would ya? Maybe we can sell it to one of those tabloids."

Emma held up her hands. "No. No pictures." All she

needed was a photo in the *National Inquisitioner* of her standing there with a box of super tampons.

Ignoring her words, the woman groped under the counter and pulled out a silver cell phone.

Emma turned to flee, but found her path blocked by a tall, jeans-clad man who suddenly strode up from the back of the store. He grinned down at her. "Looks like you fooled these guys but good, April."

"Huh?" Coquille said.

Emma stared up at the smiling man, silently echoing the clerk's sentiment. He had thick dark hair, black eyebrows, and a deep cleft in his chin, where his five-o'clock shadow dipped in like a pen in an inkwell. His face was all planes and angles, except for a disconcertingly sensuous mouth and a pair of dark, intelligent eyes that regarded her with startling familiarity. Her stomach did a cartwheel.

The man clunked a can of motor oil and a six-pack of Pepsi on the counter, right beside her box of tampons. "She loves to make people think she's Emma Jamison."

The clerk's mouth dropped open. "You mean . . . she's not?"

The man laughed. "She's good, isn't she?"

Emma gazed up at him. Aside from her grandmother and the public-relations specialist she'd hired, no one had stepped up to help her since this whole nightmare began. Here was a knight in shining armor, riding to her rescue. Unfortunately, he'd be knocked off his horse as soon as she paid for her purchase with the credit card in her hand, because it clearly identified her as Emma Jamison.

The man's smile made her feel like she was under the rotisserie lamp with the overcooked sausage. Jeezem Pete, there was some wattage in his smile.

"Go on out and get some fresh air, April," he said. "I'll take care of this."

"But . . ."

"Go on, sweetheart."

Sweetheart?

He put his hand on the small of her back, urging her toward the door. Good gravy—the wattage wasn't just in his smile. His touch jolted her like a cattle prod, and she found herself moving toward the exit.

"Wow. She's a real dead ringer," Emma heard the clerk say as the ripped screen door squeaked closed behind her. She stepped out of view and stood uncertainly on the cracked sidewalk, listening to the exchange inside.

"I know," the tall man replied. "She has a lot of fun with it."

"Sure fooled me," the clerk said.

"She fools everyone. It's kinda pathetic, getting your kicks at the expense of someone else like that, but then, everyone needs their fifteen minutes, I guess."

"She sure looks like her."

"Not once she gets her clothes off."

"Oh, yeah?" The clerk guffawed. "Too bad."

"Yeah. No kidding."

Emma's back stiffened. There was something distinctly unflattering about being imagined naked and found lacking. Was the man really trying to help her, or was he just having some fun with her himself? She should probably just get in her car and go.

She started toward her idling car, ready to do just that, when the screen door banged behind her. She turned to see the man striding toward her, the six-pack of Pepsi in one hand, the motor oil and a brown paper bag in the other. He handed her the paper bag. "Here you go."

She peeked inside. Sure enough, there were the tampons. Inwardly cringing, she folded over the top of the sack and mustered a smile. "Thanks." She opened her purse to repay him, then cringed again as she recalled why she'd been about to pay with her credit card. "I'm afraid I don't have any cash on me. I'll have to write you a check."

"Don't worry about it. It's on me." Muscles rippled under his gray polo shirt as he set the motor oil and the six-pack on the roof of a black pickup. He grinned at her. "I gotta say, though—this is the first time I've bought feminine-hygiene products for a woman before I've at least bought her a drink."

Emma's face heated. "Well, I'm glad I could add to your life experiences."

"So am I." A dimple played on his left cheek. "So . . . can I?"

The question caught her off guard. "Can you what?"

"Buy you a drink."

"No!" The answer flew out like a knee-jerk reflex, sudden and hard. Ever since this nightmare began, she'd avoided public settings like restaurants, bars, and stores.

She tried to soften her abrupt response with a smile. "Thanks, but I have my little dog in the car." Emma gestured to her silver Saturn, where Snookems stood on her hind feet, peering out the window, her long dog hair blowing in front of the air-conditioning vent. "I just picked her up at the boarding kennel, and I need to get her home."

"We could go later."

"I-I don't like to go out," Emma stammered. "It always ends up like . . ." She gestured lamely toward the store. "Like that."

"Well, hey—I know a little place where you'll be left alone." He leaned against his pickup. "The atmosphere kind of sucks, but the view's good, the beer's cold, and no one will bother you."

"Where's that?"

"My place."

It never stopped. It would never stop. For the rest of her life, men would think she'd be willing to go to bed within five minutes of meeting them. "Nice try," she said curtly. She turned to leave, her spine rigid.

The feel of his hand on her arm jolted her to a stop. It was a light touch, but the heat from his fingers seeped right through her skin and straight to her blood, warming it. "Hey—I didn't mean that the way you apparently took it. I wasn't planning to seduce you." His mouth curved in a slight smile. "At least, not yet."

But he would at some point in the future? Against her will, the thought made a tight curl of attraction unfurl in her belly.

His dimple winked at her. "I figure I'd better give you some time to get over that Bangkok crotch rot first."

Her face heated again, but the humor made her relax. "Very funny."

"That's what I thought when you said it." His gaze held hers. In the store, his eyes had looked black, but here in the sun, they were gold as whiskey, and just as intoxicating.

"I shouldn't have said that," she found herself saying. "With my luck, it'll end up as the headline in next week's tabloid. I just get so sick of being hassled, and . . ." She was babbling. Something about this man threw her completely for a loop. She moistened her suddenly dry lips. "Thanks for bailing me out."

"Glad I could help." He shot her another of those knee-weakening smiles and stuck out his hand. "By the way, I'm Max Duval."

Max Duval. The name sounded familiar, but the feel of his big warm hand wrapped around hers made it hard to think. "I'm Emma Jamison."

"I know."

Of course he did. She pulled back her hand, feeling strangely awkward.

He leaned against his truck. "You work at Sunnyside Retirement Villa, don't you?"

She nodded. "I'm the director of housekeeping there."

"That's what I thought. I just moved my grandfather into an apartment there last Friday."

Sunnyside was expecting only one new resident: Harold Duval, the founder of an internationally known plastics company. The whole center had been buzzing about it for days, because Duvalware wasn't just a household word; it was a household staple. Every refrigerator in town probably held last night's leftovers in a Duvalware plastic container.

Emma's eyebrows rose. "Harold Duval is your grandfather?"

"That's right."

"So you were the boy in all those Duvalware ads and TV commercials?"

His brow furrowed. "Afraid so."

It was silly, but Emma's pulse picked up speed. The dark-haired boy in those ads had been her first crush. When she was little, she'd taped a photo of him to the back of her closet and kissed it every night before she went to bed. And he still had the dimple that had made her heart skip.

She forced her gaze away from that dimple. "We've all been looking forward to your grandfather's arrival."

"That's only because you haven't met him yet." The

words were teasing, but his eyes looked like there was some truth behind them.

"Well, I wanted to be there to welcome him, but I had to go to a weekend seminar at the home office in Tampa. Is he all settled in?"

"He's in. I don't know how settled he is."

Emma nodded sympathetically. "It can be hard, adjusting to a new place."

And I ought to know. She'd been in Chartreuse since May, but she still felt like a complete outsider. She'd made the mistake of mentioning it to her grandmother last Thursday when she'd stopped by Grams's apartment at the retirement home.

"You moved here to start over, but all you're doing is turning into a hermit," her white-haired grandmother had chided her as she'd handed her a glass of iced tea. They'd been sitting on Grams's leopard-print sofa in her jungle-themed living room. "You need to get out and about and start building a new identity."

"I don't want an identity. I want to be anonymous."

Grams's pudgy cheeks had rounded in an elfin grin. "No one's anonymous in a town as small as Chartreuse, dear."

"So what's the answer?"

"You need to make over your life. Oprah just did a series about it."

Emma had suppressed the urge to roll her eyes. Her grandmother thought Oprah could solve all the world's problems in less than an hour.

"It only takes one little action," Grams had continued. "One action sparks another, then another, then before you know it, your whole life has changed."

"What kind of little action are we talking about here?" Emma had asked suspiciously.

"Anything that will propel you forward. It's all about momentum." Grams had leaned forward, picking up a momentum of her own. "Emma, dear, you've been dealt a bad house of cards, but you need to take the bull by the horns and make lemonade."

Her grandmother had a real talent for mangling adages. "Bulls are full of something besides lemons, Grams," Emma had said dryly.

"I'm not going to let you sidetrack me with a bunch of hooey about my mixed metaphysics."

"Metaphors."

"Metaphors, petite fours. The point is, you need to get out there and get a life."

Waiting for things to blow over sure wasn't working. Maybe her grandmother was right, Emma had silently conceded.

"Oprah says the first step is to make a commitment in writing, then set one small, specific goal with a deadline," Grams had continued.

"Such as?"

"Well, to build a new network of friends, you should decide to have coffee with one new person within the next week."

"No one wants to have coffee with me, Grams."

"You're making negative assumptions," Grams had scolded. "You need to expect good things, and then you'll start to attract them. A positive attitude is the key to working with divine providence."

There Grams went with the divine providence stuff again. "Grams—"

"You've got to make an effort." Grams's blue eyes had

taken on that balky-mule look that said she wasn't going to take no for an answer. She reached for the notepad and pen on the side table beside the phone and handed them to Emma. "Write this down: 'I, Emma Jamison, pledge to take any and all action necessary to rebuild my life. I will start by having a cup of coffee with someone new this week. And retirement home residents don't count.'"

"This is ridiculous," Emma had muttered, but she'd written down the words anyway.

"Sure I can't change your mind about that drink?" Max asked now.

The last thing she needed while she was trying to live down a man-killer reputation was to start dating the grandson of a plastics mogul, Emma thought. "Thanks, but I really need to be going."

"Well, if not a drink, how about a snowball? There's a stand down just up the street."

A snowball? The novelty of the invitation made Emma hesitate.

"Come on," he coaxed. "I won't bite. And I promise to come to your aid again if anybody harasses you."

He was so darned appealing, with those gold eyes and that dimple. And it was just a snowball—in the middle of the afternoon, in plain sight—which hardly qualified as a date. Besides, he *had* just gallantly bailed her out with the convenience-store clerk. And he *was* the boy she'd drooled over when she was eight.

And going for a snowball was the same as going for a cup of coffee. It would be an easy way to make Grams happy.

"Okay," Emma said before she could talk herself out of it. "I'll meet you there."

CHAPTER FOUR

$\mathcal{M}$ax's black Silverado rocked through a muddy pothole as he followed Emma's car to the edge of the convenience-store parking lot. He'd wanted to meet her ever since she'd moved the parish, although he couldn't exactly say why.

Aw, hell—who was he trying to kid? Her lush, do-me body was pure male fantasy, and she'd starred in more than a few of his own.

Which didn't say much for the state of his love life, Max thought ruefully. Not that he currently had one; Chartreuse didn't have many single women, and the last time he'd taken one to dinner, the whole town had their wedding planned before dessert. He'd learned the hard way that it was best to date women who lived out of town, but between his job as district attorney and his election campaign, he didn't have much time for long-distance romance.

Judging from the way he'd reacted to Emma, maybe he'd better start making the time. She wasn't dressed provocatively—she was just wearing some faded jeans and a V-necked blue T-shirt—but the outfit left her assets no place to hide, and boy, did she have some assets.

It was her face that really riveted him, though. Heart-shaped and pale, with a straight nose, a cupid's bow mouth, and big blue eyes, it was way too serious to go with that playground of a body. It was hard to reconcile the woman who'd done Ferguson to death with that somber-angel face.

Which intrigued him. Hell, he'd been intrigued ever since he'd seen that photo of her in that unbuttoned dress. Max liked to think he was pretty good at reading people, but Emma was written in hieroglyphics.

Why had she jumped in the sack with a mud-ugly old man nearly three times her age? Max had never believed the murder theory, which left a pathetic assortment of possible motives: she had a secret life as a call girl; she wanted Ferguson's ear for a political cause; she wanted a favor, such as a job or a government appointment; or she was a groupie who got a rush from sleeping with powerful men.

The turn signal on Emma's car blinked, and her head swiveled both ways before she steered her Saturn onto the two-lane highway. He eased his pickup out after her, trying to put his finger on exactly what it was about her that was so disconcerting.

Dignity—that was it. She had an air of dignity about her. Hell, she'd even managed to make Bangkok Crotch Rot sound dignified.

The memory made Max smile. "Dignified" was an odd word to describe a woman who'd screwed a hairy-assed old man on tape for all the world to see, but it fit. It was as if there were two Emma Jamisons, and he wasn't sure which one was for real. All he knew was that he had an unhealthy interest in finding out. Before he'd stopped to think about it, he'd asked her out.

Which was not the wisest move, considering that he was up for election. His campaign manager, Terrence O'Neil, had stressed the importance of maintaining a squeaky-clean image during these last six weeks. "You're running against a real mudslinger," Terrence had warned. "When Dirk Briggs ran for mayor back in '98, he discovered that the incumbent's wife was having an affair. He ran a series of ads saying that if a man couldn't keep his own house in order, he had no business running a city."

"Classy tactic."

"Yeah, well, he's a classy guy. So be careful where you go and what you do, because Briggs will be looking for ways to smear your name."

Max scowled out the windshield. He didn't like the idea of worrying about appearances or what other people thought; he'd had a craw-ful of that growing up. Man, he'd hated all those phoney-baloney Duvalware ads, where his dysfunctional family had acted like the Cleavers. What a crock. How ironic was that, anyway? A plastic family selling empty plastic containers.

He abruptly took his foot off the accelerator as Emma's brake lights flashed, indicating that her tortoise pace was slowing to a snail's. Damn, but she was cautious. Not what he'd expect from someone who indulged in reckless sexual behavior. But then, nothing about Emma was what he'd expected.

A warped plywood sign proclaiming "Sno-Ball Heaven" in red hand-lettering loomed on the right. Emma's brake lights flashed again, followed by her turn signal. He followed her onto a crushed-shell parking lot in front of a ramshackle whitewashed shack.

Emma parked under a live oak and climbed out of her car, holding a hairy scrap of a dog that looked like a blond and gray wig on a leash. As Max piled out of his truck and walked toward her, the wig stuck out a tiny pink tongue and barked.

Max winced. Man, he hated yappy little dogs. This one was all fussed up with a pink bow in her long hair.

"Meet Snookems," Emma said.

Max eyed the ridiculous little beast, unsure what was expected as a greeting. He settled for giving a curt nod in the dog's direction.

"It's okay to pet her," Emma said.

Max shoved his hands in his pockets. "Thanks, but I'll pass."

"You don't like dogs?" Emma's clear blue eyes took his measure. Those eyes were really something—as blue as her jeans, and razor sharp.

"I'm not a fan of little ones."

Big dogs—Rottweilers, Pit Bulls, Dobermans—didn't bother him. If a big dog attacked, Max could always fight back. But there was no way to fend off one of those little sissy dogs. Hitting one would be like hitting a woman, and Max could never do it.

He could tell by the look on her face that he'd lost major points.

"I was bitten by a Pomeranian a few years ago," he reluctantly added.

Emma's brows puckered. "Were you hurt badly?"

The bite had become infected, and he'd ended up in the hospital on IV antibiotics, but he wasn't about to tell her that. His buddies still razzed him about it. "Nah."

"Well, you don't have to worry about Snookems. She's only bitten one person, and he deserved it."

"Oh, yeah? What was he doing?"

"Trying to take a photo of me through her doggie door."

"Yikes. Sounds like you've really been hounded by the media."

The bad pun made her smile, transforming her face from pretty to beautiful. Her eyes were really something— little pieces of sky, floating in the heaven of her face. "If Snookems makes you uncomfortable, I'll put her back in the car."

The offer made Max feel ridiculous. "No, that's okay."

Emma bent and set the dog on the ground, giving Max a glimpse of generous cleavage as she straightened the dog's bright pink leash. Attraction grabbed him like a mugger— fast and hard and unexpected. He fought against it, irritated at his reaction. He didn't want his libido calling the shots right now.

But then, he didn't want his small-dog phobia calling them, either. He was relieved when the furball moved to the far side of Emma and cowered behind her leg.

"Why did the Pomeranian bite you?"

"I was arresting his owner."

Her eyebrows flew upward. "You're a cop?"

"No. I used to be."

"But you're not now?"

"No. I'm the local DA."

Emma hit her forehead with the heel of her hand. "Of course. You have those bumper stickers with the little apples—'Max Duval, taking a bite out of crime.' "

Max winced. "Those were my campaign manager's idea."

"I think they're cute." She tilted her head and looked up

at him. "How did the grandson of a plastics mogul end up as a Louisiana DA?"

"It's a long story." And Max had no intention of getting into it. He gestured toward the rundown shack. "We'd better go order before this place falls down."

Emma grinned and started walking toward the shack, her little dog scurrying beside her pink-polished toes. "It's looked this way all my life. I think it was designed to look decrepit."

"So you grew up here?"

"No, in Dallas. But my grandparents had a strawberry farm here, so I visited a lot." The shell gravel crunched beneath her blue flip-flops. "What about you?"

"I'm originally from Virginia. I went to law school at Tulane, and I've been in Louisiana ever since."

"How did you end up in Chartreuse?"

"My old law professor became the DA here, and he hired me as assistant DA. He died in office a couple of years ago, so I finished out his term."

"And now you're running for office yourself."

"Yeah. The election is six weeks away."

"So—are you going to win?"

"I hope so. Things look pretty good right now, but my campaign manager says they're about to get a lot tougher." Max stepped into the welcome shade of a live-oak. "Apparently my opponent plans to spend a lot of money on advertising, and he's likely to run a smear campaign."

Emma's expression grew somber. "Well, then, you probably shouldn't be seen with me."

His campaign manager would no doubt agree.

A heavyset woman with a wide, friendly face slid open the tiny window in the front of the shack as they drew near. She wore a sleeveless turquoise shirt, and her upper arm continued to flap after the rest of her arm stopped moving.

"Hello, Mrs. Boudreaux," Max greeted her.

The woman's face broke into a gap-toothed smile. "Well, hello yourself!" She turned and spoke over her shoulder. "Willie—look who's here, son!"

A large, slack-jawed man with obvious Down syndrome shuffled forward, wearing a splattered apron. "Mr. Max!" His broad face creased in a grin, exposing bright green teeth and lips. Apparently Willie had been sampling the wares. "Hey, I'm doin' like you said—keepin' the house clean an' my room nice an' neat."

"Good for you."

"An' I signed up to help on the next Habitat home."

"That's terrific."

Willie peered through the window at Emma. "Mr. Max built our new house."

"Did he really?" Emma's eyebrows rose as she glanced at Max.

He shook his head, embarrassed. "I just helped out."

"Max was the project manager," Mrs. Boudreaux said. "He coordinated all the volunteers and made sure everything went smoothly."

The praise made him uncomfortable. He shifted his stance. "Emma, this is Mrs. Boudreaux and her son, Willie."

"Nice to meet you," Emma said, sticking her hand through the window. Willie jumped forward and gave it a vigorous pump.

Mrs. Boudreaux's eyes widened. "You're Emma Jamison!"

Emma's face froze. Wow, Max thought—she couldn't go anywhere without being recognized. Even Willie was staring at her.

But Willie wasn't impressed with her notoriety. "You're pretty," he declared, still pumping her hand.

Emma flashed him a smile. "Thank you."

Mrs. Boudreaux continued to gape as Emma stepped back. "You're the girl who was with Ferguson."

Emma's smile vanished. "No," she said flatly.

"But you look just like her. And her name was Emma, too. And I read that she moved here. And—"

Emma's little dog growled. Emma's face looked strained and tense.

"If you don't mind, Mrs. Boudreaux, we'd just like a couple of snow cones," Max interrupted.

"Oh. Sure." Mrs. Boudreaux took the hint and flipped open an order pad. "What can I get you?"

"Sugar-free raspberry, please," Emma said.

"I'll have a regular cherry," Max said.

The ice machine whirred inside the snowball shack.

"Here you go," Mrs. Boudreaux said a moment later, holding out two Styrofoam cups heaped with red ice. She squinted at Emma as she handed her the darker one. "If you're not the girl who was with Ferguson, you're a dead ringer for her."

"I hear that a lot," Emma said solemnly.

"What do I owe you?" Max asked.

"Oh, nothing. It's on the house."

"Well, then, here's a tip for Willie." He shoved a five-dollar bill through the window, took the other snowball, and then led Emma away before Mrs. Boudreaux could pepper her with any further questions.

"Sorry about that," he said. "I promised to take you somewhere you wouldn't be bothered."

She lifted her shoulders. "There's no such place. I

thought it would be better in a small town, but so far, that doesn't seem to be the case."

They sat down at a white plastic table under a large green umbrella. "Is that why you moved here? For peace and quiet?"

Emma nodded. "I thought it would be easier to make a fresh start here. Plus, I needed a job after my business went under, and I liked the idea of living near my grandmother." She dug a spoon into the colored ice. "You must feel the same way about your grandfather."

The remark took Max by surprise. "What?"

"Well, you moved him here to be near you."

As if he'd had a choice. "I'm the only family he has left, and things reached the point where he could no longer live alone. His mind started kind of coming and going."

Her eyes warmed with sympathy. "He's in the Alzheimer's wing, isn't he?"

Max dipped his spoon in the flavored ice and nodded. "His official diagnosis is dementia, and he's classified as 'high functioning.' Sometimes he's fine—but other times, he's lost."

"Has he had problems for long?"

"Apparently so, but he did a good job of hiding it."

An amazingly good job. It was shocking how long it had taken for anyone to notice that Max's grandfather was losing his mind—enough to confront him or question him about it, at any rate. It wasn't until he'd run through most of his money that anyone had realized something was amiss.

Emma nodded sympathetically. "A lot of dementia patients are embarrassed and scared, so they try to hide their confusion." Emma spooned some shaved ice between her lips. "How's your grandfather doing now?"

"Surprisingly well. He actually seems happier than I've

ever seen him." Which was downright annoying, as far as Max was concerned. "Maybe the secret to happiness is losing your mind."

"I don't think so. If it were, I'd be the happiest person alive." Emma's mouth arced in a rueful smile. Her lips were red from the snowball—red and juicy-looking. Max bet they tasted just as sweet as they looked.

Down, boy, he silently reprimanded. Hooking up with Emma was a terrible idea on a couple of levels. First of all, there was the campaign to consider. And in the second place, he had no idea what kind of person he was dealing with here. Emma could be anything from a call girl to a psychopath.

"Maybe it's not losing your mind. Maybe it's just losing your memory." Max dug into his snow cone. Now might be a good time to do a little digging into her past, as well. "Which is pretty understandable. After all, everyone has something they'd like to forget."

Her eyes took on that guarded look again, the same one she'd gotten at the convenience store and with Mrs. Boudreaux. "Such as?"

"Well, I'd like to forget that run-in with the Pomeranian, and I bet you wish you'd never set eyes on Ferguson."

Her expression went from guarded to lockdown. "No," she said icily. "Because I never did." Scooping up her little dog, she abruptly rose and marched toward her Saturn.

Max's stomach sank. *Great, just great. Smooth going, Duval.* "Hey—wait up!" He hurried after her. "Emma— hold up a minute."

She paused beside her car and reluctantly turned around. Her little dog growled as Max strode toward her. He stopped several feet away, shoved his hands in his pockets, and pulled out his most sincere expression. "Look—I didn't mean to offend you."

"No. You just meant to trick me into admitting something juicy." Her eyes were as cold as the snowball she'd left on the table. "Nice try."

"I wasn't trying—"

She gave him a scathing look. "Oh, please." She yanked open her car door.

"Look—I'm sorry," Max said abruptly.

She hesitated. He was silently congratulating himself that the apology had worked when she turned and nailed him with a pointed gaze.

"For the record, I never met Ferguson, and that wasn't me in the video. I've stated that over and over, and I resent the fact you think I'm a liar." She climbed into her car, slammed the door and started the engine.

"Emma," he called, through the window.

She opened it a crack. "I forgot to thank you for the snowball," she said in a wooden tone.

The window zipped up. Her little dog stood on its hind legs on her lap and bared its teeth as she backed out of the parking lot and drove away, her tires spewing white dust from the shell road.

Terrific. He'd known her all of fifteen minutes, and she'd already decided she never wanted to see him again. He tossed his snow cone into a dented aluminum trash can and strode toward his pickup, blowing out a disgusted breath.

What the hell—it was just as well. There was no way he could get involved with Emma Jamison.

On the other hand, it was a small town, and she worked at the retirement home where his grandfather now lived. There was no way he could completely stay away from her, either.

CHAPTER FIVE

Later, that evening, Emma drove up to the three-story French-country style retirement center. An imposing structure with large windows, heavy stained-wood shutters, curved iron balconies, and a soaring terra-cotta roofline, Sunnyside Retirement Villa was something of an anomaly amid the sloping roofs and deep porches of rural Louisiana. Built and operated by a national retirement-community management corporation, Sunnyside looked more like a resort than a home for the elderly—which was the whole idea. The center's motto was "Carefree comfort in a sumptuous setting."

And sumptuous it was. The brick-and-stucco retirement center offered luxurious common areas, including a massive parlor with a full bar, a rec room, a crafts room, an exercise room, and a library, as well as an on-premises restaurant, a beauty salon, and a courtyard garden. Designed for active seniors who rented one- or two-bedroom apartments, the villa also offered various degrees of assisted living services, along with a special Alzheimer's wing that had its own rec room.

Emma parked her car in the side lot and let herself into the employee entrance at the west end of the building. As the heavy arched door closed behind her, she saw Florence Holt, a petite resident with thin white hair who reminded Emma of Betty White, ambling down the hall toward her, leaning on her walker.

"Well, good evening, Emma. What on earth are you doing here on a Sunday evening?"

It was a good question—one that Emma couldn't quite answer. She'd driven home after leaving the snowball stand, intending to spend a quiet evening at the old farmhouse her grandmother had deeded to her, but the quiet had just felt lonely. She'd telephoned her two closest girlfriends, hoping for a long chat, but Annie and her husband were hosting a neighborhood barbecue in their back yard in Santa Barbara, and Caroline had been in the middle of feeding her baby in Atlanta. The fact that her friends were busy with husbands and children had left Emma feeling more lonesome than ever.

That was what Emma wanted—a family of her own. She was beginning to wonder if that was even possible. Thanks to that photo, that ungodly tape, and the universal belief that she was the girl featured in them, she wasn't exactly the kind of girl a man would want to take home to his mom.

Thank heavens for her grandmother. Grams was her rock, and she insisted that Emma's life was about to take a turn for the better. "Once people get to know you," Grams had said, "they'll realize all this hoopla is a crock. Just be patient, dear, and this will all blow over."

Emma tried to share Grams's optimism, but episodes like today's encounter with Max made her wonder.

She'd overreacted to his assumption that she was guilty—she knew she had—and she wasn't quite sure why. Maybe it was because he was so darned attractive. Maybe it was because he'd seemed like a really nice guy, what with rescuing her from the convenience-store clerk and volunteering for Habitat for Humanity. Or maybe it was because she'd allowed herself to believe that maybe, just maybe, someone was actually interested in her, not just her notoriety.

Yeah, right. Max was just like the rest of them—a rubbernecker hoping for a drive-by look at the wreckage of her life. And Max was the worst kind, the kind who thought he was clever enough to trick her into a tawdry confession. The sheer arrogance of the ploy was almost as irritating as his presumption of guilt. Even more infuriating was the fact that for a few moments, he'd succeeded in getting her to let down her guard.

"You spend all day working around us old fogies, dear," Mrs. Holt said, pulling her thoughts back to the moment. "You ought to spend your free time with people your own age."

I'd like to, Emma thought glumly. *But the only people who don't treat me like I just got voted off* Sleeping with the Stars *are people too old to read the newspaper.*

"I was out of town at a business seminar for a few days," Emma said, "so I came by to see how Grams is doing."

The elderly woman smiled. "Oh, she's doing great."

"Sounds like everyone is." Laughter and the strains of "Strangers in the Night" poured from the parlor. Emma peered around the corner and saw a large group of senior citizens clustered around the elegant room, their faces animated. "What's the occasion?"

"No occasion. Just Mrs. Cavanaugh having one of her musical evenings."

Emma watched the withered woman hunched at the grand piano, her eyes closed, her gnarled hands moving over the keys with amazing finesse. Emma had heard about Mrs. Cavanaugh's piano playing skills, but she'd never actually heard her before. "She's wonderful."

"Yes. It's amazing, isn't it?"

"I'll say." Especially considering that Mrs. Cavanaugh had Alzheimer's so severely that most of the time she didn't even recognize her husband of sixty years.

Emma spotted him sitting in a persimmon-colored armchair near the piano. He was slight with sloping shoulders and a small paunch, his head nearly bald except for a thin fuzz of gray hair that gave him the appearance of a baby eagle.

He was never far from his wife's side. His mind was crystal clear, yet he'd moved into the Alzheimer's ward to be with her. The rapt adoration on his face as he watched her play made Emma's heart ache. What would it be like, to be loved like that? With a pang, Emma wondered if she'd ever get to find out.

"Where's Grams?" Emma asked Mrs. Holt.

"On the sofa by the wall with Mr. Duval. Those two have really hit it off. They've been thick as thieves ever since he got here."

Emma peered into the room, which was decorated in elegant shades of taupe and cream with touches of sage and persimmon. Sure enough, her chipmunk-cheeked grandmother sat beside a silver-haired man on the sofa by the fireplace, her head bent toward his, her hand on his arm. She was wearing a turquoise dress instead of her usual stretch pants and knit top, and it looked like she was even wearing a touch of lipstick. As Emma watched, Grams threw back her head and laughed at something he said. Maybe it was a trick of the light, but for a second, Grams looked thirty years younger than her seventy-eight years.

She must have felt Emma staring, because she looked over. Her face lit with a smile. "Emma, dear! What a pleasant surprise. I didn't expect to see you until tomorrow morning."

Emma crossed the room, feeling strangely awkward, as if she'd intruded on a private moment. She bent and kissed her grandmother's cheek, inhaling the unexpected scent of lavender. Since when had Grams started wearing perfume? "I came by to see how you were doing."

"I'm fine, dear. Better than fine—I'm wonderful!" Her Pillsbury Doughgirl cheeks puffed out as she grinned. "Emma, I want you to meet Harold Duval. Harold, this is my granddaughter, Emma Jamison."

The tall man stood and took her hand with a gallant bow. The resemblance to Max was unmistakable; they had the same granite jawline, the same deep-set eyes, the same high cheekbones. "It's a pleasure to meet you," he said. "You're every bit as lovely as your grandmother."

Emma glanced at her grandmother. The older woman's cheeks were pink, and her eyes were unusually bright. "Um-thank you," Emma managed. "Nice to meet you, too."

Harold waited until she sat on a tapestry-covered armchair before he sank back down on the sofa.

"Harold has the most handsome grandson, Emma,"

Grams said. "I saw him when he helped Harold move in. His name is Max, and he's a total warm-y."

"A total what?"

"Warm-y. I heard one of the aides call him that."

"Hottie, Grams. The term is *hottie*."

"That's it. He's a total hottie. You've got to meet him."

"Actually, I already have."

Grams's brows rose in surprise. "Oh?"

"We ran into each other this afternoon at the convenience store on the edge of town."

"Oh, my. *That sounds positively providential!*"

Emma suppressed the urge to roll her eyes. Her grandmother thought everything was some sort of a sign from above, especially if it tied into something she wanted to believe.

Grams leaned forward. "Tell me—was Max buying Pepsi?"

"As a matter of fact, he was. Why?"

"Because Harold loves Pepsi, but Sunnyside only serves Coke, so Max dropped off a six-pack late this afternoon. He left it in Harold's room with a note while we were out playing shuffleboard. I was so sorry he didn't stop by so I could meet him."

"I'm sure you'll get a chance."

"Isn't he handsome? I think he looks just like Harold." Grams cast the elderly man a sideways smile.

Was Grams *flirting*? Disconcerted, Emma mustered a polite smile. "There's a, uh, definite similarity."

Grams's eyes twinkled mischievously. "Well, let me tell you . . . if Max takes after his grandfather in the kissing department, you don't know what you're missing."

Kissing? What the heck had gone on in the four days

she'd been gone? Alarmed, Emma leaned toward her grand-mother. "Um, Grams—can I talk to you for a moment?"

"Of course, dear. Go right ahead." Grams settled back against the sofa cushion and looked at her expectantly.

"I mean alone."

"Right now?"

"Yes."

"Well . . . I suppose." She reluctantly turned to Harold. "Will you excuse us for a moment, Harold?"

"But of course." He stood again as Grams rose, the summer-weight wool of his gray pants swaying against his thin legs.

Emma hustled her white-haired pixie of a grandmother into the hallway. "You've been kissing Harold?"

"Why, yes, dear." Grams blinked up at her, as if it were the most normal thing in the world.

Emma's mind balked at the mental image. Her grand-mother—romantically involved?

"Is something wrong, dear?" Grams asked.

Everything was wrong! Grams was technically a widow, but still . . . She and Gramps had been married for more than half a century. How could she be interested in another man? "You've only known him two days," Emma pointed out.

"Three. We met the day he moved in, and stayed up talking half the night. I feel like I've known him all my life." Grams sighed, her face blissful. "He's a wonderful man—so considerate and sweet and attentive."

"But what about Granddad?" Emma blurted.

"Oh, honey." Grams's gaze was warm as a sympa-thetic hug. "I loved him dearly, and while he was alive, he was my whole world. But he's been gone for three years now."

It was true, and logically, Emma knew there were no grounds to object. Emotionally, though, she objected plenty. "Don't you think this is all moving a little fast?"

"At my age, sweetie, you've got to move fast."

"But Grams . . . this isn't like you."

"I know." She clasped her hands to her chest and grinned. "Isn't it wonderful?"

Wonderful was not the word Emma would have chosen. *Unsettling, shocking*, and *disturbing* were more like it. Emma looked closely at her grandmother. Her cheeks were flushed, and her eyes held an unusual glitter. "You look a little feverish, Grams. Are you feeling all right?"

"Oh, I'm feeling terrific. More than terrific."

"But—"

Grams reached out and patted her arm reassuringly. "Honey, you've got to grab the brass gusto while the grabbing's good."

"Ring," Emma muttered automatically.

"What's that?"

"The saying is, you have to grab the brass ring."

"Right. And you need to grab it with gusto. You ought to do a little grabbing of your own, sweetheart." Grams cocked her head to the side. "Say, isn't that convenience store where you met Max named the Grab 'N' Go?"

"Yes," Emma said, not following Grams's train of thought.

"Well, see there? That's definitely a sign."

"No, it isn't. It was just a coincidence."

"There's no such thing as coincidence, dear. A coincidence is just a miracle where God chooses to remain anonymous." The piano music ended. Grams glanced at her watch. "We need to get back to Harold. If I leave him alone for a second, the other ladies start crawling all under him."

"Over him."

Grams grinned. "That, too." She turned back toward the parlor.

Emma placed her hand on her grandmother's arm, feeling a little desperate. "But Grams—he has dementia."

Dorothy lifted her shoulders. "Everybody forgets things now and then."

"Dementia is more than a little forgetfulness."

"I know all about it, dear."

It was true. Emma's grandfather had suffered from dementia as his heart had failed, and Grams had devoted herself to caring for him.

"Speaking of forgetfulness," Grams said, "I hope you haven't forgotten your promise to get together with someone new this week."

Now was not the time to tell Grams she'd already fulfilled it with Max. "I haven't forgotten."

"Good." Grams motioned toward the parlor. "Come on. Let's go rejoin Harold."

"I really need to be going," Emma said.

"All right, dear—but we'll have to talk tomorrow, because I want to hear all about your trip and seminar. And I want you and Harold to get better acquainted." Grams pursed her lips thoughtfully. "We're free Wednesday night. Why don't you plan on joining us for dinner? Once you get to know him, I'm sure it'll put all your concerns to rest."

Emma doubted it, but it would give her a chance to evaluate just how demented her grandmother's new boyfriend was. "Okay."

"Terrific!" Grams raised up on her tiptoes and kissed Emma's cheek. "I'll see you tomorrow."

～

Dorothy pulled her eyebrows together as she watched Emma make her way down the hall. She'd considered telling her about that pesky reporter who'd stopped by and asked about her over the weekend, then decided against it. Emma had more than enough to worry about as it was. Besides, he wasn't a real reporter—just a college student doing a summer internship at the *Chartreuse Daily Monitor*. With any luck, he'd go to a frat party, drink himself a leg of beer—was *leg* the right word? Didn't quite seem right—and forget all about it.

She hoped so, anyway, because the last thing Emma needed was a local newshound snooping around. Life had dealt her a dirty hand, that was for sure, but she was far too young and pretty to fold the towel or throw the cards or whatever the saying was.

She watched Emma disappear out the employee exit. Maybe she shouldn't have encouraged her to move to Chartreuse and take this job, Dorothy fretted. She loved having Emma so near, but a young single woman needed a social life, and there weren't very many single people Emma's age in the area. She sure wasn't likely to meet any hanging out at the retirement center.

Emma needed a little push. Well, Dorothy was just the person to give it to her—starting with Harold's grandson. He was a real chunk, and he was single. Plus, he was the DA, and apparently he was a good one. There'd been an article in the paper today talking about how Max had the highest conniption rate—was *conniption* the right word?—of any DA in parish history. And he was a former policeman, and he'd saved a bunch of people during Hurricane Katrina, so he was bonafide hero, to boot. Harold hadn't talked much about Max—he'd just said they'd had a disagreement years ago and hadn't been close since—but he'd looked proud as punch when Dorothy had read him the newspaper article.

Yessirree, Max was just the sort of man Emma needed in her life, and since Emma had run into him, it appeared that divine providence agreed. If getting those two together was part of the cosmic plan, it wouldn't hurt for Dorothy to nudge things along a little.

Cheered by the thought, Dorothy headed back into the parlor, only to find Esmerelda Thornton sitting on the sofa beside Harold. Dorothy's mouth puckered in a frown. The gangly scarecrow of a woman wore a low-cut green dress and a blond wig, and she sat there batting her black-rimmed eyes at Harold as if she were Rita Hayworth. Dorothy supposed she should feel sorry for her—after all, Ezzy was allowed out of Alzheimer's wing only if she were accompanied by a family member or an aide—but Ezzy had been a hussy back when she had all her marbles, and she hadn't changed a lick since she'd lost them. She'd strolled naked down the hall of the Alzheimer's ward on more than one occasion, and last week, she'd been found in Arnie Moran's room wearing a see-through nighty.

Dorothy padded up on her Reebok Walkers. "Excuse me, Ezzy, but that's my seat."

Esmerelda looked up. The woman's eyelids were so weighed down with slopped-on makeup that she couldn't even open them fully, much less achieve the look of wide-eyed innocence she apparently was attempting. "This gentleman and I are having a nice chat." Esmerelda waved a hand across the room. "There's another seat over there."

"And I'm sure you'll find it just as comfortable."

Esmerelda puffed out her lower lip in a pout that might have worked for her fifty years ago and slanted a pleading glance at Harold. "You're not going to let her throw me off the sofa, are you?"

Harold looked from Dorothy to Ezzy, then back again, his eyes confused.

"Harold's too much of a gentleman to stop me," Dorothy said. "I'm sure he's hoping you'll do the right thing and move on your own."

"Well, I never!" she huffed.

Dorothy snorted. "Oh, yes, you have, Ezzy. More times than you can count."

Esmerelda sniffed haughtily but rose to her feet and teetered off.

Dorothy settled on the sofa as a baffled-looking Harold watched Ezzy's retreat.

"Was she going to a costume party?" he asked.

Dorothy laughed. "No. She used to sell cosmetics, and she thinks if she uses enough, she can spackle in her cracks and crannies."

"Well, I'm so glad you don't wear all that gunk." His gaze licked over her like a puppy's tongue. "You have such a lovely natural radiance."

Lovely natural radiance. The words made Dorothy's cheeks warm with pleasure. In her whole life, no one had ever said anything like that to her. She'd always secretly longed to be beautiful, but she'd never been a real looker. She hadn't much minded, because her late husband Wilbur hadn't; they'd known each other all their lives and were so used to each other that appearances hadn't mattered.

Besides, she hadn't had time to worry about how she looked. She'd been too busy helping Wilbur run the strawberry farm—planting, weeding, watering, spraying, picking, and packaging, not to mention keeping the books and hiring workers, all the while handling the chores of running a home and raising a child.

She'd focused on the people in her life and the things that needed doing, not on her appearance, but every now and then she'd longed for a little glamour and romance. She and Wilbur had had a good enough physical relationship, but it had dwindled to nothing in his later years, so she'd figured all that was behind her.

She'd never dreamed there could be another man in her life—much less one who'd look at her like Harold was looking at her now. It did something to her, something light and floaty and bright.

Harold's distinguished gray brows suddenly pulled together over troubled eyes.

"Is something wrong?" Dorothy asked him.

He leaned toward her. "I'm embarrassed to admit this, but I seem to have forgotten your name."

Dorothy patted his hand. She knew not to take it personally. Harold hadn't forgotten her because she wasn't memorable; he'd forgotten because he had dementia. Dementia was a thief, a sly, shifty, silent thief, sneaking in and pilfering memories like a light-fingered maid filching the silver—slowly, gradually, piece by piece.

Well, dementia might steal the past and it might steal the future, but it couldn't steal the moment, and the moment was what counted. The moment—the now—was all anyone ever had, anyway. Right now, this very instant.

Besides, there was something to be said for a man who was attracted to her all over again every time they met.

"I'm so sorry." Harold's eyes couldn't quite meet hers. "My memory sometimes just blanks out on me. I know you're someone special, but . . ."

He knew he knew her. He knew she was special. And that was enough.

"My name is Dorothy," she said softly, taking his hand. "And when you're with me, you don't have to worry about forgetting things. I know it's not your fault."

Relief flooded his face. "I feel like I'm letting people down," he confessed. "It makes me feel like an idiot."

"It's not you. It's the disease. You're not to blame."

"I'll be doing all right, and then all of a sudden, I can't remember where I am or how I got there or recognize anyone around me. I can tell you all about growing up in the Depression, but I can't remember what I had for breakfast."

She patted his hand. "I'll tell you what. I know you can read just fine, so I'll make you some notes. When you have those blank-out moments, you can look at them and figure things out."

He lifted his head. "You'd do that for me?"

"I'd be delighted to."

"That would be wonderful." He met her gaze. "You know, I feel like I've known you all my life. A lot of things I really don't mind forgetting. But you . . ." His long fingers tightened around hers. "I don't want to forget you."

"Well, then, I'll make sure you don't. I have a necklace with my name on it. I'll start wearing it, and that way, if you forget, you can read my necklace and remember."

"Thank you."

"And if you want to ask me the same question forty times, that's how many times I'll answer it."

"I can't tell you what a relief that is." He stretched his arm across the back of the sofa. "So what was your name again?"

She started to answer, then saw the corners of his mouth pull high in a grin.

"Just teasing, Dorothy." His arm slipped down around her shoulders, his hand warm on her arm. "Just teasing."

CHAPTER SIX

"*H*appy birthday to you . . ."

The off-key chorus of voices drifted out of the Alzheimer's rec room on the second floor on Tuesday as Emma headed down the corridor, a clipboard in her hand, to check the apartments her chambermaid staff had cleaned that afternoon.

"Whose birthday is it?" Emma murmured in a low voice to Teresa, the grandmotherly floor nurse who was standing in the rec room doorway. Most of Emma's co-workers treated her as if she had Ebola, but Teresa was always warm and friendly.

"Lucy Smith's," Teresa replied. "She just turned ninety-five. Her family drove over from New Orleans to throw her a party."

Emma peered in the doorway. The frail, stoop-shouldered woman sat in her balloon-festooned wheelchair, beaming as a dozen or so family members crowded around her. Mrs. Smith's gray-haired daughter, who had to be at least seventy herself, held an eight-layer chocolate doberge cake glowing with candles. Across the room, a teenage girl in jeans, a black shirt, and goth-looking black eyeliner leaned against the wall, videotaping the proceedings.

The sight of the video camera made Emma's heart pound. She jerked back as if she'd been burned.

Teresa eyed her with concern. "Are you okay?"

Emma nodded, embarrassed. "I don't want to interrupt." The truth was, her fear of being videotaped had grown more pronounced since the Ferguson debacle. She'd seen a therapist, taken anti-anxiety medicine, and even tried hypnosis, but nothing stopped the irrational, choking panic that filled her at the sight of a video camera.

"They invited the staff to join them. Why don't we go in?" Teresa urged.

"I-I'd love to, but I need to check a few more rooms."

"Well, maybe you can stop by and have a piece of cake later."

"Yeah." *Much later,* Emma thought as she hurried down the hallway. *After I'm sure that video camera has left the building.*

Drawing a deep breath, she looked down at her clipboard as she rounded a corner, then bumped squarely into something large and warm and solid.

"Whoa, there." It was a male chest, she realized as a strong hand clasped her by the arm, steadying her. And not just any male chest; she looked up and found herself staring into the all-too-handsome face of Max Duval. He wore a dark business suit and looked like he'd just stepped out of *GQ*. His left hand held a case of Pepsi. "You're in a mighty big rush," he said.

Her already erratic pulse skipped another beat. She stiffened and drew back. "I—um, sorry. I should have been paying more attention."

She stepped aside, holding the clipboard in front of her jacket like a shield, and started to walk past him.

He reached out and touched her arm again. "Emma."

What was it about this man's touch that rattled her so? The heat of his fingers burned through her gray blazer as she stopped and turned toward him.

"I want to apologize for the other day. I didn't mean to insult you."

The memory of how she'd stormed off pricked her conscience. "I-I overreacted," she admitted. Her gaze fell on the case of Pepsi in his hand. "If you're looking for your grandfather, I just saw him downstairs playing shuffleboard." *With my grandmother,* she almost added. She decided not to mention it. With any luck, Grams's infatuation with Harold would burn itself out in a week or two, and Max would never even know about it.

"I don't want to bother him. I was just on the way back to my office from a meeting and thought I'd drop this off with the floor nurse."

"You wouldn't be bothering him. I'm sure he'd be glad to see you."

"I wouldn't bet on it."

Emma looked at him quizzically.

Max shifted the case of cola to his other hand. "Before this dementia thing came up, we hadn't spoken to each other in about twelve years."

She wanted to ask him why, but the locked set of his jaw didn't invite a lot of questions. "So how are things between you now?" she ventured.

He lifted his shoulders. "Weird. I'm not even sure he knows who I am."

"I didn't think your granddad's dementia was that bad."

Max stepped aside to let an elderly woman in a wheelchair roll down the hallway. "Well, the doctors say he still has seventy percent or so of his cognitive abilities, and he's on medication that seems to have leveled things off. But apparently our history is part of the thirty percent that's gone." He lifted the red and blue Pepsi carton. "Fortunately, he still remembers the really important things, like his favorite brand of cola."

Emma smiled. "It's funny, the things they remember."

"Yeah." Max shifted his stance. "So, do you happen to know where the nurse is? Last time, she unlocked his apartment and I stuck this in the fridge."

"She's in the rec room at a birthday party. But I need to check the maid service in your grandfather's apartment anyway, so I can let you in."

"Great."

He walked beside her down the hall, then waited as she fitted the master key into the door. As the door swung open, Emma caught the scent of furniture polish. It looked like the maid had done her job, Emma thought, looking around the handsomely furnished living room. A large leather sofa and two massive leather arm chairs sat over a large, earth-toned Kilim rug. The glass-topped coffee table and the large wooden carving of an eagle atop it looked clean and well polished.

"I have to do a quick check of the bedroom and bathroom," Emma said.

"Okay." Max headed for the kitchen.

She returned to the living room to find Max standing in front of an oak side table, holding a leather-framed photo. He glanced up as Emma approached. "I didn't know he brought any pictures with him."

Emma looked at the photo. It showed a seven- or eight-year-old Max standing in front of a giant Christmas tree with jewel-like ornaments, his parents smiling beside him. All of them wore matching red plaid flannel pajamas. "Oh, I remember that!" Emma exclaimed. "It was part of a Duvalware ad campaign. There was a TV ad like that, too." She neglected to tell him she used to kiss the screen when his face flashed on it. She leaned forward and pointed. "Look—there's your Superman cape!"

Max nodded. "There was a year or so when I wore it in every ad."

※

Max distinctly remembered why he'd worn the cape. He'd thought it held special powers, and he'd hoped it would somehow make his parents become as happy in real life as they pretended to be on camera.

The memory made Max set the photo down on the table harder than he'd intended. The thud reverberated in the small apartment. "All finished here?" he asked, turning to Emma.

"As soon as I make sure the maid emptied your grandfather's dishwasher."

Emma headed into the tiny kitchen, then rejoined Max a moment later. "All set."

Max followed her out the door to the hallway, his mind still on the photo. Why the hell had his granddad brought it with him? Had his dementia-addled mind rewritten history, so that he believed his own press? It irritated the heck out of him to think that his grandfather might have happy memories of Max's lousy childhood.

Not that it mattered. It was all in the past, and Max was way over it.

His thoughts were disrupted by a surge of people in the hallway. A gray-haired woman carried a balloon bouquet, a middle-aged man held a stack of gifts, and a young man pushed a frail elderly lady in a wheelchair. Max and Emma stood against the wall and gave them room to pass.

"Happy birthday, Mrs. Smith," Emma called as the thin white-haired woman wheeled by.

"Thank you, dear," the elderly woman replied in a faint vibrato.

"Hey—aren't you Emma Jamison?" asked a teenaged girl with dyed black hair, kohl-rimmed eyes, and a gold nose ring. "Wow—you are! My friends will never believe I actually saw you!" She lifted a video camera in her black-nail-polished hands and aimed it at Emma.

The color drained from Emma's face. She drew in a ragged breath, and her hand flew to her throat.

Max stared at her, alarmed. "Are you okay?"

Emma nodded, but something was wrong. She seemed to be gasping for air. "Ex-excuse me," she mumbled. Before he could stop her, she'd turned and fled down the hall.

"Hey—what's the matter with her?" the girl asked as Emma disappeared through the metal door under the exit sign to the stairwell.

Max didn't know, but he intended to find out. She was having trouble breathing—as if she were having an asthma attack or choking or maybe even having a seizure. Intent on helping her, he pushed past Goth Girl and followed Emma into the stairwell.

She'd already made it past the first half-flight and was out of sight. "Emma," he called, his feet clomping loudly on the concrete stairs.

She didn't answer, but he heard the solid thud of a heavy metal door a floor down. He raced down the steps and through the metal door, only to see another door close halfway down the hall.

He headed toward it. *Housekeeping*, a sign on the door proclaimed. He pushed through it and entered a room that was half-office, half-entryway to a large storeroom beyond. The office side held a neatly organized desk with a pink lamp and a vase of home-grown pink roses. A white dry-erase calendar was mounted on the wall beside it, a work schedule carefully printed in a precise, neat hand.

"Emma?" Max called again, stepping into the larger room. It was a marvel of orderliness: cleaning products marched across the shelves with military precision, push brooms and mops hung from perfectly aligned hooks, and vacuums stood like a precisely spaced regiment of soldiers. Neat stacks of folded sheets and towels lined the far wall, behind three empty maid carts.

Max spotted Emma behind the carts, sitting on the floor, her face against her knees.

He hurried forward and crouched beside her. "Hey— are you okay?"

"Yeah," she muttered, keeping her head down. "I just need a moment."

He was relieved to note that she was no longer struggling to breathe. He sank onto the cold tile beside her, his back against the wall. "What happened?"

She pulled in a deep, slow breath and hugged her legs. For a moment, he thought she wasn't going to answer. "I had a panic attack," she finally said. "I have a phobia about being videotaped."

It was no wonder. Max pulled up his legs so he was sitting just like her. "I guess this whole media thing's been rough on you."

"That's an understatement. But it's not what gave me the phobia."

"No?"

She shook her head. "It started in junior high."

Junior high? That was unexpected. "Did something happen to cause it?"

"Yeah." She drew her knees tighter, her face pale against the fabric of her slim black pants, and remained silent.

Max had seen enough crime victims to know a traumatized person when he saw one. He took a stab at the cause of it. "Look, you don't need to tell me," he said softly, "but if you want to talk to a rape counselor, I know someone who—"

"I wasn't raped."

"Oh. Well, there's an abuse hotline, and—"

"It wasn't like that. I mean, it wasn't a crime. It was just . . ." She drew a deep breath and closed her eyes. She was silent so long he thought she wasn't going to elaborate. "I was humiliated," she said at length, her voice barely above a whisper.

It wasn't a response he'd expected. "Must have been pretty bad."

"It was." She leaned her head against the beige concrete-block wall and stared at the maid cart in front of her.

He knew how badly junior high could suck—he'd had some pretty traumatic experiences there himself. "Care to talk about it?" he prompted.

"No."

"Okay."

He sat beside her in silence. After a long moment, she broke it.

"Maybe it *was* a crime." she turned her head toward him. "Is sexual harassment a crime?"

"Depends on what's involved and where it happens," Max replied. "What happened?"

She blew out a long sigh and tilted her head back, her gaze on the far wall. "I was in a school debate that the local public-broadcast channel was taping, and it was my turn at the mike. These three boys—Johnny Malanto, Pete Close, and Josh Urville—were sitting in the auditorium, right behind the TV camera, directly in my line of vision. And they held out their hands in front of their chests like they were palming watermelons, and made these stupid prissy faces and started rubbing their nipples through their shirts, and everyone around them started laughing. My mother—"

Her voiced cracked. She closed her eyes again. "My mother had just died of breast cancer. I was self-conscious about the fact I'd matured early, and . . . and . . . I needed to start wearing a bra, but Dad didn't notice or know what to say, and I didn't know how to bring it up, and since Mom had died of breast cancer, I guess I had some issues, anyway." She pulled her knees tighter and rested her chin on them. "So there I was, braless in a too-tight white shirt, with lights from the camera shining right through the fabric, and these kids started mocking me."

Oh, man. A wave of sympathy rolled through Max, along with a rush of anger toward the insensitive jerks who'd ridiculed her.

"I just freaked out. I lost my train of thought and started hyperventilating." She drew another long breath and slowly exhaled. "My speech teacher had told us, 'Don't mess up, because this channel airs the same programming over and over.' Well, all I could think about was messing up, and I was nervous about being taped to start with, and then those boys started in."

She swiped her cheek with the back of her hand. "To make matters worse, the channel ran the tape for a month, and there I was, in a see-through shirt. I thought I'd never live it down. Walking to class every day became a nightmare." Her voice trailed off. "And ever since, whenever someone points a video camera at me, I have an anxiety attack."

The woman featured in the world's most famous sex tape had a phobia about video cameras? He turned it in his mind, trying to make sense of it.

Maybe Ferguson had hidden the camera. Or maybe Emma was lying, and everything she'd just told him was a crock—but if that were the case, it meant she was the best actress he'd ever seen. It was yet another warped piece in an already twisted puzzle.

"Being afraid of video cameras must have made this whole Ferguson ordeal a nightmare," he ventured.

"It sure didn't help. But it would have been a nightmare, anyway." She rested her head back against the wall. "It still is."

He could vouch for that. She'd been bothered by three people during the two brief times he'd seen her. "Can I get you anything?" he asked. "A glass of water, or a soda?"

"No, thanks. I'm—"

The office door burst open. Between the maid carts, Max saw a heavyset woman in a black-and-white maid's uniform pushing a creaking cart toward them.

Emma scrambled to her feet. Max abruptly followed.

The woman jumped back as they stood. "Oh!" She clapped her hands over her mouth.

"I'm sorry, Renee. I didn't mean to startle you," Emma said.

The woman placed her hand over her heart as if she

were about to say the pledge of allegiance, white showing around her dark eyes. "Like to scared me to death." Her gaze flew from Emma to Max, then back again. "What—what ya'll doin' in here?"

"We were just . . ." Emma hesitated, apparently stuck for a logical explanation.

"Checking a loose wheel on one of the carts," Max quickly supplied. He turned to Emma. "That ought to take care of it."

Emma bobbed her head. "Thank you."

Buttoning his jacket, Max rapidly strode out of the room. He could feel the maid's gaze following him and knew she wasn't buying the story. What kind of guy repaired a maid's cart in a Brooks Brothers suit? Damn it—they hadn't been doing anything, but it was just the sort of situation that could start all kinds of speculation and gossip.

Which was all Emma needed.

Not to mention all *he* needed.

Instead of worrying about that, though, his thoughts were fixed on what Emma had told him as he headed for the exit. He solved mysteries for a living, but Emma Jamison was an enigma—a real Rubik's Cube of a woman. He was dying to figure her out. Unfortunately, every time he saw her, he came away with more questions than answers.

CHAPTER SEVEN

I'm afraid we have a problem." The executive director of the retirement center folded her hands on her desk and regarded Max in a way that reminded him of the time he'd been hauled into the principal's office in fourth grade for putting his pet frog down Becky Talbert's blouse.

Only this time, he didn't have a frog—or a clue why he'd received a call from the retirement center that morning, asking him to come meet with Mrs. Schwartz as soon as possible.

It had taken a massive amount of reshuffling for Max to clear his schedule on such short notice, but here he was, sitting across from a stern-faced woman who looked more like a nightclub bouncer than a guardian of the elderly. "Is my grandfather all right?" he asked.

"Yes, he's fine," Mrs. Schwartz said. "But there's a behavioral matter we need to discuss."

Oh, great. The old man was probably up to his old tricks—imperiously issuing orders and generally acting like supreme ruler of the universe.

Mrs. Schwartz tapped her fingers together on her un-
adorned desk and deepened what seemed to be a perpetual
frown. She was a Rodney Dangerfield of a woman, with a
bulbous nose, a bulky build, and protruding bulldog eyes.
Unfortunately, she didn't seem to have the late comedian's
sense of humor. "Let me begin by saying that we have
certain standards here, and there are certain behaviors we
simply can't allow."

"Well, Mrs. Schwartz, he *is* in the Alzheimer's wing,"
Max said mildly, hoping to head off a long list of his
grandfather's transgressions.

"Yes, but even in the Alzheimer's wing, there are behaviors we simply can't tolerate. When we catch our residents in a situation that is, well, *compromising*, we have to
step in and correct it."

Compromising? What the heck had the old guy done?

"We're not faulting your grandfather," Mrs. Schwartz
continued, "but we need to take steps to ensure that this
kind of thing doesn't happen again."

"What kind of thing? What the heck happened?"

She cleared her throat in a delicate harrumph. "We
caught him in bed with another resident."

"In bed." Max stared at her blankly. "You mean he wandered into the wrong room?"

"No, he was in his own room."

It took a moment for Max to wrap his head around the
implications. "In his own bed . . . with another resident?"

"I'm afraid so."

Max still wasn't sure he had an accurate grasp on the
situation. "A female resident?"

"Yes."

Max started to laugh, but Mrs. Schwartz's somber
expression stopped him. He was struck by an alarming

thought. "This resident—was she another Alzheimer's patient?"

"No, she lives on the main floor."

A woman in her right mind had climbed into bed with his grandfather? Max couldn't help it. He erupted in laughter.

Mrs. Schwartz's mouth flatlined. "Mr. Duval, I don't think you understand the seriousness of this situation."

As far as Max could tell, there was nothing serious about it. "He was in his own apartment," Max pointed out. "It's his private domicile."

"Well, yes, but he's in the Alzheimer's wing, so we check in on him. The floor nurse was completely shocked when she made the eleven-o'clock rounds."

Max knew he should make a case for his grandfather's rights, but he couldn't resist acquiring just a little more information first. "Were they naked?"

"Well, no." Mrs. Schwartz shifted her bulky frame. "Not entirely."

"They were partially naked?"

"Their clothes were . . . loosened and disarranged."

"Disarranged," Max repeated. Good gravy, the old guy was getting more action than he was.

Mrs. Schwartz's brows hunkered together. "We simply can't have this kind of thing going on here."

"Why not? Seems to me the residents should be able to do whatever they want in the privacy of their own apartments."

The woman gaped at him, her thin lips parted, her bull-dog eyes widening and protruding further. Apparently it hadn't occurred to her that he might not share her outrage. "Why, because . . ." Her lips clamped together and twisted. "Because we're not operating a brothel."

Max crossed the ankle of one leg over the knee of the other. "Was there any indication money exchanged hands?"

"No, of course not."

"Well, then, you have nothing to be concerned about, brothel-wise."

"Mr. Duval, I don't know what on earth you're thinking, but—"

A soft knock sounded on the door.

"Yes?" Mrs. Schwartz called.

The door squeaked open. "I was told you wanted to see me?"

It was Emma—wearing a tailored black pantsuit and a gold name tag, with her hair pulled back in some kind of smooth twist. Her white blouse was buttoned to the neck, and her boxy jacket completely hid her figure. There was nothing provocative about her attire or demeanor, but when her eyes locked with his, his body responded as if she were buck naked.

"Come in, Emma," Mrs. Schwartz ordered, her voice as flat as her pictureless white walls. "Mr. Duval, this is Emma Jamison. Emma, this is Mr. Duval's grandson."

Max stood up as she entered the prison cell of an office. "Great to see you again."

"You two have met?"

Emma nodded.

Mrs. Schwartz shot Emma a disapproving glare, as if she'd done something wrong. "Sit down," she ordered.

Emma sank onto one of the two black vinyl chairs opposite Mrs. Schwartz's desk. Max sat back down beside her.

"As I was explaining to Mr. Duval," Mrs. Schwartz continued, "we have a problem."

"I heard what happened, and I'm very sorry." Emma leaned forward earnestly, her words coming out in a rush. "I'm sure my grandmother didn't know she was breaking any rules."

"Your grandmother?" Max stared at her. "The woman in bed with my grandfather was your *grandmother*?"

Two bright pink spots blazed on her cheeks, and her spine went rigid. "I—I'm certain that this isn't what it looks like. My grandmother has never . . . she would never . . ." Emma twisted her fingers tightly together. "I'm sure this is all a misunderstanding."

"Hmph." Mrs. Schwartz sniffed. "Misunderstandings certainly seem to follow your family."

Emma sat perfectly still. The pink spots spread across her cheeks, making her look as if she'd been slapped. "I'll talk to my grandmother and make sure that nothing like this happens again."

"I would hope so," Mrs. Schwartz sniffed.

Max leaned forward. Emma might need to bite her tongue, but he felt no such compunction. "Hold on a moment. I didn't see anything in the rules and regulations that says residents can't have a sex life."

Mrs. Schwartz couldn't have looked more shocked if he'd exposed himself. "Our rules clearly state that no resident can put the health or well-being of another resident at risk."

"I still don't see the problem. Unless you're worried that either my grandfather or Emma's grandmother has a sexually transmitted disease."

Mrs. Schwartz's mouth opened, then closed, then opened again. "That-that wasn't . . ." the older woman stammered. "I was thinking more along the lines of . . ."

She looked at Emma, then hastily looked away, as if the sight offended her. "The possibilities of overexertion."

"I recall reading that the possibility of someone having a heart attack during sex is extremely slim," Max said.

Mrs. Schwartz shifted cold eyes to Emma. "Well, as we all know, it *does* happen."

The pink on Emma's cheeks spread all the way down her neck. "I haven't talked to my grandmother yet," she said in a carefully modulated tone, " but I'm sure there's a perfectly innocent explanation for her presence in Mr. Duval's room last night."

Mrs. Schwartz gave a disbelieving snort.

"All the same, I'll speak to her and make sure it doesn't happen again." Emma's voice was low and controlled. "Now, if you'll excuse me, I need to get back to work."

Emma unfolded from her chair, stiff as an ironing board. Max stood, as well.

Mrs. Schwartz bared her teeth in an attempt at a conciliatory smile. "Thank you for coming, Mr. Duval. And if you don't mind, I'd appreciate it if you'd speak to your grandfather, as well."

"As it happens, I do mind. I mind considerably."

"What?"

"I have no intention of discussing this with my grandfather."

Mrs. Schwartz's brow rose in shock. "Why not?"

"Well, first of all, it's a private apartment, so my grandfather can entertain anyone he wants, any time he wants. In the second place, it wouldn't do any good for me to talk to him, because he probably wouldn't remember a thing I said. And finally, even if he did remember it, he wouldn't listen to me, anyway. So I suggest you advise your staff to knock before they enter his apartment." Max crossed the room to the door and jerked it open. "If you'll excuse me, I'm due in court in half an hour."

Max held the door for Emma, then closed it once they were both out in the hall. "Nasty old crone," he muttered.

"You can say that again."

"Nasty old crone."

He was rewarded with a slight smile. He smiled back. "Well, this is an interesting turn of events. I never thought of my grandfather as the romantic sort."

Emma's eyes grew wary. "I'm sure it's not what it looks like."

"No?"

"No. I'm sure there's an innocent explanation."

"Like what? They were playing tiddlywinks under the covers?"

Emma's expression turned stony. "I'm glad you find this all so amusing." Turning abruptly, she marched down the hall.

Max followed after her. "Come on, now. Don't take this so seriously."

"But it *is* serious."

"Why?"

"Because everyone in town is going to be doing exactly what you're doing—jumping to conclusions, smirking behind my grandmother's back and assuming the worst."

The heels of Emma's pumps clicked on the beige travertine tile. Max had to hustle to keep up with her. "Who says I'm assuming the worst?"

"Oh, please." She gave him a *get-real* glare. "You made it quite clear you think they were fooling around."

"So? I don't think there's anything wrong with it. I think it's downright impressive, given their ages."

Emma stopped short and skewered him with a pointed

look. "My grandmother is not the fool-around type. She was a loving and faithful wife for fifty-six years. She would never just hop into bed with a man she's only known a few days."

"But they *were* caught in bed together," Max pointed out.

Emma's arms straightened at her sides, making her look like a soldier at attention. "But we don't know what they were actually doing."

I've got a pretty good idea of what they were at least trying to do. Max wisely kept the thought to himself.

"You can just wipe that smile off your face," Emma said hotly. "It isn't like they were caught *in flagrante.*"

Max couldn't help it. His smile widened. "Wow. I never heard anyone actually call it that."

Emma turned on her heel and resumed her march down the hall. Max had to hustle to catch up with her. "Okay, okay. I probably shouldn't jump to conclusions. But the truth is, it doesn't matter what I think, because it's none of my business."

"It's nobody's business, but everybody's going to talk about it all the same." Emma rounded a corner. "Grams was probably just helping him make his bed or something, but word of this is going spread all through the retirement home and then through the whole town. Everyone's going to think the same way you do, and my grandmother's reputation is going to be ruined."

The thought of a seventy- or eighty-something-year-old woman worrying about her virtue made Max smile. "Come on, Emma—nobody cares about a reputation in this day and age."

She stopped in her tracks. "Are you always Mr. Sensitivity, or am I getting special treatment?"

"What?"

"Did you forget who you're talking to?"

Oh, man—that wasn't the most tactful thing to say to someone whose life was in tatters because of a ruined reputation. "Hell," he muttered. He shoved his hands in his pockets, then pulled them out. "Look, I'm sorry. I wasn't thinking about the Ferguson thing. I was just thinking about two old people in a retirement home and how cool it is that they even have any interest." He stepped closer and put a hand on her sleeve. She wouldn't meet his eyes, but the tightness around her mouth was softening. "I didn't mean any disrespect to your grandmother. I know they haven't known each other all that long, but it doesn't take very long for chemistry to kick in. If attraction is there, well . . ."

She lifted her eyes, and her gaze slammed into his like a sucker punch. Oh, wow—attraction was definitely there. He was suddenly aware of her body heat radiating through her jacket sleeve.

She stared at him, her pupils large black flying saucers in the blue sky of her eyes. The air between them seemed to form a vacuum. His fingers slid up her arm. Emma opened her mouth as if to say something, then changed her mind.

His eyes locked on her lips. "Sometimes, you just find yourself drawn to someone," he found himself saying.

He edged closer, close enough that he could smell her soft, flowery perfume, close enough to feel her breath, to hear the little hitch in it as she inhaled. His other hand found her other arm. Her face tilted upward, her eyes smoky. Her lips fell open and beckoned him, a plump, pink, parted invitation.

All sense of time and place fell away. Nothing else

existed, nothing else mattered, except this soft, beckoning, beautiful woman and his urgent need to kiss her. His head lowered. His lips were about to claim hers when two shrill female voices intruded.

". . . And when the night nurse opened the door, Dorothy and Harold both screamed. And then the nurse screamed."

"Do tell!"

"I'm tellin', I'm tellin'. And then security came, and they escorted Dorothy back to her apartment."

"Do tell!"

Startled, Max turned to see two elderly women on walkers, shuffling around the corner.

They stopped short. "Oh, Madge—looky there!" said the shorter one, who wore a hot pink pillbox hat with her pink velour jogging suit.

"I can't see without my bifocals," said her companion, a large-boned woman with improbably black hair piled into a high beehive. "Is it Dorothy and Harold again?"

"No, no, it's a younger couple."

"And they're spoonin', too?"

"Looks like it."

"You think there's something in the water around here?"

"I don't know, but just in case, I'm gonna drink me a gallon."

Emma's face flushed scarlet. "I-I need to go," she stammered, pulling away.

"Emma—wait."

But she'd already slipped out of his grasp and scurried down the hall.

༚

What on earth had she been thinking? Emma's heels staccatoed down the corridor, her thoughts tap-dancing through her mind. It was bad enough that she'd poured out her pathetic junior high sob story to Max, but now she'd gone and nearly kissed him. Was she out of her *mind?*

She must be. There was no other explanation. The simple fact that Max had forgotten about her notoriety for a second had somehow overridden all of her better judgment.

She was pathetic.

Beyond pathetic—pitiful, snivel-worthy, whimper-inspiring. He thought she'd slept with Ferguson and her grandmother had slept with his grandfather, and instead of behaving in a way that would disprove it, she'd given him reason to think he was right.

No, pathetic didn't begin to describe her.

Why was she wasting her time thinking about Max, anyway? She should be focused on her grandmother. Poor Grams—escorted to her apartment by security! She must be absolutely mortified. Emma understood all too well what it felt like to endure questions and sly looks and behind-the-back whispers. Grams would need all of her support and comfort.

She stopped before her grandmother's apartment door, which was decorated with a cheerful sunflower-strewn grapevine wreath and a brass nameplate that read "Dorothy Jamison." She knocked, and the door swung open. There stood Grams, wearing a bright smile, a purple top, and a necklace with her name on it that Emma had never seen. For that matter, Emma couldn't recall her grandmother ever wearing any jewelry at all, aside from her wedding ring and wristwatch.

"Oh, Emma—it's you." Was it her imagination, or

did her grandmother seem slightly disappointed? Before Emma could decide, Grams bussed her loudly on the cheek. "Come in, sweetie." Grams stepped back from the door. "I want to hear all about your trip to Tampa. How did your seminar go?"

Emma walked into the jungle-green, animal-print-strewn living room, feeling slightly uncertain. Her grandmother acted as if nothing was wrong. But then, that was just like Grams, to focus on other people rather than herself. "Fine."

"I think it's so impressive that the corporate muckety-mucks asked you to present a program for the other house-keeping directors, especially since you've only been here a couple of months. Not that I'm really surprised." Grams bustled past her leopard-print sofa and zebra-striped easy chair on her way to the kitchen. "You've certainly made a difference in the way this place is run." Grams picked up the pot from her Mr. Coffee. "Would you like a cup of jim?"

"I think you mean joe. And no, thanks. Um, Grams . . ." Emma hesitated. Her grandmother refilled her own mug, looking vivacious and happy and bright-eyed. Had she forgotten what happened last night? A wave of alarm rushed through Emma. What if Grams were developing dementia herself?

"Grams," she began. "I heard there was some kind of incident last night."

"Oh, that." Grams flicked her wrist, waving away all concern. "Silly morons, making a big deal out of nothing."

It wasn't the reaction Emma was expecting. "I understand that security escorted you back to your room."

"The night guard is a very nice man." Grams lifted the lid on her cat-shaped cookie jar and pushed it toward

Emma. "Care for a cookie? I know it's early, but they're oatmeal, so they qualify as breakfast food."

Cookies for breakfast? Her grandmother had always been a stickler for well-balanced meals. This was completely out of character. "No, thanks." Emma sank onto a giraffe-skin-printed barstool beside her grandmother's kitchen counter and eyed her worriedly. "So, what happened last night?"

Grams waved a hand airily. "Oh, a staff person walked in on Harold and me."

"I heard you were . . ." Emma found the words sticking in her throat. She swallowed and started again. "I heard you were in bed with him."

Grams took a bite of cookie and nodded.

Emma frowned, still not sure her grandmother understood the implications. "Grams, people think . . . I mean, it looked like you and he were . . ."

Grams waved her hand again. "Well, that's what they get, boating in like that without so much as knocking."

It took a moment for Emma to translate the Gramspeak. "Barging, Grams. I think you mean barging."

"That's right." Dorothy nodded. "That woman showed absolutely no respect, no respect at all for Harold's privacy. I've told him he needs to get a deadbolt on the door."

"Grams, he's a dementia patient. He can't have a deadbolt."

"Well, they ought to knock. But I suppose that from here on out, we'll just have to come down here."

"Come down here to do what?" This conversation wasn't going at all like Emma had imagined. "What were you doing?"

"We were lying on his bed, watching TV."

"Watching TV," Emma repeated. She blew out a sigh

of relief. "I knew there had to be some kind of reasonable explanation."

Grams's eyes twinkled. "Of course, we were making out a little, too."

Emma stared at her grandmother.

Grams's lips quirked up. "Close your mouth, dear, or you're going to catch a fly."

"Grams, this isn't funny."

"I wasn't trying to be funny, dear. I'm absolutely serious." She took another bite of cookie, then pulled a paper napkin from the napkin holder on the counter and dabbed her mouth. "I know, I know, you think I'm too old for nookying around. I thought so, too. But then I met Harold, and it's like . . . like the most wonderful, magical, magnificent thing you can imagine. He makes me feel like a young girl again."

"But Grams . . . he has dementia."

"You seem a might forgetful, too, dear. We had this conversation last night."

"But, Grams—people talk. You don't want people laughing at you behind your back."

"Why not? Maybe making old fogies laugh is my contribution to society." Dorothy polished off her cookie and carried her coffee cup to the sink. "Honey, one of the advantages of being my age is that it doesn't matter one whit what people think or say about me. Harold and I are both single and over twenty-one. I'm not going to apologize to anyone for anything I do or don't do behind closed doors." She stopped and frowned, apparently stricken by a sudden thought. "But—oh, sweetie, I hadn't thought how this might affect you." The lines on Grams's face pleated like a schoolgirl's skirt. "Am I creating a problem? I wouldn't want to do anything that might reflect badly on you."

"Reflect badly on *me?* Grams, at this point I'm like a vampire—I don't even have a reflection."

Grams grinned. "Good to see you haven't lost your sense of humor, dear." She glanced at her watch. "Oh, my—I'm supposed to meet Harold in the rec room for a game of ping-pong in two minutes."

Emma rose and followed Grams out the door and into the hall.

"You're still going to join Harold and me for dinner tonight, aren't you?" Grams asked as she locked her apartment door.

"Yes."

"Good! I'm anxious for you two to get acquainted. Let's meet in the parlor at seven." She gave Emma a peck on the cheek. "Have a good day, dear."

"You, too." Emma kissed her back. "And Grams—please try to behave yourself."

"I'll try." Grams gave a mischievous wink as she started down the hall in the opposite direction from Emma. "But I'm not making any promises."

CHAPTER EIGHT

Max pushed through the frosted-glass door to the DA's suite of offices in the parish courthouse after lunch to find his campaign advisor pacing the reception area.

"Sorry I had to reschedule our meeting this morning, Terrence," Max said, taking a stack of pink message slips from Jeanne, his über-efficient receptionist. "I had something of a crisis at the retirement home."

From the sweat beaded on Terrence's bald, light-bulb-shaped head, the wiry man was having a crisis of his own. But then, Terrence lived in a state of crisis. High-strung and anxious, the slight man was a walking commercial for Paxil.

Terrence had managed three successful campaigns for Max's predecessor, Ben Kovell, so Max had hired him, thinking Terrence would handle the campaign so Max could focus on criminal cases.

Boy, had he been wrong. He should have paid closer attention to Ben's reelection bid instead of keeping his nose stuck in case files twenty-four/seven, because apparently an election campaign was a full-time job in and of itself. Which irritated the hell out of Max, because there weren't enough hours in the day to handle the caseload as it was.

Terrence pulled a copy of the *Chartreuse Daily Monitor* from under his arm and waved it in front of Max as they strode down the carpeted hallway to Max's corner office. "Did you see this?" Terrence asked.

"The latest poll numbers? Yeah." Max nodded at his assistant as he walked past his office.

"Briggs is gaining on you."

The mention of his opponent's name made Max scowl. Dirk Briggs was a member of the town's wealthiest family, and he had an attitude of entitlement that reminded Max too much of his own father. A self-important a-hole more interested in recognition than results, Briggs had previously made unsuccessful bids for mayor and state representative. Those defeats had wounded his pride, and now he was hell-bent on winning this election.

Which would be a disaster. Briggs was a two-bit litigation attorney with a lousy win record and a dubious work ethic, and he hadn't handled a criminal case in years, if ever. As far as Max was concerned, the district attorney's office was no place for beginners or slackers. It was the last bastion of law enforcement, the place where all the hard work of the police and the sheriff's deputies and the FBI either paid off or went bust.

Most importantly, the DA was the protector of the people—the only thing standing between a felon and another victim. Max had seen people die because a DA let a criminal walk, and he still had cold-sweat nightmares about it.

The DA's office was just too damned important to be

handed over to the likes of Dirk Briggs, and Max intended to keep that from happening.

Terrence trailed behind Max as he made his way down the hallway, past a row of framed awards and diplomas. "People vote for folks they know or know about, and Dirk's family's been around forever."

Long enough to have a church, a school, and a street named after them, Max thought grimly. "Yeah, well, I'm the incumbent, and criminal convictions are at an all-time high. That's got to be worth something."

"Not as much as you'd think."

"That makes no sense."

"Nothing about politics makes much sense." Terrence followed Max into his bookcase-lined office. The afternoon sun shone through the large window overlooking the town square, giving the mahogany paneling on the walls a rich reddish glow.

"If you want to keep this job, Max, you're going to have to get your name out there more. Did you see the article in Sunday's paper?"

Max circled around the old oak desk he'd inherited from his predecessor. "The one where Dirk is gushing about the joys of family life and his wife is gazing at him like he's her favorite flavor of Ben and Jerry's?" His tall-backed cordovan leather chair creaked as he sat down. "What a bunch of phony schmaltz."

"Yeah, well, that stuff goes over big with voters." Terrence sank into one of the two red leather chairs on the opposite side of the wide desk. "They like candidates who come across as warm and friendly and family-oriented. You could do with a dose of that yourself."

Max leaned back in his chair and riffled through the

pink message slips the receptionist had handed him. "Spit it out, Terrence. What do you want me to do?"

"I'd like to get some photos of you with your granddad."

Max looked up. "No."

"Why not?"

"Because he has dementia, and I'm not going to exploit him."

"It's not exploitation to show you care about your grandfather," Terrence said. "We could spin something off that old ad campaign for Duvalware—'From Our Family to Yours.' Remember?"

Oh, Max remembered, all right. He remembered all too well. He remembered all the photo shoots and magazine spreads and TV commercials orchestrated by his grandfather, featuring Max and his parents as the perfect family. Never mind that his parents could barely stand to be in the same room with each other, and when they were, the insults and accusations made the air so toxic that Max could barely breathe. And never mind that when he was little, he saw his mother and father only in passing, when the nanny trotted him by on the way to bed or out the door to yet another soccer match or baseball game, where he was the only kid with no family there to cheer him on. And never mind that when he was ten, he was shunted off to boarding school and saw his family only for photo shoots and holidays.

Oh, yes, Max remembered, and the memory made his stomach knot like a pretzel. No, Max wouldn't be posing his grandfather in phony pictures.

"It would make a great story," Terrence pressed. "And there's a go-getter of a summer intern at the local paper who would do a good job. His name is Louis Ashton, and he's a photographer as well as a reporter. I could talk him into going out to the retirement home, and—"

"Forget it."

Terrence tapped his bony fingers on the arm of his chair. "But we need to do something to make you seem more touchy-feely."

"Why can't I just be good at my job?"

"Because that's not enough. Voters like people they can relate to, people they have a personal connection with." Terrence pushed out of his chair. "If you don't want to involve your grandfather, then we need to play up the sex-appeal angle." He frowned thoughtfully as he began to pace. "That might be even better. Women all go gaga over you, anyway."

Max gazed up at the ceiling and closed his eyes.

"I've got it!" Terrence stopped in midpace. "We'll find you a romantic interest."

Max grimaced. Man, he hated this whole running-for-office business. What the hell did his personal life have to do with what kind of prosecutor he was?

"It's got to be the right person." Terrence resumed pacing, his gaze fixed on the worn Persian rug, his hands clasped behind his back like Sherlock Holmes. "Someone classy, someone likable, someone with a solid career of her own. Got any ideas?"

Max opened his eyes and curled his lip in a sardonic twist. "Yeah."

"Great! Who?"

"Emma Jamison."

Terrence rolled his eyes. "Good one."

Max had made the suggestion knowing it would get Terrence's goat, but the quick way Terrence dismissed it oddly irritated him. "She's actually very nice."

Terrence snorted. "Yeah. Ferguson thought so, too."

An inexplicable sense of defensiveness washed through Max. "Hey, everyone's made mistakes."

"Yeah, but not everyone's screwed the elected leader of the free world to death." Terrence narrowed his eyes as he gazed at Max. "You can't seriously be thinking about seeing her."

Max had fantasized about it, but fantasies didn't count.

"It would be political suicide to have your name connected with hers," Terrence warned.

Max knew it. So why did he keep thinking about her? He'd never been the kind of guy who was drawn to forbidden fruit.

His chair squeaked as he pushed it back. "Let's find a way to focus the campaign on the job I'm doing. Maybe you can get the paper to run an article about how convictions are up and recidivism is down."

"That's not news."

"But showing up at the Jaycee breakfast with a date is?"

Terrence lifted his narrow shoulders. "Look, I know you don't like it, but that's the nature of politics. The public votes for people they like, so we have to make you likable."

"And I'm not?"

Terrence gazed at him in all seriousness. "Not particularly."

Max's lips quirked up. "Gee, thanks."

The intercom on Max's desk buzzed. He pushed a button and his executive assistant's voice rattled through the speaker. "Excuse me, Max, but there's someone from the retirement home on line one, and she says it concerns your grandfather."

"Again?" Max grumbled.

"Go ahead and take the call," Terrence urged. "I have to leave anyway. But think about what I've said."

Max stared at the paneled oak door after Terrence pulled it closed behind him. It was probably true; he probably didn't come across as very likable. After all, he didn't socialize a lot. He worked, he went home, he worked some more. He used to spend his weekends working on Habitat projects, but the last house was finished and the next one wouldn't start up until October. Almost all of his leisure time lately was spent in solitary pursuits—reading, fishing, playing spider solitaire on the computer. His life probably seemed pretty boring.

But that was the way he liked it. His days were full.

So why did he feel so empty?

He jabbed at the phone button, wondering what his grandfather had done this time. "Yes?"

"Max?" trilled a female voice. "This is Dorothy Jamison. I'm a friend of your grandfather's."

"Oh, yes." Max said, swiveling around to gaze out the window. Emma's grandmother. Why was she calling him? "I've heard about you."

"Well, I've heard of you, too—and I saw you when you helped your grandfather move into his apartment. I think it would be lovely if we could all get together, and I was wondering if you could join Harold and me for dinner tonight."

"Tonight?" Max took a quick look at his schedule. He had a meeting with the farmers' co-op at four, but otherwise, his evening was free.

"I know it's short notice, but I hope you can make it."

Max was curious about the woman caught in bed with his grandfather, but he had no desire to spend any time in the old man's company. "I'm sorry, but—"

"My granddaughter is coming," Dorothy added. "And I thought it would be nice if you could join us."

Emma would be there? The invitation suddenly held enormous appeal. He swiveled back to his desk. "It just so happens that my schedule is open. What time do you want me to come?"

CHAPTER NINE

$\mathcal{H}$ello, Max. I'm Dorothy Jamison."

Max wasn't sure what he'd expected his grandfather's seductress to look like, but this wasn't it. The woman waiting for him under the wrought-iron chandelier in the Sunnyside entry hall was short and plump, with curly white hair, round rosy cheeks, and bright blue eyes. She looked like Mrs. Claus, or at least one of the elves.

Max took the tiny hand she offered. The sleeve of her silky pink blouse shimmered in lamplight.

"I'm so glad you could join us. I've been looking forward to getting to know you."

He'd been more than a little curious about Dorothy, as well. What kind of woman got romantically involved with a crotchety old dementia patient? Probably one who thought Harold was still rich.

"Harold is waiting for us in the parlor." Dorothy took Max's arm and led him into the large room across from the restaurant. A cluster of women stood in the corner near the bar, laughing uproariously. As they drew closer, Max was startled to discover that the source of their laughter was his grandfather.

"Harold is quite the charmer," Dorothy said. "If I leave him alone for a moment, the other ladies are all under him."

Max raised an eyebrow. "What?"

"Maybe I meant over. I get confused about propositions. But the point is, everyone just loves his sense of humor."

Max glanced at Dorothy warily, wondering if the old woman was bonkers.

She cocked her head to the side like a parrot and glanced up at him. "You look surprised."

"I've got to say, I've never known Granddad to be particularly humorous."

"Folks often have sides to their personalities that family members don't see."

"Really."

Dorothy nodded. "Sometimes it's hard to get beyond our memories of a person. We view them through a lens of our own limited experience." Dorothy patted his arm. "Come on. Harold will be so glad to see you."

I doubt that, Max thought, but he followed her into the room anyway.

❧

Harold glanced away from the group of ladies to see Dorothy heading toward him, accompanied by a tall young man. His stomach clenched with anxiety. He knew the man, he knew he did, but for the life of him, he couldn't conjure up a name or a context.

Think, he ordered himself. *Concentrate.* But it was no use. Memories bobbed on the dark waters of his mind like flotsam and jetsam, floating just out of reach. He strained to capture them, but trying to remember only stirred the waters and sent the memories drifting further away. He had swamphead again. Just like swamps weren't land or water but somewhere in between, his head was a thought-bog, a weird shadowland where the past and present got all jumbled up.

"We have to skee-daddle, Harold," said one of the women standing beside him. She had pale apricot hair and wore dangly earrings that looked like fishing lures. "We're playing Bunco in the game room at seven."

"All right. I'll see you ladies later." Harold smiled and gave a polite bow as the group drifted away. When he looked back up, the young man was drawing nearer. A wave of panic welled inside his chest. This was someone important, someone he should know. A business associate, a rival, a friend . . . Harold just wasn't sure.

Awful, not to remember. Names and faces and relationships were the worst. He'd always lived by his brains and his wits, and now he was losing them.

The face was familiar, so familiar. Familiar . . . like family.

Family—that was it. This was a member of his family.

The man stopped in front of Harold and held out his hand. "Hello, Granddad."

Granddad. Thank God for the clue! His grandson. Of course. Unexpectedly, a chunk of memory came floating back.

This was his grandson—the grandson he'd had a falling-out with. The grandson who hadn't spoken to him in more than a decade. What was his name?

Max—that was it. Max. Oh, they'd been so angry at each other, furiously angry. Over what? Harold couldn't remember exactly. Were they still mad at each other?

Max extended his hand. Harold cautiously shook it.

"How are you doing?" Max asked.

"Good. I'm good. You?"

"I'm fine."

Max didn't seem angry. Aloof and a little ill at ease, maybe, but not angry. Apparently, something had happened to change their relationship. Thank heavens. Harold didn't know what it was, but it didn't really matter. He'd just go with the flow and carry on as if everything had always been hunky-dory.

"Have a seat," Harold urged.

Max waited until the white-haired woman with him sat down on the sofa next to Harold. What was her name? He'd known just a moment ago, but now he couldn't recall it. His memories were like the water cycle—completely evaporated, formed into wispy clouds, or raining down so hard and fast that he couldn't keep their order straight.

He watched Max settle into a nearby armchair, dwarfing it. He was a big man—tall and muscular, with dark eyes and straight, even features.

"I understand that you caused a bit of excitement around here last night," Max said to him.

He had? Harold couldn't remember. "Where did you hear that?"

"From the center's director."

What center was he talking about? The Performing Arts Center in Nottingham, Virginia? He'd been one of their biggest benefactors. Or maybe the Science Center at that university—what was the name of it?—where he'd donated so much money. He'd better hedge his bets. "Seems like people could find something better to talk about than my business," he said gruffly.

"Well, as long as you're here, they seem to think your business is their business, too."

Here? Oh, God—where the hell was he? His upper lip beaded with sweat. "Nosy old buzzards," he muttered, reaching for his handkerchief in his jacket pocket. It made a crinkling sound as he pulled it out.

"Mrs. Schwartz isn't too happy you were entertaining Dorothy in your apartment," Max said.

Mrs. Schwartz? Dorothy? Who the hell was he talking about?

Harold unfolded his handkerchief and discovered a small note tucked inside, like a secret message. Keeping the edge of the handkerchief up to hide it, he glanced down at it.

> **Where you are:** *Sunnyside Retirement Villa in Chartreuse, Louisiana.*
> **Dorothy:** *your friend. She understands forgetting. You can ask her anything.*
> **Max:** *your grandson. He brought you here from Virginia.*

"You look confused, Granddad. Do you remember any of this?"

"Of course I do."

"You sure?"

"I—" *Dorothy.* The name conjured up a feeling, a warmth, but no face came with it.

"Of course he is," said the woman seated beside him.

Harold turned toward her. She had a smile like a blessing—reassuring and peaceful. He took the hand she extended. It was soft and warm, a perfect fit in his palm.

This must be Dorothy. He decided to test the theory.

"Have you met Dorothy?" Harold asked Max.

"Yes." Max turned and nodded at the woman. "She greeted me at the door."

He'd guessed right. *Thank God,* Harold thought. It was exhausting, trying to cover up for the things he didn't remember.

Max tapped his fingers on the tan upholstery of his chair. "Mrs. Schwartz called me into her office this morning, Granddad."

"Who?"

"Mrs. Schwartz," Dorothy said. "She's the pinch-faced old sourpuss who runs this place and treats all of us like unruly children."

Harold grinned. Something about Dorothy made him feel quite unruly.

"She was upset that you had company in your room, Granddad."

He'd had company in his room? Who the heck . . . Harold looked at Dorothy. She squeezed his hand and winked.

A thrill of excitement, unexpected and young and green, coursed through him. Harold winked back. He wished to heck he could remember what they'd done. "Is that a fact."

Max nodded. "I told her that your apartment was your private residence and you could entertain anyone you wanted."

"Oh, good for you!" Dorothy beamed approvingly, then leaned forward and lowered her voice. "I understand Mrs. Schwartz also talked to my granddaughter."

Max nodded.

Her brow crinkled. "I hope I haven't caused Emma any problems. Mrs. Schwartz has it in for her."

"Why is that?" Max asked. "Didn't she hire her?"

"Oh, no. The corporate office hired Emma over her objections. This place was in shambles and about to lose its accreditation, but Mrs. Schwartz couldn't find a qualified housekeeper. Emma had all kinds of credentials, but old Schwartzy refused to even interview her because of that Ferguson fuss. So Emma sent her résumé to the corporate office, and the vice president stepped in and hired her."

Dorothy turned as an attractive woman with light brown hair walked into the room. "Oh, look—here comes Emma now!"

✧

Emma spotted Max the moment she entered the parlor, even though he was sitting with his back toward the entrance, opposite Grams and Harold. She froze in her tracks.

Great, just great. Grams had set her up. She should have suspected as much, from the way Grams had carried on about Max the other night.

Memories of their close encounter in the hallway earlier in the day made Emma consider turning and fleeing, but her grandmother's bright eyes had lit on her, and she was already waving her over.

"Emma!" Grams called. She'd changed into a hot pink sequin-spangled blouse that Emma had never seen before, and she wore matching pink lipstick. Emma wondered for a moment if she should have changed out of her black pantsuit, then quickly decided she was being ridiculous.

"Over here," Grams called.

Emma had no choice but to join them. Harold and Max both rose to their feet, looking so much alike that the resemblance was startling.

"Harold, you remember my granddaughter, Emma," Grams said.

Emma held out her hand to the lanky, white-haired man who was dressed in a dapper blue blazer, gray pants, and a starched white-and-blue striped shirt. "Nice to see you again," she said.

Harold bent over her hand in a courtly bow. "The pleasure is all mine."

"And I believe you've met Max." Grams gestured toward Max like a model on *The Price Is Right*. Unfortunately, Max looked like the grand prize, standing there in his charcoal suit, white shirt, and blue and gray patterned tie, his dark eyes burning into hers. To Emma's chagrin, her heart rate ratcheted up several notches.

"Yes." Emma clutched her hands behind her back and nodded at Max, hoping to avoid having to shake his hand. She shot her grandmother a reproachful glance. "You didn't tell me Max would be joining us this evening."

"Funny," Max said, raising an amused eyebrow. "She made a point of telling me *you'd* be here."

And he'd come anyway. The news made her heart rate accelerate further. Max's dimple flashed in an unfairly sexy fashion as he held out his hand. She reluctantly took it and once again felt an unsettling current of heat zing up her arm. What was with this man? He was like a self-contained power plant. Plug him into the wall and he could light up half the town.

"Can I get you a drink?" Max asked, gesturing toward the small bar in the corner.

"No, thanks. Employees aren't allowed to drink on the premises."

"But you're off duty."

"Yes, but rules are rules."

"I've always thought rules were made to be broken," Harold said, shooting Grams a roguish smile.

"Around here, rules are meant to be followed," Emma said firmly. She knew she sounded like a schoolmarm, but *someone* needed to act like a responsible adult. "That way, everyone knows what to expect."

Grams grinned. "Ah, but it's the unexpected that gives life its spark. Don't you agree, gentlemen?"

"Yes indeed," Harold said enthusiastically.

Max's gaze settled on Emma in a way that made her blood heat. "There's a lot to be said for the unexpected," he said.

Like that little episode in the hall this morning. Emma smoothed her jacket, trying to smooth her flustered nerves. She couldn't—*wouldn't*—let that kind of thing happen again. She shot Max a don't-fool-with-me look. "There's even more to be said for avoiding trouble."

Grams glanced at her wristwatch. "Speaking of trouble, we'd better head in to dinner if we don't want to lose our table. Our reservation was for seven."

Max's eyebrows rose. "The dining room requires reservations?"

"It's one of the changes Emma recommended," Grams said. "It's made the service much better, because the kitchen knows how many people to feed and the waitresses don't get overwhelmed." Grams took Harold's arm as they all strolled toward the bustling dining room. "Emma has made lots of improvements all over this place. In fact, she's doing such a great job that the Sunnyside big-wigs had her go to their corporate office in Tampa last weekend and conduct a workshop for the housekeeping directors of all their other retirement properties. They even offered her a job at the corporate office."

"Wow. That's impressive." Max looked like he meant it.

Dorothy nodded. "It darn sure is. Especially since she's only been here two months."

Jeez, Grams—give it a rest. Her grandmother was hawking her as if she were a slicer-dicer at the state fair.

"Are you going to take the job?" Max asked.

Emma shook her head. "I just got settled here, and I want to stay near my grandmother." *Although I might change my mind if you don't behave,* she thought with a warning look at Grams.

Grams didn't take the hint. "Doesn't the restaurant look wonderful?" she continued. "It was Emma's idea to use real linen at night, and to set the tables with little flowers and candles. And she suggested that the servers wear black shirts and pants with those clean-looking chef's aprons."

This was really getting embarrassing. Emma cast her grandmother another knock-it-off glance.

But Grams would not be dissuaded. "The restaurant was practically empty most evenings, but Emma helped the chef revamp the menu, and now it's packed."

"Grams, no one cares about all that."

"Of course they do, dear." Grams was no doubt about to offer up another glowing tidbit of embarrassment when the restaurant hostess mercifully arrived and led them to a table near the terrace window. Max held out Emma's chair, then seated himself beside her.

This felt way too much like a double date. After the menus were perused and discussed, Emma angled her body away from Max and turned her attention to his grandfather. "So, Mr. Duval—how do you like it here?"

"Oh, I'm having a wonderful time." Harold unfolded his starched napkin on his lap. "This is one of the best vacations I've ever had."

He thought he was just visiting. An awkward silence lurched in the air.

Max cleared his throat. "You live here now, Granddad. You're not on vacation."

"Oh, every day is a vacation when you're retired," Dorothy said breezily. "Right, Harold?"

Harold shot her a grateful smile. "Right."

Grams was covering for him, just as she used to cover for Emma's grandfather's confusion. The realization struck a nerve. It was overly protective, overly intimate. It was . . . well, maybe not disloyal, exactly, but still somehow *wrong*.

The waitress arrived and took their orders, and the conversation shifted to the upcoming shuffleboard tournament, then to the ballroom dancing lessons that Grams and Harold were taking in the villa's exercise room. Today's lesson had been the rhumba. Grams was trying to encourage Harold to get up and demonstrate a few moves when the waitress mercifully arrived with their salads.

Emma had just taken a bite of romaine lettuce when she heard a familiar gravel-like voice behind her. "Hello, there, Emma—Dorothy, Harold."

Oh, no—Iris Huckabee. The flame-haired resident had a voice as abrasive as her personality, and just the sound of it made Emma cringe. Iris was one of those people who never had a good thing to say about anyone or anything. Emma turned, and sure enough, there stood a tall woman with a large frame, a hooked beak of a nose, and kinky hair dyed an improbable shade of orange.

Iris was perfectly capable of walking on her own, but she loved to hijack people and grab an arm, no doubt to have a captive audience for her diatribes. Tonight she was leaning on the arm of a gangly woman in her late forties who wore a dreadful purple and yellow print shirt. From the unfortunate curve of her nose, Emma guessed she was Iris's daughter.

"Hello, Iris," Grams said with a pleasant nod. "Do you know Harold's grandson, Max? Max, this is Iris Huckabee."

Max rose to his feet to greet her.

"This is my daughter, Anise," Iris said.

Anise smiled, revealing long yellow teeth, then turned to Emma. "I hate to interrupt, but I was wondering if I could get your autograph." She placed a piece of paper and a pen on the white tablecloth in front of Emma.

Dread started a slow crawl up Emma's spine. "I-I'm sorry, but I don't sign autographs."

"Why not?" Iris demanded.

"Because I didn't do anything, so there's no reason."

The daughter's horsey smile faltered. "Oh, I don't care what you did or didn't do. You're famous, and that's all that matters."

Emma inwardly flinched. She hated to be rude, but she refused to fan the flames of her own infamy. "I can't," Emma explained. "It's a matter of principle."

"Principle!" Iris blew out a derisive snort of air. "For goodness' sake. All you have to do is sign your name."

"She said no, Iris." Grams offered a conciliatory smile to Anise. "Why don't you get Max's autograph? He's the district attorney."

"Anise wants to sell it on eBay," Iris grumbled. "Max isn't famous enough."

Anise gave Max flirtatious smile. "No offense."

"None taken." Max's dimple flickered in amusement.

"Well, how about Harold?" Grams asked. "He founded Duvalware."

"Really? Well . . . sure." Anise picked up the pen and paper and set them in front of Harold.

Harold gazed down at the blank page, his brow crinkled, his expression confused. "Is this the bill already?"

Dorothy laughed, as if he were joking. Emma was pretty sure he wasn't. "That will come later," she told him. "She wants your autograph because you're famous."

"I am?"

Dorothy laughed again. "Of course you are. You're such a teaser."

Looking more than a little bewildered, Harold scrawled his name on the paper and handed it to Anise.

The woman's purple and yellow sleeve dipped in the bleu cheese dressing on Emma's salad as she reached across the table. She shot Emma a cold look, as if it were her fault. "Sorry to have bothered you," she sniffed.

Iris leaned on her daughter's arm as they shuffled away. "Couldn't give you an autograph because of her principles—hmphh!" she muttered. "Seems a little late in the game for her to be worrying about *that*."

"Why, that old biddy—" Dorothy sputtered, starting to rise from her chair.

Emma put a hand on Grams's arm to stop her. "Let it be," she said softly. "It's okay."

"It's not okay," Grams fumed. "She can't walk around saying things like that!"

"We weren't supposed to hear her. She was talking to her daughter."

"But we *did* hear her!"

"Let it go, Grams." Emma cast her grandmother a pleading look. "Let's just forget about it and enjoy our dinner."

☙

The waitress chose that moment to refill their water glasses, and the conversation moved on to other topics. Between bites of surprisingly good shrimp Creole, Max bantered with Dorothy and pondered Emma. She didn't come across as the kind of woman likely to be motivated by a desire for fame or attention; she'd been embarrassed by the autograph request, as well as by her grandmother's bragging. So what *was* she motivated by? Why had she slept with Ferguson? It bugged the hell out of him that he couldn't figure her out.

"So, Max—I read about you in that 'Meet the Candidates' profile in the Sunday paper," Dorothy said as the waitress cleared their plates.

Max shifted uncomfortably. He loathed aren't-I-wonderful spin stories, and that profile had been a real fluff piece.

Dorothy turned to Emma. "You were out of town, so you probably didn't see it. It said Max was a hero during Hurricane Katrina. He took his fishing boat into New Orleans and rescued more than forty people from their rooftops."

Emma's gaze warmed his face. "Wow."

"He also won a distinguished service medal as a police officer," Dorothy said, "and he volunteers for Habitat for Humanity."

Criminy. The old gal was really laying it on thick. "I'm beginning to think I should hire you to handle my campaign PR," Max said.

"He's won most of the cases he's tried as DA," Dorothy continued, "and he's started a crime prevention program where someone will come out and check your property and make sure it's secure." Dorothy shot him a speculative look. "Do you ever do inspections yourself?"

Given her obvious match-matching mission, it wasn't hard to guess where this was going. "The sheriff's department handles that, but I'd be happy to make an exception in your case."

"Oh, I'm not worried about myself. But Emma has a window that won't lock."

Surprise, surprise, Max thought.

Emma's eyes widened with alarm. "No."

"Yes, you do, sweetie. The lock on your bedroom window is rusted open." Grams turned wide eyes on Max. "I worry about her, living all alone out in the country. I was wondering if maybe you could follow her home and fix it."

"No." Emma raised her hands, palms out, her expression mortified. "Not necessary."

"Yes, it is, dear. I know you like to be self-sufficient, but sometimes we all need a little help."

Not the kind you're giving me, Emma's glare clearly said.

Max grinned. Dorothy was quite the little cupid. "I'll be happy to fix it."

"There's really no need, " Emma said.

"Yes, there is, dear," Dorothy said. "I'm worried sick about it."

"Well, then, I'll hire someone tomorrow."

"Why pay someone when you have a Habitat volunteer willing to do it for free? And if Max takes care of it tonight, dear, I won't have to lie awake, worrying about you."

Emma's eyes narrowed in annoyance. "It's odd that you're suddenly so worried, since that window's been stuck since you lived there."

"Yes, but I'd forgotten about it. Now that I've remembered, I won't sleep a wink until it's fixed."

Max couldn't resist baiting Emma. "You don't want your grandmother to have trouble sleeping, do you?"

"I'm sure she'll manage to make it through another night," Emma said, shooting her grandmother a look full of daggers.

"Look at it from a time-management standpoint," Max said. "It'll take me two minutes to fix it, but it'll take ten times that long to talk your grandmother out of it."

Harold leaned toward Emma, his dark eyes earnest. "Go with the fastest, most efficient method—that's the time-management rule. And don't forget the survival rule—it's best to surrender when you're surrounded and outgunned."

Max glanced at his grandfather. He hadn't realized the old man had been following the conversation.

Emma gave a defeated sigh and held up her hands. "All right, all right."

⁓

The sun had disappeared behind the pines, and the western sky held the last vestiges of an orange and pink sunset by the time Max followed Emma out of the retirement center thirty minutes later. A slight breeze carried the faint scent of sweet olive on the hot, humid air.

"Where are you parked?" Max asked as the heavy double doors closed behind them. "I'll follow you to your place."

"You don't need to." Emma paused and adjusted her black purse on her shoulder. "Grams isn't really worried about my window."

"She acted pretty worried."

Emma shot him a get-real look. "Surely you weren't buying that."

Max grinned. "Is your grandmother always so . . ." He searched for a tactful word.

"Bossy? Pushy? Manipulative?" Emma supplied.

"I was going to say something more along the lines of *insistent.*"

"Spoken like a true politician." A stray strand of hair escaped from Emma's chignon and blew across her face, caressing the rounded apple of her cheek.

"Grams has always been full of advice, but in the past couple of weeks, she's been on a real toot."

"A toot?"

"That's Grams-speak for getting riled up about something. Oprah is running a series of stories about how to make over your life, and Grams has decided that mine needs a complete overhaul." Emma tucked the wayward strand behind her ear. She had beautiful ears, Max thought— delicate little pink shells, adorned with small silver earrings that gleamed in the light when she moved her head. "She's right, of course, but I'm not sure my life is fixable."

"Well, your window is."

Emma lifted her shoulders. "It's no big deal. I'll call a handyman tomorrow."

He should be glad she was letting him off the hook, but he wasn't. Emma intrigued the hell out of him. "Look—I gave your grandmother my word, so unless you want to go back in there and tell her you've changed your mind, I'm duty bound."

Emma blew out an exasperated sigh, apparently weighing the difficulty of dealing with him versus her grandmother. The wind loosened that strand again and sent it whipping back across her face. This time it blew against her lips—those full, rosebud, please-kiss-me lips. Once again, she smoothed away the golden brown tendril.

"Okay, okay. But just so we have this straight . . ." She fixed him with an I-mean-business, this-is-deadly-serious gaze. "All you're going to do is fix my window."

She was awfully cute when she was stern. "Understood."

"Okay." They headed for their vehicles, and Max found himself following Emma's Saturn for the second time in a week. Four miles of two-lane highway and a long stretch of heavily wooded dirt road later, he braked behind her in front of a two-story, Acadian-style house. Built of white clapboard with three upper dormer windows, it was wrapped by a deep porch. The scent of jasmine wafted on the air as Max swung out of his pickup.

"Great place," Max said, gazing at the house.

The cicadas hummed an evening chorus in the quiet night. "It was my grandparents' home," Emma said. "Grams deeded it to me when she moved into the retirement home."

If Dorothy could afford to give away property, then his initial suspicions about her being a gold digger were probably unfounded. Maybe she was just what she seemed—a slightly daffy little old lady who for some reason actually enjoyed his grandfather's company.

But what kind of person was Emma?

Hopefully, the inside of her house would give him a clue. He rounded his pickup, unfastened the tailgate, and pulled out a worn red toolbox, then slammed it shut and followed Emma up the steps to the porch. As his footsteps reverberated on the wood, muffled yaps sounded behind the beveled-glass door.

"There goes my alarm system," Emma said. "Wait here while I disarm it."

Max paused as Emma fitted her key in the lock and

crooned to the dog in the soft, high-pitched tone women use when talking to a baby. She opened the door and scooped up the little rag-mop. "All clear."

Max strode across the porch and through the doorway as Emma flipped on the lights.

The sight that greeted made him stand stock-still. "Wow."

Emma grinned. "Grams was going through an artistic phase."

"Wow," he repeated, resisting the urge to rub his eyes. The entry hall was painted in free-form triangles of turquoise, day-glow orange, and silver. The dining room to the left sported enormous yellow and green polka dots on a shocking pink background.

"Are my eyeballs bleeding?" Max asked as he followed Emma into the living room, which featured zebra-esque black and red stripes in a dizzying, squiggly pattern.

"Not yet," Emma told him. "It takes about twenty minutes before that effect sets in."

Max looked around, feeling like he'd landed in a sixties funhouse or an episode of *Laugh-In*. "Your grandmother did this?"

Emma nodded. "Right before she gave me the house. She said she was expressing herself, but I'm sure it was a deliberate effort to force me to paint it."

"Why would she do that?"

"Because she knew I'd be reluctant to change it from the way it had looked all my life. She wanted me to make the place my own."

So Emma was sentimental—and her grandmother was either truly crazy or exceedingly insightful. "Are her efforts going to help you over that reluctance thing?"

"Oh, yeah." Emma grinned. "I've already painted the

upstairs. The walls of my bedroom were so loud they kept me awake."

Max eyed the bright colors. "Bet it took a lot of primer to cover this up."

"Two coats," Emma said ruefully. "It took forever, and the fumes gave me a headache. I've been dreading doing the downstairs because I hate the thought of breathing that stuff for hours."

"I've got a couple of power painters I could loan you," Max said. "They really speed things up."

"Thanks. It's nice of you to offer."

He was pretty sure she'd never take him up on it. His gaze scanned the room. If it weren't for the walls, it'd be a great place. A worn rug in faded shades of red, green, and yellow sat in front of the brick fireplace, which was flanked by two red-checked chairs. A vase of homegrown roses and a collection of photographs perched atop a long console table against the wall.

He crossed the room and looked at the collection of photos. They were a far cry from the professionally posed and shot pictures in his grandfather's apartment. These were obviously shot by amateurs—out-of-focus, uncentered, with no attention to background or contrast or composition—but their imperfection gave them their charm.

He picked up a photo of a gap-toothed girl blowing out six candles on a birthday cake as a young couple looked on. "Is this you?"

She crossed over and joined him at the pictures, holding the dog in one arm like a football. "Yes. With my parents."

He set down the photo and looked at the others. The one on the right showed her as a toddler on her dad's lap, gazing at a book. Beside it was a picture of her on a swing, her mom pushing her. The next photo showed her in a cap and gown, with her father, Dorothy, and a tall older man, his eyes beaming with affection and pride. The pictures left him feeling like an orphan on a snowy night, pressing his face against the window of a warm home.

"Is this your grandfather?"

"Yes." Her face went soft as she picked up the silver-framed picture with her free hand. "Does it bother you that your grandfather is seeing my grandmother?"

The question startled him. "No. Does it bother you?"

"Yeah."

"Why?"

Emma set down the picture. "It feels like she's being disloyal to Granddad or something. You don't feel that way?"

He shook his head. "I never knew my grandmother, so no."

"Has your grandfather dated a lot of women?"

"He's never dated at all, as far as I know. He never had room in his life for anything but work."

"Good."

"Good?"

"That means he's not a player."

The very idea made Max grin. He picked up a photo of a three- or four-year-old Emma on the lap of a smiling lady. "You look like your mom."

"Thanks."

"What was she like?" Max asked.

"Warm and funny and vivacious." Emma's expression grew pensive. "It nearly killed me when she died."

He put the photo down, feeling awkward. "That must have been rough."

"Awful."

"So where's your dad?"

Emma gazed at a Christmas photo. "He died in a car crash when I was a sophomore in college."

"Wow. I'm sorry."

"Yeah. My folks were the greatest."

"You were lucky."

"Yeah, I was." She looked at him. "Are your folks still alive?"

"My mom is. My dad died when I was seventeen."

"What happened?"

"He mixed his two favorite pastimes—drinking and powerboat racing." Max paused and glanced at Emma. "There was some speculation it was deliberate."

"Oh, how horrible." Sympathy radiated from her eyes. "Your family always looked so happy in all those commercials."

"Yeah, well, the operative word is 'looked.' "

Oh, man—why had he opened his big mouth? Now he had to offer some kind of explanation. "Life was nothing like those ads," he told her. "My parents' marriage was a war zone."

"So they divorced?"

Max shook his head. "Granddad wouldn't allow it. He threatened to cut them off without a dime if they split. And since their whole lives revolved around Granddad's money, they did as he said."

Emma's eyes were soft and warm, and he got the feeling they were seeing way too much.

What was with him, baring his soul like this? The squiggly zebra walls must be getting to him. Uncomfortable, he shifted the toolbox to his other hand. "So where's this window that needs fixing?"

"Upstairs."

He followed her up a creaky wooden staircase, past a kelly-green and orange striped wall.

The upstairs hallway was painted a soft taupe. It was easy to tell where Dorothy's handiwork ended and Emma's began.

He followed her into a large airy bedroom painted soft yellow and cream. It smelled like Emma—green and sweet and spicy, like a combination of herbs and flowers. The room was dominated by a four-poster bed covered with a fluffy white duvet, the headboard piled with green and yellow pillows embroidered with what looked like daisies. But the thing that immediately caught his eye was a pair of pink lace panties on the bed. She scooped them up and tucked them quickly into a drawer, but not before setting off a series of provocative images in his brain. Emma in lace. Was that the kind of thing she had on now beneath that stern suit?

"The window's over here." She set her little dog on a chair in the corner and gestured to the second of two windows across from the bed.

Max walked over and examined the latch, glad to have something to do to take his mind off the mental image of Emma in those panties. Sure enough, the latch was rusted together. He gave it a tug. Solidly rusted together.

Opening his tool box, he pulled out a can of WD-40 and squirted some on the window latch. He jerked on it again, but it didn't budge. He drew out a pair of pliers and yanked once more. Nothing.

"That's okay," Emma said. "I'll call a locksmith in the morning."

Damn it, he wasn't going to be defeated by a stupid rusted lock, especially not in front of Emma. "Nah. I'll get it," he said. Fitting the pliers more tightly on the latch, he gritted his teeth and pulled with all his might.

Too late, he realized it was overkill. The latch suddenly popped free. He flew backward, stumbled over his toolbox, then tried to right himself, only to turn and crash headfirst into Emma's bedpost.

Emma screamed.

Her little dog barked.

Max's view of the room went dark.

He opened his eye to see Emma hovering over him, her blue eyes warm with worry. "Are you okay?"

He did a fast physical inventory. His forehead hurt like the dickens, but the thing that really smarted was his pride. "Yeah. I'm fine."

Her fingers, soft and gentle, touched his forehead. Her lips parted, and he could feel the warmth of her breath on his face. "Oh, no—you're bleeding."

"I'll be all right."

Her brow furrowed in concern. "You might have a concussion. Maybe I should call an ambulance."

"No!" He could just see the newspaper headline—*DA Picked Up in Ambulance at Emma Jamison's Home.* "I'm fine."

"Are you sure? Let me help you up." She knelt down, put her arm across his back, and tried to help him to his feet, but he was so much larger than she was that she nearly toppled over on top of him. "Are you dizzy?" she asked worriedly.

He hadn't been, but feeling her arm around him was making him that way. The scent of her—the heady combination of perfume and pure, desirable woman—was more intoxicating than a shot of tequila. "I'm okay," he muttered.

He hauled himself to his feet. Emma wrapped her arm around his waist, as if he were disabled and unable to walk. He opened his mouth to tell her that he was fine, that he didn't need to lean on her, then abruptly shut it. Why ruin a good thing? Her breast was pressed against the side of his chest, and her hair smelled like coconuts.

She led him to the side of her bed. "Stay here and I'll go get the first-aid kit."

He sank onto the mattress as she hurried away. A moment later, she returned with a damp washcloth and a white plastic box. Standing over him, she gently dabbed at the wound. Her breasts were at eye level, and her body heat wafted toward him. The scent of her coconutty hair and soft, green-smelling perfume wound around him like a hypnotic spell.

"It doesn't look too bad," she said. "I don't think you need stitches. But you've got a nasty bump. You're probably going to have a bruise." She gently pressed the washcloth to his forehead again.

He winced.

"I'm sorry. I don't want to hurt you."

You're not hurting me—you're killing me. "It-it's all right," he managed to grind out.

She turned her attention back to his forehead. Her brows pulled in a worried frown, and she bit her bottom lip.

He stared at that lip, wanting to bite it himself. *Stop it,* he ordered himself. He forced his gaze from her face, but when he looked straight ahead, his gaze was riveted directly on her breasts.

Damn it—he was getting aroused. He turned his gaze down, only to realize he was now staring at her crotch. Not good, either. Definitely not good. In desperation, he closed his eyes.

She misread his closed eyes for pain. "I'm so sorry. I feel terrible about this."

"It's no big deal." His voice came out strangely husky.

"No big deal to bash your head?" She pulled the backing off the Band-Aid and pressed it to his skin.

He shrugged. "It's been bashed worse."

He needed to get out of here. He started to stand up just as she leaned forward to make sure the bandage was secure, and his head collided with her breasts.

"Oh!" She staggered backward.

"Sorry." He reached out to steady her. "Are you all right?"

"Yes. I-I—" Their eyes collided harder than their bodies. Her pupils grew wide and dark, and then it was undeniably there: attraction, thick enough to eat with a spoon.

They stood there, staring at each other, long after politeness dictated that someone should have moved. It was unmistakable, this pull between them. It was gravitational. Magnetic. And entirely irresistible.

He didn't know who leaned into whom, but slowly, slowly they were coming together. His hands found their way to her waist. His blood pumped thick and heavy in his veins. His gaze slid to her lips, the lips that had been driving him crazy ever since he'd first set eyes on her. He could practically taste them. He was aching to taste them.

Her eyes fluttered closed. His heart pounded hard. Her lips were a mere breath away.

Then the tune from *Perry Mason* rent the air.

Her eyes flew open. She jumped back, her hands on her chest.

Damn it. Damn it. Damn it all to everlasting hell. He unclipped the cell phone from his belt, flicked it open, and looked at the number. It was the sheriff's office.

"Sorry," he muttered. "I've got to take this." He put it to his ear, and then after a brief conversation, he flipped the phone closed and turned to Emma. She stood by the lace-curtained window, her arms wrapped around herself, gazing out at the night.

"I have to go."

"So I gathered."

Max stood there, feeling awkward, wanting to say something about what just happened, not knowing what to say.

She turned and began packing cotton balls back in the first-aid kit. "Thanks for fixing my window," she said.

"Glad to help. I'll be happy to help paint your downstairs, too. Just give me a call."

Her head bobbed once. "Thanks."

She wouldn't call. Well, given the circumstances, it was just as well. He had no business sniffing around.

She headed downstairs, leaving him nothing to do but follow. He paused as she opened the front door. "Emma . . ."

"Thanks again. Good night." She wrapped her arms around herself in a do-not-touch sort of body language that put the kibosh on any goodbye hugs or kisses, so he just walked to his truck, climbed in, and started the engine. As his tires crunched on the drive, he couldn't help but wonder what would have happened if the phone hadn't rung.

He knew exactly what would have happened; he would have kissed her, which would have been an unwise move. A very unwise move.

He knew he should be grateful for the interruption, but he didn't feel grateful at all.

CHAPTER TEN

As Emma climbed the stairs to the Alzheimer's wing the next afternoon, she thought of Mr. Duval, which made her think about Max. But then, everything made her think about Max. Truth be told, she'd thought of little else ever since she'd nearly kissed him last night.

Which was not—repeat *not*—in her best interests. Just because he radiated enough testosterone to give her a buzz was no reason to ignore all of the other, more substantial reasons to stay away from him.

She mentally ticked them off as she headed down the hallway. In the first place, she had no desire to get involved with anyone who believed she was the woman in that video.

In the second place, she didn't want to get involved with a man who thought she was a liar, because trust was absolutely essential.

And in the third place, she did not, not, *not* want to have her name connected with anyone in the public eye, especially someone running for public office. She'd moved to

Chartreuse to lie low and get out of the headlines, not to have her name linked with another politician.

Emma stopped beside the partially opened door of the first Alzheimer's wing apartment and rapped on the door frame, but the blare of a TV soap opera drowned out the sound. She pushed the door and stuck in her head. "Mrs. Alvarez? It's Emma Jamison from housekeeping."

"Oh, yes, dear," called a wobbly voice from the back of the apartment. "Come on in."

Emma walked through the small Bengay-scented living room to the bathroom. She found the slight, white-haired woman standing on her tiptoes, her heavily rouged face tilted up, as she tried to hang three dresses in plastic dry-cleaners bags from the shower rod.

"This clothes rack is too high," Mrs. Alvarez complained.

Emma stepped forward and took the dresses from the woman's heavily veined hands. "This is your shower, not your closet," she gently explained.

"This isn't my closet?"

"No, ma'am. This is where you take a bath."

"Oh." Confusion clouded the brown eyes behind the thick trifocals. "Is that what I'm supposed to be doing? I'm supposed to be taking a bath?" Mrs. Alvarez reached for the top button on her floral housecoat, ready to disrobe.

"No, ma'am," Emma said quickly. "It's time to put your dry cleaning away. Let's go hang your dresses in your closet."

Holding the dresses high with one hand and leading the elderly woman with the other, Emma headed for the bedroom. She opened the closet door, only to have a jumble of wrinkled papers, candy wrappers, crumpled paper towels, and other trash tumble onto the beige carpet.

"This isn't the closet," Mrs. Alvarez declared. "This is the trash chute."

It certainly looked like one, Emma thought wryly. "You don't have a trash chute here, Mrs. Alvarez. You have a wastebasket in your kitchen and in your bathroom, and we empty them for you every day."

"Oh. Oh, dear. Oh, dear." Tears formed in Mrs. Alvarez's eyes. "What am I going to do? I can't keep it all straight."

"That's all right. I'm here to help you." Emma put her arm around the woman and helped her to the green-and-peach floral chintz sofa in the living room in front of the television. Emma picked up the remote and turned down the volume.

"I wish I were home. Oh, I want to go home!" Tears rolled down the woman's wrinkled cheeks, cutting a path through the heavy pink blush. "I just want everything the way it used to be."

Emma knew the feeling. She sat down beside the woman and patted her arm, searching for a way to help her. "Tell me about your home, Mrs. Alvarez. What did the bathroom look like?"

"It was pink. My Alberto painted it the most beautiful shade of flamingo pink." She rubbed her eyes. "He said it reminded him of my rosy cheeks."

That explained the overdose of blush, bless her heart. "Why don't we paint the bathroom here the same color?" Emma suggested.

The old woman's eyes lit up behind her thick glasses. "Oh—could we?"

"Sure. I'll bring some paint chips tomorrow and you can select the shade you want."

"Oh, you're such a dear!"

"It'll be fun," Emma said with a smile. "In the meantime, let me straighten out your closet for you."

Emma headed into the kitchen and located a pair of yellow latex gloves and a box of trash bags under the sink. Grabbing a white plastic bag, she pulled on the gloves and headed back to the bedroom closet. She was on her knees, bagging up the trash on the floor, when a knock sounded on the door.

She heard Mrs. Alvarez open it.

"Is Emma Jamison here?" a male voice said.

That was probably one of the contractors she'd called about repairing the hole in the rec room drywall, caused by a runaway wheelchair. "I'll be right with you," Emma called, standing and heading for the living room. Mrs. Alvarez stepped aside, and Emma saw a young man with a wiry build and a shock of dirty blond hair standing in the doorway. He wore blue jeans and a rumpled black T-shirt and had a large camera hanging from a strap around his neck.

A wave of trepidation washed over her as she eyed the camera. "Are you here to give an estimate on the rec room?"

"No. I'm here to see you." He flashed another gummy smile. "I'm Louis Ashton, and I'm a journalism major at LSU. I'm doing a summer internship with the *Chartreuse Monitor,* and I was wondering if I could interview you."

Emma's shoulders tensed. "I don't do interviews."

"I promise I won't take up much of your time."

"I'm sorry, but no."

"Please. It would really help me out." Louis 's eyes held a pleading-puppy look. "If I just could get an interview with you, it would help me land a good job when I graduate." This smile was alarmingly flirtatious. Jeez, did he really think that would work?

"I'm sorry," she repeated. "I can't."

"Well, at least let me take a photo."

"Sorry. I have to go." Emma closed the door, her heart pounding hard. She turned around to see Mrs. Alvarez standing behind her, a puzzled look on her face.

"He seemed like a nice young man," the elderly woman warbled. "You should have invited him in for some tea."

"He didn't want tea. He was a, um, salesman."

"Oh?" Mrs. Alvarez's eyes looked slightly crossed behind her thick trifocals. "What was he selling?"

His soul. "Magazine subscriptions," Emma told her. "Why don't you sit down and watch your program, and I'll finish cleaning your closet, okay?"

"Okay, dearie." Mrs. Alvarez toddled over to her seat in front of the TV and cranked up the volume. Emma returned to the bedroom closet and scooped up the last of the trash. She was twisting a tie onto the white plastic bag when a knock sounded at the front door again. Alarm skidded up Emma's spine. "Mrs. Alvarez," she called, "don't open—"

But it was too late.

⌇

Louis Ashton wiped his damp palms on his jeans as he waited outside the apartment door. It was pushy, knocking a second time, but his personal credo was WWGD—What Would Geraldo Do?—and Geraldo never took no for an answer.

Louis didn't intend to, either. If he was ever going to land a job in the big leagues, he needed better clips in his résumé than the crap he'd been writing about the

Chartreuse Ladies' League Fund-Raiser or the Pontchartrain Parish DA's race.

And he intended to get them. He wasn't working his way through college flipping burgers so he could spend his life covering Jaycee meetings. No, sirree. He had big dreams of big bucks and a big name. By the time his ten-year reunion rolled around, all of those SOBs who'd looked down on him in high school would be begging for his autograph.

He had everything it took—skill, smarts, persistence, and nerve—and he was going to show them all. He just needed a break, a big story, something with national interest, something that would make people at a city daily or news syndicate sit up and say, hey, we've got to hire this guy. Emma Jamison was just the ticket, and here she was, right in his own back yard.

He rapped on the door once more. Sure enough, the little cross-eyed granny in the baggy flowered dress opened the door again. She stared up at him through her smudged glasses as if she'd never seen him before. "Hello, young man," she trilled. "Would you like to come in?"

"Sure."

The little woman pulled the door wider. He stepped inside, just as Emma came around the corner.

She froze, a trash bag in her yellow-gloved hands, her forehead gathered in a frown. "What are you doing back here?"

Beads of sweat popped out on Louis's forehead. He put on his most sincere face and decided to take another stab at winning her over. "Ms. Jamison, you and I can help each other out. If you'll let me interview you, I'll tell your story, your way."

The creases in her forehead deepened. "I've already told you no. Please leave."

"But we could sell it to a national publication and make a lot of money. I'd be willing to split it with you."

Uh-oh. From the way she was scowling, she was seriously PO'd. "What part of no don't you understand?"

It was time to make his backup move. It was gutsy, but then, no guts, no glory.

"Well, then . . ." He quickly raised the digital camera, looked through the viewfinder and clicked. The flash went off.

"Hey!" Emma took a step back, blinking hard. "I didn't give you permission to take my picture!"

"I don't need it," he said bluntly, snapping another picture.

Emma's face darkened like a thundercloud. "Leave or I'll call security."

Louis didn't think the building had any security during the daytime, but he wasn't sure. He *was* sure that he didn't like the look on Emma's face as she stalked toward him. Something in her eyes reminded him of the way his big brother looked right before he doled out a major dose of whup ass.

"Out. Now!" Emma advanced, wielding the trash bag over her shoulder like a club.

He backed out the door and down the hall, nearly tripping over his retro high-top sneakers. "Just think about an interview, okay? You could make a lot of money."

Emma followed him into the hall. "Out!"

Louis yanked open the heavy metal door under the red exit sign, raced past a large garbage container, and scrambled down the stairwell. He would have loved to have squeezed off another picture, but Emma looked mad enough to punch him, and he'd already had his nose broken twice.

"And don't come back!" she yelled over the railing.

Oh, he'd be back, he thought as his rubber soles thudded down the concrete steps. It would be better if she cooperated, but even if she wouldn't, he still intended to get a story. At the very least, he hoped to sell something to the tabloids. They weren't the most prestigious type of publication, but the pay was awesome. If he could sell a story to, say, *The National Inquisitioner*, he could pay for his textbooks without having to ask *Do you want fries with that?* like he had last semester.

And who knew? Before the summer was over, maybe he'd convince Emma to sit down and give him a one-on-one. That would really rock. Man, that would be totally awesome.

～

Fury boiled in Emma's chest. How dare that little twerp waltz into the Alzheimer's wing, BS his way into a dementia patient's apartment, then snap her picture as if she were some kind of national landmark? Emma slung the bag of trash into the garbage cart with more force than necessary, then stomped back into the hallway—just in time to see her grandmother coming toward her, her white hair fluffed out around her face like a cloud.

Grams's smile crumpled into a worried frown. "My goodness, dear. Is something wrong?"

Oh, something was wrong, all right. "A reporter just showed up and took two pictures of me."

"Oh, dear. Was it a college kid from the *Monitor*?"

Emma's eyebrows rose in surprise. " Yes. How did you know?"

"He came by the other weekend, asking for you."

Emma slumped against the wall and sighed.

Grams patted her arm. "Don't worry, dear. The *Monitor* doesn't run that kind of stuff."

"No, but the tabloids do. And this guy looks long on ambition and short on ethics."

"Maybe none of the papers will want to buy his pictures. You haven't been in the news in a while, so maybe the whole publicity nightmare is over."

Yeah, if everyone in the world drinks a big dose of Milk of Amnesia.

"You have to have faith, dear," Grams said softly.

"For how long?"

"As long as it takes." Grams patted Emma's cheek. A whisper of lavender perfume wafted from her wrist.

Emma turned her attention to her grandmother. She was wearing lipstick again, this time a soft peach that matched her shirt. The necklace with her name hung around her neck, and her hair was poufier than usual.

"Your hair looks different," Emma said. "Did you style it a new way?"

Dorothy patted it. "I put some mouse in it."

"I think you mean mousse."

"Mousse, mouse—they both make my hair stand straight up. But don't change the subject, dear."

"I wasn't aware we were on a subject."

"Well, we're about to be. I want to dish." Grams took her arm and walked beside her past a wall sconce in the corridor. "So tell me—did you have a good time last night?"

This was obviously a loaded question. "It was a very nice meal," Emma answered carefully.

"Isn't Harold wonderful?"

"He's very charming, Grams."

Grams beamed. "I knew that if you got to know him, it would put all your worries to rest."

"I wouldn't say they're exactly at rest," Emma said cautiously. "I said he was charming, and charm can hide a lot. I wasn't sure how much of the conversation he was actually following."

"Oh, he's like everyone else." Grams airily waved her hand. "He follows the parts that interest him." Grams leaned forward conspiratorially. "So what about Max?"

Emma's stomach tightened. "What about him?"

"Did he follow you home and fix your lock?"

"Yes."

"And?" Grams asked eagerly.

"And then he left."

Grams's face fell. "That's all?"

Emma nodded.

"Shucks." Grams snapped her fingers as if a live one had gotten away. "Well, I'm sure you'll be hearing from him soon. He seemed *verrry* interested in you."

It was time to set her grandmother straight. "I know what you're trying to do, Grams, but it's not going to work. Max is running for office, and I'm the most scandalous woman in America. If he dated me, he couldn't get elected as sewer inspector."

Grams waved her hand. "That's just your negative thinking."

"No. It's reality. And here's another piece of it: being seen together wouldn't just be bad for Max; it would be bad for me, too. I'm trying to live down a hot-to-trot reputation, and a high-profile romance is the last thing I need."

Grams tipped up her chin to a pugnacious angle. "No, the last thing you need is to hole up and hide away."

"I'm not hiding away."

"You're not exactly painting the town red. Oprah says people with lots of social interaction are healthier and happier." Grams stopped short and put her hands on her hips. "You promised me that you'd take any and all necessary action to rebuild your life. Well, it's necessary for you to get out there and socialize."

"And how, exactly, would you like to me to do that?"

"Oprah said one of the best ways to meet people is to take a class or join a group of folks who share your interests. And I think I've got just the ticket."

Oh, boy. Here it came.

"I read something in the 'Town Doin's' section of the paper today that was positively providential," Grams continued. "I know how much you love to read, and it turns out that the women's fiction reading group meets at the library on Thursdays."

Wow—that actually didn't sound too bad. The group would be all women, women who shared her passion for good books. "Maybe I'll check it out."

"You *definitely* should check it out, because there was an unmistakable sign." Grams paused dramatically.

This ought to be good.

"The book they're discussing this month is Susan Elizabeth Phillips's *Kiss an Angel*, and I know you read it, because you loaned it to me." She gave Emma a triumphant smile. "If this isn't a case of divine providence at work, I don't know what is."

Grams's interpretation of signs didn't hold much weight in Emma's mind—Grams thought divine providence was at work if she got a good parking space at the grocery store—but this suggestion actually sounded like a good one.

"You promised me you'd make an effort," Grams said.

"I know, I know."

"So you'll do it?"

Heaven only knew she needed to do something, if only to get her mind off her unhealthy preoccupation with Max. She lifted her shoulders. "Sure."

"That's wonderful, dear!" Grams beamed, then gave her a quick peck on the cheek. "Now, if you'll excuse me, Harold is waiting for me."

"You're going to his room?" Emma asked, alarmed.

"As a matter of fact, I am."

Emma gazed into her grandmother's pert face. "Grams—you're not going to get caught in a compromising position again, are you?"

"Of course not, dear." Grams smiled and patted her arm reassuringly. "I have absolutely no intention of getting caught." With a mischievous wink, Grams sauntered down the hall.

CHAPTER ELEVEN

$\mathcal{A}$ few minutes before seven that evening, Emma pushed her way through the smoked-glass door of the Pont-chartrain Parish Library, across the street from the court-house square. The air conditioning, which should have provided relief after her blocklong walk in the August heat from the courthouse parking lot, raised goose bumps on her arms. Maybe the temperature wasn't responsible for her chill, she thought as she glanced at a sign in the lobby, indicating that the lone meeting room was on the second floor; maybe it was just the thought of walking into a roomful of strangers and enduring their inevitable stares.

Emma climbed the stairs and walked through the fiction section, inhaling the faint, musty smell of books, then hesitated in front of the glass doors that closed off the conference room. Through the glass, she could see seven women seated around a long conference table, chatting and laughing. A sense of longing filled her chest. Grams was right; she needed to make some friends. Her tight circle from college had married and scattered, and although they tried to stay in touch, the occasional e-mail or phone call wasn't the same as having friends she could do things with.

Well, nothing ventured, nothing gained. Emma drew a deep breath, smoothed her navy and white print skirt, tugged at the bottom of her navy twinset, and put on a smile.

Seven faces turned toward her as she pushed open the door. "Hello," Emma ventured into the sudden silence.

A couple of women nodded, but no one said a word. They all sat and stared.

Emma swallowed, unnerved by the quiet. "I'm Emma Jamison."

"We know," said a blonde in her late thirties, with classic Barbie doll looks and a condescending air. She exchanged smirking glances with the other women, then lifted a perfectly arched eyebrow. "May we help you?"

The vibe was so unfriendly that Emma was tempted to say she must have the wrong room and beat a quick retreat, but she hated the thought of explaining it to Grams. She also hated the thought of turning and running. She was not a quitter, she reminded herself. "I'm here for the women's fiction reading group," she said, deliberately widening her smile. "Am I in the right place?"

The blonde somehow managed to look down her nose at Emma, even though she was seated and Emma was standing. "Well, this is the reading group, but I'm afraid our membership rolls are closed."

Emma hadn't expected a warm welcome, but she hadn't anticipated a total freeze-out, either. It was a bald-faced attempt to exclude her, and the rudeness of it made her more determined to stay than ever. She forced another smile. "It's sponsored by the public library, so I assumed that meant it was open to the public."

The woman's glossy lips flattened with displeasure. "Well, it was—in the beginning. But now we really don't have room for another member."

Emma's fingers tightened on her handbag, a sense of resolve tightening inside of her. "Oh, there's always room for one more. And I see you have an empty chair." She crossed the room on shaky legs and sat down, then turned to the short brunette next to her and extended her hand. "Hello."

The woman hesitated, then tentatively took her hand.

"I didn't get your name," Emma prompted.

"Susan Matthews," the woman said reluctantly.

"Nice to meet you." Emma turned and held out her hand to a round-faced redhead with glasses as thick as Coke bottle bottoms.

"Hi. I'm Lulu," the redhead said, pumping her arm. Lulu seemed unaware of the anti-Emma dynamics in the room. "And that's Carrie." She pointed to the blond Barbie. "That's Ann on her right, then Sarah, Madeline, Angela, and Marie."

Carrie shot Lulu a disapproving look. "Lulu, dear, we really don't have time for all this. We're running behind schedule, and we want to get through all our questions." She glanced at a sheet of paper in front of her on the table. "Our book this month was *Kiss an Angel* by Susan Elizabeth Phillips. Ann, I believe it's your turn to begin. What was your overall impression of the book, and why?"

Ann looked over the rim of her reading glasses. "Well, it was an intriguing story, but the author went into entirely too much detail in the, uh, personal scenes."

"You mean the sex scenes?" asked Lulu. Her glasses magnified her slightly protuberant hazel eyes, giving her an odd resemblance to a goldfish. "Oh, I just loved them!

The scene where he rips off her trapeze tights reminded me of the time my husband and I went to Charleston. I put on a lacy teddy, then we watched a movie—"

Carrie placed a hand on her chest. "Lulu, dear, how does this relate to fiction?"

"Well, the movie was fiction. It was one of those naughty ones that you can get in hotels—I'm sure you know the kind—and then we played this role-playing game—"

Susan put her hand on Lulu's arm. "Honey, that's way too much information."

"Again?" Lulu's face fell.

All of the women tittered.

A blonde who was either Madeline or Marie leaned toward Lulu. "You can tell me after the meeting."

"Me, too," chimed in the brunette beside her.

Carrie turned to the woman to the right of Ann. "Sarah, what did you think about the book?"

The discussion continued around the room, each woman giving an opinion and the others responding to it, until they came to Emma. Carrie's gaze swept right over her.

"Okay, Ann, the next question is—" Carrie said.

"Wait a minute." Lulu interrupted. "Emma hasn't had a turn."

Carrie pulled her lips into an obviously phony smile. "Since Miss Jamison is a visitor, I'm sure she prefers to observe."

Wrong guess, Barbie girl. "Actually, I'd like to participate," she said, keeping her voice as cool as possible. "*Kiss an Angel* is one of my favorite books, and I think the love scenes advance the plot and show character development."

"Oh, I'm so glad you . . . ow!" Clutching her side, Lulu

turned to Susan. No one else said a word. Silence hung in the air, thick as a bug bomb.

"Well. Moving on . . ." Carrie said crisply.

It was a pattern that continued throughout the rest of the hour. Every time they came to Emma, Carrie tried to skip over her. Emma spoke up, only to have her remarks greeted with icy silence. By the time the meeting was over, Emma felt as welcome as a mother-in-law on a honeymoon.

"What's our book for next month?" Lulu asked as the women rose to leave.

"I'll call you in the next day or two and let you know," Carrie replied.

"But we always decide on the next book before we lea—ow!" The redhead shot another accusing look at Susan, who shook her dark hair and gave her a warning frown.

"I think we should consider moving the meeting to another location," Carrie said.

"Such as?" Ann asked.

"A place where we'd have more . . . privacy." Carrie cut a quick sideways glance at Emma. "Perhaps my house. We'll discuss it when I call about the book selection."

Emma froze. It was the southern cut, the cold shoulder, the modern-day equivalent of a scarlet letter—an indication of how far they were willing to go to exclude her.

Emma fought the urge to bolt. No; she wouldn't give them the satisfaction of running her off. She forced herself to sit still until the other women rose, forced herself to smile, forced herself to slowly walk out of the room. She casually wandered into the library stacks and pretended to peruse book titles, determined not to leave until they had.

From the corner of her eye, she watched the women cluster together behind the glass wall of the conference room, talking in low tones and laughing—no doubt about her—for what seemed like forever.

At length, they began to file out of the room. "Do you want to go get some coffee?" asked Susan.

"No. I need to get home and tuck the kids into bed," said Anne.

"Me, too," said Lulu.

Emma listened to their voices fade as they clattered down the stairs, each headed home to a scandal-free life they took completely for granted, a life filled with husbands and children and friends—the kind of life Emma had always wanted and now would probably never have.

That truth, cold and steely, cut her to the bone. She could change externals like her surroundings and her job, but she couldn't change the underlying facts: women didn't see her as friend material, and men didn't see her as the kind of woman they'd date in public, much less marry. Regardless of what Grams said about faith and divine providence and fresh starts, Emma was damaged goods.

The unfairness of it all formed a hard knot in her throat. Blinking back tears, she gazed blindly at the book spines until she was sure all of the women had left, then she made her way downstairs and out the door into the muggy night.

The sidewalk was mercifully deserted, as was the tree-lined square in front of the stately red brick courthouse. Cicadas and tree frogs in the sprawling oaks croaked a mournful chorus as she crossed the empty street, her navy mules making a hollow click on the concrete. The lump in her throat felt like a boulder as she paused beside her Saturn to dig her keys out of her purse.

"You shouldn't do that, you know," called a familiar voice.

She looked up to see Max approaching on the other side of her car, his white shirt gleaming in the street lamp. Her low spirits sank still further. Great, just great. Just what she needed—the embodiment of all she couldn't have, telling her one more thing she couldn't do. "I shouldn't do what?"

"Stand by your car and dig for your keys in the dark. You should already have them out so you're not such a vulnerable target."

"For what? Harrassment from you?"

His dimple flashed in the light of the streetlamp as he neared, his face still partially shadowed. "Among other things."

"What are you doing here?" she asked.

"Working late. My office is in the courthouse. You?"

"I went to the reading group at the library."

He leaned on the roof of her car. His tie was loosened and his dark jacket was slung over his shoulder. As he looked directly at her, the lamplight shone on a Band-Aid on his forehead. The sight added guilt to her mixed bag of already dark emotions. "How's your head?"

He touched the bandage. "Well, it's been quite the conversation piece. Everyone wants to know what happened."

Oh, no. "And what do you tell them?"

"Oh, nothing much." He gave a faint smile. "Just that I hit it on your bedpost."

Her stomach balled into a hard fist.

His smile disappeared. "Hey—I'm teasing."

Of course he was. He couldn't say anything like that without endangering his own career. All the same, she failed to see any humor in the fact that her reputation was that laughably bad. "That's not funny." Her keys jangled as she yanked them out of her bag. "Not funny at all."

"Hey, I didn't mean to upset you."

"I'm not up-upset." Tears welled up in her eyes, as months of pent-up emotion welled up in her chest.

"Oh, I can see that." He circled the car to stand beside her. "From the look on your face, I've obviously had a soothing, tranquilizing effect on you."

Dammit, she wasn't going to cry. Emma tried to unlock her car door, but her fingers slipped on the key pad and she accidentally hit the alarm button. The horn bleated in the night like a deranged goat. In an effort to shut it off, she dropped the keys. She bent to pick them up, only to bang her forehead against Max's as he knelt for them at the same time.

She heard him suck in a ragged breath.

Emma jerked back. "Oh, no—did I hurt you again?"

Max scooped up the keys and punched the button, mercifully silencing the blaring horn, then straightened and touched the Band-Aid on his forehead. "I'm good. How about you?"

"I-I'm fine." *For a person who's a klutz and a bad-luck magnet with a totally messed-up life—not to mention a name universally synonymous with "lying slut."* To her mortification, the tears she'd struggled to suppress since she left the library bullied their way out.

"Hey—hey." Lines formed between Max's eyebrows. "Are you okay?" He took her head in his hands and tilted it, checking for a bruise.

It was hard to breathe, standing that close to him, in the perfect posture for a kiss. She jerked away and swiped at a tear. "I-I'm fine."

"You don't look fine."

"Well, I am." Her protest was considerably weakened by the fact that her eyes were pouring like hydrants. Embarrassed to be crying and angry at him for seeing her do it, she wiped at the unwanted tears, then held out her damp palm. "Would you please just give me my keys?"

"I'm trying to apologize here."

"I don't want an apology." She was precariously close to completely losing it. "I just want to get in my car and l-leave."

"I don't think you should drive in this state."

Tears streamed down her face in rivulets, dripped off her chin, and plopped onto her blue sweater in big round drops. "I am n-*not* in a s-s-state."

"Well, I am, so let's just go sit down for a minute."

The tears made it impossible to mount a serious protest. Max put an arm around her shoulders, and even though she knew it was a bad idea, she let him guide her under the gnarled branches of the live-oaks to a wooden bench in the center of the parklike square. She sank onto the hard bench, which faced a spot-lit statue of Lady Justice in front of the red brick courthouse, and tried to will herself to stop crying. Unfortunately, willpower had melted into won't-power.

"I wish I were one of those guys who carried a handkerchief, but unfortunately, I'm not," Max said. "Do you have some Kleenex in your purse?"

Emma undid the latch, fumbled inside, and pulled out a tissue packet. He took it from her, extracted a tissue, and gently wiped her cheek. The simple kindness cranked up the volume of the waterworks. Months of pent-up emotion—anger, frustration, bitterness, and hurt—poured out in huge, gut-heaving sobs.

"Hey—hey. It's okay." He pulled her against his

shoulder and put both arms around her. She leaned in and bawled like a motherless calf. He just sat there, holding her, while her tears soaked the shoulder of his white shirt. It smelled like cotton and starch and testosterone—a heady, musky, intoxicating scent that filled her with indescribable longing. She cried for the life she'd lost. She cried for the humiliation she endured on a daily basis. She cried for her future and for all the things she was unlikely to ever have . . . like a relationship with this man.

Not that she wanted one, she thought with alarm. She didn't. She'd never get involved with a man who thought she was a promiscuous liar. But she hated the fact that he thought that about her, and she hated the fact that a relationship with any decent man, ever, seemed increasingly unlikely.

At length, her sobs morphed into full-body hiccups. She sniffed loudly and blew her nose.

"Feel better?" he asked.

"Than what?"

"Than you did a moment ago."

One of Max's arms was still around her, and his hand moved up and down her sleeve in warm, long strokes that were simultaneously comforting and strangely unsettling. The leaves of the live-oak sighed overhead. "Yeah."

"Want to talk about it?"

"No."

"Okay."

He wasn't going to press her for details. He was going to just sit there, his arm around her, and let her snivel and hiccup. Well, good. She didn't feel like talking, anyway.

She wiped her eyes, blew her nose again, and then, despite all of her intentions, the words poured out. "I went to the women's reading group at the library, and they snubbed me," she found herself saying. "They acted like I was invis—" A hiccup jolted her. ". . . invisible." The tears started anew.

His hand moved up and down her arm in a soothing caress. "Who was there?"

"I don't know their last names. The ringleader was named Ca-" Another hiccup. "Carrie."

"Blond hair and an attitude?"

Emma nodded.

"She's married to my opponent."

"Well, she was awful, and everyone followed her lead."

Max's fingers were warm on her arm. "Carrie and her posse are a grown-up version of *Mean Girls*. Don't let them get to you."

Emma twisted the Kleenex in her hands. "It's not just them. It's this whole, horrid situation. Sometimes the unfairness of it all makes me so angry and frustrated that I think I'm going to explode." A hiccup jolted her. "I tell myself there's no point in being bitter, that I've got to move on and accept things and make lemonade with the hand I've been dealt—" Another hiccup interrupted her. Great; she was mixing her metaphors, just like her grandmother. His hand reassuringly rubbed her shoulder.

"Anyway—I moved to Chartreuse because I thought life would be different here and I could start over, but everything's just the same, and there's no end in sight, and—" Another hiccup shook her whole body. She drew a deep breath, trying to stave off a sob.

"It's like I'm a criminal, but I didn't get a trial." She twisted the tissue into a thin rope. "Sometimes I wish I'd been accused of breaking some kind of a law, because then someone would be forced to really investigate things, and maybe they'd find the girl who really was with Ferguson when he died, and my life wouldn't be—" A hiccup-sob rattled through her. ". . . such a wreck."

ॐ

Max's fingers froze on her arm. Good God. Could she be telling the truth? For the first time, he seriously considered the possibility.

What if another woman really had been with Ferguson that night, and Emma was just a scapegoat? Was it possible?

The headlights of a car filtered through the low-hanging branch of the live-oak beside them, back-lighting the statue of Lady Justice. He gazed at it, turning the question in his mind.

It was possible, but not likely. Every criminal he'd ever tried had claimed to be innocent. Years as a prosecutor had taught him the truth of the old axiom: If it looks like a duck and walks like a duck, chances are, it's a duck.

But Emma didn't look anything like a duck—and nothing about her walk seemed the least bit ducklike.

What if—just *if*—she were telling the truth?

A rush of adrenaline coursed through him at the possibility. Injustices *did* happen; just last week, Max had handled the paperwork to free a prisoner who'd been convicted of rape ten years ago but had now been exonerated by DNA.

What if, just as Emma claimed, she'd never even met President-Elect Ferguson?

"Has anyone ever investigated this?" he asked.

"I hired a private investigator a month after it happened." Emma tore the Kleenex in two. "I used up all of my savings to pay him."

"What did he turn up?"

"Nothing. The Secret Service refused to cooperate, and without their help, he was roadblocked. The agency said they never make any statements about the private life of someone they protect."

"What about DNA evidence? That could clear you."

Emma lifted her shoulders. "Since no crime was committed, they said they didn't collect any."

"Yeah, right," Max muttered. He drummed his fingers thoughtfully along the back of the bench. "They've got it somewhere."

"Not where I'm likely to ever get ahold of it."

That was true.

Emma gazed down at her hands. "I took out a second mortgage to hire a public-relations expert, thinking that maybe she could help me get my name cleared."

"And?"

Emma pressed her lips together, but not before Max saw the bottom lip tremble. "I took a polygraph test, which I passed with flying colors. Instead of writing about that in a positive way, though, the media concluded that I probably passed because I was pathological liar." A large beetle charged at the spotlight shining on Lady Justice. "We lined up interviews with several so-called investigative journalists, but the results weren't much better. I decided to quit giving interviews when a reporter compared me to O. J. trying to find the real killer."

But unlike O. J., Emma apparently had tried. Guilty parties didn't run through all their assets trying to prove something they knew was unprovable.

Jeezem Pete—what if she were really innocent? He suddenly realized that he desperately wanted her to be.

He twisted toward her. "Tell me what really happened that night."

"Why? You won't believe me."

"Try me."

She flashed him a skeptical look.

"Please."

She turned her gaze to Lady Justice and stared at the ragged moths circling the spotlight. For a moment he thought she wasn't going to answer. "A Secret Service agent kept me in the front room while Ferguson went up the back stairs," she said at length. "He said it was a security measure, but I'm sure it's because they didn't want me to know that a woman was with the president-elect."

"So you never saw her."

"No. And for the record, I never saw him, either." A touch of belligerence colored her words.

"But you heard them."

Emma nodded. "I heard the bed squeaking upstairs."

"What about the video?"

"I saw a camera on a tripod in the room afterward, but I thought it belonged to the Secret Service. They were processing the room like a crime scene, and they said it was standard procedure to tape their search."

"They took the camera with them when they left?"

Emma nodded. "Along with all the bedding." The leaves rustled overhead. "Have you seen the tape?" she asked.

"No." He fully intended to, though. He also intended to Google her and run a criminal background check. Hell, he could even call his old police partner Dave Harris; Dave now ran a PI agency in D.C. and had contacts in every federal agency.

"The woman on that tape doesn't even look that much like me." Emma twirled the mangled Kleenex. "I don't have a tattoo, my hair is darker and a little longer, and my derriere doesn't look like that."

Derriere. The word made Max smile. Trust Emma to make a butt sound classy. "How's it different?"

"It's got a different shape."

"How so?"

She glared at him with mascara-streaked eyes. "It's not as big, okay? I'm not going to freaking show you."

The indignation in her voice made him grin. "What about that photograph of you coming out of the house?"

She blew out a frustrated huff of breath. "I've explained that over and over. I lost a button off my dress. I was in the bathroom, trying to safety-pin it back on, when a Secret Service agent threw me out of the house."

"You looked so upset and scared in the picture."

"You'd look that way, too, if the Secret Service had physically forced you out the door in the middle of the night and you thought a bomb was about to go off."

Everything about the way she told this rang true. She wasn't trying to convince him. She wasn't playing the pity card. She was frustrated—and understandably so.

"I assume you pointed all this out at the time."

"I tried and tried, but I didn't really have anyone to point it out *to*. I had no day in court, no forum for exonerating myself. All I had was the media, and they were only looking for sensational sound bites."

And because of her phobia about video cameras, she couldn't just sit down and do a broadcast interview, Max realized.

"I tried everything I could think of," Emma said, tucking a strand of hair behind her ear. "I kept trying until I used up all my assets. Grams deeded her house to me and told me to sell it and use the proceeds, but that was where I drew the line. There comes a point where you have to stop throwing good money after bad."

She wadded the Kleenex into a ball. "The private investigator told me I needed to face the fact that it's me against the entire U.S. government. If they want to hide the fact that the Secret Service smuggled a girl into the house, what real chance do I have? If I had a million dollars—or two million, or ten billion—I probably still wouldn't be able to clear my name."

She was right. She was absolutely right.

"I've always believed in changing what I can and accepting what I can't. Well, this is apparently one of those things I can't change, so I moved here, trying to accept it. I thought that if I could get to know people, they'd realize I'm not like that, and I could make new friends and build a new life." She gazed at the statue of the blindfolded woman. "I'm beginning to think I made a huge mistake. It's impossible to get to know anyone when no one wants to know me."

I want to know you. He was suddenly aware that her breast was pressed against his side. He breathed in the scent of her hair, and something about the combination of coconut shampoo, perfume, and warm skin set his body on fire.

To his chagrin, she stuffed the tattered tissue in her sweater pocket, then gathered up her purse and keys. "It's getting late. I'd better be getting home."

She rose from the bench. Max rose as well, and walked beside her through the deserted square. "I want to apologize again for upsetting you," he said as they stopped beside her car.

"It wasn't you. Everything had just kind of built up inside." Her eyes glittered in the lamplight as she turned toward him. "Thanks for letting me cry on your shoulder." She stood on tiptoe and leaned toward him. *She was going to kiss his cheek.*

He saw his chance, and like a ballplayer stealing second base, he reflexively went for it. Without pausing to think, he turned his face and caught her full on the mouth.

She froze. He pulled back to see her staring up at him, her eyes wide and shocked.

Shock was an asset. He didn't want her to think. He wanted her to feel. Pulling her closer, he lowered his mouth to hers again.

Her lips softened, then opened, then moved under his. *She was kissing him back.* Desire, hot and dark, kicked him in the gut. He deepened the kiss, losing himself in it, in her. She moved against him, her mouth wet and responsive.

He felt a sudden push against his chest.

"No." The word came out in a raw whisper. She stepped back, drawing her purse in front of her. Her pupils were huge, her breathing fast. "No. I can't do this."

"Emma—"

"Look—this is a bad idea. This is the last thing I need right now. And you have an election—"

A car rounded the corner, its headlights blinding them. Emma glanced at the car, then back at Max.

"I've—I've got to go."

The car slowly cruised past as she opened the door of her Saturn and climbed inside. This time he didn't stop her.

Because, damn it, the person he should have stopped was himself.

CHAPTER TWELVE

*E*mma poked her head in Mrs. Schwartz's colorless office a week later. "You wanted to see me?"

"Indeed I do." The woman's brow hunkered ominously low over her protuberant eyes.

Uh-oh. Emma entered the office as if it were a shark tank and perched nervously on a chair across from Mrs. Schwartz's desk, smoothing the skirt of her putty-colored suit.

The burly woman picked up a tabloid and smacked it down on the desk in front of Emma. "I assume you've seen this?"

Emma gazed down at a copy of the *National Inquisitioner* and winced. Oh, no—there was her photo. She was standing inside Mrs. Alvarez's apartment, a bulging white trash bag in her yellow-gloved hands, her face contorted, her mouth open as if she were yelling. She looked like a bag lady on crack.

"Trashy Butler Cleans Up," the headline read.

Emma briefly closed her eyes, then forced herself

to open them and read the rest of the caption: *"Emma Jamison, the sexy butler who shagged President-Elect Ferguson to death, has given up her glamorous job with the super-wealthy to work as the housekeeping director at a retirement home in the tiny town of Chartreuse, Louisiana. Emma is shown here doing a little dirty work—and doesn't look too happy about it."*

"Oh, no," Emma groaned.

"My reaction exactly." Mrs. Schwartz glared at her. "And it was the reaction of Mrs. Alvarez's daughter, who called me from Shreveport this morning. She recognized the antique dresser in the background, and she was extremely upset to see her mother's apartment featured in the *Inquisitioner*." Mrs. Schwartz drummed both sets of sausage-like fingers on her desk. "Needless to say, she was even more upset that her mother had been subjected to your angry outburst."

"It wasn't an outburst. I—I was telling the photographer to leave."

"In none-too-pleasant terms, apparently." Her fingers continued to clog-dance on her desk. "This puts you in a very bad light, Emma—a very bad light indeed, which reflects badly on all of Sunnyside. You look . . . menacing, I believe Mrs. Alvarez's daughter called it. She threatened to move her mother to another facility if she couldn't be assured that reporters would not be crashing into her apartment and employees would not be subjecting her to shouting matches."

"I wasn't shouting. I had gathered up her trash, which she'd stashed in her closet, and a reporter knocked on the door. Mrs. Alvarez opened it, and—"

Mrs. Schwartz waved her hand. "I'm not interested in your excuses."

"I'm not making excuses. I'm trying to explain."

"There is no satisfactory explanation for this." She thumped the paper with a stubby forefinger. "This is *your* fault, because the photographer came to take *your* picture. I hold you entirely responsible, and I simply will not tolerate this kind of thing."

Emma swallowed back her frustration. "I understand."

"I hope you do, because there will be serious repercussions if this happens again." The coarse skin on Mrs. Schartz's red nose had deepened to crimson. "Have I made myself clear?"

"Very clear." It would do no good to point out that if it were in her power to stop photographers from stalking her, Emma would have done so long ago—just as it would do no good to point out that she'd spent most of last Saturday painting Mrs. Alvarez's bathroom. There was also no point in mentioning that she'd stayed late every evening this week labeling drawers for Mr. Duval, putting cedar chips in Mrs. Brown's closet so it would smell like her old cedar closet, wallpapering Mrs. Hildegarde's kitchen, and taping pictures of the items inside the cabinets to Esmerelda Thornton's kitchen doors.

Emma left Mrs. Schwartz's office-slash-interrogation chamber, her fingernails digging into her palms. Mrs. Schwartz had been trying to get rid of her ever since she'd arrived; she'd been peeved that Emma had been hired over her objections and annoyed that the executives at the corporate office liked her innovations. Maybe she should reconsider taking the job at corporate headquarters in Tampa, Emma thought. She'd talked to the VP last week, and he'd told her the position was still hers if she wanted it.

On the other hand, she hated the idea of letting Scwhartzilla run her off. Emma loved being near her grandmother, she liked having a lovely home with no monthly payment, and she thoroughly enjoyed working with the residents, especially the Alzheimer's patients.

She would not let the old crone win, Emma decided hotly. She'd dig in her heels and do some damage control. She'd write a letter to Mrs. Alvarez's daughter and explain the situation, and then she'd call the corporate VP so he'd have all the facts and not just Mrs. Schwartz's twisted version.

Her back stiffened with resolve as she strode toward her office. As she walked past the parlor, she spotted an empty Styrofoam cup on the coffee table and a newspaper sprawled on the sofa, so she veered into the empty room to straighten it. A housekeeper checked the room three times a day, but Emma never walked past if she saw something out of place. She fluffed a sofa pillow, then reached for the newspaper. Her pulse fluttered as she glanced at it. There, on the front page, was a photo of Max.

She sank onto the sofa and stared at it. She hadn't seen Max since that evening in the courthouse square, but he'd called her at her office the following morning.

"I got the impression I was out of line last night," he'd said.

Emma had struggled to sound unruffled, although her pulse was galloping. "That's because you were."

"Well, I apologize. It won't happen again." He'd paused a moment. "Look—we're bound to run into each other, what with our grandparents dating and you working at the retirement home and this being a small town and all, and I don't want things to be awkward between us."

"Me, neither."

"Good."

"Good."

An awkward silence had beat between then.

"Well, then, it's settled," he said. " We'll go back to just being friends and forget that kiss ever happened."

Yeah. Right. As if. Agreeing to forget about it had just made her think about it more than ever.

She pulled her eyes from his picture in the newspaper to the headline below. "*DA Race in Political Spotlight*." Looked like divine providence was trying to warn her off, she thought wryly, because the last thing she needed was to be anywhere near a spotlight.

Crumpling the newspaper and picking up the lipstick-smeared Styrofoam cup, she marched to the trash receptacle behind the large column separating the parlor from the hallway. As she pushed the trash through the metal flap, she heard the unmistakable rasp of Iris Huckabee's voice.

". . . and they've got that hussy who killed Ferguson working right here at Sunnyside."

Emma peered around the pillar to see the obnoxious old biddy coming out of the hair salon, leaning on the arm of a stylish brunette about Emma's age.

"Well, in all fairness, I don't think anyone ever proved it was Emma," the brunette said.

Surprised, Emma craned her neck to get a better look at the woman who'd just defended her. Slim and pretty, she wore brown cropped pants and a fitted white blouse, topped with a low-slung jeweled belt.

"What more proof do you need?" Iris's voice grated like Brillo pads on Emma's eardrums. "They have a porn tape showing her in the very act!"

"Why, Iris," the brunette said, her eyes wide, her voice shocked. "I didn't know you watched porn."

The elderly woman's mouth opened in surprise. Emma suppressed a laugh.

"From what I can see, Emma's doing a wonderful job here," the brunette continued. "This place looks a thousand percent better than it did the last time I was here."

"Well, she's a tramp, and her grandmother's no better," Iris huffed as they stopped by the elevator. "The way Dorothy is carrying on with that Duval man is positively indecent."

Emma tensed. It was one thing to hear malicious gossip about herself, but it was entirely another to hear it about her grandmother.

"I don't think it's a bit indecent." The brunette pressed the elevator button. "I think a late-in-life romance is just wonderful!"

The old woman gave a loud snort. "She's making a fool out of herself, and out of him, too. If you ask me, she's after his money."

Emma stepped out from behind the column, ready to give Iris a piece of her mind. She stopped short when she heard her grandmother's voice.

"Somebody ought to wash your mouth out with Lysol for talking such trash, Iris." Emma saw Grams approach from the side, a shuffleboard stick in one hand.

Iris started as if she'd seen a ghost. "Dorothy! I—I didn't know you were there."

"Apparently not. Next time you decide to spew your venom, you'd better be a little more careful about who's in earshot."

The elevator dinged.

"Your elevator's here," Dorothy said. "I think you'd better get on it."

"Dorothy, really, I—"

"Have a good day, Iris."

"That old blowhole!" Grams muttered as soon as the elevator door closed.

Blowhard, Emma silently corrected, stepping into the hallway.

"Don't take it personally." The brunette patted Dorothy's back. "She never has a good word to say about anyone."

"Oh, I know," Dorothy replied. "But she makes me so mad I could spit screws."

The brunette's brow puckered in a confused frown.

"Nails," Emma translated as she walked toward them. "She means spit nails."

"Emma, dear!" Grams kissed her cheek. "Have you met Katie Charmaine?"

"No, I haven't." Emma smiled at the woman and stuck out her hand. "But thank you for standing up for me."

Katie gave Emma's hand a vigorous shake. She had a round, pretty face, short, stylishly choppy hair, and friendly brown eyes. "My pleasure."

"Katie owns the Curl Up 'N' Dye hair salon in town," Grams said. "The hairdresser who comes here most mornings works for her."

"Sheila's on vacation this week, so I came instead," Katie explained. She smiled at Emma. "It's so nice to finally meet you. I've heard a lot about you."

"I'm afraid everyone has."

Katie laughed. "In my line of work, I hear everything about everybody. I take it all with a grain of salt."

"I've been trying to introduce Emma to some people her own age," Grams said, shifting her shuffleboard stick to her other hand. "This is positively providential. You two ought to go to lunch and get better acquainted."

Emma's face heated. She didn't want to put Katie on the spot. "Grams, I'm sure Katie's got plans."

"Actually, I don't, and I think that's a great idea. Want to go to the Chartreuse Café and grab a bite?"

"Now?"

"If your schedule allows it. I don't have an appointment until one-thirty. A real sit-down lunch would be a treat."

It would be one for Emma, as well.

"Go ahead," Grams urged.

What the heck? "Sure," Emma said. "Let me stop by my office and grab my purse."

⟋⟍

Twenty minutes later, Emma and Katie handed their lime green menus to a harried-looking waitress in a chartreuse apron.

"Thanks, Cindy," Katie said. "That'll be all." As the waitress hurried off, Katie leaned across the table. "This was a great idea. I'm so glad you were free to join me."

Emma gave a rueful smile. "My social calendar isn't exactly packed."

Unlike the Chartreuse Café. The tables were filling up quickly, and a line was queuing up at the door. The quaint Main Street diner smelled of Cajun spices and fried seafood, and the décor looked like it hadn't changed in four or five decades. The walls were painted a pale shade of the town's namesake color, a green Formica lunch counter ran the length of the restaurant, and the wobbly tables were set with chartreuse plastic placemats. Emma and Katie sat at one of the four black vinyl booths in the back.

"So how do you like Chartreuse?" Katie asked.

"Well, the town isn't exactly rolling out the red carpet

for me." Emma unfolded the paper napkin and placed it in her lap.

Katie nodded sympathetically and squeezed a slice of lemon into her iced tea. "I heard you had a hard time at the library last week."

"Wow. Bad news really travels."

"I think there's some kind of tongue-relaxer in the shampoo I use." Katie grinned as she reached for a blue packet of sweetener. "I hope you didn't take it too hard. I know what it feels like to get the cold shoulder from Carrie and company."

"Really?" Emma looked at Katie's vivacious face, wondering how anyone could dislike her.

She nodded. "My family was what's commonly known as white trash."

The blunt statement took Emma aback. "Oh, I'm sure—"

"Trust me. We really were," Katie said in a matter-of-fact tone. She ripped the packet and poured the white granules in her glass. "My father was in prison, and my mother was an alcoholic party girl."

Emma opened her mouth, then closed it, at a loss for words.

"People acted like my folks' behavior was contagious or something. Other kids' parents didn't want their kids playing with me, and by high school, I was trying to live up to everyone's low opinion of me. I ended up running away at fifteen, and I vowed to never come back."

"Oh, Katie—I'm so sorry."

"Oh, don't be." Katie picked up her iced-tea spoon. "I came back ten years ago, and it turns out Chartreuse is where all my dreams came true. Some of the very people who used to snub me are now good friends. And five years ago, I married the love of my life."

"That's wonderful."

"Yeah." She stirred her tea and smiled wistfully. "It'll be more wonderful when he gets home from Iraq in sixty-eight days and . . ." She glanced at her watch. ". . . thirteen and a half hours. Not that I'm counting."

Emma smiled.

"The point I'm trying to make is, public opinion in this town can be turned around."

"How?"

"Well, we can put some positive stories out on the grapevine. See that woman in the white jacket at the table on the right?"

Emma cautiously glanced over at a woman with frizzy black hair and horn-rimmed glasses, talking in a secretive fashion to her two lunch companions. "Yeah."

"That's Nellie. She's the cashier at the drugstore, and she's one of the biggest gossips in town."

"Note to self: don't buy any personal items at the drug-store," Emma said dryly.

Katie laughed. "You're not kidding. But when I drop by and mention that Iris was in a snit because you're doing such a good job at the retirement home that she didn't have anything to complain about, the word will be all over town in four hours."

Emma's heart warmed. "Thanks."

"No problem. It might take a little while, Emma, but after people get to know you, most of them will accept you. And as for the ones who won't . . . well, who cares?"

The blond waitress returned with steaming bowls of sea-food gumbo and a basket of French bread. She paused as she set a bowl in front of Emma. "You're Emma Jamison, aren't you?"

Emma nodded, dread mounting in her chest.

"I've got a copy of the *National Inquisitioner* in the back." She hitched her thumb toward the kitchen. "Would you mind signing it for me?"

Jeez, but she hated this. Emma mustered a regretful smile. "I'm sorry, but I don't do autographs."

The waitress's expression soured like week-old milk.

"See, Cindy, the thing is, Emma is trying to live all that down," Katie cut in. "You wouldn't like it if people asked for your autograph because you lost your virginity to Charlie Henton on prom night, would you?"

Cindy blanched and took a step back. "I—I didn't!"

"Of course you didn't." Katie's tone was warm and re-assuring. "But people said you did, and I'm sure that was awful for you. Well, that's just the situation Emma's in. So I'm sure you can understand why she wants to play down the rumors."

"Oh. Sure." Cindy's throat worked as she swallowed. Her eyes darted to Emma. "Sorry. I didn't mean no harm."

"I know you didn't," Emma said warmly. "It's okay."

Cindy bobbed her head and edged away. "Well, y'all enjoy your meal."

Emma leaned across the table as Cindy left. "I can't believe you said that!"

"Well, people need to put themselves in your shoes." Katie reached for the bread basket. "Cindy's another of the town's big gossips. She'll spread the word, and you won't be bothered by any more local autograph hounds." Katie placed a slice of French bread on her plate. "So how do you like your job?"

Emma was still marveling at the way Katie had handled the autograph request. "Better than I thought I would. Aside from Mrs. Schwartz, the staff is great, and I really like working with the residents."

"You must be super-organized to have a job like director of housekeeping."

Emma gave a modest shrug. "Organizing is the one thing I'm good at."

"Well, I'm so disorganized it's embarrassing." Katie ripped off a morsel of bread and picked up her knife. "The back of my shop is so crammed with stuff it's hard to reach the bathroom. I keep planning to deal with it, but I don't even know where to start."

"I could help, if you like," Emma offered.

"Oh, I couldn't ask you to do that."

"You're not asking. I'm offering. It's the sort of thing I love to do."

"Really?"

Emma nodded. "It's my creative outlet. Some people paint, some people sing, some play an instrument. I organize."

"Well, in that case—I'd love your help!" Katie grinned widely. "But you have to let me reciprocate with styling services."

"It's a deal."

"This is terrific!" Something at the entrance caught Katie's eye. She leaned forward and lowered her voice. "And speaking of terrific, there's District McDreamy."

Emma followed Katie's gaze to the entrance. There, standing beside a thin, balding man, was Max, wearing a gray suit and a burgundy striped tie. Her heart jumped like a jackrabbit.

"I understand you two are already acquainted," Katie said.

"Where did you hear that?" Emma asked.

"Well . . . I heard you two had dinner with your grandparents. And Marie said Anne went back to the library for her sweater, and she thought she saw you with Max by the square, and she said you two looked ver-ry cozy."

Emma's heart pounded. "Oh, no." Anne must have been in the car that drove by after they kissed.

Katie's brows pulled together. "What's the matter? Max is a friend of my husband's. He's a great guy."

Which was exactly the problem. "He's running for office. I could hurt his campaign."

Katie glanced back at the door. "He doesn't look worried about it. He's coming this way."

Emma looked up to see Max heading toward their table. As their eyes met, he lifted his hand and waved at her. Emma tentatively waggled her fingers in response. The diminutive man beside Max frowned and murmured something to him.

Max continued toward them, smiling and talking to people along the way. The little bald man tagged after him, his brow wrinkled like a Sharpei's.

"Hi, Max," Katie said brightly.

"Hello, Katie." Max stopped at their table and looked at Emma. "Emma."

A furnace blast of attraction made her mouth suddenly go dry.

Max gestured to the slight man beside him. "This is my campaign manager, Terrence O'Neil."

Katie and Emma murmured greetings. Terrence responded with a terse nod.

"How's Paul?" Max asked Katie.

"He's good. I got an e-mail from him last night," Katie said.

"Tell him hello, will you? And let him know we're all pulling for him."

Katie nodded. "Sure will."

Max's gaze returned to Emma.

Terrence cleared his throat and took a step back, ready to go. "Well, it was nice meeting you two. Max and I had better go grab a table before they're all gone."

"Maybe we could pull up a couple of chairs and join them," Max said.

Terrence's frown deepened. "Actually, Max, we have a couple other people planning to join us."

"We do?" Max's eyebrows rose. "Who?"

"A, um, couple of major contributors. We need to get a table of our own and wait for them."

Terrence was trying to keep Max away from her, and Emma couldn't blame him. But Max had a stubborn look in his eye, the same one he'd gotten when Emma had tried to dissuade him from following her home to help with her window.

"Actually, I was kind of hoping to talk to Katie about a private matter." Emma flashed Max a tight, dismissive smile. "Maybe another time."

❧

Max saw right through Emma's indifference; she was giving him a graceful out. He should feel relieved, but instead, he just felt disappointed. "Sure." He dipped his head in a curt nod. "Didn't mean to interrupt."

He followed Terrence to a small table by the side window. "That would have been a bad move, a very bad move," Terrence hissed as Max pulled out the chartreuse vinyl chair. "What were you thinking?"

Max unbuttoned his suit jacket as he sat down. "Hey, Katie's husband is a pal, and Emma works at the home where my granddad lives. It's no big deal to share a table with a couple of friends."

"It's a big deal if one of those people is Emma Jamison."

Max unwrapped the napkin from around the dented flatware. "Emma's gotten a bum rap." He placed the paper napkin on his left thigh. "I don't think she's the woman on the tape."

"What?"

"I watched it the other night, and they don't even look all that much alike. Everyone's just assuming it's Emma because she was there and she was photographed in that unbuttoned dress." After viewing the video on the Internet, he'd been so convinced the woman wasn't Emma that he'd called up his old police partner in Washington.

"Hey, Dave, how's the detective business?" Max had asked.

"Going gangbusters."

"That's great. Glad to hear it. Look, Dave—I need a favor. Do you have any contacts at the Secret Service?"

"Yeah. What's up?"

Max had explained.

"I'll give them a call and see what I can find out," Dave had said. "And while I'm at it, I'll do a complete workup on Emma."

"I hate to break it to you, Max, but most people think the fact Emma left the mansion nearly undressed is pretty compelling evidence," Terrence said now.

Max glanced over at Emma, who was sitting with her back toward him. "There's more evidence that it *isn't* Emma than that it is. She has an affidavit from her doctor that she doesn't have a tattoo, her hair is lighter, and she's slimmer."

"Hell, Max—everyone said that tattoo could have been temporary, and women change their hair all the time. Not to mention gain or lose five or ten pounds; my wife has two separate wardrobes, depending on what time of the month it is." Terrence picked up his glass of water and took a big gulp. "Why are we even talking about this? Emma could be Little Bo Peep or pure as extra virgin olive oil, and it wouldn't matter, because everyone—"

"Excuse me. Are you Max Duval?"

Max looked up to see a scrawny young man standing by the table. He had crooked teeth and hair that looked like he'd stuck his finger in an electric socket. "Yes."

He stuck out his hand. "I'm Louis Ashton with the *Chartreuse Daily Monitor*."

"Oh, yeah," Terrence said. "You're the summer intern from LSU, right?"

The young man's hair bobbed like a rooster comb as he nodded.

Terrence introduced himself. "You're supposed to cover Max's talk to the Daughters of the American Revolution next week, aren't you?"

"Yeah." Louis looked curiously at Max. "I was sitting at the corner table way in the back, and I just saw you talking with Emma Jamison."

Tension coiled in Max's stomach.

"He knows the lady she's with," Terrence said before Max could speak. "Her husband's a soldier in Iraq."

Max shot Terrence an annoyed look.

"So what are you working on now, Louis?" Terrence said, obviously eager to change the subject.

"The usual small-town stuff. Plus I'm doing some freelance work."

"Oh, yeah?"

Nodding, Louis rocked back and forth on his P.F. Flyers, puffed out his thin chest and showed his gums in a smile. "I just sold a photo of Emma to the *National Inquisitioner*. "

Max felt his blood pressure rise. "That's—"

"Terrific," Terrence quickly supplied.

"Yeah." Louis's mouth curved in a self-satisfied smile. "I made more money on that one photo than I'll make at the *Monitor* all summer."

The lowlife little twerp. Every muscle in Max's body tensed. "Selling photos to a tabloid is—"

"—very lucrative," Terrence interjected. "Congratulations. But we're in the middle of a discussion here, son. If you'd like to interview Max about anything pertaining to the DA's office or the election, give me a call, and I'll be happy to set it up." He pulled out a card, handed it to him and shook his hand. "Nice meeting you."

Max glowered at Terrence as the young man strolled out the side exit, the elastic of his red underwear visible above the saggy butt of his jeans. "I can't believe you just encouraged that jackoff to sell more tabloid photos."

"I distracted him, and you ought to be thanking me for it," Terrence hissed. "It's four weeks until the election, and Dirk Briggs would love to smear your name any way he can. I don't care if Emma Jamison is the reincarnation of Mother Teresa; you can't afford to be connected to her.

Especially with young Clark Kent there lying in wait to sell a story to the tabloids."

Terrence was right. It was good advice, and Max knew it. All the same, his gaze kept darting toward Emma, and over the next few days, his thoughts did the same.

CHAPTER THIRTEEN

*H*arold braced himself on the dashboard as Dorothy's red Jeep Wrangler convertible lurched over yet another pothole in the dirt road. "Great balls of fire, girl, you drive like a bat out of hell! Any faster and we'll go into orbit."

Dorothy cast him a sideways grin. "You told me you always wanted to be an astronaut."

That had been his boyhood dream, all right. His memory was sharp today, sharp and clear. He could almost smell the ink of a Buck Rogers comic book, almost feel the pages in his hand, almost hear the cigar-choked voice of the newsstand owner—"If you wanna read it, kid, you gotta buy it." He hadn't had two cents to rub together, so he'd convinced the man to let him read the comic book in exchange for half a day's work every Saturday. It had been his first business negotiation.

Another bump jostled the Jeep. Dorothy bounced in the air, her curly white hair peeking out the edges of a pink chiffon scarf, the kind Grace Kelly used to wear. The ends of the sheer fabric blew carelessly in the wind—or maybe in the air conditioner; Dorothy had it going at full blast, even though the Jeep's rag top was down. She made quite a sight, all decked out in those Jackie O sunglasses, barely tall enough to see over the steering wheel. Just looking at her made him smile. "What did you used to daydream about?"

"Being a movie star—or at least looking like one." Her mouth curved in a dreamy smile. "I wanted to turn heads and feel pretty."

"You *are* pretty."

"Oh, Harold." She glanced over at him, and he could see her blue eyes twinkle out the side of her sunglasses. "You know what? You make me feel that way."

A rush of pleasure burned through him like good bourbon. "I'm glad. Because I'd like to make all your dreams come true."

"You're doing a darn good job of it."

Harold smiled as the Jeep rounded a bend at a speed that should have lifted the left tires off the dirt road. A moment later, he braced himself again as Dorothy braked to a jerky stop before a two-story white frame house. She killed the engine. "Here it is. This is my old home."

Harold gazed at the classic Acadian structure, admiring the deep porch and the way jasmine twined up the two red-brick chimneys on either end. Light dappled through the tall trees overhead, making patterns on the gray shake-shingle roof. "This is lovely."

Dorothy nodded. "I have a lot of good memories here."

"So why did you move to Sunnyside?"

Dorothy lifted her shoulders. "It was time."

"How did you know?"

"Well, I think divine providence always gives you signs."

Harold had never believed in things like signs and providence, but Dorothy did, and she'd piqued his curiosity. "Such as?"

"Well, I was tired of all the upkeep on the place, and I felt lonely out here after Wilbur died. I had to make an effort to get out and see people, and as time went on, I was doing it less and less. And then one of my good friends moved to Sunnyside, and she just loved it. Whenever I'd go out to see her, I'd hate to come home."

Dorothy raised her sunglasses to the top of her head. "Those were pretty obvious signs, but I didn't take the hint. So God started giving me more direct little nudges."

"Such as?"

"Well, I was flipping through the TV channels one night, and I landed on an old movie called *Sunny Side of the Street*. And the next week, I was going through Wilbur's old albums, and there was Ella Fitzgerald's record *The Sunny Side of the Street*. But the clincher was when I met a friend at the Chartreuse Café for breakfast and the waitress asked how I wanted my eggs, and I found myself saying, 'Sunny side up.'" Dorothy looked at him, her eyes the blue of deep water. "And I got to thinking, that's how I want my life. Sunny side up. So I moved to Sunnyside. And I've never regretted the decision."

"You were wise," Harold said, gazing thoughtfully at the house. "If I hadn't been forced to move, I would have stayed in that big old mausoleum of a house until I died."

"Do you miss it?"

"No. It's funny. I insisted on staying there for so many years, and now I wonder why."

Dorothy propped her elbow on the open Jeep window. "Sometimes familiarity can become a trap."

He'd never thought of it that way, but then, Dorothy had a way of seeing things he'd overlooked—little, beautiful things, like the seed star inside of an apple that she'd shown him just yesterday. "I've probably asked this before, but I don't remember the answer. You and your husband—were you happy here?"

"Very happy."

"What was he like?"

"Quiet. Kind. Real low-key." Dorothy pulled her scarf off her head and grinned. "And you know me—I'm a shake-things-up kind of person. We balanced each other out real nice."

Harold nodded. "Myrtle and I were different, too. I always thought we were beauty and the beast."

Dorothy smiled and touched his arm. "You could never have been a beast."

"Oh, I'm afraid I was. Maybe not so much when Myrtle was alive."

"You showed me her picture," Dorothy said softly. "She was definitely a beauty."

Harold nodded. "Inside and out." It still amazed him that she'd had anything to do with him. "Did I tell you how we met?"

Dorothy nodded. "At a USO dance in England. You married her two weeks later."

Harold could still remember every detail of the way she'd looked that night—like a princess out of a fairy tale, a star straight out of the movies. She'd worn a pink, floaty dress that shimmered in the light, with matching pink high heels. The skirt had belled out when she twirled on the dance floor, and her light brown hair had bounced on her shoulders, like Katherine Hepburn's. When he'd danced with her, he'd been so nervous he'd stepped on her foot.

"Her parents were titled and wealthy, and I was an illegitimate American bastard. They told her she could do better, that I was beneath her, that I'd never be able to provide her with the quality of life she was accustomed to."

Dorothy's mouth curved up. "But she married you anyway, smart girl."

"I don't know what she saw in me, but I vowed I'd prove her parents wrong. I wanted to give her everything her heart desired."

"You loved her."

"Oh, I did." Harold stared out the window. "And I worked my tail off to build a good life. Unfortunately, I worked so hard that I wasn't around much. Then, Myrtle died when Mike was twelve, and after that—" He shifted on the seat. "It was like the bottom fell out of my world. Like a part of me died, too."

"I know how hard it is to lose a spouse," Dorothy said softly.

"It was probably even harder on Mike, losing his mother." Harold looked down at his hands. "I'm afraid I was too torn up to be much use to him. Poor guy, it was like he lost both parents." The image of his son's sullen face rose up in his mind.

"He was sad and angry, and he got angrier every day, and I didn't know the first thing about dealing with him." The failing report cards, the arguments, the fights at school . . . Harold felt like he was sinking in quicksand, just remembering it. "I thought boarding school would help, but after he went away, well, we just grew further and further apart. I'd see him at Christmas and in the summer, and I always tried to make those times special, but he wanted nothing to do with me. He was just mad at the world."

He glanced up at Dorothy. Her blue eyes were soft, her expression sympathetic and understanding.

"He got a girl pregnant when he was in college, and I insisted that he marry her. No grandchild of mine was going to grow up being called a bastard." Harold knew only too well how that could scar a child's soul. "I hoped he'd settle down and be a good husband and father, but it just wasn't in him. All he wanted to do was drink and race speedboats." Harold blew out a sigh. "I did my best to keep him in line, but I wasn't very successful."

"How did you keep a grown man in line?" Dorothy asked.

"I controlled his cash flow."

Her lips quirked up. "Oh, my. I bet that went over well."

Harold's mouth curved in a rueful grin. "Can't say that it did. Not with my son, and not with his wife. She could spend money like a drunken sailor on leave. 'Course, my son could, too." Harold leaned back against the headrest. "They fought like a couple of greedy pirates. About the only thing they could agree on was that they both hated me."

"Did they get a divorce?"

Harold shook his head. "I insisted they stay together for Max's sake." At the time, he'd been so sure it was the right thing to do. Now it seemed like the height of arrogance. "They retaliated by keeping Max away from me as much as possible."

Dorothy's soft hand tightened on his arm. The breeze whispered through the leaves of the oak overhead.

"Max was a great kid—conscientious and hard-

working and self-disciplined, the exact opposite of his father. It was probably his way of rebelling." Harold closed
his eyes for a moment. He could picture Max as a boy,
somber and self-contained, his nose buried in a book.

"I pinned all my hopes on Max. I wanted him to come
to work for the company when he got out of college, because I planned to turn the business over to him. Turns
out he didn't want it." The irony of it still burned. "All
I'd worked for, all I'd built to pass on, and neither my son
nor my grandson wanted it. It felt like a slap in the face."
It still stung to think about it. "Max and I argued, and it
got ugly. I tried to control him like I controlled his dad—I
threatened to cut him off without a cent." Harold stared
through windshield at a lopsided oak tree. "And damned if
he didn't call my bluff."

"Max doesn't seem like a guy who can be bullied,"
Dorothy said softly.

"No." Harold sat in silence for a moment, then turned
toward her. "I blew it, Dorothy. I missed the boat. I wanted
to give my family everything, and I ended up giving them
nothing. I turned them all against me. Sometimes I think
all the good in me died with Myrtle."

"That's not true." Dorothy gazed at him intently. Her
eyes were bluer than the sky above, blue and clear and
bright. "I see good in you every day."

She was the one with all the good—a kind heart, a generous spirit, and an upbeat personality that brightened the
day of everyone she encountered. The thought of letting
her down weighed like a stone in his chest. "I couldn't
stand it if you grew to hate me, Dorothy, and I'm afraid
you will. I seem to always end up hurting the people I
love."

"Harold Duval, you listen to me." Her cherub cheeks

shook with indignation. "You make me smile and laugh. You give me a reason to get up in the mornings. You make me happy in ways I can't even put into words. And the only way you could hurt me would be if you said you didn't want to be with me anymore."

"Really?"

"Yes, really." She touched his face. Her palm was cool on his cheek. "Everyone's made mistakes, Harold. The important thing is that you learn from them and stop repeating them. If you've hurt someone, you make amends, forgive yourself, and do things differently in the future."

Forgive yourself. How could he ever forgive himself for screwing up his family? And as for amends—how the hell was he supposed to do that?

Dorothy seemed to read his mind. "You need to talk to Max and clear the air."

Talk—as if that would help. The word *sorry* never changed a thing. All that please-forgive-me, I'm-so-angst-ridden crap was a waste of time and energy, an exercise better left to whiners and losers. Real men stood by their decisions and lived with the consequences. "There's no point in talking. What's done is done, and it's too late to change it."

"It's never too late." Her voice was soft and sure. The blue in her eyes was like healing balm to his soul.

"What the hell would I say to him?"

"When the time is right, you'll just know. All you have to do is get willing, and divine providence will give you the right words at the right time."

He used to think that people who believed all that stuff were morons, but now he wasn't sure. The truth was, he envied Dorothy's faith. He wished he could believe in a benevolent Almighty who gave guidance and help and forgiveness.

Harold looked at Dorothy's sweet face, so sure and so certain. He believed that she believed. Maybe that was a start. "I'll think about it."

"Good." She flashed him a bright smile, then pushed those enormous sunglasses down on her nose, tucked the Grace Kelly scarf back over her white curls, and turned the ignition key. "Ready for another ride in the Road Rocket?"

She knew just when to drop a topic and move on. She had a real knack for keeping things sunny side up, for making life fun and light and exciting. He grinned back at her, his heart tight and tender. "You betcha, beautiful."

She might not believe it, but he thought she was the loveliest woman alive.

CHAPTER FOURTEEN

"How long do you think this will take?" Dorothy tapped her fingers on the arms of the chair across from Mrs. Schwartz's desk later that afternoon, impatience welling up inside her. "Oprah is about to come on."

Mrs. Schwartz folded her meaty hands on her ink blotter. "We're waiting for your granddaughter and Mr. Duval."

"No need to wait on me. I'm here already," Harold said. He gave Dorothy a little wink, letting her know that he was fully present and accounted for. Dorothy grinned back.

"I meant your grandson," Mrs. Schwartz said, her voice condescending.

"Oh." Harold gave the stern-faced woman a deliberately blank look. "But I'm here, too, aren't I?"

"Yes, you are."

"Good." Harold shot Dorothy another wink. "Just checking."

The office door opened and in walked Emma, wearing a navy pantsuit, her hair pulled back in a low ponytail, her expression worried, her face pale.

Poor Emma, Dorothy thought; this Ferguson thing had squeezed all the brightness out of her. Emma needed something or somebody to bring out her shine, and Dorothy had her hopes set on Max.

Yessiree, Max Duval was just the ticket. Divine providence had picked him out and arranged all the circumstances, Dorothy was sure of it. They'd met at the Grab 'N' Go—and hadn't she told Emma to grab the brass gusto, before she'd ever known that? And then they'd gone for a snowball—and hadn't she overheard that nasty old Iris say that Emma had a snowball's chance in hell of ever being considered respectable? Those were definitely signs.

Emma glanced quizzically at Dorothy and Harold, then looked Mrs. Schwartz. "I understand you wanted to see me?"

"Yes," Mrs. Schwartz said coldly. "I'm afraid we've had another incident."

The door opened again and in walked Max. Oh, my, what a handsome man—handsome enough to give Dorothy's pacemaker a workout. She'd seen pictures of Harold in his younger days, and he'd looked just like Max. Dorothy glanced at Harold and noticed he was regarding Max with a wistful expression.

For his part, Max's gaze was riveted elsewhere. "Hello, Emma," he said. His eyes locked with hers for a long moment, and the chemistry in the air was like a living, breathing thing. *Ooh, I knew it.* Dorothy's mouth curved in a triumphant little smile. *I just knew he had a thing for her. And Emma likes him, too, or she's no kin of mine.*

"Hello," Emma replied, her voice just a tad bit breathless.

Yes. Dorothy silently exulted. *Knew it, knew it, knew it!*

Max nodded greetings to everyone else in the room,

then seated himself beside Emma in one of the four austere chairs arranged to face Mrs. Schwartz's desk. "We've got to stop meeting like this, Mrs. Schwartz." He flashed the old broad a smile that would have melted her heart, if she'd had one.

He was just as charming as his grandfather. Dorothy cut a glance at Harold. He was sitting perfectly still, staring down at his hands.

He'd clammed up the moment Max had stepped into the room, Dorothy realized. Poor man; guilt and regrets were eating him up. The argument he'd had with Max years ago was water over the bridge—or was the water supposed to be under the bridge? Never mind. The point was there was a bridge, and it could span troubled water, and whatever had happened between them in the past needed to be forgiven and forgotten.

Mrs. Schwartz's expression looked dark as a thundercloud. Apparently she was immune to the charm of the Duval men. "If your grandfather associated with residents who obeyed the rules, I wouldn't have to keep calling you. As it is, I'm afraid we have to discuss another infraction."

Max cast a sideways glance at Emma, his expression amused. "What did they do this time?"

"Your grandfather left the premises without authorization."

Max shot a concerned look at Harold. "He wandered away?"

"No. He left in a vehicle with an unauthorized person."

"That would be me." Dorothy raised her hand. "I'm completely unauthorized."

Harold chortled. Max's mouth curved in a smile.

"This isn't a joke," Mrs. Schwartz barked.

"Well, for heaven's sake, it isn't a war crime, either,"

Dorothy said. "We went to lunch in Hammond, then I drove him around and showed him all my old haunts. We had a perfectly lovely time."

"I don't see why this is a problem," Max said.

The jowls on Mrs. Schwartz's bulldog face trembled. "We have rules about dementia patients leaving the property. We need to know where they are at all times."

"So next time, they'll let you know where they're going." Max spread his hands. "Problem solved."

"Not quite yet," Mrs. Schwartz said firmly. "You have power of attorney. I can't release your grandfather to the custody of anyone without your authorization."

"I have no objection to Granddad going out with Mrs. Jamison. I'll put that in writing, if you like."

"Good!" Dorothy scooted to the edge of her chair and started to rise.

But the old shrew wasn't through trying to ruin everyone's day. Her hamlike hands sprawled on her desk. "Mr. Duval, I don't think you've fully considered the dangers of allowing a person of Mrs. Jamison's age to drive your grandfather anywhere."

Dorothy bristled. "Hey! Just because I'm older doesn't mean I'm incontinent."

"I think you mean *incompetent*, Grams," Emma softly corrected.

"Yes. Thank you, dear. The point is, Mrs. Schwartz, I haven't gotten a ticket in more than twenty years. I have a legal driver's license, and I'm in full compliance with the law."

"Sometimes that's not enough." Mrs. Schwartz sniffed.

"Excuse me, but do I get a say in this?" Harold said abruptly.

Everyone turned and looked at him.

"I'm going to die sooner or later, and if it's all right with everyone here, I'd prefer to die in a car with Dorothy instead of sitting alone in my room."

The words squeezed her heart. Dorothy reached out and did the same to his hand. "I feel exactly the same way, dear. That's how I want to go, too." Too late, she realized how the remark sounded. "Not that I'm planning to kill anyone with my driving. I'm a very, *very* safe driver."

She glanced over at Emma, who was a white-knuckle passenger. Emma rolled her eyes.

Well, I am.

"I have no problem with Mrs. Jamison driving my grandfather," Max said.

"Oh, good. That's settled." Dorothy jumped out of her chair. "Let's go, Harold. Oprah's about to come on, and it's kind of stuffy in here."

၂

Emma followed her grandmother and Harold into the hallway, a headache pounding in her temple. Her day had started off badly and progressively gotten worse. The two-hundred-pound floor polisher had lost a wheel in the hallway of the Alzheimer's wing, both day-shift janitors had called in sick, and the laundry service somehow had turned half the white table linens an unsightly shade of gray.

When Mrs. Schwartz had discovered that Harold was missing, she'd blamed Emma and thrown a full-throttle hissy fit. Thank God Grams and Harold had returned when they had, because Mrs. Schwartz had been ready to put an APB out on them.

And now Grams was eyeing Max with a mischievous

twinkle in her eye that could only spell more trouble. "Thanks for your support in there," she said.

Max rubbed his jaw. "No problem."

Grams batted her eyes in that innocent, I'm-not-up-to-anything way that set Emma on high alert. "While you're here, Max, maybe you could help Emma move a broken floor polisher."

"That's not necessary," Emma said quickly. "The janitor will deal with it tonight."

"Why wait till then, when you've got a big strapping man here right now?"

"He's busy, Grams. I'm sure he needs to get back to his office."

"It'll just take him a minute," Dorothy said. "And I'm sure he won't mind spending a moment or two alone in your company."

Wow, Grams, could you possibly be any more obvious?

Max's dimple flashed at Emma. "Remember the time-management rule."

"Go with the fastest, most expedient method," Harold chimed in.

Emma sighed. "All right, all right." She shot her grandmother an exasperated look, then motioned to Max. "Come on. It's upstairs in the Alzheimer's wing."

ॐ

Max winked at Grams, then followed Emma up the main staircase, admiring the view as he went. Emma was right—her backside *was* smaller than the one on the video.

He thought about saying as much, then decided it wasn't the sort of comment she was likely to appreciate.

At the top of the stairs, she turned to the left and gestured to a hulking orange machine in the hallway. "I was afraid I'd damage the floor if I tried to drag it, and it's too heavy for me to lift. If you can load it on a cart for me, I can take it from there."

"Sure. Where's the cart?"

"In a storage closet in the Alzheimer's rec room."

They turned and headed toward it as an elderly woman with scarlet lips and black rimmed eyes sauntered toward them. Her low-cut red dress sagged on her skeletal frame. "Hello, Miss Thornton," Emma called.

Ignoring Emma, the woman fixed her gaze on Max. Her sloppily made-up eyes simmered with a come-hither look that made Max recoil in alarm.

Her gaze raked him over. "And who might you be?" she purred.

"This is Max Duval," Emma said. "Max, this is Esmerelda Thornton."

The woman stepped closer. "Would you like to buy me a drink?" She put a bony hand on his chest and fingered his tie.

Whoa. "I—uh . . ." How the hell was he supposed to handle this? Max looked at Emma for help.

"I'm afraid he doesn't have time today, Ms. Thornton," Emma said, taking Max by the arm. "Maybe another time. Have a nice afternoon!"

Emma pulled him down the hall and around the corner, then abruptly dropped his arm.

Max adjusted his tie. "Thanks for the save."

"You're welcome."

"Is she always like that?"

"Sometimes she's worse."

Max was about to ask how when an apartment door opened and a fiftyish brunette in a red-and-white striped blouse and a denim skirt stepped into the hall. Her dark eyes locked on Emma. "You're Emma Jamison, aren't you?"

Emma's expression grew guarded. "Yes."

"I'm Marie Alvarez. I'd like to have a word with you."

Emma sucked in a deep breath, twined her fingers together, and spoke in a nervous rush. "Mrs. Schwartz told me you were upset about the photograph in the *National Inquisitioner,* and I completely understand. I was upset, as well. That reporter just showed up, and your mother opened the door—"

"I got your note." Marie's brown eyes softened as she smiled. "I'm afraid I overreacted."

Emma's face visibly relaxed.

"I hope I didn't cause you any problems with Mrs. Schwartz."

Emma lifted her shoulders. "None that I couldn't handle."

"Well, I blame her for the whole incident."

Emma's eyebrows rose. "You do?"

The middle-aged woman nodded. "When I moved Mom here a year ago, the Alzheimer's wing had three more aides than it does now. Mrs. Schwartz keeps cutting the staff to save money, and now there are barely enough aides to provide care, much less security. Mom would open the door to Jack the Ripper if he knocked."

"You should write a letter to the corporate office," Emma suggested.

"Good idea. I'll do that. But that's not what I wanted to talk to you about, dear. I wanted to thank you for painting Mom's bathroom the color of the one in her old home."

Her face creased in a wide smile. " It was ingenious! It's really cut down on her confusion. And the floor nurse told me you did it on your own time."

Emma looked away, apparently embarrassed by the effusive praise. "I'm glad it helped."

"Like a charm." Marie's gaze turned to Max. "You're Harold Duval's grandson, aren't you?"

"Yes," Max said.

"I've met your grandfather—what a charming man!"

There was that "charming" thing again, Max thought. Amazing. It was hard to believe so many people used the word to describe a man he'd always thought was cold and distant.

"I understand that Emma did some work in his apartment last week, too," Marie said.

Max glanced at Emma and raised an eyebrow. "Is that a fact."

The older woman nodded. "Emma's done something to help just about every resident in the wing." Down the hall, the elevator chimed, signaling its arrival. Marie turned toward it. "Well, I have to run. Thanks again!"

Max looked at Emma as they continued down the hall. "So you're painting Alzheimer's patients' bathrooms in your spare time?"

She lifted her shoulders. "Just a couple of them. It helps the residents remember which room is which."

"What did you do to Granddad's apartment?"

"I labeled things for him. He has trouble remembering where things are, but his reading comprehension is still good." She shot him a reproachful look. "If you visited him more often, you'd know."

Max looked away. "He doesn't want me to visit."

"How do you know?"

Max stepped aside to let a woman in a wheelchair pass. "You just saw him. He completely ignores me."

"Maybe that's because you ignore him."

"I don't know what to say to him," Max admitted. How had this conversation gotten all turned around, anyway?

He followed Emma into the moss-green rec room at the end of the hall. A ping-pong table and a pool table were positioned under Tiffany lamps at the front. In the center of the room, a tiny man with a weak chin and a prominent Adam's apple sat at a large table, pasting pictures onto construction paper.

"Hello, Mr. Arnie," Emma called.

He looked up and gave a gap-toothed smile. "Hello, dear."

In the back of the room, two elderly women sat on a plaid sofa, watching a blaring rerun of *The Golden Girls* on the wide-screen TV. Emma waved to them but got no response. Max followed her across the room to a pair of doors.

"Why did you use your own time to paint her apartment?" Max asked.

Emma pulled a key ring out of her pocket. "Mrs. Schwartz doesn't want me 'wasting time' doing things for individual residents. She says I should only work on things that benefit the center as a whole. And she thinks painting apartments is an unnecessary expense, because, and I quote, 'They're just going to get worse and die, and then we'll have to paint all over again.'"

Max shook his head. "She reminds me of Nurse Ratched in *One Flew over the Cuckoo's Nest*. How did a woman like that end up running a retirement center, anyway?"

The keys jangled as Emma searched through them. "Sunnyside bought this place from a smaller chain of retirement homes, and Mrs. Schwartz was one of the employees they inherited."

"Well, they need to disinherit her. They should give her job to you."

Emma glanced at him warily, as if she were trying to determine whether or not he was joking. "Thanks," she said at length, inserting a key in the lock and twisting it. "But that's not likely to happen."

"Why not?"

She tugged the doors open, then gave him a you-can't-be-serious gaze. "Would you have considered moving your grandfather here if you knew I was in charge of the place?"

No, he realized. Before he'd met her, he never would have considered entrusting his grandfather to the woman on that videotape. "I would now."

Her eyes softened. "Thanks."

He followed her into the dark closet, which smelled of pine disinfectant. A large pushcart sat against the wall in the back, between neat shelves of sheets, towels, and cleaning supplies. "If people could see what you're really like, Emma, your public image would change. If you could overcome your fear of cameras, someone like Diane Sawyer could interview you, and—"

"I've tried to overcome it," she interjected.

"How?"

"Well, let's see." Turning to face him, she raised a hand and held up her index finger. "I saw a therapist, but it didn't help." She raised another finger. "I tried medication, but it had too many side effects." She held up a third finger. "I tried hypnosis. No results." She raised her pinky. "And I had Grams videotape me, thinking that I could gradually become accustomed to it. Unfortunately, the next time I encountered a stranger with a camera, things were just as bad as ever."

Hell. "You need to clear your name, Emma."

"Yeah." Her mouth twisted in a sardonic smile. "I'm working on finding a time machine so I can travel back and be a thousand miles away from the Mullendorf estate last December. Any ideas where I can get one?"

This was too serious to joke about. "You need to find the woman in the video."

All traces of humor left her face. "I tried to get to the bottom of this, Max. I ran through all my money and got my hopes up again and again. You can only bang your head against a brick wall for so long before you lose your mind." She turned and yanked on the red handle of the pushcart. "There comes a point where you have to just accept things and move on."

Max wanted to tell her he'd talked to Dave, but from the sound of things, she'd just think he was interfering. He'd better wait and see what Dave turned up before he broke the news.

He helped her pull the cart out of the closet. "Do you need help with any of the painting or labeling and whatever else you're doing in the apartments?" he asked. "I'm between Habitat houses, so I could help out."

Emma shook her head. "I'm finished."

"So you're back to painting your walls?"

"Not yet. I've been helping Katie organize the storage room at her salon. It's taking a while because we can only work on it when the salon is closed, but we should finish up this Sunday."

"So what are you doing Saturday?" Max asked.

"I thought I'd start priming the walls at my place."

"Then I'll come over with my power painters." The metal cart clattered as he rolled it down the hall.

Her eyes grew wary. "I don't know if that's a good idea."

"It's a great idea. The job will go faster with two people."

"I don't mean that. I mean . . ."

Max knew exactly what she meant. "I promise not to put any moves on you, if that's what you're worried about. I just thought I'd keep you from getting another primer headache."

Her eyebrows rose. "I'm surprised you remembered that."

He stopped the cart beside the broken floor polisher. "I remember everything you've ever told me."

Her lips parted in surprise. The remark surprised him, too, but hell, it was true. His interactions with Emma were all written in bold type and italics in his mind. He bent and hoisted the heavy orange machine onto the rubber-lined cart. When he looked up, he found her watching him.

She quickly averted her eyes, as if he'd caught her checking him out. Had she been? The thought made his heart beat faster.

She put her hands on the cart handle and tugged, trying to turn it around. The weight of the polisher made it difficult to maneuver.

"I'll get it. It's too big for you to handle alone." And so was this whole Ferguson situation. The only way to ever clear her name was to find the woman in the video, and that was going to take inside connections.

"Thanks, but I can manage." She leaned against the cart, putting her whole body weight into it, and pushed. It awkwardly swung around.

"You just don't trust yourself alone in that dark closet with me again," he teased.

She flashed him a dry grin. "You have a rich fantasy life, don't you?"

Yeah. And it completely revolves around you.

She finally got the cart turned around and started pushing it down the hall. "Thanks for your help," she called over her shoulder.

I hope you feel that way when you learn about Dave, Max thought as she disappeared through the rec room doorway.

CHAPTER FIFTEEN

*I*t was only ten o'clock in the morning, but sweat dripped off Louis's forehead as he focused his camera on the two men in front of the Pontchartrain Food Bank. Man, it was hot. He'd wanted to take this stupid photo inside, but his editor had told him to get the sign over the door of the ramshackle building in the shot, so here he was, steaming like human broccoli in the August heat.

"Stand a little closer," Louis directed. "And Mr. Briggs, can you turn the basket a little more toward me?" Both men in his viewfinder complied. This was a totally bogus assignment—Dirk Briggs handing a basket of food to the local food bank director. This wasn't news; this was pandering. Apparently, Briggs's family owned the bank, which pretty much meant they owned the town, and the newspaper covered whatever Briggs wanted. Since he was running for DA, he wanted daily coverage of his amazing benevolence and generosity.

"Don't they have to give his opponent equal time?" Louis had asked his editor.

The short, potbellied man had lifted his suspender-striped shoulders. "No law to that effect, although most newspapers do. But Dirk has a way of working around the rules."

Yeah, he just bet he did. Louis knew the type—fraternity boy, silver spoon, thought he was better than everyone else. He'd always hated that kind of guy—mainly because he wanted to be one himself.

No such luck for the Lou-meister. Instead of a silver spoon, he'd been born with a plastic spork. He'd had the lousy luck of being the fourth son of a mechanic in Bayou La Tête whose idea of a big social occasion was a night of beer and bowling. Instead of an investment portfolio, his old man had a '57 Chevy on concrete blocks in the back yard and permanent grease stains under his fingernails. No matter how hard he scrubbed with Lava soap, his nails remained black and ragged.

Those nasty nails had always embarrassed the hell out of Louis. Two years ago he'd invited a friend from college home for Thanksgiving, and the sight of his father carving the freaking turkey with his freaking nasty hands had made Louis want to crawl under the table and puke.

And his mother—man, she was just as pathetic. She worked in the coffee shop where the rich high school kids hung out, and she took demeaning crap on a daily basis. The overprivileged jerks thought it was funny to mouth off and treat her like dirt, making her step and fetch it to remake a stupid cappuccino because the foam was too wet or some other bogus BS, only to leave an insultingly small tip, if they left one at all.

Well, Louis wasn't going to spend his life having other people look down on him like that. No, sir. He was going to be somebody, somebody people looked up to and envied. He was headed for the big time. He might not have the looks for TV, but he could damn sure make a name for himself in print. In print, things like a big nose, crooked teeth, and acne scars didn't matter. Besides, when he hit it big, he could afford to have all that stuff fixed.

"Say, son—move to the left and take another picture," Briggs told him. "That's my best side."

Louis fought the urge to roll his eyes. Man, what a dick. But this guy was buds with the newspaper's owner, so he'd better suck it up. "Sure." Louis squeezed off another shot. "Got it."

The manager of the food bank, a friendly looking Andy Griffith type, smiled. "Well, if that's all, I need to get back to work. We're doing a delivery this afternoon to the soup kitchen in Mireau, and I need to get everything packed up." He shook Mr. Briggs's hand. "Thank you very much."

"My pleasure, my pleasure." Briggs hitched up his khakis over his barrel of a belly as the manager disappeared into the whitewashed, tin-roofed building. His editor had said that Briggs had been a big shot on the local football team when he'd been in high school, but his athletic build, if he'd ever really had one, had gone completely to pot.

Briggs ambled toward him, his comb-over drooping in the heat. "Say there, son—let me see those photos."

Man, this guy really thought he ran the show. Swallowing his distaste, Louis held out the camera and showed Briggs the three photos.

"Use that last one," Briggs said.

"Sure." Like hell he would. Sorry sonuvabitch, telling him what to do.

Briggs put one foot on the step of the building, showing off shiny alligator cowboy boots. He probably wore the boots just to make himself look taller, Louis thought with disdain.

Briggs leaned forward conspiratorially. "I understand you sold a photo of Emma Jamison to the tabloids."

"Yeah."

"I also understand you're looking for another angle."

"Where'd you hear that?"

"You mentioned it to some girl you work with, who gets her hair cut at the salon where my wife goes. News travels real fast in a small town."

No shit. Man, the way gossip spread through this town, it was a wonder they even needed a newspaper.

Briggs's voice dropped lower. "I have a little something that might interest you."

Louis's ears perked up. "Oh, yeah?"

Briggs stepped closer, close enough that Louis could smell last night's garlic on his breath. " 'Course, this is strictly off the record. You didn't hear it from me."

"Sure. What is it I didn't hear?"

"Well, apparently Emma and the DA are getting pre-e-e-ety cozy."

"No kidding." A little rush of adrenaline kicked into Louis's bloodstream. "What's this based on?"

"A couple of things. Thing one: one of my wife's friends saw Emma and Duval standing reeee-eal close the other night in the town square, after she busted the reading group."

"Busted it? What do you mean?"

"Crashed it. Showed up uninvited."

Now, this might be news. Louis dug his notebook out of his pocket. "Where was it?"

"At the public library."

Oh, man, that was lame. "I don't think you can crash something at the public library."

"Well, it's a group of regulars, and nobody invited her. But that's not the story." He shifted closer, his breath fetid in the humid air. "The story is, one of the women had to go back to the library because she forgot her sweater, and she saw Emma and Duval standing by her car, and she swears it looked like they were kissing."

"Kissing? The DA and Emma Jamison?"

"Yeah. He had his hands on her arms and they were standing this close." He held up his index and middle finger, all squished together.

"Hmmm." More adrenaline dumped into Louis's veins. That was exactly the kind of thing he needed—something that tied Emma into real news. A political sexcapade might be the launch pad he was looking for. Oh, yeah—he was liking the sound of this.

He'd better play it cool, though. If Briggs thought it was really a big deal, he might take it to his buddy the publisher, and before Louis had a chance to break the story, it would get assigned to a staff reporter. "That's really interesting, Mr. Briggs, but it doesn't sound like there's any proof to back it up."

"Well, how about this: Emma's grandmother and Duval's grandfather are a hot item at the retirement home."

Louis's eyebrows rose. "They are?"

Briggs nodded. "Everybody there knows they're fooling around. They were caught in the old man's room a few weeks ago."

"No kidding." This could be a story in and of itself.

"Serious as a heart attack. Max and Emma were called into the executive director's office and everyone got their wrists slapped."

It would be pretty easy to check this out. He'd run into a loudmouthed redhead named Orchid or something—Iris, that was it—during his first visit to Sunnyside, and she'd be thrilled to give him the four-one-one.

Louis tried to steer the conversation back to the bigger story. "Well, that's sure interesting, but it doesn't mean anything's going on with Max and Emma."

"Trust me, something's going on." The garlic fumes hit Louis's face in a gagworthy blast as the older man leaned closer. "If you tail one or the other, I bet you'll catch them together."

Louis had already tailed Emma a couple of times. He knew what she drove and where she lived, but as far as he could tell, her life was a total snoozefest. She went to work, she hung out at the beauty salon with that soldier's wife, and she went home. But maybe he ought to tail Max.

He could do it this weekend. He worked half a day Saturday and was off on Sunday. Weekends were when they were likely to get together, anyway.

In the meantime, he'd try to get something on the grandparents. That could be worth another paycheck from the tabloids. "Thanks for the tip."

"You're welcome." Briggs slapped him on the shoulder in a way that made him flinch. "Follow up on it, and I guarantee you'll strike gold." He winked at him. "But you never heard it from me, right?"

"Right." Louis gave him a smile. Man, what an ass. "Absolutely."

❧

Emma awoke before six on Saturday morning and, after a breakfast of oatmeal and coffee, dressed in navy stretch shorts and a white LSU T-shirt. She combed her hair into a ponytail, washed her face and brushed her teeth, then pulled a brown eyeliner pencil from the immaculately organized makeup bag she kept in her bathroom drawer. She leaned toward the mirror, pencil in hand, and caught her own gaze in the mirror.

No. She wasn't going to put on makeup for Max. If she started primping for him, that would mean she cared what he thought about her.

But you do, her mind taunted.

Well, she didn't have to act like it. They were friends, that was all, and she intended to keep her mind on the reason he was coming over—to help her quiet her screaming walls. If her home didn't feel so chaotic, maybe she'd feel more in control of her life, and heaven only knew she needed all the control she could get.

She tucked the liner back in the bag and started to put the bag in the drawer, then impulsively reopened it and pulled out her pink lip gloss. She needed to keep her lips moisturized, she reasoned. She was about to put the bag away again when she decided to add just a smidgen of mascara, as well, because . . . well, she didn't really have a reason, but she'd already put it on one eye and might as well do the other.

She padded downstairs and into the kitchen, her little dog trailing at her heels. She made two ham-and-cheese sandwiches, figuring the least she could do was offer Max lunch, then spent the next hour covering the hardwood floor with a plastic tarp and stretching blue painter's tape along all of the baseboards. She'd just set up a stepladder in the polka-dotted dining room and started taping off the crown molding when Snookems yapped out a warning.

From her perch on the ladder, Emma saw Max's truck in her drive. Ignoring the way her heart picked up speed, she climbed down, scooped up her dog, and opened the door.

"Hi," she called as Max emerged from his pickup.

"Hi, yourself."

Wow, but he looked good. He wore old jeans with a worn fly and a gray New Orleans Zephyrs T-shirt. His forearms were muscled and tanned, and the shirt stretched taut over his broad chest as he opened the tailgate. He hoisted himself into the truck bed and hauled out a long-handled paint roller with a hose, and something that looked like a vacuum cleaner, then jumped down and strode toward the porch. As he stepped into the multicolored foyer, Emma felt a heady buzz of attraction.

Snookems growled.

"Glad to see you, too, fuzzball," Max said to the dog.

Emma focused on the equipment in his hands. "Is that your super painter?"

"It's a power painter." His dimple flashed as he lifted it. "*I'm* the super painter."

"Oh, yeah?" Emma grinned. "Where's your cape?"

"Left it at home. I didn't want to get primer on it."

Emma's grin widened as she closed the door. "So are you wearing tights under your jeans?"

"Maybe. Want to check?"

The concept held a dangerous amount of appeal. "I'll pass."

Max set the paint contraption on the tarp, then walked into the dining room, eyeing her handiwork. "Looks like you nearly have the place all prepped."

"I haven't finished taping the crown molding or the windows or doors."

"It'll go a lot faster with two ladders and two pairs

of hands. I'll go get the rest of my equipment out of the truck."

He returned a few moments later with a Home Depot bag and a wooden ladder tucked under his arm. He set his ladder beside hers in the living room, and they worked in tandem, each picking up the tape at the end of the other's reach. In thirty minutes flat, they were putting the final strip on the downstairs ceiling.

Emma lowered her aching arms. "Wow. Do you prosecute criminals as fast as you tape off ceilings?"

"I wish. Unfortunately, that saying about the wheels of justice grinding slowly was invented for a reason."

Emma stood on her ladder and admired his biceps as he pressed down the last bit of tape. "You really like it, though, don't you?"

"Slow grinding?"

She rolled her eyes. "Your job."

His mouth pulled in a sardonic grin. "I must, to go through all this election BS."

"What attracted you to the law-and-order business in the first place?"

"The shiny badges."

"Seriously. Why didn't you go to work at your grandfather's business?"

She heard him blow out a harsh breath. "Because I wanted to live life on my terms. I'd grown up surrounded by plastic, and I wanted to do something real." He climbed down his ladder, his jeans straining against his muscled thighs. "I wanted to feel like I was making a difference in the world."

"Why did you pick criminal justice?"

He folded the ladder tray and pushed up the rung

hinges. "Because I hate seeing innocent people being victimized."

"Do you have some personal experience along those lines?"

He shot her a teasing grin. "Sounds like you're trying to establish a motive. Have you thought about a career in law enforcement?"

He was avoiding answering, which meant she'd hit the mark. "So what happened?"

His ladder screeched as he closed it. "Nothing much."

"Well, then, you shouldn't mind telling me."

He lifted the ladder and carried it into the foyer. He was trying to evade the question, which made her all the more curious. She followed him. "You might as well tell me, because I can be very persistent. Besides, I told you all the sordid details of my video phobia."

☙

Yeah, she had. And refusing to tell her his story was turning it into a bigger deal than it really was.

"I was bullied when I was a kid," he said. The moment he said it, he felt like a moron. He halfway expected her to make fun of him.

But her eyes held nothing but sympathy. "How old were you?"

"Not quite eleven. I'd just gone to boarding school, and I was smaller than everyone else because I'd skipped a couple of grades."

"What did they do to you?"

"You name it. Beat me up, framed me, gave me swirlies . . . It was a hellacious year."

"And the teachers didn't help?"

"They didn't know, and I didn't dare tell." He leaned

the ladder against the wall. "It went on the whole year. Then most of them graduated and went to another school. Which was actually a shame, because over the summer, I took karate and grew about a foot."

Emma followed him back into the foyer. "Let me guess," she said. "The next year, you stood up for the new kids."

He looked at her, surprised. "Yeah, I guess I kind of did."

"And you've sympathized with victims and underdogs ever since."

If she'd been anyone else, he would have thought she was mocking him, but her tone was warm, her gaze warmer still.

Her eyes turned somber.

"Is that how you see me—as an underdog?"

The question jarred him. "What?"

"Are you hanging around me because you feel sorry for me?"

She was serious. His eyes ran over her fitted T-shirt, her low-riding shorts, and her long stretch of leg. He drew in a deep breath and inhaled the scent of her faint perfume and coconutty hair, and the attraction he'd been fighting all morning kicked into high gear. "Believe me, sweetheart, pity is the last thing on my mind when I look at you."

Her lips parted, then closed, then parted again. She turned to the window and smoothed down an already smooth piece of tape on the side of the window frame. "Well, good." Her tone was overly bright, an obvious attempt to override the sexual energy crackling in the air. "I wouldn't want to be an object of pity."

How about an object of desire? He stifled the words, and tried to stifle the thought. *You're here to help her, Duval, not add to her problems.* He needed to focus on the job at hand and not think about the way she looked and smelled.

He crossed to the other end of the foyer and knelt down beside the cans of primer. "Ready to tackle the messy part?"

Emma nodded. Max pulled a screwdriver out of his toolbox and pried the lid off a can. An acrid scent filled the air, mercifully masking her heady scent.

Emma wrinkled her nose. "I'd better put Snookems outside so she won't get into that stuff."

"Good idea. This type of primer is next to impossible to get out of your hair, and I don't think your little dog would look so good with a buzz cut."

He inserted a hose into the can of paint, then snapped a lid over it. He was connecting the hose to the roller when she came back into the room.

"So how does this thing work?" she asked.

"I'm getting ready to show you. But first I want you to put this on." He pulled a metallic gray-and-black gas mask out of the Home Depot bag and handed it to her.

"You're kidding, right?"

He shook his head. "It's a paint respirator. It'll keep you from inhaling the fumes."

Emma gingerly took the thing and turned it in her hands. It was mainly made of soft, clear plastic designed to fit over the mouth and nose, with small black barrels jutting out on each side.

"Some people are sensitive to primer, and apparently you're one of them. I had a couple of unused respirators left over from the last Habitat project in my truck, so I brought you one."

Emma eyed the contraption. "I'll look like an ant eater in this."

Max grinned. "Actually, you'll look more like an ant. But hey, it's better than getting sick."

"True." She started to slip it over her head, then stopped. "So where's yours?"

"This stuff doesn't bother me."

"You said you had a couple of these things, right?"

He could see where this was leading, and he didn't like it. "Well, yeah, but . . ."

She put her hands on her hips. "I won't wear one if you don't."

"Because you're worried about my safety, or because you want me to look as goofy as you?"

She grinned. "Both."

It was hard to argue with such blatant honesty. He sighed. "Okay. I'll go out to the truck and get it."

"That's more like it." Emma fit the mask over her face and followed him to the door.

᠅

A hundred yards away, Louis tensed as the front door opened. He'd been crouched in the bushes for nearly an hour, sweating like a sumo wrestler in a steam bath, waiting for just this moment.

He'd gotten up at six this morning and parked on the two-lane highway that led to Max's private drive—the SOB had an electric gate in front of his property—then waited for him. He could hardly believe his luck when Max had driven straight to Emma's house. Louis had been so excited that he'd goosed the accelerator and nearly rear-ended Max's truck when Max had turned onto the dirt road. To play it safe, he'd parked on a turnoff behind a clump of bushes a half-mile up the dirt road and walked down through the woods, lugging his camera, a tripod, and the new telephoto lens he'd ordered off eBay. The August heat was a bitch; his shirt clung to him like wet plaster, and his pants were so sweat-soaked it felt like he'd whizzed in his shorts.

But it was all about to pay off. He lifted the camera and struggled with the heavy lens, trying to get it in focus. Man, this was great—better than great. It was just what he'd hoped for—just the kind of the thing the *National Inquisitioner* had said they'd buy.

He'd e-mailed the editor after his conversation with Briggs last Wednesday, explaining that a rumor was circulating that Emma was seeing the DA and asking if they'd be interested in an article.

The editor had phoned him back, telling him to never discuss potential assignments in writing. "E-mails can come back and bite us on the butt," he'd said in a fast Brooklyn clip. "Call me from now on."

"Sure," Louis had said, grinning with pride. Wasn't this some shit—having phone access to an editor at a national news publication? Okay, so it was a tabloid, but hey—the pay was great, and the circulation was amazing. No one else in his journalism class was making this kind of money, that was for freakin' sure.

"Just a story won't work," the editor had told him. "But if you can get us a photo of them together—especially if they're doing something real friendly, if you know what I mean—and maybe some comments from locals who are outraged or shocked, well, then, we might have something."

"No problem," Louis had said, hoping to hell that silver-spoon boy Briggs hadn't been just blowing smoke.

His pulse pounded as he twisted the long lens, trying to get the shot wide enough to catch both Max at his truck and the woman in the doorway. As the shot came into focus, he nearly dropped the camera.

"What the hell . . ."

Emma—or someone, or *something*—stood at the door, wearing what looked like a gas mask. It was scary-looking, like something out of a war film or a movie about aliens. As Louis watched through the lens, Max emerged from his truck, wearing a similar weird mask.

"Holy shit." What the hell were they doing—operating a meth lab? Louis overcame his shock to snap a couple pictures, but he got only the back of Max's head. Max's truck was parked sideways, so Louis couldn't get the license tag or a bumper sticker or anything that would prove it belonged to him. And Emma—if it even *was* Emma—was totally unrecognizable. The pictures were worthless.

He watched Max close the door behind him. Should he try to sneak up and peer in the window? The *Inquisitioner* wouldn't buy any pictures shot through a window—it would leave them wide open to an invasion-of-privacy lawsuit—but if he knew what was going on, maybe he could somehow use it in his story. On the other hand, he could end up in jail if the DA caught him window peeping.

Or trespassing. Oh, hell—he might be trespassing right now. He hadn't thought of that. He didn't know where Emma's property began or ended. For all he knew, the dirt road marked the beginning of it.

He looked at his phony Rolex watch and muttered an oath. He was due at work in an hour, and he was so sweaty that he'd have to go back to his dinky, dingy apartment to take a shower and change clothes. He had two choices: He could leave now, or sneak up and peer in the window.

WWGD?

There was no question. Geraldo would look in the window. But hell—would Geraldo feel this scared? Louis's hands shook as he unscrewed the bulky lens from his camera and put it in the case around his neck, along with the camera. He folded up the tripod, then crept toward the house, ducking behind trees, sweating like crazy.

He jumped as a branch snapped under his sneaker, then crept up to the back of the house and cautiously peered in a window. Nothing but an empty kitchen. His back against the wood siding, he slowly inched his way toward the front of the house. He paused by the first window, then leaned forward and looked in.

There they were! Their backs were toward him, and he could clearly see that they were . . . painting.

Shit. That's all they were doing? He craned his neck for a closer look. Max was on a ladder, painting the wall with some kind of souped-up extra-long roller, and Emma knelt a short distance away, using a brush along the floorboard.

Well, big whoop-de-do. They were wearing dumb-looking, overly cautious masks and painting a stupid wall.

Damn. He'd really hoped he'd catch them cooking chemicals—or at least rolling around in a steamy embrace.

Still, this wasn't all bad, Louis consoled himself. Max wasn't spending a Saturday painting Emma's house for nothing. Something was going on between them, and he'd get a photo soon enough. He'd come back and see if Max's car was still here after work, and if it wasn't, he'd stake out Max's home again tomorrow.

CHAPTER SIXTEEN

Around three o'clock in the afternoon, Emma plopped her paint roller in the tray and breathed a sigh of relief. The respirator made her sound like Darth Vader. "Done at last."

Max pulled off his mask. His cheeks had red creases where the plastic had pressed into his skin. "Sounded like you just said, 'Duh, alas.'"

"I can't talk through this thing."

He grinned. "That sounded like 'Icon tall. Boo, disdain.'"

Smiling, Emma lifted her mask. She cringed at the odor.

"Better keep that on until you get out of here," Max suggested. "Why don't we go outside and clean up?"

"Okay." Emma put the mask back over her face, then picked up the paint tray and roller as Max gathered up the power painter, the roller, the can of primer, and the lid. Max followed her through the kitchen and out the back door. Snookems barked sharply as Emma peeled off the mask and drew in a deep breath of fresh air. "This is much better."

"Yeah. I can actually understand you."

"Hey, I wasn't the only one who was incomprehensible." Emma peeled off her plastic gloves and headed to the faucet at the side of the deck that they'd used earlier when they'd cleaned up to eat the sandwiches. "When you told me the wall needed another coat, it sounded like you said you needed an otter Coke."

Max grinned back. "Oh, yeah? Well, you told me I had kissed a lot."

"What?"

"I think you were trying to say 'missed a spot.'"

She swatted at him, smearing more primer on his already primer-streaked arm. Her arms were even more coated in the thick white stuff, she noticed as she picked up the garden hose.

He stood behind her as she bent to turn on the faucet. "I hate to tell you this, but you have a big streak of dried primer in the back of your hair."

"Oh, no." Emma started to raise her hand to touch it, then realized she'd only be making it worse. "How do I get it out?"

"The best method is to soak your hair in water for about an hour, then use a fine-toothed comb." He held the water hose while she rubbed her hands under the stream. The wet primer washed off, but the dry stuff stuck like superglue.

She looked up at him. "You're telling me to go soak my head?"

Max smiled. "I usually just go for a swim."

"You have a pool?"

"Better than that. I have a whole lake." He watched her

scrub primer off her arms. "I live on a houseboat on Lake Pontchartrain. Why don't you grab a swimsuit and we'll head over there?"

Emma hesitated. "Oh, I don't think—"

"What else are you going to do?" he asked. "Your house is filled with fumes, and you're too much of a mess to go anywhere."

"Gee, thanks for the compliment," Emma said, but looking down at her primer-splattered legs, she knew he was stating the obvious.

"You can bring your dog. She looks ready to keel over from heat exhaustion."

Emma glanced at Snookems, who was lying in the shade on the corner of the deck. Sure enough, the poor thing's tongue was hanging so far out it looked like it would never fit back in her mouth.

She shouldn't accept the invitation. It was a bad idea to spend any more time alone with Max. On the other hand, she hated to just sit in her back yard while the primer dried, and a swim *did* sound wonderful. "Okay," she found herself saying. "I'll go get my swimsuit."

"Atta girl."

She started for the house.

"You're forgetting your resting gator," he called.

She turned around. "What?"

He lifted her mask and held it out. "Your respirator."

She walked back and took it from his hand, grinning. "Very funny."

"Hairy bunny?"

She rolled her eyes, but she was enjoying the silly exchange. "You've obviously inhaled too many fumes. Breathe deeply while I'm gone, and maybe oxygen will restore your brain cells."

"Rebore my brain meld?"

"You're insane." She fitted the mask back over her face.

"Inane?"

"Completely." Grinning behind the mask, she headed inside.

Snookems stood on Emma's left thigh, her tiny front paws on the window, as Emma followed Max's Silverado down the two-lane highway twenty minutes later. Emma had insisted on taking her own car instead of riding with Max, so that no one would see them together. Plus, it made it seem less like a date.

Which, of course, it wasn't. Well, okay, maybe it sort of was, but since Emma had her own car, she could leave any time she wanted, and since Max wouldn't bring her home, they wouldn't have any of that awkward kiss/don't kiss goodbye stuff at her door.

Not that there would have been any of that, anyway. They were friends, that was all. Hadn't they just managed to spend the morning and half the afternoon together without getting the least bit romantic?

Well, maybe there'd been a little mild flirting. And she'd caught him looking at her legs a few times when she'd been up on the ladder, and she'd taken more than a few peeks at his buns and pecs, and there had definitely been some flammable chemistry brewing in the air.

But nothing had happened. And nothing *would* happen.

The left rear signal light on Max's truck blinked. Emma slowed and followed the pickup onto a dirt road, which really wasn't a road at all, but wheel ruts cut through a thick forest of pines and cypress. Emma followed it around a bend, then saw a wrought-iron gate blocking the road.

Max swerved off the path, climbed out and unfastened the gate, then waved her through. She waited for him on the opposite side of the gate, then followed his pickup for a half mile or so, down a road so bumpy that Snookems was jostled off her hind-leg stance.

The dense forest thinned. Emma followed Max's truck around a long curve, then drew in her breath. The lake stretched in front of her, smooth and shiny as an endless mirror, so vast that the far shore was invisible. A long wooden pier jutted out into the glassy expanse of water. Docked beside it was a small white fishing boat and a two-story white and blue houseboat.

Emma pulled her Saturn to a stop beside Max's pickup. Reaching for the canvas tote holding her swimsuit, she climbed out, the little dog in her arms. The scent of salt water and warm vegetation filled the steamy air.

"What do you think?" Max asked.

"This is beautiful! It must be hard to leave this place every morning."

He smiled. "Sometimes it is."

"Where on earth did you get your houseboat?"

"On eBay."

She looked at him, certain he was teasing. "No way."

"Way. It was part of a fleet of houseboats that people could rent at a lake in Arkansas. It's got two bedrooms, two baths, a kitchen—all the conveniences of home." He motioned toward it. "Come on. I'll give you the grand tour."

Emma's flip-flops slapped on the wooded pier as they headed toward the houseboat. Max stepped onto the boat first and held out his hand to help her aboard. Cradling Snookems in one arm, she took his hand and felt his palm swallow hers in solid warmth, sparking a familiar tingle. He released her hand to open the sliding-glass door.

"After you," he said with a gallant sweep of his hand.

Emma stepped inside and looked around. A navy blue sofa lined one wall, flanked by two end tables. A built-in bookcase and entertainment center sat on the opposite wall, near a desk and leather easy chair. An oval table and six chairs filled the dining area adjacent to the galley. "It's terrific," she said.

"It came fully furnished," Max said, snatching a stray T-shirt off the sofa. "Pots and pans, sheets and towels, dishes and everything."

Emma noted that some of those dishes were in the sink and the desk was covered with papers, but all in all, the place was pretty neat for a bachelor pad.

She stepped into the kitchen and ran her hand over the cool smoothness of the stainless-steel countertop. "It's hard to believe it's a boat. You've got a dishwasher and an oven and a refrigerator . . . it's a full kitchen."

"You can't call it a kitchen," Max said with a teasing grin. "If you're on a boat, you have to call it a galley. It's a law."

She grinned back. "I'll keep that in mind. I don't want you siccing the boat language police on me." She gestured to the galley appliances. "How do you power all this?"

"I use land utilities while I'm docked, but the boat has its own generator and water storage. Want to see the rest of it?"

"I'd love to."

She followed him through the living room to the front of the boat. "This is the captain's quarters."

"You being the captain."

"And first mate and deckhand and cook and chief bottle

washer." A king-sized bed was permanently affixed to the wall, along with built-in nightstands on either side.

"I'm impressed," Emma said, fingering the bottom of his navy blue comforter. "You actually make your bed."

He lifted his shoulders. "Guess boarding school's good for something."

Few personal effects were visible. No pictures graced the walls, and the top of his large mahogany dresser held only a few scattered receipts and loose coins. She peered into the bathroom on the right and was surprised to see an oversized tub and shower. "I never knew boats had such big baths."

"This one's more house than boat." He jerked his thumb toward the back. "There's a smaller bath and bedroom at the opposite end of the boat—along with a deck and swim launch. Want to see?"

"Sure."

She followed him back through the living room. He opened a door on the right that led to a smaller version of his bedroom, complete with the same comforter she'd seen in the master.

"The swim deck's back here." He led her to the far side of the living room and opened a sliding-glass door perpendicular to the one by the pier. Emma stepped onto a deck with two white resin lounge chairs and two small matching tables, surrounded by white railing. Max opened a gate in the railing, then bent down and flipped out a small wooden platform with a water ladder attached.

"This is amazing," Emma said.

She glanced up at a set of ladder-like stairs leading to the upper level.

Max followed her gaze. "That leads to the sundeck. Want to see?"

"Sure." Emma set Snookems on the nearest lounge chair, then scrambled up the steps.

Eight wrought-iron chairs sat around a large table shaded by a tan and green striped sun umbrella. Two lounge chairs with matching cushions sat on the other side of the deck near a set of barbells and a built-in barbecue grill. Emma fingered the stainless-steel hood of the grill. "Wow. What a great place for entertaining."

"It was a party boat," Max said. "It came with a jet ski and all kinds of water sports equipment."

"Oh, it has a slide!" Emma clapped as she looked at the two-story curved slide. "Is the water deep enough to use it?"

"Yeah. It's about ten or twelve feet here. Can you swim?"

Emma nodded. "I was on my high school swim team."

Max pulled his mouth into a disappointed frown and snapped his fingers. "There go my hopes of mouth-to-mouth resuscitation."

She shot him a pained look, but butterflies took flight in her stomach. Her gaze inadvertently flew to his lips.

"Ready to change into swim gear?" he asked.

No. She should probably rethink this whole thing. Instead of stripping down to her bikini, she should probably grab her little dog, get in her car, and go home. If she knew what was good for her, she'd do just that. But self-preservation was not top of mind at the moment. "Sure," she found herself saying.

"You can use the guest room. I'll meet you back up here in a few moments."

※

Max changed in record time and was busy wetting down the slide with a water hose when Emma joined him a few minutes later. Her upper body was covered with her T-shirt, but her legs were bare beneath a black bikini bottom, and the sight of her made his mouth go dry.

"You look great," he said.

"Thanks." Her gaze darted to his bare chest, then her face colored. "You, um, too."

He crouched to shut off the water, and she climbed on the slide while his back was turned.

"Here goes nothing," she said, pushing off. She squealed as she slid down the slide, then hit the water with a splash.

Max watched her bob to the surface and smooth her hair out of her face, a wide grin on her face. "That was a blast!" she called.

It was a blast watching her. Max climbed over the railing and executed a perfect dive into the water. As his head emerged, he heard Snookems bark from the lower deck swim platform.

"Can you swim as well as you dive?" Emma asked as he swam toward her.

"Only one way to find out."

"I'll race you to that buoy and back." She pointed to a red-and-white ball floating about fifty yards away.

"You're on."

"Okay—ready. Set. Go!" He let her get a head start, then took off after her. She was a good swimmer—strong and graceful. He had to pour on the power to catch up with her. All the same, he touched the buoy seconds before her.

"No fair," she said, breathing hard. "You have greater upper body strength."

"Maybe, but you have the greater upper body."

A splash of water hit him upside the face.

He splashed her back.

Her mouth curved in a mischievous grin. "You're going to regret that."

"You started it."

She splashed him again, then dove underwater before he could retaliate. He turned to go after her, only to feel her tug on his legs, pulling him under.

He popped to the surface, but she'd swum away. She treaded water, laughing.

"You've asked for it now," he warned, heading toward her.

A bark sounded from the boat. Max turned his head to see a small splash, then a tiny gray head bobbing on the water.

"Snookems is coming to save me!" Emma said.

"Good, because you're going to need all the help you can get," Max said, grabbing her around the waist.

Emma kept her eyes on the dog. "I've never seen her swim before."

Max was about to follow through on a payback dunking when Snookems's head disappeared. It bobbed up a moment later, only to vanish again.

"She's having trouble." All playfulness left Emma's voice.

Oh, hell—he couldn't let anything happen to her little dog. Max released Emma and propelled himself through the water at top speed. The dog's head surfaced once more, but as Max neared her, the little beast disappeared from view.

Max dove down and strained to see in the murky water, the salt in the brackish water stinging his eyes. He was about to come up for air when he spotted something sinking to the bottom, something so still that it looked like a seaweed-covered piece of wood. Fighting the urge to surface, Max dove deeper, close enough to see that it was the limp dog, her long hair floating out around her. Max scooped the tiny Yorkie under her front legs and shot to the surface, gulping in air.

"I've got her," he yelled to Emma. She was behind him, her face drawn and pale. Holding the dog close to his chest, Max one-arm crawled to the boat. He hoisted the motionless animal onto the swim platform, then hauled himself up after her.

The dog wasn't breathing. Max rolled the lifeless Yorkie onto her back and pushed on her tiny rib cage. *Nothing.* Dread, sick and sour, clutched his throat. Dammit, he couldn't let the little beast drown. Without pausing, he put his mouth over the dog's muzzle and blew. *Still nothing.* He pushed on the dog's chest again, afraid of cracking her tiny ribs, then blew again.

The little dog stirred, rolled to her side, and coughed out a lungful of lake water. Max sank to his knees in relief.

"Thank God!" Emma breathed. Max looked up to see her standing beside him on the swim platform, water dripping from her shirt and hair.

Snookems coughed again, scrambled to her paws, then looked at Emma and wagged her tail.

"Oh, baby!" Emma scooped up the little dog and cradled her in her arms. "Are you all right?"

The dog wagged her wet stub of a tail and licked Emma's face.

"She looks okay."

Emma gazed at Max, her blue eyes brimming with relief and gratitude, her cheeks wet with more than just lake water. Her heart was in her eyes, and what Max saw there took his breath away.

"Thank you," she said softly.

"No big deal." But it was. Seeing her look at him like that did funny things to his insides, and it felt like a very big deal indeed.

Emma set the little dog on the deck. Snookems shook, spraying water like a lawn sprinkler. Emma reflexively put out her hands.

Max seized on the chance to lighten the mood. "Atta girl," he told the dog. "I never got a chance to pay Emma back for dunking me."

Snookems wagged her tail and stuck out her tongue.

Emma shot Max a wry grin. "When you said it might be fun to do mouth-to-mouth resuscitation, I thought you meant on me."

Oh, man—had he really just given mouth-to-mouth to a *dog?* The thought made him wince. "What's the matter?" he asked Emma. "Jealous?"

She gathered up her dripping dog and laughed. "I can hear it now. 'DA caught French-kissing dog. Film at eleven.'"

"You realize that if you tell anyone about this, I'll have to kill you," he said with mock seriousness.

"I won't. I promise." Her eyes held a softness—a tenderness, almost—that made his heart do a funny patter. "But I do reserve the right to tease you about it mercilessly."

The way she was looking at him, though, wasn't teasing. There was a light in her eyes that made him feel as if someone had just poured meat tenderizer on his heart. If he hadn't just been mouth-to-muzzle with a dog, he'd pull her to him and kiss her.

Instead, he pushed off the deck and rose. "If you'll

excuse me, I'd like to go have a little personal time with my toothbrush and some heavy-duty, germ-killing mouthwash."

"Why don't you just chew a Milk-Bone?"

He looked up at the sky with a pained expression. "You're going to hound me about this, aren't you?"

"You're doggone right." Grinning, she made a shooing motion with her hand. "Go deal with your dog-breath issues."

A few moments later, Max rejoined her on the deck and found Emma drying the dog with the towels. In his absence, she'd called the vet, who'd said that as long as Snookems was showing no ill effects, she didn't need to be checked.

"In that case, want a rematch on that race?"

"I should probably be getting home." Emma set the dog on the deck chair and straightened. Her T-shirt clung to her like a second skin, her black bikini clearly visible through the wet white fabric. Looking at her made his mouth go dry, again.

"I understand. You probably don't want to lose again," he said, hoping to goad her into staying.

She leaned against the railing and shot him a sardonic smile. "You just got lucky. Next time I'll leave you in my wake."

"Oh, yeah?"

"Yeah."

"Well, let's put it to the test. Put your dog inside so she can't try to commit hara-kiri again and let's have a rematch."

He saw her hesitate.

"Unless you're afraid of losing," he added.

She met his challenging gaze with one of her own. "You're on."

&

He deliberately let her win the next race. She called him on it, he denied it, and Emma launched another underwater attack. A raucous water fight ensued. When they tired of dunking and splashing and chasing each other, they took turns on the slide, competing to see who could make the bigger splash. After a while, Max got out the jet ski, and Emma climbed on behind him, holding onto his hard-muscled stomach as they flew across the water. She was pretty sure that the excitement zinging through her veins had more to do with the feel of Max's bare skin against hers than the speed of the jet ski.

She'd tried to keep from staring at his body all afternoon, but it was a losing battle. Apparently he put the barbells on his sundeck to good use. His chest was broad and tan, his stomach taut and muscled. His dark blue swim shorts stopped a little above midthigh, revealing strong tanned legs covered with a light dusting of dark hair. If he ever got tired of prosecuting criminals, Emma thought, he could start a career as an underwear model.

They played until the clouds looked like pink cotton candy and the jet ski was nearly out of fuel. By the time they climbed back onto the boat, dripping wet and laughing, the sun had disappeared over the horizon.

Emma felt Max's eyes on her as she reached for a towel. A sudden wave of self-consciousness hit her, causing her to wrap the towel around herself, then sink onto a chaise lounge. Max disappeared into the kitchen, then returned a moment later with two beers and a fine-toothed comb.

"Scoot over," Max said.

She looked at him askance. "Get your own chair."

"I can't comb the primer out of your hair from over there."

"Oh." The concept disconcerted her. "You're going to do it for me?"

"Well, it's in the back and you can't see it."

He popped the top on her beer and handed it to her, then straddled the chaise lounge behind her. She took a nervous sip and set the can in the drink holder in the chair arm, keenly aware of the muscled thighs stretched on either side of her. A shiver chased up her spine as he lifted a strand of her hair and gently eased the comb into it.

"I can't remember the last time I played in the water like that," she said, trying to lighten the suddenly sensuous mood.

Max slowly drew the comb through her hair. "Me, neither."

"Yeah, right." She shot him a skeptical glance over her shoulder. "You probably do this every weekend."

Max shook his head. "That's the first time I've gotten out the jet ski this summer. And I haven't been down the slide since I first got the boat."

His knuckles brushed against the back of her neck, sending a quiver of awareness through her. She reached for her beer and took a long drink, hoping to soothe the tension coiling in her stomach. "You expect me to believe that you live on a party boat and you never get wet?"

He lifted his shoulders. "It's no fun to play alone."

"So why are you? Alone, I mean."

The comb hit a tangle, pulling her hair.

"Ow!" She turned her head and looked at him. "If you don't want to answer the question, just say so."

"Sorry." He grinned. "I hit a snag."

"With the comb, or with your love life?"

"Both," Max admitted, backing the comb out of her hair and starting over.

"So why *are* you alone?"

His fingers bumped against her neck again. "I guess I just haven't met the right person."

"Ever thought you had?"

"Yeah. I was engaged a while back." He gently pulled the comb through her hair. "Like you."

Emma watched a dragonfly flitter on the water. She would never get used to people knowing things about her that she hadn't told them.

"Wasn't your ex-fiancé a psychiatrist?" Max prompted. "And didn't he write a book?"

Emma nodded glumly. *"The Ultimate Aphrodisiac: Why Women Sleep With Men in Power."* The jerk had gone on talk show after talk show, supposedly psychoanalyzing Emma and hawking his book. "He made a fortune off me."

"You two had already broken up before this Ferguson thing happened, right?"

Emma nodded. "I'd called things off in May—about seven months earlier."

"Why?"

Emma gazed at the fading orange clouds on the horizon. "I found out he'd been fooling around with another woman. A former girlfriend had cheated on him, and he had this weird fear that I was going to do the same, so he slept with someone else as a preemptive strike."

"Wow. Sounds like he needs a shrink himself."

"No kidding."

"What did you ever see in him?"

It was hard to remember, sitting between Max's thighs

as he gently combed her hair. "He was great at first—charming, considerate, amusing. I think I fell in love with the person he pretended to be." She glanced at Max over her shoulder. "So tell me about your fiancée."

"Ex-fiancée," Max corrected. He wiped primer off the comb with a towel. "What do you want to know?"

"Well, does she live here?"

"No. In New Orleans."

Good. It made no sense, but Emma was glad she wasn't someone Max ran into on a daily basis. "How did you meet?"

Max inserted the comb in her hair again and gently brushed a strand. "She was a defense attorney."

"Wow. So opposites really do attract."

"I didn't think of us as opposites at the time. We were both attorneys, so I thought we had more similarities than differences." The tree frogs in the woods hummed a warm-up chord as he eased the comb through her hair. "I was wrong."

"What happened?"

"Just what you'd probably expect. We broke up over a case."

"Must have been a bad one."

"Yeah." He paused for a moment, and then continued. "She represented a guy accused of rape and aggravated assault. He was a total sociopath, but Dana got him off on a technicality. We both knew he was guilty and that he'd do it again if he got the chance." Another pause. "And sure enough, he did."

"She must have felt awful."

"Well, that was the deal breaker. She didn't. She didn't feel the least bit bad—or at least, she claimed she didn't. And looking at it professionally, that's a good attitude for a defense attorney to have." He eased another piece of primer out of Emma's hair. "I knew she was just doing her job, but I couldn't get past it. When all is said and done, we are what we do."

"Or don't do," Emma said wryly.

"Maybe especially that." Max's hands stilled in her hair. Emma felt his fingers on her shoulders, and she turned toward him. His eyes were dark as chocolate, except for a little ring of gold around his pupils. The gold gleamed in the twilight as his gaze met hers. "You didn't do it, did you?" His voice was low and soft. "You're telling the truth about Ferguson."

"Yeah."

His chocolate gaze poured over her, melting and warm. "I believe you."

❧

I believe you. Amazing, how those three little words affected her. It was like breathing fresh air after being locked in an airless vault, like coming out of an underground bunker and seeing the sun.

Max's finger tipped her face toward him. "Hey—I didn't mean to upset you."

She wiped at her suddenly tear-filled eyes. "I'm not upset. I'm-I'm . . ."

Touched. Overwhelmed. *Falling in love with you.* Without stopping to think, she twisted more toward him, and then—*Oh, God.* He hauled her around to face him and claimed her lips with his.

He tasted salty and sweet and sexual. He smelled like sunshine and saltwater and every erotic dream she'd ever had.

His mouth sloped over hers, hot and hungry and wet,

teasing her lips apart. His lips moved to her neck, trailing a hot path up her throat, to her ear, then back to her mouth. His hands slid up the sides of her chest, cupping the sides of her breasts, as his tongue ravished her mouth. A shiver chased through her.

"Are you cold?" he murmured.

"Hot," she whispered. "Burning up."

A growl rumbled deep in his throat. He put one arm under her knees, the other behind her back, and lifted her. Cradling her against his chest, he carried her to the sliding-glass door. He propped her on his thigh as he opened it, then again after he stepped through the doorway to close it.

She clung to his neck as he carried her through the living area to the front of the boat, then set her down inside his cabin. Her hips sought his as his mouth reclaimed hers. She was on fire. She couldn't get close enough, couldn't get naked fast enough. She tugged at her T-shirt, trying to work the wet fabric over her head.

"Let me," he murmured. He pulled up the hem and lifted it over her head. Her nipples puckered through the black fabric of her bikini top as his gaze ran over her.

He unhooked her bra, and she felt a moment of sudden shyness. All of the junior-high taunts, all of the unwelcome attention, and all of her insecurities about the size and shape of her breasts—too large, too heavy, too low—came rushing to the forefront of her mind as he peeled off her bikini top. She started to wrap her arms across her chest, then stopped as she heard a hitch in his breath.

"My God, you're gorgeous," Max murmured, reaching out a hand and reverently touching her. "Beyond gorgeous."

The heat in his eyes burned away her trepidation. His

mouth moved over hers and an ache, sweet and demand-ing, overrode all conscious thought.

She felt his manhood press against her belly, hard and warm, and she edged closer. With a groan, he reached for her bikini bottom and slid the wet fabric down her legs. She tugged his swim trunks down, as well. He was hugely aroused, and the sight of him turned her insides to liquid fire. She stood on tiptoe and pressed herself intimately against him, one leg wrapped around his, her mouth seek-ing his.

He moaned against her lips. Cupping her bottom, he lifted her and carried her to the bed. She pulled him down with her, her legs curling more tightly around his, her body arching closer.

He suddenly broke the kiss and buried his face in her damp hair. "Hell." He hissed the word against her ear.

"What?"

"I don't have any condoms." He rolled away and looked at her, his eyes dark with frustration.

Emma reached for him, unwilling to give up physical contact.

"Come on," he said, abruptly rolling off the bed and taking her hand.

She blinked up at him, her mind not fully functioning. "What?"

He tugged her up and off the mattress. "We don't have any condoms, so we'll have to do something else."

"Like what? Play Canasta?"

His eyes crinkled as he grinned. "Not exactly what I have in mind." He pulled her hand. "Come on."

"What? Where—"

"The shower." He led her into the bathroom, pulled back the blue shower curtain, and turned on the water.

Water sprayed down from a showerhead attached with a flexible hose. He tested the temperature with his hand, then pulled her in.

Warm water streamed down on her skin. Max pulled her against him and covered her mouth with his. Her pelvis once again arched into his, aching for him.

"Uh, uh, uh," he whispered. "Can't go there."

Stepping back, he picked up a white bar of soap and dragged it slowly over her body. Leisurely, thoroughly, he soaped first one breast, then the other. Slowly, langorously, his hand slid down the slope of her belly, turning her insides to molten lava. Down, down, down he slid, down to the cleft hidden in her intimate curls. She shivered as his fingers stroked her, stoking her aching need.

And then he knelt in front of her, parting her secret self with his fingers.

It was almost too intimate to be endured. She leaned against the white tile and tensed.

"Please," he murmured. "Let me."

She was beyond refusing him anything. She trembled as his five o'clock shadow rasped against her thighs. Her hands curled in his hair as sensation, exquisite and keen and almost unbearably good, swelled and billowed within her. She cried out as the wave of pleasure crested and broke, and her legs started to give out from under her.

He caught her as he rose to his feet. She was still trembling as he pulled her into a kiss.

"I never . . ." *Felt like that. Let a man do that. Felt so close, so intimate, so connected.*

Words could not convey all that she felt. She would have to find another way to tell him. She reached for the soap, lathered her hands, then ran slippery fingers across his hard chest, down his muscle-rippled belly, down further to his jutting manhood. He moaned as she took his hard length in her palm, and she felt a thrill as he throbbed in her fingers.

"Wait," he murmured. "Sit on the edge of tub."

She did as he asked. He unhooked the flexible shower head from its holder, pulled her legs apart, and knelt before her, aiming the warm stream of water at her most intimate center.

"But I already . . ." *Ahhh.* Desire flared to life once more. She gave herself over to the exquisite sensation of warm water, warm fingers, and hot desire. Pleasure blazed through her, growing and spreading like wildfire, until she exploded again.

She opened her eyes to see him watching her. She looped her arms around his neck, and he lifted her to her feet, his mouth on hers. He paused to put the showerhead back in its holder, then reached for her breasts. She was struck by inspiration.

"Your turn to sit," she murmured. He sank to the edge of the tub. Kneeling beside him, she ran the bar of soap between her breasts, then fit his manhood in her cleavage. Holding her breasts together with both hands, she moved up and down.

"Good God, Emma." He moved with her, thrusting hard between her breasts, as warm water rained down. His breath came fast and hard until he climaxed with a loud moan.

He cradled her face in his hands as she straightened. "That was amazing," he murmured, his eyes warm and smoky and tender. She nodded, her heart too full to speak. He helped her to her feet, then wrapped one arm around her back, the other around her head.

"*You* are amazing," he whispered, curling a lock of her wet hair around his finger.

"You are, too."

Smiling, he leaned down and rested his forehead on hers. "I guess we're just amazing together."

Together. Was it even possible? Not until after the election, that was for sure. Even afterward, being with her could jeopardize Max's career—and being with him would put her back in the public eye.

But she wouldn't think about that tonight. Tonight, she would simply revel in their closeness, savor every kiss, and relish every moment. Because tonight, she didn't have to be Emma Jamison, the celebrity; tonight she could just be Emma Jamison, the woman.

The woman who was falling head over heels for Max Duval.

❧

"Dave, It's Max." Max paced the upper deck of his houseboat the next morning, the cell phone to his ear. "What have you found out about Emma?"

"Sheesh, man." Dave's voice was thick with sleep through the phone line. "Couldn't you call at a decent hour?"

Max winced against the sun reflecting off the water. "It's nearly nine your time."

"Yeah, well, it's a Sunday morning," Dave grumbled. "Most people like to sleep in."

"Sorry. So did you find out anything?"

Max heard a rustling through the phone and pictured Dave pushing upright in bed. "Not a lot, but what I've got supports your theory."

"Let's have it."

"I checked into the Internet porn site that aired the video. Apparently the investigator Emma hired had already questioned the site's owner about how he got the tape."

"And?"

"He insists that it just showed up in the mail."

That figured. "What about the postmark?"

"He said it was illegible and he threw the envelope away."

"Yeah, right." Max stopped and drummed his fingers on the railing. That was no doubt the standard spiel every porn site operator used for celebrity videos. But if the Secret Service had sent it to quiet the growing demand for an investigation, this time it was probably the actual truth. "What else do you have?"

"Well, I checked Emma's bank records. She hasn't made any suspicious deposits or opened any new accounts since this happened, so apparently she didn't make a profit from selling the video or servicing Ferguson or taking any payoffs in exchange for keeping quiet."

"You didn't need to check out her finances." Max started pacing again. "She had nothing to do with it."

"Hey, I'm just covering all the bases," Dave said. "I told you I was going to do a full investigation. I figured you needed all the facts."

Max ran his hand through his hair. He could see where Dave was coming from, and ordinarily, he'd appreciate the thoroughness, but hell—he didn't like the idea of sniffing into Emma's private business behind her back. "Yeah, well, don't do any more checking up on Emma. Anything else?"

"Yeah—and this could be major if it pans out. I've got a lead on a Secret Service agent who just retired. This guy was supposedly in New Orleans on the Ferguson detail, and he's unhappy with the way the whole thing was handled. I'm trying to set up a meeting with him. I should hear something the first part of the week."

"Oh, man—that's great!" This could be the break he was looking for. "Thanks, Dave. Thanks a million."

"Yeah. Glad to help." He paused. "So—it sounds like you're really into this girl." He waited for Max to respond, but Max didn't take the bait. "Guess that means it's probably too late for the advice I was about to offer," Dave continued.

"Which is?"

"Be careful, okay? Because regardless of what she's like, her reputation stinks, and it's the kind of stink that can rub off on you. Maybe you should wait and see what we can find out before you get too deeply involved."

It was already too late. Max had never been a love-'em-and-leave-'em kind of guy; when he made love to a woman, he was into her more than physically. Besides, on a gut-deep level, he knew that Emma was innocent. He just needed the evidence to prove it.

"Thanks for your help. Let me know as soon as you hear something."

Max said his goodbyes, closed his cell phone, and climbed down the ladder to the lower deck. Emma's little dog jumped off the sofa as he entered the living room and trotted toward him, her stub of a tail beating back and forth.

"So you've decided I'm not so bad after all, huh?"

Snookems wagged her tail again. Max bent down and held out his hand. The little dog cautiously advanced toward him, her black nose twitching. Max stroked her long hair, pleased beyond all reason that the dog was letting him pet her.

"I bet you're ready to go outside," Max said. The little dog thumped her pathetic excuse of a tail. Max crossed the room and picked up the rhinestone-studded pink leash Emma had left on the side table. Snookems sat down, her back toward him. "I take it that's a yes." He carefully fastened the leash to the dog's hot pink collar, then opened the door to the dock. The little dog trotted beside him as if Max walked her every day.

Max grinned as he stepped out into sunshine. Who would have thought he'd get such a kick from walking a frou-frou little mutt? Not him, that was for sure.

"You're okay," Max told the dog. "But you still have the lamest name I've ever heard."

CHAPTER SEVENTEEN

*E*mma awoke to a warm, tickling sensation on her cheek. "Stop it, Snookems," she muttered, rolling over.

"Sure thing, honey bunch," said a deep male voice.

Emma's eyes flew open. She wasn't in her own bed, she was in Max's. And it wasn't her Yorkie kissing her face, but Max. He was leaning over her, his lips curved in a teasing smile.

Her eyes locked on his mouth—the mouth that had done such amazing things to her for much of the night before. So she hadn't dreamed it, after all. The night of mind-blowing, sexier-than-actual-sex lovemaking had actually happened.

He bent over and kissed her. He smelled of shaving cream and toothpaste. "I didn't know you were into pet names, sugar britches."

She threw a pillow at him. "I thought you were my *dog*."

"An understandable mistake. There's only a 180-pound difference between us, and we *are* both wearing collars."

She sat up and brushed her hair out of her eyes. He was standing by the bed, dressed in a light blue shirt and a blue-striped tie.

"Where are you going?"

"To a pancake breakfast at First Church. I'm speaking about victims' rights."

"You should have awakened me when you got up."

"I figured I kept you awake enough of the night."

And he had. They'd moved from the shower to the bedroom and started all over again. Around midnight they'd raided the kitchen, grilled a steak on the deck, and devoured it under the stars, laughing and talking and feeding each other small bites. They'd ended up back in each other's arms, making love again in long, slow, inventive, everything-but-intercourse sex.

He held out a steaming mug. "I made you some coffee."

"Thanks." Clutching the sheet to her naked chest, she sat up and wrapped her fingers around the warm ceramic.

"And I took Snooks out for a walk."

"You did?" The thought of Max holding a hot-pink rhinestone-studded leash with a tiny Yorkie on the end made her laugh.

"Yeah. We're buds now."

At the mention of her name, Snookems ambled into the bedroom. The Yorkie had lost the rubber band holding her topknot, and her hair hung in her eyes, the bow dangling by the bottom of her left ear. Emma laughed. "Looks like you had a wild night, too, Snookems."

Max opened the closet door and pulled out a navy sports jacket. "I'll be back in a couple of hours. Just make yourself at home."

Emma set the coffee mug on the nightstand and swung

her feet to the floor. "I need to get going myself. I promised Katie I'd meet her at her salon this morning."

"Well, if you want to grab a bite before you go, there's cereal in the pantry, and I don't think the milk is past its expiration date."

"Okay. Thanks."

"Maybe we can get together back here or at your place this evening." His tie swung forward and tickled her chest as he bent and kissed her again. "I'll call you later."

She smiled up at him. "Thanks for dinner and . . . and everything."

His dimple flashed. "The pleasure was all mine."

"Not all of it."

She waited until he left the room, then grabbed a towel off the floor, wrapped it around herself, and went to the window to watch him walk to his truck. The sight of him striding down the dock, his jacket slung over his shoulder, made joy champagne-bubble through her veins.

"Uh-oh. You've got it bad," she murmured, but there didn't seem to be anything bad about it. Grinning to herself, she did a little happy dance as she located her shorts and the green Tulane T-shirt Max had loaned her last night. They would need to be circumspect until after the election, she thought as she got dressed, but that was just a few weeks away. After that . . . well, she didn't know, but for the first time in a long time, she dared to believe that she might, just might, actually be getting a life.

Grinning like a Cheshire cat, she carried the coffee mug to kitchen, where she found Max's pantry door hanging open.

Well, well, well—Mr. Perfect had a flaw. Boxes of cereal, cans of soup and stew, bags of chips, and packages of beef jerky were piled into the small space willy-nilly, jumbled on the shelves and splayed all over the pantry floor.

Humming happily, Emma set to work, and in twenty minutes' time, the pantry was completely organized. She was about to start in on his cabinets when she glanced at the clock on the stove and realized she barely had to time to race home and change clothes before meeting Katie at the salon.

"Come on, Snookems." Scooping up the little dog, she gathered up her wet bikini and T-shirt from the day before and headed out the door. The sky was overcast and the air smelled like rain as she strode down the dock to her car, but the gloomy weather didn't make a dent in her high spirits.

Max had left the gate open, so she drove through, then stopped on the other side and scrambled out of her car to close it. As she fastened the gate's metal latch, she heard the rumble of an approaching vehicle. She looked up to see an old red Chevy round the corner.

Oh, no—it was the reporter who'd barged into Mrs. Alvarez's apartment. Emma watched in frozen horror as the gel-haired punk climbed out of the car, a camera in his hand.

"Good morning, Emma." He snapped a picture. Her heart in her throat, she ran on leaden feet to her Saturn. He clicked off another shot as she climbed in. "What are you doing here?"

"I-I—" Shock blurred Emma's mind. All she could think was that she was being photographed leaving Max's place at nine o'clock on a Sunday morning, wearing Max's shirt. Ducking her chin, Emma slammed the car door as he snapped a picture through the windshield. His car blocked the drive. Panicked, Emma backed up, jerked the car into forward, then steered off the road and around the dusty Chevy, her Saturn lurching over a large branch.

Her stomach lurched, as well, as a single, heart-sinking thought played through her mind: she might have just cost Max the election.

꒰꒱

Emma showed up at the Curl Up 'N' Dye an hour later, carrying a long box of shelving she'd picked up at the Home Depot in Hammond earlier in the week. Katie yanked open the pink door before she could even knock, her face concerned. "I heard about you and Max."

"Oh, no." Emma set the long box on its end and slumped in the doorway.

Katie took one end of the long cardboard box and pulled her into the campy pink and black salon, then closed the door. Emma plopped onto a pink vinyl stylist's chair. "How did you find out?"

"I got a call from Lulu, who'd had a call from Ruth, who'd heard at the Chartreuse Café that Louis took a picture of you at Max's gate this morning."

Emma covered her face with her hands. "This is terrible, Katie. I'm going to ruin Max's life."

Katie sank into the adjacent pink styling chair. "We won't let that happen," she said decisively.

"It's already happening."

"No. Louis didn't actually see you *with* Max; he just saw you leave his place. So all we have to do is come up with a plausible explanation for why you were there."

"In his clothes?"

Katie frowned. "What were you wearing?"

"A Tulane T-shirt. My own shirt was still wet from

yesterday's swim." She blew out a sigh. "I should have put it in the dryer while I organized his pantry."

Katie shot her an incredulous look. "You organized Max's pantry?"

Emma nodded sheepishly.

"Girl, have you got some kind of OCD problem or what?"

Emma put her head against the back of the chair and sighed. "No. At least, I don't think so. Organizing things just feels creative and meaningful and . . . I don't know. I just like to do it."

Katie snapped her fingers and leaned forward. "That's it!"

"What?"

"The reason you were at his place!" Her eyes gleamed. "He saw what a great job you did organizing his grandfather's apartment, and he asked you to come over and do the same for him."

"Oh, right. Like anyone's going to believe that. What kind of bachelor gets someone to organize his closets?"

"A sloppy one who can't find anything."

"Max isn't really all that sloppy," Emma said defensively.

"That's not the point!"

"Katie, this story is full of holes. Even if the premise were plausible—which it's not—isn't it a little suspicious that I was there that early on Sunday morning?"

"Well, you'd already made plans to help me here, so you had to get an early start in order to squeeze him in."

Emma shook her head. "No one will believe it."

"We'll make them believe it."

"How?"

Katie had already pushed herself out of the chair,

grabbed her purse off the counter and headed for the front door. "I'll be right back."

"Where are you going?"

"To the drugstore. I'll buy some shelf-lining paper and drop a word in Nellie's ear about how you've organized my salon and all the Alzheimer patients' apartments, and I'll tell her you're starting a side business as a professional organizer."

It was a sweet idea, but it would never work.

"I'll happen to casually mention that you did such a great job with Mr. Duval's apartment that Max hired you to do his place," Katie continued. "And then I'll tell her that Louis took a picture of you leaving there this morning and that this unfounded rumor is already circulating, and isn't that just the funniest thing, how people can get things all wrong? Nellie loves to set people straight. She'll be peeing all over herself in her eagerness to make sure everyone gets the real story."

Emma had to admit, the plan got points for creativity. "Katie, you have a frighteningly cunning mind."

Katie's mouth curved in a mischievous smile. "I'm pretty good, aren't I?"

"You're scary good. Remind me to never get on your bad side."

Katie pulled her purse on her shoulder and looked at her thoughtfully. "To make this really work, though, we'll need to shore up this professional organizing thing. You might need to actually take on a few paying jobs."

"No one's going to pay me to clean their closets."

"Sure they will. The only question is, will you do it?"

"Well . . ." Why not? With all of her reserves depleted, Emma's finances could use a boost. "Sure. Absolutely."

"That's all I need to know." Katie flashed a roguish

grin. "I have a positively brilliant idea for making this story solid. Can you come by the salon tomorrow morning at ten?"

Getting away from Sunnyside wouldn't be a problem, since her job often took her off property. "Sure. But why?"

"Because that's Carrie's appointment time." Katie rubbed her hands together and gave a villain-in-an-old-movie grin. "Oh, this will be so much fun!"

Fun was not the word Emma would have used to describe the tension coiling through her the following morning as she stood outside Curl Up 'N' Dye.

But then, *fun* wasn't the word she would have used to describe her conversation with Max, either, when she'd called him yesterday afternoon.

She'd drawn a deep breath and just blurted it out: "The photographer for the *National Inquisitioner* took a photo of me leaving your place today."

A moment of silence had greeted her announcement. "We'll deal with it," Max had said.

The fact he took the news so well made Emma feel worse. "Katie's already put a plan into action. I don't know if it will work or not, but maybe it'll mitigate the damage." She'd briefly explained Katie's strategy.

"I'm not going to lie," Max had said.

"You won't have to. If anyone asks what I was doing there, you can honestly say I organized your pantry."

"That's not what they're going to ask," he'd replied dryly.

"Well, if they ask if we're involved, you can tell them we're not. Because as of now, it's the truth. "

"Now wait a minute. That's not—"

"Max, we can't see each other until after the election."

Pulling her thoughts back to the present, Emma drew a bracing breath and pushed on the door. The pink salon buzzed with female voices and laughter as it swung open, but as soon as she crossed the threshold, a deathly silence fell across the room.

"Emma—hello!" Katie waved a pair of scissors at her from the first of the salon's three hair stations. Carrie sat in the styling chair, a black and pink polka-dot styling cape around her neck like giant bib, her damp bangs hanging in her face. With her pinched mouth and narrowed eyes, Carrie looked like a wet weasel. "That conditioner you wanted finally arrived, Emma. Just a moment and I'll get it for you."

Emma nervously took a seat in the waiting area by the door, near a woman wearing a red knit top with a lady-bug motif. The woman regarded Emma as if she were the one with bugs crawling all over her. The hairdresser at the station next to Katie's—a friendly-faced, middle-aged woman named Beth whom Emma had met while working on the salon storeroom—smiled at Emma in the mirror, and Rachel the manicurist gave Emma a little wave, but no one spoke. The silence in the room stretched out like an overextended rubber band.

Katie snipped a fraction of an inch from the bottom of Carrie's hair. "Carrie, I believe you know Emma."

The woman refused to look at her. "We've met."

"Nice to see you again, Carrie," Emma said in her friendliest tone.

The woman kept her eyes averted.

"Carrie is chairing the annual fund-raiser for the local women's league," Katie said, combing Carrie's hair.

"They're going to auction off goods and services to raise money for underprivileged children."

"That sounds like a wonderful cause," Emma said.

Carrie's lip tweaked into something that was probably supposed to be a smile but made her look as if she'd eaten some bad shrimp.

Katie's eyes widened, as if she'd had a sudden brainstorm. "Oh, I have an idea!" She whirled around Carrie's chair to face Emma so abruptly that the wet-haired woman grabbed the chair arms in alarm. "Carrie, you ought to ask Emma to donate her services!"

"I don't think she provides the kind of service our members would want to purchase," Carrie said coldly.

The woman in the ladybug sweater tittered. So did a brunette soaking her nails at the manicure table, along with an apple-faced woman with sheets of tin foil layered in her hair like a radiator grill in the next stylist's chair.

Katie pretended not to understand the innuendo. "Oh, yes, she does," she said earnestly. "Emma has tremendous organizational skills. She's done wonders with the apartments in the Alzheimer's wing at Sunnyside, and it was such a hit with the families that she's started doing professional organizing in her free time. You've got to see what she did to my storeroom."

"She tackled your storeroom?" The tin-headed woman looked up from her copy of a fashion magazine.

"Did she use hip boots and a snake kit to do it?" asked the brunette at the manicure table in a high-pitched voice. All of the women laughed, apparently familiar with the condition of Katie's storeroom.

"You have to see it to believe it." Katie motioned to Carrie. "Go take a look."

"Maybe some other time," Carrie said.

"Well, I want to see it," said the bug lady. She rose from her chair and disappeared around the corner. A tall woman with a towel around her hair waiting at the shampoo sink stood and trailed after her, followed by the brunette getting the manicure.

"Oh, my stars. I can't believe this!" came the brunette's high-pitched voice.

"It's like something from a makeover show!" said another woman.

"Everything is so beautiful!" said the bug lady.

"Told you," Katie called.

Emma pretended an intense interest in the contents of the product display case, but inside, she was high-fiving herself. In keeping with Katie's kitschy decor, she'd painted the louvered doors of the new storage unit black, with pink and black polka dots inside to match the fabric on Katie's window shades and styling capes.

"I had no idea you had so much space back here, Katie!"

"Look at those little wooden labels! They're just exquisite."

Emma had found the wooden discs at a crafts store and hand-painted them, then hung them from slender ribbons in front of black-lacquered baskets.

"And the polka dots—oh, I *love* the polka dots!" said the brunette.

"This I've got to see," said the woman with foil in her hair.

"Me, too," said the woman getting her hair cut at Beth's station.

More *oohs* and *ahhs* emanated from the back of the salon.

"Carrie, you've got to take a look at this!" the bug lady called.

"Oh, all right." With obvious irritation, Carrie huffed out of the chair and marched across the salon, the polka-dot styling cape flapping.

Katie winked at Emma.

"Isn't it wonderful?" One of the women cooed.

"Well, anything would have been an improvement," Carrie grumbled.

"Yes, but this is positively inspired!"

After an exchange of more superlatives, the women returned to the main part of the salon.

"I think a closet reorganization would be a big hit at the auction," Katie prompted as Carrie resumed her seat on the styling chair.

"Oh, I don't think—" Carrie began.

"Oh, Carrie, it's a fabulous idea," said the foil-haired woman. She turned to Emma. "How much do you charge?"

Emma thought fast. "It, um, depends on the job."

"Normally a reorganization like she did for me would cost at least eight or nine hundred dollars, plus materials," Katie contributed.

Emma bit her lips to keep her mouth from falling open.

"It's worth every penny," the bug lady said. "What would you charge to do my office?"

"I'd, um, have to see it before I could give you an estimate."

The woman pulled a Realtor's card out of her purse and handed it to Emma. "My cell number is at the bottom. Give me a call and we'll set up a time."

Emma nodded and took the card.

"So, Emma—would you consider donating a reorganization to the auction?" Katie prompted.

"Sure."

"But I don't think—" Carrie began.

"Oh, Carrie—you can't possibly pass this up!" the tin lady said.

"Well, then . . ." Carrie looked at Emma as if she were regarding a particularly loathsome reptile. "Thank you."

"You're welcome."

"Don't forget to send Emma a complimentary ticket to the auction," Katie said.

Carrie gave a sickly smile.

Emma glanced at her watch. "I really ought to be going."

"Let me get that conditioner for you." Katie put down her scissors, once more leaving Carrie with wet bangs hanging in her eyes, and scurried to the front of the shop. She pulled a pink plastic bottle of conditioner out of the product display cabinet and handed it to Emma, giving her a subtle thumbs-up sign. "Give this a try and let me know how you like it."

"Okay. Thanks." Holding the bottle, Emma pulled on the door, jingling the bells on the dried-flower wreath that adorned the outside. She smiled as she stepped into the hot August sunlight. Maybe, just maybe, this was actually going to work.

CHAPTER EIGHTEEN

The citizens of Chartreuse deserve a district attorney who shares their morals and family values," Dirk Briggs proclaimed to the thirty Daughters of the American Revolution who'd gathered for lunch in the upstairs meeting room of the Chartreuse Café a week later.

From his seat at a front table, Max saw Dirk's paunch strain against the buckle of his belt. Max had heard through the grapevine that Dirk was suing the local dry cleaner for shrinking his suits. He'd outgrown his clothes a good fifteen or twenty pounds ago, but he was in denial about his waistline size.

Just like he was in denial about his hair. The man must have no mirrors in his house. How could he possibly look at his sparse patch of follicles and think his ear-level side part was fooling anyone?

"The voters of this parish deserve a DA who won't bring disgrace and scandal to the office." Briggs held up a copy of last Tuesday's *National Inquisitioner*, open to page eight.

Max stiffened. Oh, no—The headline over the incriminating picture of Emma was large enough to be read by the ladies in the back of the small room: *Hotsy-Totsy Butler Straightens Politician's Drawers.*

Murmurs filled the room. Beside him, Terrence mopped his brow.

Max put on his courtroom poker face. Katie, bless her heart, had mitigated the damage by buying up all the copies of the tabloid at the town's grocery store, drugstore, and convenience store, so most of the town's populace hadn't seen the article.

The ladies leaned forward to stare at the photo of Emma standing at his gate, looking bedraggled and alarmed. In case anyone didn't recognize the location, his mailbox, clearly labeled "Duval," was in plain sight next to the gate. A campaign photo of himself, probably lifted from his Web site, was printed beside the picture of Emma.

Max closed his eyes. Every word of the awful article was etched in his memory: *Emma Jamison, the voluptuous former butler who gave President-Elect Ferguson a heart attack in the sack, was caught leaving the residence of hunky Pontchartrain Parish District Attorney Max Duval early Sunday morning. The usually impeccably dressed Ms. Jamison wore an man-sized Tulane T-shirt. (Hmm. Mr. Duval is a Tulane graduate. Was she wearing his shirt or just busting out in support of his alma mater?)*

When contacted, neither Ms. Jamison nor the DA would comment on what she was doing at his home or whether she'd spent the night there. Some sources in the sleepy south Louisiana town say that Emma, who is now employed as the head housekeeper at a local retirement home, has begun a sideline business as a professional organizer and she was simply organizing the DA's home.

Yeah. And while she was at it, we bet she straightened his drawers.

"We don't need a DA who garners this kind of publicity," Briggs said, waving the newspaper in the air. "We need a DA who will represent the people with honor. And if you vote for me on election day, that's what you'll get."

A polite round of applause erupted from the audience. Briggs gave a little bow, his beefy lips pressed in a self-satisfied smirk.

Max's courtroom experience had taught him the importance of appearing unruffled by an opponent's attack. He pasted on a smile, casually rose from his chair, and strode to the front of the room at a leisurely pace.

"Well, now, Mr. Briggs seems to have a lot to say, but none of it pertains to being district attorney. I was under the impression that that was what we'd come here to discuss." With that, Max launched into his standard speech, citing the reduced number of crimes, increased numbers of convictions, and new crime-prevention programs his office had initiated.

When he finished, the ladies applauded. Max's internal applause-o-meter told him that he'd gotten a bigger hand than Briggs, but not by much. He was losing his edge.

Max spent the next twenty minutes shaking hands and schmoozing. He'd nearly made his way to the door when he heard a man call his name. He turned to see Louis Ashton, a camera around his skinny neck, his gelled hair standing up like porcupine quills. The sight of the little twerp made his blood pressure rise.

"Mr. Duval," Louis called loudly. "What was Emma Jamison doing leaving your property last Sunday morning?"

A hush fell over the room, and all heads swiveled in

Max's direction. Max forced himself to adopt a relaxed posture. "I thought you were a serious journalist, Louis."

"I am."

"Well, then, you need to stick to reporting the news."

His receding chin did its best to jut out. "Emma Jamison *is* news."

"Only to two-bit gossip rags. I hate to see a young man with such a bright future sink to the level of paparazzi."

The young man scowled. "Are you seeing her?"

"I'm going to do you a favor, Louis, and not answer that, because this kind of story is beneath you."

Max turned and pushed his way through the door into the searing August heat. Terrence trailed right behind him.

"Thank God that hairdresser took some quick action," Terrence said as he scurried down the sidewalk beside Max, his forehead beading with sweat. "Not everyone is buying that organizing story, but at least it creates some doubt. But, Max, you can't—"

"Don't even say it," Max warned. He didn't need Terrence to tell him he couldn't see Emma until after the election. Emma had told him as much on the phone right after Louis had taken her photo at his gate.

"We can be discreet," Max had argued.

"We thought we *were* being discreet," Emma had responded.

She was right, damn it; as much as he hated it, they needed to keep their distance for the short term. But there was no reason they couldn't talk on the phone—so every evening, they burned up their cell minutes, discussing everything from UFOs to politics, describing their likes and dislikes, filling each other in on their pasts, laughing and joking and teasing. Emma was bright and witty and insightful, and their conversations were the best part of Max's day.

Max talked to Dave on a regular basis, too, and thank God he was making some progress. The retired Secret Service agent had agreed to meet with him, and Max was flying to Washington next week to accompany Dave to the meeting.

Dave had tried to discourage Max from attending the meeting. "No offense, but you're pretty intense about this whole thing. I don't want you trying to strong-arm this guy into coming forward and making a public statement."

"But he needs to make a statement."

"Not going to happen." Dave's voice had been adamant. "He agreed to talk on condition of anonymity, and I've got to honor that."

"But—"

"Look, this guy would risk losing his retirement benefits or maybe face jail time—or worse."

"Worse?"

"Max, there's no telling what the Secret Service will do to one of their own who rats them out."

"Oh, hell."

Terrence's voice brought Max back to the moment. "It's just a little over two weeks until the election, and Briggs is looking to smear you any way he can." The light changed, and they stepped across the street toward the courthouse. "Try not to end up in any more tabloid headlines."

"Believe me, Terrence, I'm doing my best."

∽

"It's too bad Max won't be back from D.C. in time for the auction," Katie said Thursday evening as she and Emma sifted through a rack of dresses at the Pour Elle dress store in downtown Chartreuse. "What's he doing up there, anyway?"

"Attending a meeting. It's about a case that's under investigation, so he can't talk about it yet," Emma said. He was free to talk about everything else, though, which they did on a nightly basis. She no longer thought she was falling in love with him; she knew it for certain. She was heart-and-soul, head-over-heels, crazy, madly in love with Max.

Emma looked at a white knit dress, then slid it down the clothes rack. "Even if he were in town, though, he wouldn't go to the auction," she said. "We don't want to stir up gossip two weeks before the election."

"It's probably wise for you two to stay away from each other," Katie shot her a knowing grin. "Anyone seeing the two of you in the same room would pick up on the vibes between you. And you're going to be the center of attention, because your donation is going to be the hit of the auction."

Emma winced. "I'm worried no one will bid on it."

Katie shot her an *oh, please* look. "You're in demand. You've already gotten two organizing jobs from people who've seen my storeroom."

It was true. Emma had already organized the real estate woman's office and was working evenings on the grocery manager's home closet. Redoing Katie's storeroom had been the best PR move Emma could have made; it had created some positive buzz about her, defused that awful picture in the *Inquisitioner,* and earned her some much-needed extra cash.

"I think you're going to be deluged with bids." Katie pushed aside a gaudy floral dress. "And I'm hearing lots of nice things about you. Just yesterday Anne said that she'd visited her great aunt at Sunnyside and that you're doing an amazing job there. And Nellie from the drugstore said that you sometimes stop by to pick up prescriptions and toothpaste and other items for the residents."

Happiness welled inside of Emma. She scarcely dared believe it, but maybe, just maybe, her life was on the upswing.

Katie moved to the next rack of dresses. "I think this auction is going to be a real turning point, so we need to find you an extra-special dress to wear to it." Katie lifted a hanger holding a red-and-white print sundress. "And this just might be it." She held it out. "Here—go try this on."

Emma regarded it dubiously. "It's not really my style. And it looks awfully fitted."

Katie raised an eyebrow. "Here's a newsflash, Em. Clothes are supposed to fit."

Emma still hesitated. "I don't want to look trashy."

"Honey, you couldn't look trashy if you wrapped yourself in a Hefty bag. Now, go try it on."

Katie was right—the dress looked amazing. It had a halter neckline and a wraparound skirt, and although it wasn't exactly low-cut, it did show a hint of cleavage. Emma bought it, along with a pair of strappy red sandals.

After she got home with it, though, she had second thoughts. She decided to take it to Sunnyside the next day and get Grams's opinion.

∽

She found Grams in her apartment the next afternoon, eating Chex Mix, drinking Pepsi, and playing Scrabble with Harold on her dining room table.

"Oh, that's lovely!" Grams said as Emma pulled the dress out of its plastic wrap and held it up. "Go try it on."

Emma changed into the dress in the bathroom, then came out and twirled around.

Grams clapped. "You look gorgeous!"

"Very nice," Harold approved.

"You don't think it's too revealing?" Emma asked.

"I think it's beautiful, and you're beautiful in it."

Emma changed back into her pantsuit. When she came out, Grams beamed at her. "I'm so glad to see you out and about, going places and meeting people."

"It feels good," Emma admitted, folding the plastic-wrapped dress over her arm. "I don't want to jinx things, but I actually think things are looking up."

Grams gave her a coquettish smile. "I don't suppose Max has anything to do with that."

He had everything to do with it. Emma grinned. "When you're right, Grams, you're really right."

"I told you that divine providence would work everything out." Grams tilted her head to the side. "Speaking of which, Oprah had a show the other day that I think was providentially inspired."

Uh-oh. Emma picked a peanut out of the Chex Mix bowl and braced herself.

"It was a show about breathing," Grams said. "Remember, Harold?"

"No. But that's okay, because that's the one skill I have down pat."

Emma grinned and gave him a thumbs-up. "And you're doing an excellent job of it."

Grams rolled her eyes. "This is serious. One of the guests was talking about different breathing techniques to help people cope with pain and anxiety. I immediately thought of you and your fear of video cameras."

Just the topic made Emma feel queasy. "Nothing works, Grams. "

"You haven't tried patterned breathing, like women in labor use. This guest on Oprah suggested six short inhales, then one exhale. Like this." Grams sucked in six short spurts of air, her eyes getting larger with every breath.

"Run for cover. She's about to blow!" Harold said.

Grams huffed out a long breath. "See? It's very relaxing."

"Not for the people watching you," Harold said.

Grams slapped him playfully on the wrist. "The point is, if you focus on your breathing, dear, you'll take attention away from your fear. Plus you'll get enough air, so you won't hyperventilate."

"I'll keep that in mind," Emma said.

"Another woman on the show said that if you stick out your tongue as far as it will go, that will help you relax, as well."

"Oh, that's just what I want recorded on video," Emma said dryly.

"Why don't you demonstrate that, too?" Harold said to Dorothy, with a wink at Emma.

Grams stuck out her tongue at Harold.

Emma laughed. Harold and Dorothy played off each other like Laurel and Hardy. Emma was still a little weirded out by the romantic aspect of their relationship, but her initial concerns had dissipated. Harold made Grams happy, and as long as they kept things casual, the friendship seemed good for both of them.

Emma kissed them each on the cheek, then headed back to her desk. Her phone was ringing as she entered her office.

"Ms. Jamison?" said a male voice as she answered it. "This is Steve Gordon at First Parish Bank."

It was the bank she'd used before she'd moved to Chartreuse. Figuring this was nothing more than a we-want-your-business-back solicitation call, she picked up a laundry invoice and only half listened.

"I hate to tell you this, Ms. Jamison, but we've inadvertently had a breach of security on your account."

Emma dropped the invoice and tightened her grip on the phone. "What do you mean, a breach of security?"

"Well, one of our tellers inadvertently gave out information about your checking and savings accounts to an unauthorized party earlier this month."

Alarm skittered up her spine. "What happened?"

"Someone working with the Pontchartrain Parish DA's office called, wanting the history of your account. So the clerk went ahead and gave him the records."

Max had gotten someone to check up on her? A cold sweat broke out on her face. "I closed those accounts when I moved here."

"Yes, I know. And I'm sure that's why the clerk thought it would be all right to give out the information. But I assure you, it's our policy to completely protect the privacy of our clients, both past and present."

"What records did he want?"

"Deposits, withdrawals, and transfers on your account over the past year."

"Did he say why?"

"No. Just that it was part of some kind of investigation."

It was a good thing Emma was sitting down, because she was certain her legs would have given out from under her. "He has no right—" she sputtered.

"Exactly. Without a subpoena, we're not supposed to give out any private information." His voice held a note of please-don't-sue-us grovel. "I can't tell you how much we regret this incident. Our policy requires us to notify our clients, past and present, of any errors concerning their account, so that's why I'm calling."

Emma sat there, stunned and sick, her thoughts climbing all over each other like crabs in a bucket. Max was checking up on her. Why? What did he think her bank records would show?

Not that it mattered. Only one thing mattered, one critical, basic, essential thing, the thing that was the foundation of everything else: Max didn't trust her.

"I believe you" had all been a lie. Her stomach felt as if she'd swallowed a boulder.

"I'm very sorry this happened," the bank representative said.

Not as sorry as I am. She dropped the phone back in its cradle, feeling as if her heart had just been dropped from the Mississippi River Bridge.

❧

"There's got to be some kind of explanation," Katie said Saturday afternoon as she ran a wide-toothed comb through Emma's wet hair.

Emma hunched down in the pink vinyl chair, trying not to look at her equally pink eyes in the salon mirror. She'd barely slept a wink last night, but by this morning, she'd channeled her hurt into anger. "Oh, there's an explanation, all right. Max is a sneaky jerk who doesn't trust me."

"Emma, honey, you need to talk to him." Katie parted Emma's hair into three sections and secured them with large aluminum clips.

"Why? So he can lie to me some more?"

"So he can explain what's going on."

"I don't want to hear a phony explanation or a sorry-you-found-out apology."

Katie combed the bottom section of Emma's hair and parted it again. "You're going to have to talk to him eventually."

"I know." Emma blew out a sigh. "But I'm not ready."

She was hurt and confused and, above all, angry. She was mad at herself and mad at him, not to mention disappointed, disillusioned, and distraught. If Max didn't think she was innocent, their entire relationship was phony, and everything she'd thought about him was wrong.

Just like she'd been wrong about her former fiancé. She'd promised herself that she'd never fall for another man who didn't trust her, but here she'd gone and done exactly that. Once again, she'd shown lousy judgment in men.

"It's going to be okay, Emma. You just need to have some faith in Max."

"Why? He doesn't have any in me."

"Well, I have faith in both of you. You're going to talk tomorrow and work this out." Katie met Emma's eyes in the mirror, her expression firm and convincing.

She spun the chair around so that Emma faced her. "But this afternoon, you're going to get ready for the auction. You're going to let me layer your hair, then Rachel's going to give you a manicure and a pedicure, and then we're going to give you a facial to deflate your puffy eyes. After that I'm going to do your makeup, and you're going to go home and put on that beautiful new dress and those hot new shoes. Then you're going to the auction, where you'll be the belle of the ball."

Katie's gaze was steady and sure, and some of that sureness rubbed off on Emma. Katie might not be right about Max, but she was right about one thing: Emma was not a quitter. She'd come a long way this summer, and she wasn't going to let Max ruin her progress.

Emma nodded. "Okay."

"Terrific!" Katie spun her back around and picked up her scissors. "Let's get started on *Extreme Makeover, Emma Edition*."

✑

Loud Cajun music assaulted Max's eardrums as he walked into the jambalaya-scented VFW Hall a little after nine that night and waited for his eyes to adjust to the dim lighting. The cinderblock building was all spiffed up: long strips of gauzy white fabric billowed from the ceiling; white-clothed tables were arranged on the concrete floor; and a ravaged buffet table sat against the left wall, next to a beer and wine bar.

At the back of the room, a row of potted ficus trees lined the base of a spotlit stage where a long-haired guitarist, a suspender-wearing accordion player, and an elderly fiddler played a raucous zydeco tune. Women in bright summer dresses and men in short-sleeved shirts danced in front of the stage, under a disco ball lit by an enormous rotating colored spotlight. Both the silver-faceted ball and the rotating light had been jury-rigged to the ceiling, where they hung precariously, casting alternating hues of red, blue, green, and yellow on half of the room.

As Max scanned the crowd for Emma, he saw Terrence's glistening chrome dome heading toward him, lit in disco ball yellow. "What are you doing here?" the wiry man demanded.

"Nice to see you, too," Max responded as the man's head turned Smurf blue. "Have you seen Emma?"

Terrence's forehead creased. "Everyone in the place will be watching you two to see if anything's going on. If you so much as say hello to her, you're going to start gossip."

"If I don't, it will, too. Everyone knows we know each other."

"Which is why I thought you'd decided not to come."

That was before Emma quit taking his calls yesterday. He'd left message after message on her cell phone and her home phone, and he'd e-mailed her more than a dozen times. And then he discovered the curt, cryptic message she'd left on his voice mail at his office—obviously a ploy to avoid speaking to him directly.

"Don't call me again," she'd said in cold tone. "And do not—I repeat, *do not*—come by my house. If you do, I'll call the police."

What the hell had happened? Last he knew, things had been great between them—better than great. He intended to get to the bottom of it.

"Don't screw things up, Max," Terrence warned him. "You're in the lead, and the election is just ten days away."

Max had had it with this whole worrying-what-other-people-think thing. His grandfather was the one who worried about keeping up appearances, not him, and he was sick of letting the opinions of others dictate his actions.

He scanned the room, looking for Emma. His eyes lit on the back of woman in a red-and-white printed dress on the dance floor with Harris Frisk, the local veterinarian. For a moment he thought she was Emma, but she looked a little taller than Emma, her hair was cut differently, and her dress was definitely not Emma's conservative style.

"Hi there, Max."

Max turned to see Dorothy standing beside him, wearing a shimmering blue pantsuit and clutching his grandfather's arm. His grandfather wore a navy sports coat, a starched blue-and-white striped shirt, and gray slacks. Max kissed Dorothy's lilac-scented cheek, then shook his grandfather's hand. "I didn't expect to see you two here."

"Oh, I've been coming to these auctions for nearly forty years," Dorothy said. "You're the one we didn't expect to see."

"I caught an early flight, so I thought I'd drop by." Max's gaze skimmed over the crowd.

"If you're looking for Emma," Dorothy said, "she's on the dance floor with Harris Frisk."

Max's gaze flew back to the woman in red and white. Frisk spun her around, and Max's heart spun, as well. It was Emma, all right—all glammed up and dazzling. Her dress flowed over her curves, showing bare shoulders and a tantalizing bit of cleavage. Her hair was partially pulled back from her face in a style he'd never seen before, and her high heels made her legs look a mile long. As he watched, Frisk spun her around again, and she laughed up at him.

Jealousy stabbed his gut. He was surprised at the force of it.

Dorothy leaned close. "I told her to dance with anyone who might ask. I thought it might help squelch rumors about you two."

It was probably a good idea, but that didn't mean he liked it.

Dorothy's elfin face curved in a wry grin. "It's not going to work if you keep staring at her that way, though."

Dorothy was right, but damn, it was hard to take his eyes off her.

The music ended. Harris kept his arm around Emma's waist as he escorted her off the dance floor. Flames of jealousy licked at Max as the man whispered something in Emma's ear.

As if she'd sensed his gaze, Emma looked up. Max wasn't sure if the lights in the room really dimmed or if it just seemed that way, but Emma's smile abruptly vanished the moment her eyes met his.

❧

Emma stopped in mid-stride, her heart fluttering traitorously. What was Max doing here? She looked away, determined to ignore him, only to find Harris gazing at her, his vanilla MoonPie face crinkled in concern. "Are you okay?"

"Sure. I was just, uh, looking for Katie."

Which, now that she thought of it, she was. Katie had received a phone call from her husband in Iraq and had gone outside to take it just before Harris had invited Emma to dance. Katie had promised Emma that she'd make a bid on her donation when it came up for auction, and Emma was afraid the auction would start while Katie was out of the room.

A man with a video camera crossed the room to the stage, causing Emma's heart to jump.

"Who's the person with the camera?" Emma asked Harris.

"It's a guy from Dirk's ad agency. They're going to

get some footage of his wife to use in his new campaign commercials."

Briggs's current commercial emphasized his family's deep roots in Pontchartrain Parish and portrayed them as pillars of the community. Apparently the new ads would do more of the same. Emma nervously watched the videographer unfold a tripod and aim the camera at the stage. She wasn't sure which made her more anxious: Max or the video camera.

As long as they both stayed away from her, she could deal.

"Want something to drink?" Harris asked.

God, yes. "Sure."

They threaded their way to the bar, moving away from Max. Harris had just handed her a glass of wine when the stage microphone squawked.

Emma turned to see the fiddle player adjusting the mike stand for Carrie Briggs, who stood beside it, looking as perfect as a Stepford wife. She wore a little black dress that probably cost more than Emma earned in a month. She smiled and tapped on the microphone with perfect pink nails, then lifted her hand and gave a beauty queen wave. The room quieted as the light on the video camera in front of her blazed on. "Ladies and gentlemen, I'm Carrie Briggs, the president of the Women's League. It's time for the evening's main attraction—the auction!"

The crowd applauded and gravitated toward the stage. Emma looked worriedly for Katie as she and Harris made their way across the room. What if Emma's service came up for auction before Katie came back?

Instead of Katie, Emma's eyes fell on Max. He was staring at her with laser-like intensity, his mouth pulled in a tight, angry line.

Her stomach knotted. What right did *he* have to be angry? *She* was the one who'd been wronged.

She whirled around and faced the stage, where Carrie was smiling as if she'd done everyone a great favor by gracing them with her presence. "Thank you all for coming tonight. As you know, this benefit will help the underprivileged youth of Pontchartrain Parish, so bid generously, and bid often."

The audience cheered and applauded.

"Most of you know the routine. As we announce each item, we encourage anyone familiar with it to give an endorsement. It's our way of thanking the businesses that so generously donated gifts and services."

Lulu climbed up on the stage, wearing an orange dress with a tulip skirt and carrying a stack of poster boards. She placed the poster boards on an easel beside the microphone, then pushed her thick glasses up her freckled snub nose.

The top poster featured a photograph of a Labrador Retriever with a bone in his mouth. Below the picture were the words "No bones about it—Dr. Frisk helped me retrieve my health."

"Cute poster," Emma said to Harris.

He flashed a modest smile. "Thanks." Harris was a pleasant man in his mid-thirties, with sandy hair, a ruddy complexion, and a short, stocky build. Unlike Max, Harris was exactly the sort of man who'd be good for her—low-key, low profile, and low maintenance. Also unlike Max, however, Harris also gave her low libido.

She reflexively cast her eyes over the crowd for Max and discovered with some alarm that he'd moved closer. What did Max think he was doing?

Emma forced her attention back to the stage. "First up

is a free pet health check," Carrie was saying. "Anyone care to say a few words about Dr. Frisk's clinic?"

A large woman in a dress that looked like an orange and pink muumuu raised her hand. The disco ball colors cycled over her, turning her red, then blue. "Dr. Frisk has been Fluffy's veterinarian for years. When Fluffy got ringworm, he not only gave me a salve that fixed her right up—he gave me enough to cure the ringworm she'd given me, as well."

The crowd laughed.

"Thank you, Mrs. Potter," Carrie said. "Do we have an opening bid?"

"Twenty dollars," called an elderly man in the back.

"I'll bid twenty-five," called Mrs. Potter.

"Thirty," said a voice near the stage.

The auction was off and running. The gavel came down at fifty dollars.

"They paid more than I charge," Harris told Emma.

"Maybe you should raise your rates." She looked around again for Katie, hoping she returned before Emma's donation came up for auction.

"Next we have a case of Community Coffee, donated by Shed's Groceries," Carrie announced.

A man at the back raised his hand. "Everybody knows Community Coffee is the best there is."

"That's right. And if you put a little whiskey in it, it's even better," said the fiddle player from the back of the room.

Everyone laughed.

"I'll bid ten dollars," said a woman in yellow by the front.

"Fifteen," said another.

"Twenty."

A carwash and five gallons of house paint were auctioned in quick succession, each supported by glowing comments.

Harris's phone buzzed. He took the brief call, then turned to Emma apologetically. "I'm afraid I have a patient with an emergency. But maybe we can get together another time."

Emma politely nodded, even though she had no intention of ever going out with Harris. She turned and eyed the back door as Harris left. Still no Katie. Max, however, was closer than ever.

Lulu whisked away another poster. The very next one read, "Closets by Emma." Emma's palms grew damp.

"Next up is a closet reorganization by Emma Jamison." Carrie's voice lacked the enthusiasm that had marked her announcement of the other auction items. "Does anyone care to say anything about this?"

Silence covered the room like a FEMA roof tarp. Emma's mouth went dry. From the corner of her eye, she saw Max's hand move. Emma curled her damp palms into fists and closed her eyes. *No. Please God, no.*

Carrie's lips curved into a feral grin. "Mr. Duval."

Emma's knees shook.

"Emma organized my apartment," piped up a voice from the back. Emma's head turned, along with everyone else's.

Harold. Thank heavens. He stood beside Grams, his thin frame straight and commanding. "She labeled things so I can find them, and it was a real help."

"I hired her to organize my office," the bug lady Realtor called out. "She set up a system that's easy to follow, and now we keep things nice and neat."

"She painted and organized my mother's apartment at

Sunnyside," called Mrs. Alvarez's daughter. "Mom doesn't confuse the bathroom and closet anymore."

"She straightened up the storeroom at my salon, and my clients can actually get to the restroom now!" Katie called from the back doorway.

"I've seen Katie's storeroom, and if she can do that, I'll bid two hundred dollars," called out a blonde, whom Emma recognized as the woman with the foil in her hair at the salon. The crowd laughed.

"Two-fifty!" called out Lulu from the stage.

To Emma's amazement, the bids went up and up—and up. Grams, Harold, and Katie made their way through the crowd to Emma's side as the bids continued to climb.

"You've started a bidding war among the *Mean Girls*," Katie murmured. "That means you're cooler than cool."

A few minutes later, the gavel finally came down. "Sold for twelve hundred dollars," Carrie proclaimed.

"That's a record," Grams told Emma. "In the forty years we've been doing this, we've never had an item go for more than a thousand dollars."

Emma soon found herself surrounded by losing bidders.

"Do you have a card?" asked Susan from the library club.

"I want one, too," Lulu said.

"Me, too," said Anne. "I want to buy a gift certificate for my sister's birthday."

"Do you do garages?" asked a man at her side.

This was amazing, Emma thought. She never would have believed that this organization business would take off, much less be a ticket out of infamy.

She jotted down her number again and again as person after person came up to her, inquiring about her services and telling her about their overflowing closets, garages, and attics.

"Well, well, well." Grams beamed as Emma's potential clients drifted away at last. "Looks like people have really warmed up to you."

"I told you," Katie added.

It was amazing. It was just what Emma wanted. By all rights, this should be one of the happiest nights of her life.

Yet it wasn't.

And here came the reason why. Her heart thudded as Max walked toward her, looking all too handsome in an open-necked white shirt.

"Congratulations," he said.

"Thank you," Emma said stiffly. She started to walk away.

He placed his hand on her arm, stopping her. "Not so fast. What the hell is going on?"

She glared at him. "You're such a super sleuth, I'm sure you can figure it out."

Max's brow drew together in bewilderment. "I'd figure it out a lot faster if you'd tell me."

"You need to tell him, Emma," Katie urged.

"Tell him what?" Grams looked from Katie to Emma to Max, then back at Katie again. "What does she need to tell him?"

Emma drew in a deep breath through her teeth, glowered at Max, then turned to her grandmother. "The bank called to tell me that Max has been snooping into my account."

"What?" Max's eyebrows flew upward in bewilderment. A second later, he jammed his hands in his pockets, blew out a breath and looked up at the ceiling. "Oh, hell. Hell, Emma—that wasn't me. That was my friend Dave."

"Oh, well." She gave a derisive huff. "That makes me feel much better."

"Emma, I can explain . . ."

"You should let him," Grams urged.

"You know what . . . you two better take this somewhere else," Katie said looking around worriedly.

"No need," Emma snapped. "I have nothing further to say to him."

Max's eyes narrowed. "Well, I have a few things to say to you."

"I don't want to hear it."

"Too bad, because we're going to talk." His eyes were hard as black diamonds, his voice ominously low. "We can either go someplace else and talk in private, or we can stand right here and let the whole town hear us, but trust me, sweetheart, we're going to talk."

Emma glanced around the crowded room. She was cornered. The fact made her furious.

"Pick a place," Max ordered.

"Better do it," Katie urged her. "People are starting to stare."

Max looked fully capable of making a scene—which made no sense, since he was the one with the most to lose. Emma blew out an angry breath. "The park across the street." Grams and Gramps used to take her there when she was a child.

Max gave a single curt nod. "I'll go out the front door. You can go out the back in a few minutes."

A brisk breeze carried the muggy scent of rain through the air as Emma crossed the street to the small neighborhood park a few minutes later. A storm was brewing. Well, that was fitting, because a storm was brewing inside her, as well. She didn't know which made her angrier—the fact that Max had asked his friend to check into her finances, or the fact that Max somehow thought that was an acceptable thing to do.

She picked her way through the clump of pines that separated the street from the park, making her way toward a tall swing set illuminated by a streetlamp. Its plastic seats were forlorn and empty, swaying haplessly in the wind.

She saw Max standing in the shadows beside the slide. He must have seen her at the same moment, because he straightened and walked toward her. She folded her arms across her chest. "You have five minutes, so talk fast."

"Look, Em—I'm trying to clear your name."

She jutted up her chin. "By checking out my bank account?"

"No. My old partner Dave is a private investigator in D.C., and he has a lot of connections, so I asked him to see if he could learn anything about Ferguson from the Secret Service. That whole bank thing—he did that on his own. I didn't even know he was going to do it."

Max was trying to get information from the Secret Service? She stared at him as she processed the information. He looked like he was telling the truth, but if he was, why had he gone behind her back? "You asked a private investigator to look into my life and you didn't tell me?"

"I was going to. I kept waiting for the right time."

A fresh wave of indignation flared within her. "We talked on the phone every night and you couldn't find the right time?"

"Every time I started to tell you, you'd say something about how well things were going here, so I thought it was best to keep quiet and not get your hopes up."

"*You* thought it was best?"

"Damn it, Emma, I'm trying to help." The breeze ruffled his dark hair. "I decided to wait and tell you when I had something to report."

The wind clattered the swings together. She'd loved that swing set when she was a child—loved the creak of the metal chains, the whoosh of wind on her face, the thrilling moment at the very top when the tension loosened before the swing changed direction. But most of all, she'd loved the sensation of pumping her legs and propelling herself into flight. She'd never liked to be pushed.

She glared at him. "You don't get to decide that. You don't get to choose what I do or don't need to know about my own friggin' life. I get to make those choices."

"Emma, I just want to find the girl who was with Ferguson."

She hated the glimmer of hope that flickered in her chest.

"I've got some leads." He stepped forward and put his hands on her arms. "That's why I was in Washington. Dave and I talked to the Secret Service agent who was with you in the kitchen."

Against her will, the hope flared to a flame. "The guy whose name was Graw-something?"

He nodded.

"What did he say?"

"He was the limo driver that night. He told us he picked up the girl at the Hyton Hotel and took her to the mansion with Ferguson."

At last—someone had backed up her story. "I told you!"

A giddy joy rushed through her. She stepped closer and anxiously peered into his eyes. "So is he going to come forward and give a statement?"

"No." Max's hands moved gently up her arms.

"Can't you make him?"

"He'll stick to the official story even under subpoena."

"Why?"

"Because the Secret Service would make him the fall guy."

His words were like fire-extinguisher foam, dowsing the hope that had burned so brightly just a few moments ago. Her heart felt freshly charred and sodden.

"Our best shot is finding the girl," he said.

Best shot? There was no shot. "Do you know her name?"

"Her working name is Amber."

"Do you know her last name?"

"No."

"Do you know where to look for her?"

"Since she's local, chances are she's still in New Orleans."

"But you're not sure."

Max's fingers moved down her arms. "I'll find her, Em. I swear I will."

A gust of wind made the tall end of the teeter-totter clank to the ground. Blinking back tears of disappointment, Emma fastened her gaze on the buttons of Max's shirt, unwilling to look him in the eye. "Look—I know you mean well, but you're just making things worse."

"How? If we can clear your name . . ."

"If." The word burned her throat. Hot tears blurred her vision. "I'm tired of living in *If*-land, Max. It's like believing in the If Bunny or waiting up Christmas Eve for

If Claus." The wind sent leaves scuttling across the playground. "I've been making progress. Tonight was a big step. People here are starting to accept me. *I'm* starting to accept me, scandal and all." Thunder growled in the distance. "I'm starting to feel like I'm finally getting a life. And then here you come, holding out an impossible dream that makes all my progress seem like nothing. It's like you're dangling a carrot in front of me—a carrot that makes me want what I can't have and keeps me from being content with the things I *can* have."

"Emma—"

A tear streaked down her face as lightning streaked across the sky. "You don't have that right. You can't just swoop in like some caped crusader and promise you'll fix the unfixable."

Max's hand slid around her back. "Emma, if you'll just listen for a moment—"

A light, brighter and closer than lightning, suddenly glared in her eyes. Another light flashed. And then, in the pool of light from the streetlamp, she saw the three of them: Dirk Briggs, the punk from the newspaper, and a man with a video camera.

The light on the front of the video camera glared like a headlight. She jerked back, fight-or-flight panic rushing through her veins, separating herself from Max.

Briggs's teeth gleamed in a smarmy grin. "Smile pretty, 'cause I intend to use this footage in my ad campaign."

Nausea crawled through Emma's stomach.

"Care to tell us what you two are doing out here?" Briggs asked.

"Having a conversation," Max said.

"Uh-huh." Briggs waved the cameraman closer. "Looks like a reeeeal cozy conversation."

Air wouldn't flow through Emma's windpipe. She tried to remember what Grams had said about breathing, but panic overrode coherent thought. She turned and ran, awkward in her high heels, her small evening bag bumping against her ribs as she fled into the trees that lined the park.

"Emma!" Max called.

It was like running on stilts, but the sandals were buckled firmly over her instep, and she couldn't stop to take them off. Fat drops of rain splattered down on her head. She stumbled over a tree root, then righted herself and kept running, praying that Max wasn't creating another photo op by chasing after her.

CHAPTER NINETEEN

Later, that evening, the door to Harold's apartment opened slowly, so slowly that Harold wasn't sure if it were really opening or if he were dreaming. In the sliver of light, he saw a shadowy figure. "Who's there?" he called.

"It's me," called a soft woman's voice.

It wasn't Myrtle—was it? No, Myrtle was gone, but it was someone like Myrtle. He strained to see in the dark, but the woman seemed murky. No, it was his head that was murky. He had swamphead again.

He heard the sound of a zipper being unfastened, felt the give of the mattress, felt the warmth of her body. She nestled beside him and wrapped her arms around him.

A little trill of excitement sang up his spine. He could feel bare arms and bare legs and something silky skimming her torso. He turned toward her and felt the warm press of an unfettered breast against his pajama top. She wasn't Myrtle—Myrtle had been thin and frail, especially the last few years. Touching her had felt like touching a tarp over a bundle of kindling. This woman—oh, hell, what was her *name?* It bobbed just out of reach—was soft and round and warm. And Myrtle had smelled like white—jasmine and ivory soap and white cold cream. This woman smelled like purple—lilacs and lavender.

And then, suddenly, he had it. *Dorothy.* That was it. Her name was Dorothy, like in *The Wizard of Oz*. And she felt like Myrtle because she made his insides warm. She chased the cold from his bones, the lonely from his soul.

She moved her hand down his chest, unfastening the buttons on his pajama top, untying the drawstrings on his pants. His breath quickened.

"You feel really good, Harold," she murmured.

"You, too, Myrtle."

"I'm Dorothy," she said.

Remorse coursed through him. "I knew that! I mean, I had it just a second ago, and then . . . I'm so sorry."

"It's okay. I'm flattered that you confuse us."

"You are?"

"Yes." She ran her hand, soft and cool, across his chest. "You loved her very much. And if I stir up those feelings in you, too, well, I think that's the biggest compliment you can give me."

Harold smiled in the dark. "Oh, you definitely stir up those feelings." He pulled her close and kissed her. She tasted warm and minty and sweet, and in the midst of that kiss, all barriers fell away. He was once again young and free—free of the restraints of decorum, free of the limitations of age, free of the foibles of memory.

A crack of light caught the corner of his eye. The crack grew wider, and he realized the door was opening again—opening wide.

Light spilled in from the hallway, illuminating a woman. She was tall and wrinkled and walking-stick thin, and she wore a see-through red negligee edged in red feathers. The light shone through it, and underneath the diaphanous fabric, she was stark raving naked.

"You cheating bastard!" she shrieked. "You've got another woman in our bed!" She charged toward them, thin gray hair flying out behind her head, long, flat breasts flapping against her ribs under the sheer material. "You cheap little tramp, get away from my man!"

Harold rolled over on top of Dorothy, wanting to protect her. The intruder tugged at Harold's arm.

"He's mine," she shrilled. "He doesn't love you. He loves me. He loves *me,* and you have no claim."

Fingernails dug into Harold's skin as the skinny woman pulled and pinched and prodded, trying to pry him off Dorothy. Harold held fast, determined to protect her, but Dorothy shimmied out from under him, her thigh-high white camisole hitching up as she rose from the bed.

"For Pete's sake, Esmerelda, leave him be." Dorothy grabbed the taller woman around the waist and hauled her off the bed.

Harold sat up and stared. Dorothy's nightie was sheer as a window curtain, providing a view of big breasts, generous rolls around her middle, and legs like blue-veined tree trunks. She tugged the wild-eyed, bony-assed skeleton of a gal toward the door, sending red feathers flying.

Harold blinked. He'd seen photos of two gals wrestling in a girlie magazine once, but they hadn't looked anything like these two. He must be having a dream. He wasn't sure if it was a good dream or a nightmare, but it sure was fascinating.

The tall woman grabbed the little round one by the hair, and the round one grabbed the bony one's arm. They spun around like a couple of bottles about to tip over. "Ow!"

Dorothy shrieked. "Turn loose, Ezzy, or I swear I'll bust your chops."

The overhead light abruptly flicked on. A woman in blue-flowered pants and a matching shirt—the kind medical people wear—stood in the doorway, her mouth hanging open, her eyes big as quart containers.

"Good God in heaven!" she gasped.

The nearly naked women toppled to the floor, the thin one pinning Dorothy to the carpet. Good gravy, but this was an interesting dream.

"Harold, do something!" Dorothy cried.

The distress in her voice made him jump out of bed. The flowered medical person yelped, threw up her hands, then turned tail and ran.

Harold looked down. Land o'goshen, his pajama bottoms had fallen down, pooling around his ankles. Yessiree, this was quite a dream.

"Help me, Harold!" Dorothy called.

A gentleman had to help a lady in distress, even in a dream. He took a step forward and grabbed the skinny woman under an arm. She was so stick-thin that it was like grabbing the crotch of a tree. "Come on now, ma'am. Turn loose and let her go."

"Don't you ma'am me!" The woman flapped her arm like a chicken wing, trying to keep Dorothy pinned with the other one. "How dare you bring another woman into our bed?"

Harold tugged harder. Old Rattlebones loosened her grip on Dorothy long enough to throw a hard right to his stomach.

The flower lady was back in the doorway—this time with a stocky man in green scrubs who had arms like a longshoreman, his biceps as big as hams. Another lady in that floral medical getup peered over his shoulder.

The man's eyes bulged like his muscles. "Holy Moses!"

"I'll teach you to mess with my man." The scraggly woman lunged for Dorothy again.

Harold protectively threw himself over Dorothy, only to end up sandwiched between the two women. Shrieks and gasps sounded from the doorway. More faces gathered there and stared, their mouths open like baby birds'.

"Don't just stand there like a bunch of peeping Johns," Dorothy yelled at the gaping crowd. "Get in here and do something!"

The large man lumbered forward. "All right, all right— that's enough, now. Let's go."

The man hesitantly lifted the lanky woman around the waist, but she'd wrapped her legs around Harold's thighs, and Harold found himself being lifted, too.

"Throw some water on 'em!" one of the women in the doorway yelled.

Another woman dashed forward and grabbed the pitcher by Harold's bed. The next thing he knew, a cold blast of ice water hit his butt, and thin gal released her thigh-clutch on him.

"Ow! Ow! Ow!" the skinny woman yelped as the large man hauled her away.

"All right, Mr. Duval—time to break this up." A female nurse with short, mannish hair and a deep voice tugged at his armpits.

Harold shrugged her off, intent on protecting the modesty of the woman beneath him. "Get me a blanket or a towel," he said.

"We'll get you one when you get on your feet."

"It's not for me. It's for Myrtle. If I stand up, she'll be exposed."

"Who's Myrtle?"

"My wife," Harold said. Why didn't they know that? Who were these people, anyway? And where the heck was he? He was suddenly confused. The only thing he recognized were the warm eyes looking up at him.

"You don't have a wife," the mannish nurse said, as if he were a child. "You're lying on top of Mrs. Jamison."

"Jamison?" He gazed down at the sweet face, the only thing in the room that seemed familiar, and felt a welling sense of panic. Oh, dear Lord—swamphead was back, sucking him under, dragging him into a tangled bayou of bewilderment and powerlessness. "Myrtle, what are they talking about?"

"It's okay, Harold," she whispered.

But it wasn't. He was lost—lost and afraid and surrounded by strangers, strangers who were telling him that everything he thought he knew was wrong.

The other nurse rushed forward. "Okay, Mr. Duval— here's a blanket. You can use it to cover Mrs. Jamison."

Mrs. Jamison? Why did they keep calling Myrtle that?

"It's okay," whispered the woman beneath him. "Just hand me the blanket and stand up. We'll sort everything out later."

Anxiety clenched his chest in a death grip. "You won't leave me, will you? Promise me you won't leave."

"Mrs. Jamison has to go back to her apartment now," the mannish nurse said. "You can see her in the morning."

Myrtle who wasn't Myrtle patted his cheek. "It looks like I have to leave for a little while, but I won't be far, and I promise to come back first thing in the morning."

"Promise?"

"I promise."

"Because I love you and I don't want to live without you." The fierceness of his emotion burned Harold's eyes, and they started to water. "I love you."

Dorothy's blue eyes gleamed up at him. "Oh, Harold—I love you, too." Her fingers brushed through his hair. "We'll work out a way to be together."

"Promise?"

"I promise."

ॐ

Mrs. Schwartz folded her hands on the desk and looked at Max, then leveled a contemptuous gaze at Emma. "As you know," Mrs. Schwartz intoned, "we had another incident last night. A very *tawdry* incident."

The old biddy was talking to Max and Emma, Dorothy thought hotly, as if she and Harold weren't even in the room. "Only tawdry thing about it was Esmerelda," Dorothy piped up. "Speaking of Ezzy, why isn't *she* here? Seems like she ought to be getting her wrists slapped instead of us."

Mrs. Schwartz's eyes nailed her like ice picks. "Alzheimer's patients can't be held accountable for their actions. You, on the other hand, are a different story."

Dorothy tilted up her head. "You are, too."

"What?"

"You're accountable for keeping folks from bursting into other people's apartments in the middle of the night, aren't you?"

Displeasure oozed from Mrs. Schwartz's eyes like sleep kitties. "That isn't the issue here. The issue is your unseemly behavior."

Dorothy bristled. "Now, just a cotton-pickin' minute.

What Harold and I do in the privacy of his apartment is nobody's business but ours. And I resent having my behavior called unseenly, because it wasn't meant to be seen."

Mrs. Schwartz gave a derisive snort.

Max's lips quivered, as if he were fighting back a smile. "Dorothy has a valid point," he said. "The residents have an expectation of privacy within their own homes."

"That doesn't give them a license to—to—to *fornicate* on our property," Mrs. Schwartz sputtered.

"Mrs. Schwartz, we've discussed this before. They have every right—" Max began.

Dorothy held up her hand. "There's no point trying to talk any sense into that woman, Max. Besides, Harold and I have come up with the perfect solution."

Max raised a questioning eyebrow. Emma's forehead crinkled in a puzzled frown.

Dorothy reached over and took Harold's hand. His fingers curled around her palm, warm and solid and reassuring. "Harold and I are getting married."

"*Married?*" Max and Emma exclaimed simultaneously.

"Yes, married."

The silence was so thick and heavy it would have made a thud if it had been dropped.

Dorothy squeezed Harold's hand. "He told me last night that he loved me and didn't want to live without me, and I feel the same way. So we talked about it at breakfast, and we've decided to tie the knot."

"Grams, I need to talk to you," Emma said firmly. "Alone."

Uh-oh. She hated it when Emma got that adult-about-to-set-a-child-straight tone to her voice. "In a minute, dear." She turned to Mrs. Schwartz and mustered her sweetest smile. "I assume you won't have any objections to us sharing an apartment when we're married?"

"Well, I-I—" Mrs. Schwartz's mouth opened, then closed. She looked at Max. "Mr. Duval can't get married. He's not in his right mind!"

Harold stirred beside her. "Is she saying I'm in my wrong one? Because I don't remember where I put my spare."

Dorothy laughed and squeezed his hand.

"Surely you're not going to allow this!" Ms. Schwartz said to Max.

"Thank you for your concern, Ms. Schwartz, but we'll take things from here." Max rose from his chair.

"But—" Mrs. Schwartz said.

"We'll handle it." Max's tone left no room for further discussion.

Following Max's lead, they all traipsed out of the dragon's lair.

Emma grabbed Dorothy's arm and drew her down the hall, away from Max and Harold. She looked awfully upset, poor dear. "Grams, you can't marry Harold!" Emma's eyes were the color of Lake Pontchartrain during a rainstorm. "The nurses said he wasn't even calling you by the right name last night."

"He might get confused about my name, but he knows me—the *real* me, the me inside. His heart recognizes mine."

Emma's eyebrows pleated together. "He thinks you're his wife."

Dorothy grinned. "So that's what I'll become. He loves me, and that's all that matters."

"It *isn't* all that matters!" Emma's voice held a note of desperation. "He has dementia. If you marry him, you won't be getting a husband, Grams; you'll be getting a patient."

"He's on medication, and he's stabilized. Besides, honey, there's no obstacle that love can't overcome. You put love first, and everything else takes care of itself."

"Grams, I admire the sentiment, but it's just not practical."

"Who said love was practical?"

Emma closed her eyes, as if she were gathering her thoughts, or maybe her patience. "Grams, you moved here because you wanted to be free from responsibilities and burdens. If you marry Harold, you'll be taking on the biggest responsibility of your life. His dementia is only going to get worse."

The girl meant well, Dorothy knew she did, but Emma just didn't understand, and Dorothy didn't know how to explain it. Some things just couldn't be translated into words; some things were just matters of the heart. "Emma, sweetie, when you love someone, responsibility is a privilege. Their burdens are yours, and yours are theirs, and it's your heart's desire to help them any way you can."

"But Grams—"

Dorothy held up her hand. "None of us knows what the future holds. Why, I might have a stroke tonight and be paralyzed. Or I could have a heart attack or an aneurism or go bonkers like Esmerelda and start running naked through the halls."

"And if that happened, would Harold be able to take care of you? Marriage is supposed to be a two-way street."

"Honey, he already takes care of me, in ways I can't even describe. Two-way streets aren't always divided right down the middle."

Around the corner, the elevator binged, heralding its arrival.

". . . and they found them all in a heap on the floor," Dorothy heard a familiar voice drawl as the doors swooshed open.

"In heat on the floor?" replied a higher voice with the same thick southern accent.

"That's the Evans sisters, Pearl and Ruby," Dorothy whispered to Emma. "They're both deaf as toast."

"Posts," Emma whispered back.

"Yes, indeed," said the first voice around the corner. "They were all nude!"

"Stewed? Well, I'm not surprised. I heard they were naked."

"It's just obscene."

"A scene? I bet it was. I'm trying to picture it."

"No, don't think anyone took any pictures. Wish they had, though. Always wondered how those threesomes work."

Emma blew out a sigh as the voices faded in the distance. "Well, there goes all hope this will be kept quiet."

Dorothy flapped her wrist. "Oh, honey, there was never any chance of that."

Over Emma's shoulder, Dorothy saw Harold shuffling around the corner, his normally straight spine sagging. Max walked beside him, his face tense.

Harold gazed at her with troubled eyes. "Maybe they're right, sweetheart. Maybe I'm no good for you."

"Now, that's just not true." Dorothy looped her arm through Harold's. "You're one of the best things that ever happened to me, and don't you ever forget it."

"But I will, sweetheart." Harold's eyes were forlorn, his voice defeated. "I forget everything."

"Well, you've never forgotten that you care about me, and that's what matters." She tugged on his arm. "Come on, Harold. Max and Emma have to get back to work, and we have to get back to being happy."

"But—"

"No buts about it. These are our lives, and we'll live them as we see fit."

⌇

Emma was still mad at him, Max thought as the older couple toddled down the hallway. Throughout the meeting in Mrs. Schwartz's office, she'd refused to meet his gaze, and now she was standing with her arms crossed, bristling like a porcupine.

Might as well live dangerously. "Your grandmother's right, you know," Max said casually.

"What?" Emma's eyes were angry blue sparks.

"Our opinions don't really count. They need to make their own decisions."

"Your grandfather's not capable of making them!"

"That's not for us to say. That's your grandmother's call."

Emma put her hands on her hips and glared at him. "So let me get this straight. In your esteemed opinion, a man with Alzheimer's gets to decide the course of his own life, but I don't."

Hell. Max had replayed that scene from last night over and over in his mind and he was still clueless about what he should have done differently. "Emma . . . I contacted Dave because I was just trying to help. I should have told you earlier what I was doing, and I apologize that I didn't, but the key thing is, I think there's a chance we can find this girl. You can't just give up."

"Is that what you think I'm doing? Giving up?" She was a pillar of indignation—eyes flashing, mouth tight, chin tilted up. Her hands moved from her hips to her waist. "For your information, there's a big difference between giving up and accepting reality."

"But—"

She was too wound up to stop. "If I'd lost a leg or an arm in an accident, would you be telling me to keep hoping it would grow back, or would you encourage me to accept my handicap and get on with my life?"

"There's no comparison, Emma."

"Yes, there is. This Ferguson thing is my handicap. And this"—she held her arms down at her sides, palms facing him—"is my reality. This is the way my life is. And if you can't handle that, well, just stay the hell away from me. Which is what you need to do, anyway." She pivoted and stalked away.

A nerve jumped in Max's jaw as he watched her go. Like hell he would. He was going to find that girl. He'd go to New Orleans this weekend and start nosing around, and he'd go back every weekend until he got results. Whether Emma liked it or not, he was going to vindicate her.

CHAPTER TWENTY

*E*mma Jamison's Grandmother Caught in Sex Orgy."

Emma looked up from the headline on the front page of the *National Inquisitioner*, her heart somewhere in the vicinity of her toenails. She was huddled with Katie in the pink polka-dotted salon bathroom, away from the curious eyes of Katie's staff and clients. She'd known that the story was coming out—Iris Huckabee had bragged that she'd talked to that demon boy reporter, and the weekly tabloids were replaced at the drugstore and grocery store every Tuesday morning—but Emma hadn't had the heart to read it without moral support, so she'd come to Katie's salon on her lunch hour.

"This is even worse than I thought it would be," Emma moaned.

"You don't have to read the story, Em," Katie said.

"Yes, I do." As much as it hurt, she needed to know what was being written about her and—more importantly—her grandmother and Max.

Emma hesitantly turned the page and winced as she

saw a large photo of her grandmother and Harold plastered across the page. Apparently the intern from hell had taken the elderly couple's photo at the auction, because it showed them on the dance floor, cheek to wrinkled cheek; their arms were extended in a tango, grinning like a pair of doddering village idiots.

The infamous photo of herself clutching her dress and fleeing the Mullendorf estate was beneath it, along with a photo of her next to Max on the playground, a look of horror on her face. Emma thrust the newspaper back at Katie. "Read it to me. I can't bear to read it myself."

Katie flipped down the toilet lid, sat down, and began to read. "*Emma Jamison, the bodacious butler who gave late President-Elect Ferguson a heart attack in the sack . . .*" Katie paused and looked up. "*Bodacious* is good. I'd be thrilled if someone called me bodacious."

Emma fiddled with the cuff of her tailored blue shirt and smiled weakly.

Katie resumed reading. "*. . . seems to come by her randiness naturally. Sources in Chartreuse, Louisiana, say that her seventy-eight-year-old grandmother was caught in a three-way sexcapade with a man and another elderly woman at their retirement home. The man was none other than eighty-one-year-old Harold Duval, the millionaire founder of Duvalware. Sources say that all three were nearly naked and writhing on the floor when the staff burst into Mr. Duval's bedroom.*"

"Writhing?" Emma moaned.

"*'We heard a commotion,' said a retirement home employee who asked to remain anonymous. 'We literally had to throw cold water on them to break them up.'*"

Emma buried her face in her hands.

"*'It looked to me like the two women were fighting,' said*

another employee. 'Or maybe they were just into rough sex. One of the women was wearing a see-through red nightgown with feathers, and the other one was in a short baby-doll camisole kind of thing. Mr. Duval's pajamas were around his ankles.'"

"Oh, no!"

"Not to be outdone by her grandmother, Emma Jamison is apparently dallying with Mr. Duval's grandson, Max Duval, who happens to be the local district attorney. As the Inquisitioner *reported two weeks ago, Emma Jamison was caught leaving his residence early Sunday morning, wearing a man-sized shirt from Mr. Duval's alma mater. The* Inquisitioner *also caught the two of them in an intimate embrace on—appropriately enough—a playground.*

"Emma seems to have a penchant for politicians. Mr. Duval is running for office against local attorney Dirk Briggs.

" 'This is a disgrace. A district attorney's behavior should be above reproach,' Briggs said. 'The people of Pontchartrain Parish deserve a DA who shares their family values and isn't involved with people of questionable character.'"

"Duval's office refused to comment." Katie put down the paper, her eyes troubled.

Emma stared up at the ceiling and shook her head. "Oh, God, this is awful. Beyond awful."

Katie's eyes grew moist. "I'm afraid there's more."

Emma's heart had already sunk to her toes. Now it dropped through the floor and started digging. "What?"

Katie blew out a sigh. "Carrie came in to have a nail tip replaced this morning and showed around the script for Dirk's latest TV commercial. It starts airing tonight."

"How bad is it?"

Katie's hesitation spoke volumes. "Not all that bad."

"It is, too. What's in it?"

"Well, I sneaked off and made a copy of it while she was in the bathroom."

Steeling herself, Emma held out her hand. "Let's have it."

Katie hesitantly pulled a folded piece of paper out of her pocket. Emma took it, biting her lip as she unfolded it.

Dirk Briggs Commercial

Spot Length: 30 seconds
Placement: Pontchartrain Parish Cable TV
Schedule: Hourly during primetime,
*   August 25–Sept. 5*
Format: Voiceover and B-roll

Born and raised in Chartreuse, Dirk Briggs exemplifies the family values of the citizens of Pontchartrain Parish. (Footage of Briggs shaking hands in front of courthouse). His wife is a leader in charity functions (footage of wife onstage at auction), his children are honor roll students at the local public school (little Briggses getting on the school bus), and his family founded and still operates the Chartreuse Bank and Trust. (Footage of elder Briggs in front of bank). A respected attorney, Dirk has represented the interests of local people for over twenty years. (Footage of Briggs rising from desk in office, shirtsleeves rolled up, to shake hand of elderly client.)

Max Duval is an outsider. (Videotape of Duval standing alone in the rain, scowling, on the play-

ground). The former assistant of the late DA Harold Jenkins, Max wasn't elected to office, but is only filling out the term after Mr. Jenkins died. (Footage of former DA.) A party-loving bachelor (footage of Duval with a beer in his hand at Fourth of July picnic), Duval lives a lifestyle of questionable morals. (Photo of Emma outside his gate.)

When you go to the polls this Saturday, ask yourself: Do you trust a man like this to uphold the law (video of Max with his hands on Emma's back, jumping apart as they turn toward the camera with alarmed expressions) or this (Dirk playing football on the lawn of his home with his two boys)?

Briggs speaking to camera: "I'm Dirk Briggs, and I'll uphold family values as the Pontchartrain Parish district attorney. I hope you'll vote for me this Saturday."

Emma wadded up the script, a gumbo of anger and frustration boiling in her chest. "I hate this, Katie." She tossed it in the trash, then turned and braced her hands against the bathroom countertop, her head down. "I hate this! I'm poisoning the lives of everyone I care about."

"It's not your fault."

"It is. If it weren't for me, none of this would be news. Just being around me is ruining their lives." She pushed off the counter and turned to face her friend. "I wonder if that corporate job in Tampa is still available."

"No," Katie said quickly. "That's no solution. Max is here, and your grandmother, and you're making friends, and—"

Emma shook her head. "I'm the Typhoid Mary of reputations. You're probably going to be next." Tears pooled in her eyes as she turned toward her friend. "It's time I faced it, Katie. I'm never going live this whole Ferguson thing down."

Katie's eyes flashed with indignation. "You shouldn't have to live it down. You should be living it up! You're young and beautiful and bright, and you didn't *do* anything." Katie spun the roll of toilet paper, pulled off a few sheets, and handed them to Emma. "Just hang in there, Emma. Max is going to find the girl who was actually with Ferguson, and this whole thing is going to be cleared up."

Emma dabbed at her cheeks. "Yeah, and maybe he'll leap a tall building while he's at it."

"I don't think you're giving Max enough credit."

The truth was, she was scared to. She was afraid to open the door of hope, because it would smash her heart again when it inevitably banged closed. "Max doesn't have much more to go on than my detective did. He has no last name, no address, nothing."

"He knows the girl's first name is Amber and that they picked her up at the Hyton. That's something."

"It's not much. He doesn't even know where to look for her."

"He knows she apparently lived in New Orleans, so she's probably still there." Katie looked at her thoughtfully. "I wonder why she hasn't come forward. Seems like she'd want to sell her story to the tabloids and make some big money."

Emma sat on the counter beside the sink. "The Secret Service probably scared her within an inch of her life. They hired her and picked her up and smuggled her into the mansion, and they don't want their involvement exposed."

"So they deliberately made it look like you were the woman?"

"I don't think they planned it; I think an opportunity fell into their laps. When my picture came out in the paper, I made the perfect scapegoat, and they just ran with it."

Katie scrunched up her forehead. "So where did the video come from?"

"Ferguson had a reputation for taping himself having sex. The Secret Service took the video, edited it, and sent it to an Internet porn site. Once everyone could see how he died, there would be no need for an investigation."

Katie stared thoughtfully at the Betty Boop picture hanging opposite the toilet. "So this girl is out there, not getting the huge bucks a tabloid would pay her for her story, while your life is being ruined."

Emma sighed. "That's pretty much the size of it."

Katie's face took on a determined look. "Well, we have to find her."

"How? By dressing up as ladies of the evening and going undercover?"

Katie's eyes grew large. "That's brilliant!"

"I was being sarcastic."

"But it could work!" Katie rose from the toilet seat. "If we go out and mingle with hookers, we might run into this girl, or at least find someone who does."

"We?"

"Sure. I want to help."

Emma rolled her eyes. "I'm sure your husband would love the idea of his wife impersonating a hooker while he's in Iraq."

"What he doesn't know won't hurt him."

"I was kidding, Katie. The whole thing is ridiculous. We don't even know where ladies of the evening hang out."

"We'll start at the Hyton, then look in bars at other hotels, and maybe check out some strip clubs. And if we look like prostitutes, maybe we can infiltrate their ranks and find someone who knows her."

"Do you really think there are ranks of hookers?" Emma asked dryly.

"Well, everyone likes to hang out with people they have things in common with."

A knock sounded on the bathroom door.

"Just a minute," Katie yelled.

Emma rose from her perch on the counter.

"Just think about it," Katie urged.

"There's nothing to think about. This is ridiculous. Besides, right now I need to be thinking about how I can break the news about this story to Grams as gently as possible."

But in the back of Emma's mind, the idea started to take root and grow.

$\backsim$

"Oh, I've already seen this. Iris gave me a copy," Grams said when Emma showed up at her door twenty minutes later, clutching a copy of the *Inquisitioner*. Grams wore hot pink yoga pants and a matching stretch shirt, and when she pulled the door wider, Emma saw two rolled-up yoga mats sitting by the door. "Come on in, dear. I'm warming up for yoga class."

Emma stepped into the apartment. Grams closed the door and moved onto the zebra-striped rug in the center of the living room, where she put up her arms and reached toward the ceiling. Her nonchalance disconcerted Emma. "Aren't you upset about it?"

Grams bent over to the side, her arms still out. "The thing that really irons my shorts is how they flat-out say you hotsy-totsied that old bugger to death, as if it's a proven fact."

"That's nothing new." Emma moved to the leopard-print sofa and sank down in the soft cushions. "But this mention of you and Harold—"

"Aw, that's no largie." Grams stretched forward and tried to touch her toes. She made it to just below her knees.

"No biggie," Emma corrected.

"Everyone around here knows Esmerelda, so no one believes that three-way business. But I hate that they let that Dirt guy spout off about you and Max."

"Dirk."

Grams straightened and reached for the ceiling again. "Well, it really ticks me up."

"Ticks you off. The expression is ticked *off.*"

"Well, I have half a mind to call up that reporter and give him a piece of my brain."

"Piece of mind."

"What?"

"The expression is give him a piece of your mind."

"I don't want him to have peace of mind. I want to tell him up."

"Off. And you can't. If you talk to him, you'll just be giving him fodder for a new story."

"Well, I want to do something." Grams stuck her arms straight out to the sides and twisted her torso to the left. "This is all my fault."

"No, it isn't. It's mine."

Grams twisted to the right. "How do you figure that?"

"Esmerelda's run around naked before and it didn't make the papers. It's only news now because I'm con-nected to it."

"But you never should have been news in the first

place, because you didn't do anything. Harold and I did something." She shot Emma a sly smile as she twisted to the left again. "At least, we were about to."

Emma wanted to stick her fingers in her ear and yell, "Na na na na na," just to shut out the image.

Grams bent over for another knee touch. "Well, things will settle down once Harold and I are married."

Emma gazed at her in dismay. "You're still considering that?"

"Why, yes, dear."

"Please don't get married to try to help me!"

"Oh, I wouldn't, dear." A knock sounded on the door. Grams straightened, her face lighting with a smile. "Here's Harold now."

Grams opened the door and Harold strode in, dapper in a crimson jogging suit. "Sorry to rush off, sweetie, but we need to go." Grams picked up the rolled-up yoga mats and handed one to Harold. "If we don't get to class early, we'll have to put our mats in the front of the room, and then everyone will talk behind our backs for sure."

Emma followed the couple into the hall and watched them scurry off toward the exercise room. As they disappeared around the corner, Katie's words ran through her mind: *You shouldn't have to live it down. You ought live it up.*

If we can find the girl, we can clear your name, Max's voice chimed in.

Her own words floated through her thoughts: *Maybe I should dress up like a lady of the evening and go undercover.*

She'd tossed off the suggestion in jest, but the idea had been simmering on the back burner of her mind. If Amber were in New Orleans, Emma might, just might, be able to find someone who knew her. And if she could find her, Emma was sure she could convince her to go to the media. If Amber went directly to the press, the Secret Service couldn't harm her, because if anything happened to her, they'd be the first suspects.

Of course, the whole plan was crazy. Could Emma convincingly look and act like a lady of the evening? She wasn't sure she could pull it off, and if she did, it was a long shot at best. A lot of things could go wrong, and results were far from guaranteed.

But if there was a chance—even a prayer of a chance—didn't Emma owe it to herself and the people she loved to take it? If Max were willing to look for the girl, shouldn't she do the same?

"I think there's a chance we can find this girl," Max had said that night in the park. *"You can't just give up."*

His words had run all over her. If there was one thing she wasn't, it was a quitter. She'd used all her resources trying to clear her name, and even though her hopes had been dashed time and time again, she'd exhausted every possible course of action before she'd abandoned the fight and turned her efforts toward accepting the situation.

Did she have the courage to change course yet again— to really believe she could clear her name, and to put her heart and soul into the effort?

How could she, when it was so unlikely?

On the other hand, how could she not?

CHAPTER TWENTY-ONE

The bored-looking bartender at the New Orleans Hyton Hotel leaned toward Emma in order to be heard over the piano music and chattering hubbub in the darkened bar. "What can I get you?"

"A soda with lime, please," Emma said, brushing back a wayward strand of the long blond wig that she'd ordered from the Frederick's of Hollywood Web site. She started to cross her legs, then thought better of it; the short black skirt and teal halter top, also courtesy of Frederick's express mail delivery, didn't leave much room to maneuver on the barstool. How did women sit in skirts this short? She looked out over the room and saw several men eyeing her, apparently hoping she'd pull a Britney.

Good grief, but this was embarrassing. They were looking at her as if she were . . . well, exactly what she was pretending to be.

Get over it, she admonished herself. She hadn't dressed up like this and driven an hour and a half from Chartreuse to worry about a bunch of gawking conventioneers.

For the umpteenth time since she'd left home, though, Emma wished she'd brought Katie with her, but she hadn't wanted to drag her friend any deeper into her troubles. Enough people that she cared about had already had their names tarnished because of her.

She scanned the room, trying to determine if any call girls were present. Four women in business clothes sat by the window overlooking the Mississippi. A handful of other women sat at tables with groups of men or in couples.

In the corner, two women clad in shorts and tank tops caught her eye. They were in their mid- to late thirties, and they were laughing uproariously. Were they call girls, or tourists? She couldn't exactly walk up to them and ask.

"Hey there, babe."

Emma turned to see a hefty man standing beside her, a beer bottle in his hand. He looked like a plus-size George from Seinfeld.

"You look lonely sitting here all by yourself."

"I'm waiting on someone."

"Sure, sure. Me, too." He winked at her. "While you're waiting, how 'bout a drink?"

"I've already ordered one."

He squinted at her. "Ya know, you look really familiar. Have we met?"

"No."

"So . . . do you want a little company?"

When she'd concocted this little scheme, she hadn't counted on men actually hitting on her. She shook her head and took a sip of her drink.

"Oh, right." He gave her a wink. "You're waiting for someone." He lifted his beer and took a swig. "Too bad. I'm looking for a good time and I have money to burn."

"You might try those ladies in the corner." Might as well let him determine their status as working girls or not.

"Really? I thought they were hotel guests."

He probably had a better eye for this sort of thing than she did. She shrugged.

He winked again, then tipped his beer at her. "Well, have a good one."

He sauntered off as the bartender placed a fresh napkin in front of her. Emma decided to see if he knew anything.

"I'm looking for a friend named Amber," Emma said, leaning forward confidentially.

The bartender regarded her with flat eyes.

"I heard she comes in here a lot, and I was wondering if you'd seen her lately."

"I have no idea who you're talking about."

"She's about my size, and she has long brown hair—or at least she did last time I saw her. She's with a . . ." What the heck were they called? This had never been covered on *Law and Order,* which was where she'd learned all she knew about hookers. ". . . a phone service."

He swiped at the bar with a faded red rag. " You mean like Cingular?"

"No! I mean she's a call girl."

"Uh-huh." He folded the towel and cocked his unibrow. "You know what, sweetheart—I think you'd better go."

"But—"

He waved his hand in a shooing motion. "The drink's on me. Go on, now."

She was being kicked out of a bar! She knew she was pretending to be a prostitute, but still, being treated like one kind of stung. Emma pulled her purse up on her shoulder and squirmed off the barstool with as much dignity as the short skirt allowed. Tugging it down, she marched out of the bar, painfully aware that every male eye in the place was following her.

Her stilettos clicked on the terrazzo floor as she crossed the lobby. A security guard gave her the skanky eye, and she hurried to the revolving-door exit, not wanting to risk being thrown out of the same place twice.

The night air was hot and sticky and smelled like river water, old buildings, and, faintly, fried seafood. She turned and walked down Canal Street toward Bourbon against the traffic, headlights glaring in her eyes. Katie had said that working girls congregated in strip clubs; maybe she'd have better luck at one of the so-called gentlemen's clubs on Bourbon Street.

Rap music thumped from an approaching Ford Mustang. The car pulled alongside her, and three young men yelled out the window. She ducked her chin and picked up the pace, ignoring the catcalls.

She turned onto Bourbon Street and merged into a throng of tourists. Music spilled out of doorways and blended with the sound of laughter. A cart rattled down the street, pulled by a clomping horse in a flower-bedecked straw hat. She jostled her way through the beer-toting crowd for three blocks until she saw a pink fluorescent marquee announcing Dick's Cabaret. Crossing the street toward it, she stared at the airbrushed photos of nearly naked women in the lit display cases beside the entrance. With more than a little trepidation, she approached a muscle-bound man with dark hair and a narrow Fu Manchu–style beard who stood in the doorway.

He looked her up and down with a frankly assessing eye. "If you're here to apply as a dancer, interviews are held in the mornings."

"Oh, I'm not here for a job. I'm looking for a friend."

His lip curled. "Yeah, aren't we all."

"Is there an admission charge?"

"I can't let you inside."

Emma's back stiffened. "What?"

"Better move along, sweetheart."

"Why?"

"No working girls allowed."

"I'm not . . ." Oh, yeah. She was. Or least she was supposed to be. Still, she bristled. "You can't keep me out because of the way I look. That's illegal."

His lip curved in a scoff. "Like you aren't. Move it."

"Wait." Emma grabbed his arm. He angrily yanked it away. She apologetically stepped back. "I-I'm from out of town, and I'm looking for an old friend named Amber. She's about my size, with long brown hair—at least, it used to be long and brown—and she was with a, um . . ." What the *heck* did they call it? ". . . a call service. Do you have any idea how I could find her?"

He glared at her. "What do I look like, a pimp?"

Emma drew herself up and glared back. "No, but you look like someone who could tell me where girls with a, um, service are likely to hang out." Emma batted her eyes at him. "Please. I'd appreciate whatever help you could give me."

His hooded eyes scanned her, locking on her cleavage. "I've heard that some girls hang out between jobs at a place called Pete's. It's on St. Jude's near Esplanade."

At last—maybe she had some kind of lead. Emma smiled. "Thanks." She started to turn away.

"Hey—don't I get nothin' for my trouble?"

He held out his hand, palm up. She started to shake it, then realized he was looking for a tip. "Oh." She pulled her purse off her shoulder, dug out her wallet, and handed him a ten-dollar bill, then turned back around.

"That was worth at least a twenty," he called after her.

It was a good six blocks, and by the time Emma found the neon sign proclaiming "Pete's Place," her feet were killing her and she'd been hit on three times. The club was in a seedier part of the Quarter, but from the outside, it looked almost upscale. A poufy purple-and-black striped awning hung over the black double doors, and twinkle lights glowed in cone-shaped potted bushes on either side of the entrance. Chained to a black wrought-iron bench under the awning, as well as to each other, were two garden statues of cherubs.

Cherubs in chains. Emma wondered about the significance as she pushed through the front door.

The bar was dim and noisy, and it smelled like cigarette smoke. The walls were painted purple and inset with gold-framed leopard-print fabric. The ceiling and one wall were mirrored, making her feel slightly off balance.

As her eyes adjusted to the dim lighting, she was surprised to discover that the clientele was largely made up of tall, beautiful, heavily made-up women.

The bartender was a willowy redhead in a purple chiffon blouse. She looked at Emma, smiled, and aimed both index fingers at her like guns. "The diva, right?"

The voice was low and masculine. As Emma walked closer, she noticed a five-o'clock shadow under the redhead's makeup.

"Your hair," the bartender said in response to her baffled look. "It's Frederick's of Hollywood's Diva, right?"

Emma fingered a strand of her faux blond hair as she perched on a purple velvet bar stool. "Oh. Yeah."

She/he nodded knowingly. "I know someone who can

custom cut it to make it fit your face. When he's through it'll look like a three hundred-dollar job."

"Oh. Really." Emma looked around, wondering if the strip club doorman had deliberately given her a bum steer.

"Yes." The redhead leaned forward. "But between you and me, natural-hair wigs are so much better, they're worth every penny."

"I'll keep that in mind," Emma said.

" So . . . what can I get you?"

"A, uh, club soda."

He smiled approvingly. "Good choice. Always best to start slow and work your way up." He pulled a glass off the back bar, scooped some ice into it, and, with an elegant curve of his wrist, punched a button on the hand-held soda dispenser.

"You're new here," he said, his purple chiffon sleeve gracefully wafting against his hairy arm as he handed her the glass. "Are you one of Dillon's new girls?"

She was tempted to say yes, but feared the consequences. She shook her head. "I'm looking for a friend named Amber."

"I knew an Amber. I haven't seen her in a while."

Emma's fingers tightened around the cold highball glass. "How long a while?"

"A couple of months." He fiddled with a purple plastic bangle on his wrist. "She was real messed up, if you know what I mean."

Emma wasn't sure she did. "Drinking? Drugs?"

"Both, honey, and God knows what else. She looked like she was on the edge of some kind of breakdown."

"What do you mean?"

"She kept muttering something about the Secret Service taking her kid."

Secret Service? Emma's heart pounded. That had to be her! "She has a kid?"

He lifted his shoulders. "I guess. I never really knew anything about her, other than the fact she worked for Miko. Holly might know more."

"Holly?"

"Yeah. Hey, Holly." He motioned to a thick-waisted woman in spray-on-tight jeans who stood chatting with a table full of women—or were they men?—under the gaudy chandelier attached to the mirrored ceiling. Holly turned and sauntered over. She had dark brown hair, a phony-looking tan, and white frosted lips, but she appeared to be biologically female.

"She's looking for Amber." The bartender cocked a head at Emma. "You seen her lately?"

Holly shook her head. A hank of hair flopped in her eye. "Not since Miko let her go."

"Miko?"

Holly gave an inelegant snort. "He was our agent. Took our money and ran about two months ago, the cheap scum."

"Do you have any idea where Amber lives?"

Holly shook her head. "Don' know nothin' about her, 'cept she had a kid she adored. A little boy, two or three years old. She always pretty much kept her personal life separate from work, which is a wise move, if you ask me."

"When was the last time you saw her?"

"Oh, gee—'bout a month ago, outside the Marriott. She was gettin' into a cab, so we just said hi and that was it. Her hair had grown back."

"Grown back?"

"Yeah. She cut it in a bob after Christmas. Said she was gonna get a regular job, get out of the life." Holly snorted. "As if."

"You don't think she did?"

She rolled her eyes. "Honey, if you could make this money doin' anything else, would you be here?"

At least she'd passed as a pro. "No."

"Well, trust me, neither did Amber. An' when I saw her, she sure wasn't dressed for no job at Wal-Mart."

Emma's hand curled around her drink glass. "Any idea how I might find her?" She tried to keep her excitement from showing. "Did she have any friends, or hang out anywhere in particular?"

"I've told you all I know." Holly narrowed her eyes. "What's with all the questions?"

Uh-oh. "I just—" Emma was relieved when the woman's phone rang.

Holly pulled out a rhinestone-studded phone, looked at the number, then pursed her frosted lips. "Time to make the doughnuts."

Emma pulled out a pen and jotted her phone number on a paper napkin. It was a long shot of the longest proportions, but she had to try. "Here—if you see her, would you ask her to call me?"

"What's your name?"

"Emma Jamison."

"Good one." She looked up with an amused half-grin, then narrowed her eyes appraisingly. "You know, if your wig was brunette, you might actually pass for her." She tucked the card in the side of her purse, then hoisted it on her shoulder. "See ya." She swaggered to the door on four-inch platform heels.

The bartender snapped his red-polished fingers. "Emma Jamison—that's who you remind me of." His brow pulled in a puzzled frown. "But if that's your gig, why the blond wig?" His eyes suddenly widened, and his lipsticked mouth opened in a little "oh." He sucked in a fast breath. "Oh, my God—you're really her!"

She'd probably get further by just admitting it. She nodded.

"Oh, my God!" he yelped, flapping his hands.

Heads swiveled toward him. Emma leaned forward. "Shhh. I'm trying to be incognito."

"Oh, this is so exciting!" he whispered. "So what are you doing here?"

"I'm trying to find Amber because I think she was the woman who was really with Ferguson."

His eyes grew as round as bagels. "Get out!"

"I'm serious."

"So it really wasn't you?"

"No." Emma scribbled down her cell number on another napkin. "If you see Amber, would you give her my number? Tell her she's passing up an opportunity for fame and fortune."

"Ooh, this is so exciting!" He looked at the napkin as Emma handed it to him. "Can I get your autograph for myself?"

What the hell. It was probably the only way to ensure he'd actually give the number to Amber, if he saw her. She picked up another napkin and scribbled her name. "I'd better not see this on eBay," she warned.

His hand fluttered to his chest. "Oh, trust me, honey— I'm going to take this home and frame it. And I'll call you if I see Amber or hear anything about her."

"Thanks." She pushed out the smoked-glass door into

the muggy air, stopped under the purple-and-black-striped awning, and pulled out her turned-off phone to check for messages.

She'd had multiple calls from Max—which was nothing new, since he'd called her several times a day since last weekend's debacle; the fact that she wouldn't take his calls hadn't deterred him in the least. Four calls in the last hour seemed excessive, though, even for Max. She also had a text message from Katie: URGENT. Call ASAP.

Emma's chest tightened. Katie wasn't an alarmist; something must have happened. To Grams? To Katie's husband? To Max? Emma pressed the call button.

"Emma," Katie began, without even saying hello. "Your grandmother and Harold have eloped."

"Eloped?" It took a minute for the meaning to sink in. "To where? When?"

"To New Orleans. This afternoon. Your grandmother took the van, and ten residents are with them."

"No!"

"It's true. Mrs. Schwartz called Max, and she's furious. She says your grandmother stole the van, that she's not authorized to drive it, and that she's endangering the lives of the other residents. Plus she has Mr. Ernie with her, and he's an Alzheimer's patient, and he wasn't signed out and he doesn't have permission to be with your grandmother. Max is on his way to New Orleans. In fact, he should be there by now. Where are you?"

Emma stared at the chained-up concrete cherub, her head swimming. "I'm—I'm in New Orleans, too."

"You are?" Katie's voice rose incredulously. "What are you doing there?"

"I'll explain later."

"Oh, my God—are you trying to find the prostitute? *Alone?*"

Her voice was so loud that Emma held the phone out from her ear. "I'll tell you all about it later. Where were Grams and Harold going?"

"First to the Gretna courthouse, where they had an appointment with a judge to get married at four."

"So—they're already married." Emma stepped back under the awning and sank down on the wrought-iron bench. Some part of her mind had thought her grandmother wouldn't really go through with it.

"I guess so." Katie paused, apparently waiting for Emma to speak. "You still there?"

"Yeah."

"She loves him, Em," Katie said softly. "I think you should support her and be happy for her."

It was just so weird. Her grandmother, married—to someone other than her grandfather. And Grams hadn't even invited Emma to the wedding.

Not that she didn't understand why, Emma thought with a pang. She would have tried to talk her grandmother out of it, and Grams's mind had been made up.

The bar door opened and a woman—or was it a man?— in skintight white pants sauntered out. Emma watched him or her swagger down the street in high heels. "Do you know where they were going afterward?" Emma asked Katie.

"To the French Quarter. I don't know exactly where, but they're having a combination bachelor/bachelorette party and wedding reception. And it has a theme."

"I'm scared to ask."

"It's 'Fulfill your Fantasies.'"

"Oh, Lord."

"They planned to stop by a costume shop and rent outfits," Katie continued.

"Outfits? What kind of outfits?"

"You tell me. What are your grandmother's fantasies?"

It was the sort of thing that fell into the don't-ask, don't-tell, don't-even-think-about-it category. "I have no clue."

"Well, Mrs. Schwartz is going to report that the van was stolen and Mr. Ernie was kidnapped if they're not back by midnight."

"*Kidnapped?*"

"Yes. And Max said that since they're out of his jurisdiction, the state police would be involved, and it would turn into a huge hassle with lots of publicity, and your grandparents would most likely spend their wedding night in jail."

"Holy mackerel."

"You and Max need to find them," Katie urged.

The last thing Emma wanted to do was call Max, but she didn't see any alternative. "Okay. Thanks, Katie."

Drawing a deep, bracing breath, Emma punched in Max's cell number.

CHAPTER TWENTY-TWO

$\mathcal{M}$r. Duval, I think we've located your party," Max heard through his cell phone. "There are about a dozen elderly people in costume at the Dog and Cat Karaoke Bar on Bourbon and St. Catherine."

Max blew out a relieved sigh. "Thanks, Sergeant. Thanks a lot."

Max closed his phone and looked down the street for Emma, then glanced at his watch. Ten-twenty. She'd called at ten and agreed to meet him in fifteen minutes at the Bienville Street entrance of the Royal Sonesta Hotel, but there was no sign of her.

He paced the sidewalk, worry gnawing at his gut. He'd damned near imploded when she'd called and told him she was impersonating a hooker. Was she out of her *mind?* She had no concept of how rough the underbelly of a city could be, no idea of the things he'd seen as a policeman and district attorney.

A group of businessmen wearing convention tags, laughing loudly, walked past, leaving the scent of whiskey and beer in their wake. On the sidewalk across the street, a couple strolled together, their arms curved around each other's backs, their heads close together. A curvaceous streetwalker in a tight miniskirt and an obvious blond wig appeared around the corner. "Hi, Max," she said.

Holy cow. He'd known Emma was dressed to thrill, but he was unprepared for the actual sight of her. Her top plunged nearly to her waist and tied around her neck, leaving her entire back and much of her chest exposed. Her scrap of a black skirt barely covered the essentials. Her eyes were rimmed with black liner, and her impossibly full lips were painted a lurid red.

He stared at the fake blond hair streaming from her head like a grass hula skirt. "Nice hair."

Emma's hand flew to the wig. "I didn't want to be recognized."

"Mission accomplished." His gaze skimmed to the generous cleavage exposed by her plunging red top and scowled. "Where did you find that outfit—Hoochies 'R' Us?"

She regarded him with obstinate eyes. "I'm pretending to be a call girl."

"I hate to tell you, but you overshot the mark. You're in the ten-dollar streetwalker range."

Her chin tilted up. "I'm afraid I'm not up on the finer distinctions."

"That's not all you're not up on." He fixed her with a dark scowl. "Damn it, Emma, this is a stupid stunt. You could have gotten killed, walking around looking like that. Prostitutes are favorite targets of serial killers and rapists."

"Oh, please. I can take care of myself. Besides, I was careful."

His gaze raked over her. "If that's your idea of caution, I'd hate to see you walk on the wild side."

Her black-rimmed eyes flashed at him like blue flames in a ring of charcoal. "You're the one who said I shouldn't give up."

"I didn't say you should stroll the streets looking like a porn star!"

"Well, it just so happens I found a bartender and a pross who were willing to talk."

"A *pross?*"

Her chin tipped up belligerently. "That's what they called them on *NYPD Blue.*"

Oh, brother. "What did they say?"

"The girl saw Amber in the Quarter just last month. She said she'd cut her hair around Christmas, but it's grown back. The bartender said she has a drug or alcohol problem, and the last time he saw her, she muttered something about the Secret Service threatening to take her child."

Adrenaline pulsed through Max's veins. "Her child?"

Emma nodded. "Apparently she has a two- or three-year-old boy."

A child—of course. Suddenly everything clicked into place. A child would give the Secret Service the perfect leverage for keeping Amber quiet.

"Guess it wasn't such a stupid stunt, after all," she said with a smug smile.

He frowned at her, jarred once more by her hoochiefied appearance. "It was dumb and it was dangerous."

She put her hands on her hips. "Because I did it myself instead of waiting for you to rescue me?"

"No. Because even trained undercover officers don't work without backup. Damn it, Emma, you could have found yourself in a situation you couldn't get out of."

"Well, I didn't, so get over it. Are you going to help me find Grams and Harold or not?"

Max sucked in a frustrated breath. There was no point in arguing with her further, but damn it, she made him crazy. "I think I know where they are."

"You do?"

"Yeah." A scruffy-looking man walked by, ogling Emma. Max glared at him until he looked away. "I called a buddy with the French Quarter police, and he had his mounted patrol look for them. Unless there's another dozen elderly people partying in costumes tonight, they're at a club called the Cat and Mouse."

"Great. Let's go."

They set off down the sidewalk. Emma stalked silently beside him for half a block, then stumbled and pitched forward in her high heels.

Max caught her. "How the heck do you walk in those things?"

"Apparently not well."

Max grinned, glad that the cold war between them seemed to be thawing. He kept his hand on her arm, painfully aware that every straight man they passed was drooling like a St. Bernard.

"So I guess Grams and Harold are already married," she said as they entered the throng on Bourbon.

"For the meantime," Max replied.

She cast him a sideways look. "What do you mean?"

"I have power of attorney. I can override any contract my grandfather enters into."

"So—are you going to?"

"Do you want me to?"

A street musician's saxophone wailed over the hubbub of the street. Emma pondered the question for nearly a quarter of a block. "No," she finally said. "It's not our decision to make. And if Grams exchanged vows with Harold, then in her heart, they're married, legal contract or no legal contract." Emma glanced up at him as they stopped at an intersection. "Are you worried that the marriage isn't in your grandfather's best interests?"

"Are you kidding? This stunt aside, Dorothy's the best thing that's happened to my grandfather since my grandmother died."

The traffic cleared and they crossed the street. Four college-aged young men crossing in the opposite direction leered at Emma and nudged each other, sloshing their beers in the process. Max tightened his grip on Emma's arm, his stomach clenching like a baseball glove around a ball.

Another block up Bourbon, a red neon sign of a cartoon cat and mouse came into view across the street. "There it is," Emma said, wobbling in her heels as she picked up speed.

Even by Bourbon Street standards, the bar was loud and rowdy. The tune "Rocket Man" blasted out the open door, accompanied by shrieking, shaky vocals. A crowd stood in the doorway, clapping along to the music, occasionally bursting into boisterous cheers.

Max held Emma's hand as they waded into the crowd. As bars went, this one was brightly lit, largely because a lighted stage took up half of one red-lacquered wall. The decor was that of a 1950s diner, all black and white and red, but it was hard to see the actual room for all the people in it. Max's eye scanned the mob of faces, looking for Harold or Dorothy.

Emma suddenly clapped both hands over her mouth, her eyes as round as whitewall tires. "Oh. My. God."

He followed her gaze to the stage, his mind immediately following her thoughts. A skinny man in a silver lamé spacesuit wagged a pancake-flat backside at the crowd. Beside him, a short, roly-poly Marilyn Monroe impersonator in a blond wig and the classic white halter dress teetered on four-inch heels. The spaceman jerkily bumped and ground to the rhythm, while the round Marilyn impersonator wiggled an ample fanny at the shrieking audience.

"No. No way." Emma had to be mistaken. His grandfather had always been the picture of decorum, overly concerned about appearances and the perceptions of others. Hadn't he insisted that they portray a perfect family despite all their problems? He would never do anything so undignified.

The spaceman did a fast spin and shimmied to the front of the stage. And there, through the open window in the round Plexiglas space helmet, shone the grinning, eighty-one-year-old face of his grandfather.

"Holy Moses," Max gasped.

The crowd burst into a raucous round of applause. His grandfather bowed and held out his silver-gloved hand to his dancing partner. The blonde spun around and sure enough, Dorothy's elfin face beamed out from under the wig. She put her hands on her knees and gave her best imitation of Marilyn's smile. His granddad punched a button on a remote-control device attached to his wide metallic belt, and the back of Dorothy's' skirt flew up in the air, à la Marilyn's famous pose. The crowd erupted in applause.

༂

"Work it, Granny!"

"Wooo-hoo!"

Dorothy's heart floated above her, riding the wave of

whistles, cheers, and applause. She blew air kisses with both hands as she straightened from the cheesecake pose, then curtsied to the crowd. My goodness, she'd never had so much fun in her life. Pushing a lock of fake blond curls out of her eyes, she shot Harold a sultry smile, then leaned close to the microphone. "Thank you, thank you very much," she said in a breathy Marilyn voice, setting off a fresh roar of cheers. She handed the microphone to Harold.

"I want to thank ground control for a successful mission," Harold intoned in somber astronaut fashion. "But mostly, I want to thank this lovely lady, because when she's by my side, I don't have to leave Earth to feel out of this world."

The crowd burst into more cheers. Harold leaned forward to kiss her, causing Dorothy's heart to somersault. The helmet opening was too small for their lips to meet, so they settled for sticking out their tongues and touching the tips. An explosion of laughter, cheers, and applause shook the room.

"You make me see stars," Dorothy murmured to Harold.

"You send me to the moon."

A heavyset man with a beard took the stage, a microphone in hand. "Let's hear it for Dorothy and Harold!" he said. The crowd whooped and hollered again. "And now, Brad from Boise is going to sing 'Cracklin' Rosie.'"

A balding man in a white business shirt and loosened tie climbed onstage as Harold helped Dorothy down.

"Grams," she heard someone in the crowd say.

Dorothy stopped in her tracks.

"What's the matter, dear?" Harold asked.

"I thought I heard Emma." Dorothy craned her neck,

trying to see over the head of a floozy-looking blonde right in front of her.

"Grams, it's me."

The voice seemed to be coming from the blonde. "Emma?" Dorothy's hand flew to her chest. Lord have mercy—what was the child doing, dressed up like a trollop? And there was Max, standing behind her.

Oh—they must have learned about their wedding plans and decided join in! With a delighted grin, Dorothy hugged Emma. "I'm so glad you came to help us celebrate! We were afraid you wouldn't approve, or we would have invited you to start with."

Dorothy released Emma and hugged Max, then stepped back and looked him over. "Why aren't you in costume?"

"I, uh . . ."

He looked a little flummoxed. Poor dear—he was probably too uptight to cut loose and get silly.

"Never mind. It's not everyone's thing." She turned back to Emma. "Are you supposed to be someone famous, dear?"

"No. I'm actually—" The off-key notes of "Cracklin' Rosie" boomed from the man on stage. Dorothy cupped her hand to her ear to hear over the nasal tenor. "Never mind," Emma said. "I'll tell you later."

Dorothy patted her arm. "If you'd rather keep your fantasy private, well, that's all right with me. I'd suggest you share it with Max, though." She winked at him. "The important thing is, you're both here."

Max cleared his throat. "So—the deed is done?"

"The deed?" My goodness, but young people were nosy. "Well, not yet. We just got married."

Max laughed, as if she'd said something funny. "Congratulations and best wishes to both of you."

Oh, how wonderful! Max had power of attorney, and Dorothy had been half afraid he'd raise a ruckus. "Thank you."

"Yes. Thanks." Harold stuck out his silver-gloved hand, and Max shook it.

Emma's black-rimmed eyes looked suspiciously damp. "I second that."

Dorothy gave her another tight squeeze, then held out her left hand, pinky and fourth finger extended. "Harold and I bought matching rings. What do you think?"

Emma took her hand and gazed at the wide gold band. "It's lovely."

Harold put his arm around Dorothy. "Not as lovely as my bride."

Oh, how she loved this man! Dorothy placed her palm on his silver lamé chest. "Don't I have a dashing groom?"

Emma grinned as her gaze moved over Harold's costume. "You certainly have a distinctive one."

"I never knew you wanted to be an astronaut, Granddad," Max said.

There were probably a lot of things Max didn't know about his grandfather—and a lot Harold didn't know about Max, Dorothy thought. Hopefully that would all change once the two of them cleared the air.

"I've always been fascinated with outer space," Harold said.

"And I always wanted to be glamorous, if only for an evening," Dorothy added.

Emma looked from one to the other. "So . . . were you two dressed like this for the ceremony?"

"Oh, no," Dorothy said. "I wore a lovely cream-colored dress, and Harold wore a dark suit. Ruby and Pearl took pictures, and then we all went to the costume shop."

"Speaking of Ruby and Pearl, where are they?" Emma asked.

"They're with the other girls at that table over there."

Dorothy turned and pointed across the room, where her five friends sat laughing and sipping enormous hurricanes.

☙

Emma turned as well, and immediately felt her jaw drop.

"Saints preserve us," Max murmured beside her.

It was a saint-invoking sight, all right. Lena's enormous breasts spilled out of a black-and-red Playboy bunny outfit, her gray hair topped with rabbit ears. Beside her sat Helga, dressed as a lumpy Catwoman, her plastic glasses perched over her black mask. Marjorie was crammed into a fluffy pink tutu, the spaghetti straps digging into her plump shoulders like knives into meatballs. The two sisters, Ruby and Pearl, were decked out as naughty nurses. Their tight white dresses ended at the top of their drumstick-shaped legs, revealing red garters attached to sheer white hosiery.

"You missed Pearl and Ruby's performance of 'St. James Infirmary,'" Grams said. "They were a little off-key because they're hard of hearing, but they were very entertaining. The other gals sang 'What's New, Pussycat?'"

"That had to be a crowd pleaser," Max said dryly.

"Where are the men?" Emma asked.

"In the back with some new friends," Harold said.

"Friends?" Max asked warily.

Harold nodded. "Some very nice fellows are buying them drinks."

"I think we'd better check this out," Max murmured to

Emma. He took her arm and followed Grams and Harold through the loud crowd as Brad from Boise butchered the song at the top of his lungs.

"There they are," Grams said brightly. "Don is dressed like a cowboy because he admired John Wayne." The heavy-set elderly man wore a child-sized cowboy hat, a bandana that looked like a bib, and a pair of tight suede chaps over his navy Sansabelt pants.

"Buster loves motorcycles, but he has a plate in his head, so he can't ride them." The potbellied little man next to him wore a fringed black leather jacket, black leather pants, enormous aviator sunglasses, and a do-rag.

"And Arnie says he applied to the police academy when he was young, but he couldn't pass the physical." The diminutive former accountant sported a blue policeman's uniform with an oversized badge and a too-large police hat sitting sideways on his head.

"Oh, Jeez," Emma muttered. "They're the Village People."

"Oh, no, dear," Dorothy said earnestly. "They're all natives of Chartreuse."

Three impeccably groomed young men sat at the long table with them. Max leaned close to Emma's ear. "Do you think the old guys have any idea those men are hitting on them?"

"No." The idea shocked Emma as well. "Do you think they really are?"

"My guess is they're male prostitutes thinking they've found some deep pockets."

A shirtless young man in a black leather vest and a gelled mohawk sauntered up to Harold. "Nice duds, dude." He fingered the silver lamé on Harold's sleeve.

Harold's eyebrows flew up behind his helmet. He pulled back his arm. "Umm—thanks."

The young man smiled, revealing a tongue stud. "It's great to see a guy your age embracing your orientation. Been out long?"

"Out of what?" Harold asked.

"You know." The young man winked. "Out."

Harold furrowed his brow. "I get out all the time."

The man laughed. "I mean out of the closet."

"Oh, they don't keep me in one. I have my own apartment."

Max stepped forward and took Harold's arm. "Come on, Granddad. Let's go join your buddies."

Buster lifted a whiskey glass as they approached, his mirrored sunglasses crooked on his nose. "Won'erful party!" he slurred.

"Yeah." Don nodded. The motion made the John Wayne wannabe totter on his chair. "We've met some t'rific people!"

They were soused. Emma's brow buckled in a worried frown. "Mr. Rouquette, I think you've had enough," she said gently. "And Mr. Arnie, are you supposed to be drinking with your blood pressure medicine?"

"Oh, I'm feelin' just fine!" Arnie said as his police hat dipped over his left eye.

Max cleared his throat. "I hate to be a party pooper, but it's time for all of you to go back to Sunnyside."

"It's way too early!" Grams exclaimed.

Emma put her hand on her grandmother's arm. "Grams, Mrs. Schwartz is very upset that you took off in the Sunnyside van."

"Why on earth would she care? It's there for the residents of the center, and ten of them are with us. That's more than go on the Monday Wal-Mart outing, and we'll have it back before then."

"But you're not the authorized driver, and you didn't get approval to take it. And you shouldn't have brought Arnie. He's on the Alzheimer's floor, and he can only leave if he's signed out."

"But look at him. He's doing fine."

The slight man did, indeed, appear to be feeling no pain. His policeman's hat hung over his eyebrows, and a handcuff dangled from his left wrist as he lifted an enormous hurricane. Arnie tried to put the straw in his mouth but only succeeded in poking his ear.

"That's not the issue," Max said. "The issue is, if you're not back by midnight, Mrs. Schwartz is going to call the state police."

"Oh, fooey," Grams said.

"Thaz ridicaloose," Arnie slurred.

"Well, that's the way it is," Max said firmly. "Not to mention that all three of you are inebriated enough to be arrested for public intoxication. It's time to go."

It took considerable effort, but Emma and Max finally got the men on their feet and moving, albeit unsteadily, toward the ladies' table. The bunny, the ballerina, and Cat Woman were ready to go, but the naughty-nurse sisters put up a fuss.

"We wanted to sing again," Ruby complained, straightening the starched nurse's cap atop her thin white curls.

"I'm sorry, but if we don't leave, Harold and I will have spend our wedding night in the pokey."

"What did she say?" Ruby asked Pearl.

"She doesn't want to do the pokey," Pearl said loudly.

"Why not? I thought that was what wedding nights were all about."

Max extended his hand and helped the ladies, one by one, to their feet. Every eye in the bar followed them as they herded the bizarre group to the exit.

"You'd better drive the van, since you're an employee of the center," Max said to Emma. "I can bring you back for your car tomorrow."

"Oh, I can drive Emma's car back tonight," Grams said. "I'm the designated driver, so I stayed sober."

The thought of Grams behind the wheel of her Saturn made Emma cringe.

Grams saw it. "I'm a very safe driver," she said huffily.

"So was Mario Andretti," Harold said.

Grams sniffed. "I haven't gotten a ticket in more than twenty years." She turned to her new husband and batted her eyes. "Besides, Harold, if you and I drive back together, we can have a little private time."

The tender look they exchanged made Emma cave. "Okay. Fine. Where's the van?"

Dorothy named the parking garage. Max took her keys and parking receipt, then returned with the van a few minutes later.

As the elderly people piled in, Max handed the keys to Emma. "I called Mrs. Schwartz and told her you were on your way."

"Thanks," Emma said, grateful he'd handled the dreaded task of talking to the old witch. "I'll drive Grams and Harold to my car and see them off, then head back to Chartreuse."

"I'll be along in a while."

He was up to something. Emma narrowed her eyes. "What are you going to do?"

"Just check out a few things. I'll talk to you tomorrow."

He was going to follow up on what she'd found out.

"Why do I have the feeling your Superman cape is about to come out of retirement?"

"Drive carefully."

He was the one who needed to be careful. "Max—maybe we should just table this whole thing until after the election."

"This isn't Chartreuse. No one's going to recognize me." He opened the driver's door to the van.

"But—"

"I'll be fine," he said as she climbed in. "What happens in New Orleans stays in New Orleans."

That hasn't been my experience, she thought as he shut her door and ambled away.

༶

Louis ducked around the corner as Emma drove off with the vanload of old geezers, barely able to contain his excitement. Oh, man—this was awesome. Thanks to that old lady Iris who'd tipped him off, he'd followed the gang of old folks from Chartreuse and documented their every move. And now he had shots of Emma dressed like a pole dancer with the DA, as well.

He leaned against the brick wall in the alley and clicked the review feature on his camera. Oh, yeah, he had some great stuff. He had photos of Emma's grandmother and her friends coming out of the courthouse, piling into the van at the costume shop, dancing and singing in the French Quarter, and generally looking like a bunch of inebriated idiots. That was a big enough coup in and of itself, but catching Emma dressed as a ho, with Max Duval—well, it was enough to make headlines in the mainstream press. He could sell this to some big mags—*People* or *USA Today*, maybe. At the very least, he'd get a premium from the tabloids. He might even get a bidding war going.

"Louis, my man, you are a total rock star," he murmured proudly to himself. No doubt about it; this was his ticket to the big leagues.

He was about to step out of the alley when he saw Max striding purposefully down the street, like a man on a mission. Where the hell was he going? Louis couldn't imagine that this story could get any better, but you never knew. While he was here, he might as well see what Max was up to.

Taking care to stay at least a half block behind him, Louis slunk out of the alley and followed Max.

CHAPTER TWENTY-THREE

*T*he side street smelled of stale beer and urine. Max stepped over a suspicious puddle as he made his way down the sidewalk to the ratty end of the French Quarter, toward a bar named the So Cool Club. One of his contacts at the Orleans Parish DA's office had told him that it was a between-johns hangout for high-dollar prostitutes and call girls. With a little luck, maybe he'd find someone who knew Amber's whereabouts.

The sign was small and wooden, hanging from two hooks under the black wrought-iron balcony of the two-story building. He pushed open the heavy door and was hit by a cloud of cigarette smoke and twangy country-western music. He blinked against the sting of the smoke and paused, letting his eyes adjust to the dim lighting.

It was a real dive. The music came from a backless radio sitting on the concrete floor, propped against the scuffed, '70s-era paneled wall. A Spanish-looking iron chandelier hung off-center in the room, dangling from a black chain looped onto a ceiling hook. About five of the small tables that dotted the room were occupied, several by obvious working girls.

The brightest spot in the long, narrow room was the mirrored bar at the back, lined with lighted shelves of whiskey bottles. Two women sat on barstools on the left side of the long bar. On the other side, a woman in a black tank top and a short jeans skirt stood between one of the two empty barstools and a burly man with a shaved head.

Max's gaze fixed on the jeans-skirted woman. From the back, she looked just like Emma—straight dark hair, good legs, and a slim build. Her butt was more pear-shaped, but then, so was the butt of the woman in the video.

Max's pulse quickened. Could she be Amber? Nah. That would be too much of a coincidence. The odds had to be . . . what? He mentally tried to calculate them. What were the chances of finding a call girl who looked just like Emma from the back, in a bar where call girls were known to congregate?

Max's heart rate shifted into even higher gear. Maybe it wasn't such a long shot, after all. It was worth checking out before he showed his hand.

Max made his way to the back and slid onto on empty barstool beside the woman. The bartender, a frizzy-haired blonde in her mid-forties, looked up and flashed Max a flirtatious smile. "What can I get you?"

"A draft, please."

Max looked over at the miniskirted woman. Her nose and chin were both long and sharp, and the predatory smile she shot him did nothing to soften them. "Hi, handsome. Don't think I've seen you here before."

Max automatically went into undercover mode. "That's because this is my first time in New Orleans."

"Where're ya from?"

The Cracklin' Rosie singer came to mind. "Boise."

"In town on business?"

Max nodded. "A sales conference."

The bartender set an icy mug in front of him. Max pulled out his wallet, extracted a five and handed it to the bartender. The woman eyed his wallet. "What do you sell?"

What the hell did people buy in Boise? Max shoved the wallet back in his pocket and took a stab at it. "Tractor parts."

She nodded and lifted a wine glass to her lips. "So . . . are you looking for some company?"

"I might be." He took a sip of his beer. "What's your name?"

"What do you want it to be?" She bent forward to give him a better view of her cleavage. "I can be anyone you like, sugar."

"Oh, yeah?" He looked her up and down, as if he were considering it, then leaned close. "I like girls with tattoos. Do you have any?"

"I sure do, sugar."

"Oh, yeah? Do you have one on your ass?"

She put a hand on her hip and gave him a seductive smile. "You'll have to find out for yourself."

"I was hoping you'd just tell me."

"No telling. Just showing."

Max gave her what he hoped was a charming smile. "So show me."

"Have you got a car or a room?"

"We can just go to the restroom. All I want is for you to moon me."

"Shoot, sugar—why settle for the moon, when you can have the sun and stars, as well?"

Max thought fast. "I, uh, don't want to cheat on my wife."

She nodded as if this were a plausible explanation.

Max edged forward. "I'll give you twenty-five dollars."

The bulky bald man sitting on the other side of her abruptly stood up, his barstool squeaking on the concrete floor. "Okay, pervert. Put up your hands."

Shock shot through Max. "What?"

The man stepped toward Max and flashed a badge. "You're under arrest for soliciting a lewd and lascivious act."

A barstool crashed to the floor as the two other women at the bar scurried for the exit. Most of the other patrons jumped up from their tables and hustled out the door, as well.

Max's stomach sank. "You don't understand. This is all a big mistake."

"You bet it is, buddy. Maybe the biggest of your life. "

"No, you don't understand. I wasn't soliciting. I was just—"

"Save it for the judge." Cold metal snapped around his wrists. "Let's go."

The cop and the woman ushered him outside. This couldn't get any worse, Max thought as they exited the bar.

And then a flashbulb went off in Max's eyes.

CHAPTER TWENTY-FOUR

*E*mma awoke the next morning to the sound of Snookems barking. She opened her eyes and squinted against the sunlight streaming through her sheer lace curtains, then groggily eyed her alarm clock and bolted upright. Ten minutes to nine. Had she overslept? Was it a weekend? And then the events of the night before came flooding back.

She hadn't gotten the van back to Sunnyside until after midnight, and then she'd had to endure half an hour of Mrs. Schwartz's ranting and raving—not to mention her scathing remarks about the way Emma was dressed. Emma had pulled off the wig, tried to wipe off as much makeup possible, and borrowed a ten-sizes-too-large sweater from Ruby, but she'd still looked like she'd just serviced the entire seventh fleet. It had taken Emma another half hour to convince the old battle ax that Grams and Harold were legally married and there was no reason her grandmother couldn't spend the night in Harold's room.

Snookems went into another frenzy of barking, and the doorbell sounded. Emma's pulse quickened; maybe it was

Max. Pushing her hair from her eyes, she grabbed her yellow chenille robe and stumbled down the stairs, Snookems trailing behind her. She scooped him up and peered through one of the sidelights beside the door.

It wasn't Max, it was Grams—wearing a pink t-shirt embroidered with butterflies and twisting the strap of her hot pink purse, her face uncharacteristically solemn. Emma pulled the door open.

"Oh, did I wake you, sweetheart?" Grams flashed what was meant to be a smile, but she was a terrible actress. Her eyes were troubled, her bouncy demeanor unusually flat.

"What's wrong?" Emma asked. "Are you okay?"

Grams stepped into the foyer and petted Snookems's head. "I'm fine, dear, but I need to talk to you."

"What's going on? Is something wrong with Harold?"

"Not Harold, dear." Grams headed for the living room.

Not Harold, but someone else. Emma's heart pounded as she followed after her. "Max? Is Max okay?"

Uh-oh. Grams' eyes darted evasively away. "Well, he's gotten himself into a bit of a pickle."

"What kind of a pickle?"

"I don't think I can really explain it."

This was completely out of character. Grams was never at a loss for words.

"Why don't you sit down, dear, and I'll show you a tape of the morning news." Grams pulled a video tape from her purse.

Emma's internal terror alert rose from orange to red. "Something about Max was on the news?"

"Instead of trying to explain it, I think it's best for you to just see it for yourself." Grams put the tape in the VCR, then sat down on the sofa and patted the adjacent cushion. Moving like a wooden doll, Emma sank down beside her.

Grams picked up the remote and pushed the button. "Take a deep breath, dear."

If she were breathing any deeper, her lungs would explode.

The screen flickered to life. A middle-aged news anchor with an unnatural tan stared out with a self-important air. "The district attorney of Pontchartrain Parish was taken into custody at a New Orleans bar last night for soliciting a lewd and lascivious act."

Emma gasped. "Oh, no."

The image shifted to a man wearing a white shirt, business trousers, and handcuffs being assisted into a police car. He turned toward the camera, a deep scowl etched on his face. *Max.* Emma covered her mouth with both hands.

"Pontchartrain District Attorney Max Duval was arrested at the So Cool Club in the French Quarter after he allegedly propositioned an undercover police officer. We have an unconfirmed report that he asked the woman to expose her bare buttocks in exchange for cash. Mr. Duval's spokesman, Terrence O'Neil, said the incident was a misunderstanding. Mr. Duval was released this morning. No charges have been filed against him."

The screen went back to the anchor desk, where a chipper blonde sat beside the male anchor. "He's up for election this Saturday, isn't he?"

The man nodded. "That's right. And he's scheduled to debate his opponent in two days."

"He'll have to give some kind of explanation then," the blonde said perkily.

The man nodded. "I would imagine so——if he doesn't withdraw from the race."

"Is that a possibility?" the female anchor asked.

"His opponent, Dirk Briggs, is calling for that. We'll have an interview with Briggs later this evening."

Grams clicked off the video. They both sat there, staring at the blank screen for a moment.

"Why on earth would Max do a thing like that?" Grams asked.

"Because of me." Emma sat motionless as the implications sank in. This was a campaign-tanking debacle, a disaster of titanic proportions. Max's career was scuttled, and she was entirely responsible.

"I don't understand," Grams said.

Emma twisted her fingers together. "He's trying to find the girl who was with Ferguson. He was looking for the tattoo."

"Well, thank heavens!" Grams blew out a sigh of relief. "I knew there had to be a logical explanation."

Except there was nothing logical about it. It was completely illogical for a man with an upcoming election to risk it all to find a hooker with a tattoo. He'd become an object of ridicule and scorn. He'd put himself in the very situation he was trying to get her out of.

It was irrational. It was reckless.

It was wonderful.

Because there was only one reason he'd do a thing like that. He loved her.

The thought flooded her heart, expanding and stretching it, filling up empty chambers she didn't even know it had. *Max loved her!* How amazing. How awesome. How . . .

Awful. Loving her had cost Max his career—a career he'd devoted himself to, a career he believed in, a career he was fighting to keep.

"He just needs to go on television and explain he was trying to help you out," Grams said.

"He does, but he won't." Emma was sure of it, surer than she was of her own name. "He won't put me at the center of another scandal."

"Well, you need to convince him."

Conviction swelled in Emma's chest. "I need to do more than that." If Max had been willing to put everything on the line to help her, how could she do any less? She couldn't—she *wouldn't*—let him lose his good name because of her.

Grams's words swirled through Emma's mind: *When you love someone, their burdens are yours, and yours are theirs, and it's your heart's desire to help them any way you can.*

Helping Max was the pure desire of her heart and soul.

Emma tightened the sash of her bathrobe, squared her shoulders, and turned to her grandmother. "Grams, can you show me that patterned-breathing exercise again?"

CHAPTER TWENTY-FIVE

$\mathcal{M}$ ax, you have to say something." Terrence paced the carpet in Max's office Thursday afternoon as Max sat at his desk, turning a boat-shaped paperweight in his hands, staring at his image on the TV recessed into his mahogany bookshelf.

The footage of a policeman putting Max into the back seat of a patrol car, along with video of Dorothy, Harold, Emma, and the entire freakish wedding party, had aired on every newscast all day—not only on the local channels, but also on CNN, MSNBC, Fox News, the major networks, and probably every station on the face of the planet. That punk reporter Louis had been interviewed again and again, describing how he'd surreptitiously followed the van, documented the wedding, and tailed Max to the bar. The sneaky little snot had not only shot still photographs but also videotaped some of the proceedings on his handy-dandy cell phone. He was even scheduled to be on tomorrow's *Today Show*.

The story was a sensation—the bizarre, can-you-believe-how-crazy-these-people-are story of the day. Make that of the week. Hell, maybe of the whole freakin' year.

And the TV coverage wasn't even the worst of it. Max looked at the stack of newspapers piled on his desk. *USA Today,* the *Wall Street Journal,* the *New York Times,* the *Washington Post,* the *New Orleans Times-Picayune*—all of them carried a photo of Max in handcuffs, the newlyweds onstage at the karaoke bar, the elderly folks in costume, and worst of all, Emma in that hooker getup. The photos featured captions like, "Go Granny, Go Granny, Go Granny Go*!*," "Arresting Development for Parish DA," "DA's Booty Quest a Bummer," "Retirees Go Wild," and "Geriatrics Get Jiggy."

Max had tried to call Emma repeatedly, but her cell phone was turned off. He'd tried to reach Dorothy, as well, but she and his grandfather had apparently taken their phone off the hook, and when he'd gone by Sunnyside, they were nowhere to be found.

Terrence sank into a chair across from Max's desk as Max hit the TV's mute button. "The debate is tomorrow, and the media are crawling all over this town. You can't keep refusing to talk. You have to make a statement."

Max turned his boat paperweight in his hand. "I wasn't charged with a crime." It had taken two hours of questioning, four hours of waiting around, and five minutes of speaking with the New Orleans DA, but all charges had been dropped. "As far as the law is concerned, it's a nonevent."

Unfortunately, as far as the voters were concerned, it was huge.

Terrence rubbed his brow. "It would have been bad enough just having your name linked with geriatric swingers and the woman who boffed Ferguson to death, but this booty-flash business needs an explanation. I think that if you just put your relationship with Emma in the context of your grandparents, the voters will—"

Max interrupted. "I'm not going to drag her into this."

"*She* dragged *you* into this."

"No. This was my decision. She didn't want me involved."

"Wish to hell you'd listened to her," Terrence muttered. "Bet she wishes so, too."

Max's chair squeaked as he leaned back in it and blew out a sigh. Damn it, he'd only been trying to help her. If he could find the call girl, he could clear Emma's name, and all of her problems would be solved.

He suddenly froze as Emma's words ran through his mind: *"You don't get to decide that. I get to make those choices."*

Where did he get off thinking he knew what was best for her? He'd been trying to tell her how to live her life—which was exactly the same thing his grandfather had done to him.

He stared blankly at his desk, staggered by the realization. More of Emma's words steamrolled through his mind. *"You don't have that right."*

Damn it, she was right. He didn't. And he, of all people, should have known that. She never would have been in the French Quarter dressed up like a streetwalker if he hadn't meddled in her life. The end result was that he'd sabotaged her efforts to lie low and fit into the community.

Terrence pushed out of the chair, shoved his hands in his pockets, and paced in front of the bookcase. "We've got to implement some serious CYA here, Max."

"Well, I can't implicate Emma."

"Can't, or won't?"

"Same thing."

Terrence suddenly froze. "Looks like she did it for you."

"What?"

Terrence pointed at the TV screen. "There she is."

Sure enough, Emma's face filled the screen. She was seated at the end of the Channel Four anchor desk, her hands clasped on top of it, wearing a cream jacket with a soft raspberry top underneath, her eyes large and scared. Max dove for the remote and clicked the volume on.

"Joining us for an exclusive interview this evening is Emma Jamison, the woman at the center of President-Elect Ferguson's death," the news anchor said. "Ms. Jamison claims to have information about the arrest of Pontchartrain Parish DA Max Duval last night. What can you tell us about that?"

Emma's throat visibly contracted as she swallowed. "I-I—" Her voice broke. The color drained from her face, and her fingers gripped the desk top. She drew in a series of short, panting breaths, then exhaled.

The news anchor stared at her, clearly disconcerted. "Are you all right?"

She looked like a cornered puppy about to puddle the floor. She drew in more rapid, shallow breaths and blew out again. "I-I'm sorry," she gasped. More short breaths, followed by a long exhale. "I have a-a phobia a-about TV cameras. I-I get panic attacks."

The reporter's eyes rounded with alarm. "Are you having one now?"

She nodded, then sucked in six more fast breaths. She looked like she was about to pass out. The reporter glanced over his shoulder, as if he were looking for off-set direction.

Emma exhaled. "This is why—why I've never given a TV interview."

"Really? So this is a first?"

She nodded, closed her eyes, and did that Lamaze-like pant again. "C-could I have some water?"

Someone's arm appeared on set and handed her a glass. Emma's hand shook as she lifted it to her mouth.

"What can you tell us about Mr. Duval's arrest?" the reporter asked.

"He was try-trying to help me."

"How?"

Emma inhaled more shallow breaths. "H-he was trying to find the woman who was with President-Elect Ferguson. He was looking for a call girl with a tattoo like the one in the video."

"Why?"

Emma's chin lifted. "B-because he believes it wasn't me, and he thinks that a good district attorney should protect the innocent as well as prosecute the guilty."

"If that's what he was doing, why won't he just come out and say it?"

"Be-because he doesn't want to drag me into another scandal."

"If there *is* another woman, why hasn't she come forward?"

"I th-think the Secret Service threatened her, in order to hide their role in hiring a call girl."

The anchor held his hand to his ear, as if he were listening to something in his earpiece. "Back to Mr. Duval—how would you describe your relationship with him?"

"We know each other through our grandparents, and we're friends." Emma swallowed and took another deep breath. "And for what it's worth, we're about to become long-distance friends, because I've taken a new job out of state."

The music came up, signaling the end of the newscast. "I'm afraid we're out of time, but we'd like continue this interview and share it with the viewers at ten o'clock," the anchor said.

Emma nodded.

"Thank you very much for joining us, Ms. Jamison."

Emma gave a tremulous smile.

"Well, I'll be damned," Terrence muttered, clicking off the TV.

"Yeah." Max slumped back in his chair like a man who'd been shot. Emma had just faced down her worst fear, and she'd done it in front of millions of people.

For him. She'd done it for his sake. And now she was planning to move away because she thought it was in his best interest.

It took him a moment to realize that Terrence was talking. "I gotta say, I never would have believed that having your name associated with hers would help you, but I'll be damned if it didn't. You're still in a hell of a mess, Max, but it's a better mess. It's still a long shot, but at least now there's a shot."

Max rose from his chair. "I've got to go find her." By the time he drove to the TV station in New Orleans, she'd be long gone, but Dorothy would know what her plans were. Hopefully Dorothy was back at Sunnyside. Max grabbed his jacket and headed for the door.

"Hey, Max. You can't go. We need to form a new strategy."

"Later."

"But this is urgent!"

Max continued out the door. As far as he was concerned, nothing was more urgent than getting to Emma.

⌇

Harold opened his apartment door to find a pretty young woman and a hefty man with a large camera standing in the hallway. The girl had dark hair and the whitest teeth Harold had ever seen. Real teeth couldn't be that straight and blindingly white, so they must be fake. Poor dear, how awful to have lost her natural choppers so early in life.

"Are you Harold Duval?"

"Yes, that's me."

"I'm Lisa Leblanc. I'm a news reporter with MSNBC."

"Oh. Well, I don't have much news to report."

She gave a little half-smile, as if she weren't sure whether he was kidding or not. "Can we come in and ask you a few questions?"

Harold peered at the man behind her. The camera on his shoulder sort of looked like the kind used in the Duval-ware TV commercials. The thought made time start to roll back like a window shade.

"Mr. Duval?" the young lady repeated. "Can we come in and talk to you?"

Harold knit his brows, trying to hold his thoughts together. Those ads had been shot a long time ago—hadn't they? Yes, he was pretty sure it had been a while. These folks weren't here to shoot a commercial. All the same, it would be rude not to let them in for a chat. He stepped back and pulled the door wider. "Sure."

The cameraman turned on a bright light on top of the camera as he crossed the threshold. Harold squinted against the glare as the gal with the dentures connected her microphone to the camera. "Can we sit at your dining room table?" she asked.

"Of course." Harold held out a chair for her, then sat down himself. The cameraman squatted beside them, that blasted light shining in his eyes like high noon at the beach.

"I understand you got married last night," the woman said.

Was it just last night? He couldn't keep track of time.

"You and your wife and your friends apparently had quite a party in the French Quarter," she prompted.

The spaceman suit was hanging on the door of his coat closet. Harold looked over at it and grinned. "Oh, yes. It was a humdinger."

"After you left the French Quarter, your grandson Max was arrested," she said. "What can you tell us about that?"

Arrested? Harold frowned. He and Dorothy had watched something on TV this morning, but he'd had swamphead and he hadn't quite followed it. Dorothy had said it didn't matter, it was all a misunderstanding, and Emma was going to clear it up.

Where *was* Dorothy? Seems like she'd said she had to go somewhere with Emma.

"Can you tell us anything about Max's arrest?" The woman asked, holding out the microphone.

"What was he arrested for?" Harold asked.

"Soliciting an undercover policewoman to expose her, umm, backside."

Good God Almighty! Harold squinted at her. "You're pulling my finger."

The cameraman laughed. "I think you mean leg."

Did he? That's not how Dorothy said it. Finger, leg—it

didn't much matter, when they were talking about Max asking to see a policewoman's patootie.

"It's not a joke, Mr. Duval."

"Why on earth would Max do a thing like that?"

"Emma Jamison says Max was trying to help clear her name. Do you know Emma?"

"Emma? Oh, yes. Yes, indeed!"

"What can you tell me about her?"

"Well, she's a real peach, that girl. She's been a god-send to the people who live here."

"Really?" The reporter's eyebrows rose in surprise. "In what way?"

"Oh, she's helped all of us confused folks find things better—she's painted walls and reorganized closets and labeled things. She's gone above and beyond the call of duty, that one."

The woman jotted something down in a long, skinny notebook. "How would you describe her relationship with your grandson?"

Harold scratched his jaw. "Well, now, that's a real puzzler. I'm not even sure they have one, although Dorothy says—"

A knock sounded at the door. Boy, his apartment was busier then Grand Central Station today. "Come in," he called.

Why, there was Max. A smile broke out on Harold's face. Max didn't come to see him too often, other than to drop off his Pepsis. "Hi there, son. These people were just asking about you."

Max didn't look too happy to see them. His jaw got some kind of little muscle spasm. "Turn that thing off," he ordered the cameraman. "You're in a private residence, and you don't have permission to shoot."

"But he said—"

"Off." It wasn't a request; it was a command. "Now."

The light clicked off.

Max turned to the reporter, his face dark, his voice verging on ominous. "You need to leave."

The girl scrambled to her feet, the microphone in her hand. "Mr. Duval, if you don't mind, I have a few questions I'd like to ask you."

"I do mind." Max's face looked hard as the Rock of Gibraltar. "And you ought to be ashamed of yourself, barging into a dementia patient's home and trying to coerce him into an interview."

"I—" the girl stuttered.

Max held the door open. "Goodbye."

Max closed the door behind them, then turned to Harold. The old, uncomfortable awkwardness settled between them.

Max cleared his throat. "Those people are barracudas."

"Well, then, it's good they're gone."

Silence hung like an overstarched shirt, stiff and stodgy. Harold waved a hand to his brown leather sofa. "Have a seat. Can I get you a Pepsi?"

"No, thanks. I can't stay. I came by to see if Dorothy knew where I could find Emma."

"Dorothy's not here, but she left me a note." Harold bustled over to his refrigerator, glad to have a task to perform. He plucked a sheet of lined yellow paper from under a magnet and held it up. "Let's see. It says, 'I've gone to New Orleans with Emma. We plan to stay the night there to avoid the media in Chartreuse. See you tomorrow. Love, Dorothy.'" That last part—the love part—made Harold's chest feel warm and fuzzy.

Max gazed up at the ceiling and heaved a sigh. "Okay.

Thanks." He turned toward the door, his shoulders slumped.

"Max—wait." Harold's heart thumped hard against his ribs. He didn't know how to say the things that were pressing on his heart, but he urgently needed to try. "I have something I need to tell you before I forget."

For a moment, Max looked like he was about to give an excuse and bolt.

"I won't take up much of your time," Harold said. "Please. Have a seat."

Max reluctantly sank onto the sofa. Harold sat down across from him in a leather club chair, the glass coffee table between them, topped by the three-foot-high wooden eagle carving that Myrtle had given him on their fifth anniversary.

It felt like there was a lot more between them than a piece of glass-topped furniture and a carved bird. Harold looked down at his hands, then up at his grandson. "Max—I know you don't have much use for me, and I can't say that I blame you. All that stuff that happened between us . . ." Harold swallowed around a lump in his throat. "Well, I was bossy and obstinate and just plain wrong, and I want to apologize."

Surprise registered in Max's eyes. He shifted his weight, obviously uneasy. "I didn't think you remembered any of that."

"Sometimes I don't," Harold admitted. "But all too often, I do. And when I do, well, I guess it's just been easier to pretend I don't." He stared at the framed Duvalware magazine ads on the side table, his gaze settling on the photo of Max in his Superman cape. He'd been pretending long before he had dementia, he realized sadly. "I messed up something awful with your dad, and then I did the same with you."

Max wore his expressionless lawyer face, but he seemed to be listening.

"It's no excuse, but I wanted him to have all the things I didn't have growing up. I thought being a good father meant being a good provider, so I focused on business and let Myrtle handle everything at home. And that worked real well for a while, but then she died." Harold's voice broke off as the memory of those days sucked him down like quicksand. He shook his head, trying to keep from going under.

"After she was gone, I didn't know how to be a parent, and I was too heartsick to have been any good at it, anyway. I gave your father whatever he wanted, and, well . . . he grew up spoiled." The memories threatened to drag him down again. He kept talking, hoping that words would be a lifeline.

"I should have cut him loose and let him sink or swim when he became a man, but instead, I tried to put the brakes on his wild behavior. At the time, I thought I was doing the right thing. I wanted you to have the family I'd never had—the family I'd hoped to give my son. I wanted your life to be like those commercials." He gazed at the geometric shapes on the rug visible between his thin legs. "But I screwed it all up."

He looked up to see Max staring at the carved eagle. He still couldn't read his expression.

"I'm sorry, Max," Harold said. "I had no right to tell you what do with your life. I understand why you rebelled. Hell, you had to, in order to be your own man. I understand that now." Harold swallowed around a lump in his throat. "Truth is, I guess I understood it at the time, but I was too damn stubborn to admit I was wrong. But I was. I was wrong."

Max's gaze didn't waver from the carving. Harold couldn't tell what he was thinking, but it didn't matter. He had to get it all out, had to say everything that needed saying. "All these years—well, I thought it was too late. I thought I'd made my bed and I had to lie in it, that what was done was done. But since I've met Dorothy, I've learned a few things."

He glanced up and discovered that Max was looking at him, really looking at him, straight on, eye to eye. "I've learned it's never too late. The part of us that counts—the part of us that loves and learns and wants to give—well, that part doesn't get old or feeble or worn out. That part just keeps on growing, and it can grow bigger than all the other stuff if you let it."

Harold's voice grew thick with emotion. "So, Max—I don't know if you can forgive me or not, and I'll understand if you can't. But I want you to know that I love you. I'm proud of the man you've become. Hell, I'm proud you had the guts to stand up to me. And no matter how befuddled my mind might get, my heart will always keep that straight." He drew a shaky breath. "I just wanted you to know."

Max's eyes glittered. The next thing Harold knew, his grandson had rounded the coffee table, pulled him to his feet, and wrapped him in a bear hug. Max's arms were strong and hard, but Harold could feel a bit of Myrtle's tenderness in his grandson's embrace.

At length, the two men drew apart. Max cleared his throat. "While we're playing true confessions here, I need to apologize, too. You're not the only Duval who's hardheaded and stubborn."

"Well, you come by it honestly." Harold clapped him on the back and pulled back, then ran his hand down his face, because his eyes seemed to be watering. "We better not tell the women about this touchy-feely crap, or they'll expect us to be Nancy-boys all the time."

The side of Max's mouth quirked up in a grin. "We can't have that."

"No, we can't." Harold sniffed. "Don't know why women like all this emotional stuff, anyway. It's awkward as hell, if you ask me."

"Yeah."

Harold gave his cheek another swipe and decided to lighten things up. "Speaking of women—did you really try to get a policewoman to show you her rump?"

Max shoved his hands in his pockets and nodded. "I wanted to see if she had a dragonfly tattoo on her left cheek."

Max had a thing for tattooed ladies? Well, now, that was odd, but Harold had heard of odder things. Why, back in '52, he'd known a man who wanted his lady friends to wear jock straps and spank him with a flyswatter.

"I've gotta go." Max patted Harold's shoulder and turned toward the door. "See you later, Granddad."

"Don't be a stranger."

"I won't."

Harold watched the door close behind him, then scratched his head. Out of all the women in the world, why would Max hit on a policewoman? Why would he think she might have a butt tattoo, and why would he bribe her to show it if she did?

Harold shook his head as he turned toward his kitchen. "And people think *I'm* crazy," he muttered.

CHAPTER TWENTY-SIX

Someone needs to tell that D.A. in Louisiana that dating Emma Jamison, whooping it up in the French Quarter with a bunch of inebriated senior citizens, and asking a policewoman to moon you is not what they mean by political party.
                              —JAY LENO, *The Tonight Show*

After his escapades in the French Quarter this week, that Louisiana DA is going to change his campaign slogan. Instead of "Max Duval—Taking a Bite out of Crime," it's going to be "Max Duval: Taking the Dentures out of Your Shorts."
                              —DAVID LETTERMAN,
                                 Late Show with David Letterman

He's also considering a slogan based on the one Teddy Roosevelt used during the Great Depression—"A Chicken in Every Pot." It's going to be "A Defibrillator in Every Closet."
                              —DAVID LETTERMAN,
                                 Late Show with David Letterman

"I just came from the town hall, and you won't believe all the press that's here for the debate," Terrence said the next morning as he walked into Max's office. "All the major networks, CNN, MSBC, Fox News, and I don't know who all else."

"Great," Max said dryly.

"Normally I would think so." Terrence plopped in a chair opposite Max's desk, pulled out his handkerchief, and wiped his forehead. "But you know why they're here."

Oh, Max knew, all right. He'd stayed up until the wee hours of the morning, watching the late night comedians have a field day:

I hear all the night spots in the French Quarter are changing their marketing strategies because of Emma Jamison's grandmother and all those old folks partying in New Orleans. They're going to start adding early-bird specials to the stripper poles.
          —JAY LENO, *The Tonight Show*

You know the favorite song of all those old people partying at that karaoke bar with Emma Jamison's grandmother? "I'm Too Sexy for My Walker."
          —DAVID LETTERMAN,
               Late Show with David Letterman

What's the biggest problem after those senior citizens with Emma Jamison have an orgy? Trying to figure out whose dentures are whose.
          —JON STEWART, *The Daily Show*

Did you know that Emma Jamison and her

grandmother are the subject of genetic research? Scientists are trying to determine if skank always skips a generation.
　　　　　—STEPHEN COLBERT, *The Colbert Report*

After those party shots of Emma Jamison's grandmother hit the media, historians want to exhume Calvin Coolidge and see how he really died.
　　　　　—CONAN O'BRIEN,
　　　　　　　Late Night with Conan O'Brien

Max was a public figure, so he was fair game, but Dorothy, his grandfather, and Emma were not, and it was eating him alive that he'd caused them to become objects of ridicule.

Especially Emma. He was dying to talk to her, but she wasn't answering her cell phone, and Dorothy didn't have one because she thought cell phones ate your brain. He'd called Katie last night, but she hadn't been much help, either.

"All I know is that Dorothy went with Emma to the TV station to give her moral support, and they're trying to avoid the media," Katie had said. "I don't know when they'll be back."

"Has Emma really quit her job?"

"I'm afraid so." A forlorn sigh wafted through the phone receiver. "She's going to work at the Sunnyside corporate office in Florida. Both Emma and the company officials think she can keep a lower profile if she's not working directly with residents."

Max had hung up feeling worse than ever. How could he have been such a dolt? He'd ruined Emma's life just as she'd started to rebuild it. He'd meant to help her, but Emma had ended up having to help him.

Damn it, *he* was the one who did the rescuing. He wasn't supposed to be the rescuee. He didn't like being out of control. He didn't like feeling vulnerable. He didn't like being needy.

And when it came to Emma, he was all of those things.

"We need to go over your media statement," Terrence said, tapping a gnawed-to-the-quick fingernail on his bony thigh. "It's less than an hour before the debate begins, and you still haven't told me what you're going to say."

That was because Max wasn't entirely sure himself. His cell phone rang and he yanked it out of his pocket, praying it was Emma.

It wasn't. It was Dave. Max punched the button. "Hey, Dave. What's up?"

"Lots. I found her."

"Emma?"

"No. Amber."

Max jumped out of his chair, his heart pounding a mile a minute. "*The* Amber?"

"Yeah."

Max let out a whoop. "How . . . Where . . ."

"When I heard what a mess you were in, I decided to fly down to New Orleans and see what I could find out. Long story short, a transvestite bartender who'd talked to Emma had subsequently found out Amber's last name—it's Reynolds, by the way. On a hunch, I checked with Social Services, figuring that if she was a crackhead with a kid, chances were she'd had some run-ins with the system. And I hit pay dirt."

"Oh, man." Max stared out his office window at the

courthouse square, where the leaves of the giant oaks cast a dappled light over the statue of Lady Justice.

"Her little boy's in the foster system, and Amber is staying with a friend in Covington. I tracked her down, and thanks to Emma's interview on that newscast, she's semi-receptive to meeting with you. I'm with her now."

"Where are you?"

"At the IHOP in Covington. She's kind of skittish, though—I think she's afraid I'm Secret Service. You'd better hurry."

"I'm on my way."

Max hung up the phone to find Terrence staring at him in wide-eyed alarm. "You're going to have to postpone the debate," Max told him.

Terrence's already bulging eyes popped out further. "Are you crazy? I can't do that."

"You have to."

"There's no way. The networks are all here. This starts in less than an hour."

"You're an expert at stalling. You'll think of something."

The whites of Terrence's eyes looked like egg whites around a yolk. "If you're a no-show, they'll crucify you."

"My buddy found the woman who was with Ferguson," Max said, grabbing his jacket from the back of the chair. "If I don't meet her now, I'm afraid she'll change her mind."

"If you miss this debate, it's over," Terrence warned. "This debate will decide the election."

"Yeah, well, this meeting could decide the rest of Emma's life." Max strode to the door and opened it.

"And that's more important to you?"

"Hell, yes."

"You're walking away from your career," Terrence called as Max headed down the door.

Max knew it, yet at the same time, he knew something else, something bigger and more powerful and more life-changing than any job.

He loved Emma. And nothing, absolutely nothing, was more important than that.

❧

"I thought Max was going to be here," Harold murmured to Dorothy an hour and a half later. His mind was a little swampy, and he wasn't sure exactly where he was, but he was pretty sure it had something to do with Max. He craned his neck, trying to see around the rows of people sitting in front of him on folding chairs in the crowded meeting hall. A herd of TV news cameras huddled in front of a stage hung with red, white, and blue bunting, where some lame political hack with a gawd-awful comb-over stood behind one of the two podiums, yacking on and on. A female moderator in a blue suit sat in the center of the stage behind a red-draped table topped with a microphone and a glass of water.

"Max is running late," Dorothy whispered. "They delayed the debate as long as they could."

"I know I've probably asked this before, but where is he?"

"That's what everyone wants to know."

Worry tugged at Harold's stomach. "Do you think he's okay?"

"I hope so. The moderator said Max was detained because of a personal emergency."

"Personal emergency." Sometimes repeating a phrase

could help Harold remember it, at least for a little while. "I wonder what that means."

"I don't know."

"If he were our age, it might mean he'd wet his pants."

Dorothy tittered. The sound made Harold smile. He loved to hear her laugh, and knowing that he had been the cause of it made the sound all the sweeter. That was one thing dementia had taught him—enjoy the moments as they unfold. The past might be a blur and the future might be uncertain, but that wasn't such a bad deal, because joy was strictly a here-and-now proposition.

"By not showing up today, Max Duval has proven he's a coward," the man onstage said.

Indignation flooded Harold's chest. By God, no one was going to get away with saying that about his grandson. "That's a bald-faced lie!" he shouted.

"Shh!" The woman in front of him turned around, her face puckered like she'd just sucked a lemon.

"You'll have to be quiet or leave," the woman onstage said.

"I'll leave when I've had my say." Harold stood and glared at the man behind the podium with that Donald Trump hairdo. A murmur went through the room as every head turned in his direction. "My grandson is a hero. He saved his partner's life when he was a policeman, and he rescued more than forty people during Hurricane Katrina. What the heck have *you* done, besides fill the room with hot air?"

A roar of laughter arose from the audience. "Hey— that's Max's granddad," someone said.

The TV cameras swiveled toward him. The moderator tapped a pencil on her water glass and leaned toward her microphone. "Security, please escort this man from the building."

Dorothy jumped to her feet beside him. "We don't need an escort. We were just leaving." Two policemen headed toward them as they edged their way out of the row. One of them tried to take Dorothy's arm as she reached the aisle. She yanked it away. "Unhand me, young man!"

The audience erupted in laughter. A man with a TV camera scurried in front of them and walked backward, taping them, as the policemen meekly followed behind. They had nearly reached the exit at the back of the building when the steel double doors burst open with a metallic clang.

Dorothy stopped short. "Here's Max now!"

A buzz rippled through the audience as Max strode into the building.

Harold watched him march down the center aisle, accompanied by a scraggly brunette wearing scuffed white sandals, a short flowered skirt, and what looked to Harold like two men's undershirts. Her face was thin, her eyes had dark shadows, and her eyebrows looked like they'd been shaved off and drawn on. A tall, muscular man wearing jeans and a dark green polo shirt followed behind.

"Who are those people with him?" Harold asked.

"I don't know," Dorothy murmured.

The windbag at the podium froze as Max and the brunette climbed the side steps to the stage. Max said something to the moderator and then stepped up to the empty podium. He adjusted the microphone, then spoke into it. "I apologize for being late, but something urgent came up."

He paused as the audience hummed, then gestured to the tall man, who was standing on the edge of the stage. "My friend and former police partner, Dave Harris, has located the person I was searching for Monday in New Orleans. Ladies and gentlemen, I'd like to introduce Miss Amber Reynolds." Max waved his hand at the woman on the edge of the stage. "Amber is the woman who was with President-Elect Ferguson when he died."

Harold could almost feel the depletion of air as the entire room gasped. Dorothy let out a shriek, then started jumping up and down.

"What's going on?" Harold asked.

"That's the girl who had sex with President-Elect Ferguson!"

Harold frowned. "I thought Ferguson was dead."

"He is."

Sex with a dead man—why, that was the most perverted thing Harold had ever heard. How was that even possible? Rigor mortis—that must be the answer. Maybe that was why dead people were called stiffs.

But why should all this make Dorothy so happy? Harold wanted to ask her, but she was tugging on his arm, pulling him to the front of the stage. He was so confused; he'd obviously missed something or forgotten something important. A feeling of anxiety clawed at his chest, but before it dragged him into muddy waters, a thought tugged him to higher ground. He didn't need to understand everything to be happy; Dorothy was happy, and Max looked happy, and that was reason enough for him to be happy, too. He followed Dorothy as she elbowed people out of the way and hurried forward to the side steps of the stage.

Max tapped on the microphone and waited for the crowd to settle down. "The Secret Service told Amber that she'd lose her three-year-old son if she ever came forward about this," he said. "Well, that happened, anyway; she was arrested for drug possession a couple of months ago, and Social Services put her child into foster care. She has since gotten clean and sober, and she's trying to turn her life around. So she decided to come forward and set the record straight."

The media surged forward in a loud, mad scramble. Camera lights shifted, photographers rushed the stage, and reporters shouted questions.

Max raised his hands. "Amber is retaining counsel, and her attorney will negotiate an exclusive interview with an appropriate media outlet. So for now, she just wants to say one thing."

The young woman stepped to the microphone, twisting her fingers nervously together. "I'm the woman who was with Mr. Ferguson, and I have the tattoo to prove it." She turned around, tugged up the left side of her skirt, and thrust out her thong-clad hip. And there, in winged glory, was a dragonfly tattoo.

The room roared. The media climbed all over each other like tackles on a quarterback, trying to get the best shot. The moderator banged her pen on her water glass, but it was to no avail.

"That's all for now," Max said into the microphone. "Don't forget to vote." He escorted Amber toward Dave, and the two men took her through the curtains at the back of the stage.

Dorothy grabbed Harold's arm and pulled him up the stage stairs. Red fabric flapped around his face as she drew him through the stage curtains and down the back steps. She tugged him through the open fire exit into the blazing sunshine.

Harold looked around, breathing hard. They were in a parking lot, and heat wafted off the asphalt in waves. Max was helping the tattooed woman into a dark blue sedan, and Dave was climbing into the driver's seat. Max slammed the door and waved, and Dave drove off.

Dorothy threw herself at Max like a cannonball. "Thank you, thank you, thank you!" she exclaimed, hugging him.

Max's face folded in a wide smile as he hugged her back. "Don't thank me; you need to thank Dave. And Emma gets a lot of credit, too. She made the initial contacts that led us to Amber."

A surge of reporters started pouring out of the building. "When will Emma be back?" Max asked Dorothy.

"She's at Sunnyside now, saying her goodbyes," Dorothy told him.

Swamphead was washing in, making it hard for Harold to follow what was going on. He watched in confusion as Max dashed to his pickup, jumped in, and peeled out of the parking lot.

"Where's he going in such a hurry?" Harold asked. "He acts like his pants are on fire."

Dorothy's face was practically sending out light rays, she looked so happy. "They probably are, but that's okay, because his heart's on fire, too."

Harold pulled his brow together, still puzzled.

"He's going to see Emma," Dorothy explained, "and I wouldn't be a bit surprised if he told her he loved her."

Finally—something he understood. Harold smiled. "In that case, he'd better drive faster."

CHAPTER TWENTY-SEVEN

The TV blared through the door as Mrs. Alvarez cautiously opened it.

"Mrs. Alvarez? It's Emma Jamison with housekeeping."

"Oh, yes." The stooped little woman in the pink floral housedress smiled broadly, then clicked off the television and widened the door. "Come in, come in, dear. Would you like a cup of tea?"

It was Emma's sixth offer of tea that afternoon. She smiled regretfully. "I'd love to, but I'm afraid I don't have time."

The old woman's face fell. "No one has time for tea anymore. Do you have time to sit down?"

"I'm afraid not." Emma fiddled with the button on her fitted blue blouse. "I just stopped by to tell you goodbye."

"Are you going on a trip?" The elderly woman blinked behind her thick trifocals.

"Actually, I'm moving to Tampa. I was offered a wonderful job there."

The woman's face crumpled in confusion. "I thought you had a job here."

"I do. I mean, I did. But I've gotten a promotion, so I'm moving."

Mrs. Alvarez pushed her glasses up on her stub of a nose and tilted her head to regard her quizzically. "Was I imagining things, or did I see you on the news?"

"I was on channel four yesterday." Emma could barely believe she'd gone through with it, but she was so glad she had. The news stories today had painted Max in a much more favorable light. She only prayed it helped enough.

Mrs. Alvarez smiled. "I knew it! And Harold's grandson was on the news, too."

"That's all cleared up," Emma assured her. "His arrest was all a mistake."

"Arrest? No, no, dear, you must be confused."

Boy, that was a case of the pot calling the kettle black. Emma suppressed a grin.

"He was just talking," Mrs. Alvarez continued in her high, shaky voice. "Just now."

"Oh. Is the debate being aired live?"

Mrs. Alvarez shook her head. It wasn't a debate. He found the girl who gave that president fella a heart attack."

Poor old soul. Mrs. Alvarez was having a bad day and was all befuddled. "He probably said something about looking for her."

"No, no. I'm certain he found her."

"It's true," said a deep, familiar voice behind her. Emma whirled around to see Max standing in the doorway, his tie loosened, his shirtsleeves rolled up, his dimple winking.

Emma's heart stood still. "You found . . ." She couldn't say it. She didn't dare think it.

"Amber." Max stepped closer, his dimple deepening. "I found Amber. Well, actually, you and Dave did. She was staying with a friend in Covington. I drove there and met her."

Emma's hand flew to her chest, covering the buttons of her blue shirt. "No way."

"Way. She came with me to the debate, and I introduced her, and, well . . . it's breaking news on all the channels."

"Told you," Mrs. Alvarez said brightly.

Max shot the elderly woman a charming smile. "Would you excuse us for a moment?"

"Oh, certainly."

Max pulled Emma down the hall and around the corner. "Emma, this whole Ferguson nightmare—it's over. Amber said in front of a dozen TV cameras that she was with him that night, and she showed off the tattoo."

Emma stared at him, trying to absorb it.

Max's hands were warm on her arms. "You're exonerated, Emma. Fully and completely exonerated."

"For real?"

"For real."

"I-I can't believe it."

"Well, there's only one thing that you need to believe right now." His fingers slid down her arms. He took both her hands and gazed into her eyes. "I love you."

She stared at him, not sure if she were awake or dreaming.

"I love you, Emma," he repeated, tightening his grip on her hands. "I love you and I can't live without you, and I want the whole world to know it."

Joy, wild and fierce and all-consuming, burned through her like a forest fire. "Oh, Max," she whispered. "I love you, too."

His arms closed around her and his mouth covered hers in a hard, exuberant, winning-touchdown-at-the-Superbowl kind of kiss. He lifted her off her feet and spun her around, and she laughed against his lips.

At length he set her back on her feet. "Emma—I'm going to drop out of the race."

She knew how much his job meant to him, knew how well it fit his skills and his passions, knew how it defined who he was and what he believed. She scrunched her brows together. "Why on earth would you do that?"

"Well, I know how much you hate being in the public eye, and—"

"Don't you dare quit because of me!" she said fiercely. She touched his cheek. It wasn't even noon, but the rasp of a five-o'clock shadow tickled her palm. "You can have both, Max. You don't have to choose."

Max's dimple deepened. She gazed into his brown eyes and saw everything she'd ever dreamed of seeing in the eyes of the man she loved.

"God, I love you," he whispered against her lips. Her arms wound around his neck, and she pulled him closer, joy fizzing through her veins like bubbles in champagne. And then, through half-shut lids, she saw vivid pops of light.

At first she thought she was just seeing stars, but then she heard clapping and cheers. She opened her eyes to see a cluster of photographers surrounded by a crowd of elderly residents.

"I'm afraid another picture of you is going to make headlines," Max murmured as they drew apart.

"At least this time, my dress is buttoned," she whispered.

"Only until I get you alone," he whispered back.

*E*PILOGUE

Two years later

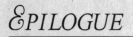ey, Sleepyhead." The mattress beneath Emma squeaked as Max sat on the edge of the bed, holding a tray of orange juice, coffee, and an English muffin.

Emma opened her eyes and smiled up at him, then scooted up against the mahogany headboard and arranged the pillow behind her. "Watch it. You're going to spoil me."

Max's eyes crinkled as he grinned. "I keep trying." He placed a folded newspaper on the tray. "There are a couple of stories in today's paper that you might be interested in."

"Oh, yeah?"

Max pointed to an article that he'd circled. Emma read the headline. "Photojournalist at the *National News Magazine* Fired for Faking News Story."

"It's about Louis Ashton," Max said. "He won an award for a heartbreaking story about a young girl who sold her baby to pay her mom's medical bills—only it turns out the girl was never pregnant, and her mom was never sick."

"Oh, wow."

"The magazine's considering filing charges against him."

"I guess what goes around comes around." Emma took a sip of orange juice. "What's the other story about?"

"Us." Max handed her another section of the paper. "We're in the 'Best of Everything' issue of the *New Orleans Times-Picayune*."

Emma read the article Max had circled. "*Our readers have named Max and Emma Duval Louisiana's most admired couple. And what a couple they are. Mr. Duval is the State Attorney General, while Mrs. Duval is the hostess of the syndicated TV show* The Butler's Guide to an Organized Home."

"*Together, the Duvals coauthored the runaway bestseller* The Butler Didn't Do It. *The couple say their most important achievement, however, is their thirteen-month-old daughter, Sophie.*"

Emma put down the paper and grinned. "Wow. That's a whole lot better than the stuff they used to write about us."

"No kidding."

It was amazing how things had turned around. In two years' time, Emma had gone from thinking her life was over to living a life beyond her wildest dreams. She smiled at her husband. "I wonder how our little achievement fared on her first sleepover with Grams and Harold."

"Let's call and find out. You know she's got them awake."

Max picked up a phone, hit speed dial, and handed the phone to Emma.

Grams answered in a cheery voice.

"How are things?" Emma said.

"Oh, just dandy. Sophie's had breakfast, and she's playing blocks with Harold."

"We'll come get her in an hour or so."

"No rush, no rush. But I'm glad you called. Harold and I have been talking, and we've decided to write a book of our own. We think folks our age might like a guide to late-in-life romance and marriage."

"Oh, I think that's wonderful!"

"We only have one problem. We can't decide on the title."

"Do you have any ideas?"

"A couple."

"Well, let's have them. "

"The Kama Sutra for Seniors, or *Did We Do It Already?"*

Emma laughed so hard that Max grabbed the breakfast tray and set it on the nightstand. "Maybe you should use them both," Emma said.

"Oh, that's a jim-dandy idea!"

"We'll see you in a bit, Grams."

"You know, I've been meaning to tell you . . . Oprah had a show last week that was positively providential." Grams's voice had that I'm-about-to-meddle tone that Emma knew so well. "It was about the benefit of having brothers and sisters. I know you want little Sophie to have every benefit, so—"

"I get the drift, Grams." Emma smiled. "See you soon."

Max looked at Emma as she hung up the phone. "What did she say?"

"She said Oprah and divine providence want Sophie to have a little brother or sister."

Max lifted a strand of her hair and twirled it around

his finger, the hint of a dimple winking in his cheek. "I've been thinking the same thing. What do you think?"

She gazed at Max, all stubble-faced and bed-rumpled, and her heart felt full enough to burst. "I think," Emma said as she twined her fingers around his neck, "it's positively providential."

ABOUT THE AUTHOR

Before becoming a full-time writer, Robin Wells was an advertising and public-relations executive, but she always dreamed of writing novels—a dream inspired by a grandmother who told "hot tales" and parents who were both librarians. When she sold her first novel, her family celebrated at a Chinese restaurant. Robin's fortune cookie read, "Romance moves you in a new direction"—and it has. Robin has won the RWA Golden Heart Award, two National Readers' Choice Awards, the Holt Medallion, and CRW's Award of Excellence.

She lives just outside New Orleans with her husband, her two daughters, and an exceedingly spoiled dog named Winnie the Pooh-dle.

Robin loves to hear from readers and can be reached at robinwells.com or by writing her at P.O. Box 303, Mandeville, LA 70470-0303.

THE DISH

Where authors give you the inside scoop!

♥ ♥ ♥ ♥ ♥ ♥ ♥ ♥ ♥ ♥ ♥ ♥ ♥ ♥ ♥

From the desk of Shannon K. Butcher

Dear Reader,

Some things are innately sexy: Long, slow kisses. The warm glide of skin on skin. A man in pain.

Okay, maybe I'm a little warped, but I really love to make my heroes suffer—a fact I'm sure my husband can attest to. Caleb Stone in NO CONTROL (on sale now) was a particularly engrossing project for me. Poor guy.

The idea of forgiveness has always intrigued me, probably because I make so many mistakes. It's almost magical the way something we can't see or touch can change people's lives. And the fact that it's a gift involving no physical construct or action seems counterintuitive. How can something that illusive be so powerful?

The little things are easy to forgive—like forgetting to put the milk away. No sweat. It's the bigger mistakes that give us pause, but usually, as long as we know they're mistakes, we can let those slide by, too. But what about the things we do purposefully? The decisions we make knowing someone is going to get hurt? The decisions we would make exactly the same way if we had to do it all over again?

Those are the questions that drove me to create Caleb. I knew from the moment he sparked to life inside my head that he was destined for a very special kind of hell—one of his own making. He was designed to be a walking, talking example of action meeting consequence in a messy collision, like the ones they show you as a warning in Driver's Ed class.

Thankfully, Caleb is tough and never complains, no matter how much I heaped on him. Which was why I had to give him a second chance. If anyone deserved one, it was Caleb, and there was only one person in the world who was capable of giving it to him.

But it couldn't be that easy, right? I mean, what fun would that be? So, Lana had to have her own heaping helping of suffering, just to make things interesting. I believe in equal opportunity, so it was only fair that I share the torment equally.

Not many people would have been strong enough to survive what Lana has. Terrorists abducted her and tortured her for days while she watched her friends die one by one, knowing she could be next at any time. Caleb was there. He saw it happen and did nothing to stop it and that decision has haunted him ever since. He knows he doesn't deserve forgiveness—not because what he did was too terrible to forgive, but because if he had to do it all over again, he'd make the same hard choices—but that doesn't stop him from wanting it all the same.

He gets his second chance with Lana, but even that is its own kind of hell. Being forced back into the life of the woman he nearly killed is not a comfortable place to be—for either of them. But they don't have a choice. Lana is hiding something and it is Caleb's duty to find out what it is before it can get her killed again. He refuses to fail her a second time.

Writing the book was great fun, which, I guess, makes me a sadist. I'll leave you to judge for yourself. I'm still intrigued by forgiveness. I'm not sure exactly what makes it so powerful even after spending way too much time thinking about it. In the end, I don't think I learned much, because I'm off to torture some more characters and I don't feel bad doing it at all.

Shannon K Butcher

www.shannonkbutcher.com

♥ ♥ ♥ ♥ ♥ ♥ ♥ ♥ ♥ ♥ ♥ ♥ ♥

From the desk of Robin Wells

Dear Reader,

The idea for my latest romantic comedy, BETWEEN THE SHEETS (on sale now), came to me while reading the tabloid headlines standing in a grocery store checkout line. Those poor celebrities, I thought; how awful to be humiliated in front of the whole world! And then a worse scenario occurred to me: What if a totally innocent woman suddenly found herself on the front page of one of these scandal sheets? What if she simply had been at the wrong place at the wrong time, but the whole world thought she had done something horrifically scandalous— something, like, say, giving the president-elect a heart attack in the sack during an illicit tryst? And what if she tried to rebuild her life by moving to the small town where her grandmother lived, and falling for a handsome, straight-arrow DA, a man who absolutely, positively, could not afford to have his name tainted by scandal? The story was off and running!

Unfortunately, it limped to a halt when Hurricane Katrina hit Louisiana. I live just outside New Orleans and many of the scenes are set there, so the catastrophe impacted the novel as well as its author. Lots of unexpected things were affected. Where would Grams and Harold get a wedding license, for instance, since New Orleans' city hall was destroyed? Could I mention the streetcar or would it still be out of commission? Would I ever be able to write funny stuff again?

It took a while, but the story finally started rolling once more, and then the characters took over and began misbehaving. Emma turned out to be a lot more smart-mouthed than I'd originally thought, Max had issues with his grandfather, and Grams was impossible to control. Louis was a late arrival to the story, he didn't show up until the last draft, and in typical Louis fashion, he caused problems all around. As for Katie, she might just need a book of her own. (Let me know if you agree!)

The secondary romance between the elderly couple was inspired by a true story. My late mother-in-law, Barbara Mix Wells, found new love in her eighties with a man who had mild Alzheimer's. They met at an assisted living center and lit up each others' last years. Here is a poem Barbara wrote about their late-in-life romance:

> How can I stay in this moment of bliss?
> A time I never dreamed
> Would happen in my elder years.
> I found and was found by another soul of my vintage
> Who needs me as much as I need him.
> We are tuned alike, parted from our mates
> After giving loving care for a lifetime.
> And now, alone, have found a company of two
> To enrich the years that are still ahead.
> —Barbara Mix Wells

Sigh. How sweet is that? Just goes to show, it's never too late for love.

I'd love for you to drop by my Web site— www.robinwells.com—to read a sample chapter of my next novel, share your thoughts, or just say hi!

Happy reading and all my best,

Robin Wells

Dear Reader,

Hope you enjoyed my book! For a
sneak peek at my next one, please
visit my Web site at robinwells.com.

All my best,

Robin Wells

---

*Want to know more about romances at
Grand Central Publishing and Forever?
Get the scoop online!*

GRAND CENTRAL PUBLISHING'S
ROMANCE HOMEPAGE

Visit us at www.hachettebookgroupusa.com/romance
for all the latest news, reviews, and chapter excerpts!

NEW AND UPCOMING TITLES

Each month we feature our new titles
and reader favorites.

CONTESTS AND GIVEAWAYS

We give away galleys, autographed copies,
and all kinds of fun stuff.

AUTHOR INFO

You'll find bios, articles, and links to personal
websites for all your favorite authors—and
so much more!

THE BUZZ

Sign up for our monthly romance newsletter,
and be the first to read all about it!